The Chocolate Thief

LAURA FLORAND

KENSINGTON PUBLISHING CORP.
www.kensingtonbooks.com

KENSINGTON BOOKS are published by   \

Kensington Publishing Corp.
119 West 40th Street
New York, NY 10018

ISBN-13: 978-0-7582-6940-9
ISBN-10: 0-7582-6940-4

First Kensington Trade Paperback Printing: August 2012

10 9 8 7 6 5 4 3 2 1

Printed in the United States of America

4-14 (14)
4-16(23)

AUG – 9 2012

The Chocolate Thief

With *mille mercis* to Jacques Genin and Michel Chaudun,
two master chocolatiers in Paris who
so very kindly allowed me inside their *laboratoires*
and patiently answered all my questions.

Thank you also to Sophie Vidal, *chef chocolatier* for Jacques Genin,
who was patience personified.

Chapter 1

Sylvain Marquis knew what women desired: chocolate. And so he had learned as he grew into adulthood how to master a woman's desire.

Outside, November had turned the Paris streets cold and gray. But in his *laboratoire,* he brought his chocolate to the temperature he wanted it, smooth and luxurious. He spread it out across his marble counter. With a deft flick of his hand, he stroked it up and spread it out again, glowing and dark.

In the shop, an elegant blonde whose every movement spoke of wealth and privilege was buying a box of his chocolates, unable to resist biting into one before she left the shop. He could see her through the glass window that allowed visitors a glimpse of the way artisan chocolate was made. He saw her perfect teeth sink into the thumbnail-sized chocolate and knew exactly the way the shell yielded with a delicate resistance, the way the ganache inside melted on her tongue, the pleasure that ran through her body.

He smiled a little, bending his head to focus on his chocolate again. He did not see the next woman as she entered his shop.

But as it turned out, she wasn't about to let him miss her.

The scent of chocolate snuck out onto the rainy street. Boot heels broke their rapid rhythm as passersby, bundled in long black coats, glanced toward the source and hesitated. Some stopped. Some went on. Cade's momentum carried her inside.

Theobromine wrapped around her like a warm blanket against the chill. Cacao flooded her senses.

She hugged herself. The aroma brought her home, belying her own eyes, which told her she couldn't be farther from the steel vats of the factory, the streams of chocolate ejecting without break in tempo from spouts into molds, and the billions of perfectly identical bars and bold-printed wrappings that had formed her life.

Something, some tension she carried with her, unknitted in her shoulder muscles, and the shiver from its release rippled all the way through her body.

Someone had molded chocolate into giant cacao bean halves that graced the display windows and added drama to the corners of the shop. She could imagine the hand that had shaped them—a man's hand, strong, square, long-fingered, capable of the most delicate precision. She had a photo of that hand as her laptop wallpaper.

On the outside of each bean, he had painted a scene from a different country that produced cacao. And on the surface of the horizontal beans, he had placed thumbnail-sized chocolates, exactly where he wanted them.

She looked around the shop. Tucked in corners here and there, black brands on shipping crates spoke of distant lands. Real cacao beans spilled from the crates, reminding customers that chocolate was an exotic thing, brought from another world. Cade had seen those lands. The black brands brought their scents and sights back to her mind, the faraway people she had met, the sounds of machetes on cacao trees, the scent of fermenting cacao husks.

He had scattered cocoa nibs here and there, as a master chef might decorate a plate with a few drops of sauce. He had spilled vanilla beans and cinnamon bark on multiple surfaces, wantonly, a *débauche* of raw luxury.

Every single element of this décor emphasized the raw, beautiful nature of chocolate and thus the triumph of its ultimate refinement: the minuscule squares, the *chocolats* worth $150 a pound, from the hand of Sylvain Marquis.

Sylvain Marquis. Some said he was the top chocolatier in Paris. *He did, too,* she thought. She knew he had that confidence. She knew it from that picture of his hand she carried on her laptop.

His boxes were the color of raw wood and tied with shipping string. The name stamped on them—SYLVAIN MARQUIS—dominated them, the color of dark chocolate, the font a bare, bold statement.

Cade breathed in, seeking courage from the scents and sights. Heady excitement gripped her but also, in strange counterpoint, fear, as if she were about to walk naked onto a stage in front of a hundred people. She shouldn't feel this way. Chocolate was her business, her heritage. Her dad often joked that her veins ran with the stuff. A significant portion of the global economy actually did run off the chocolate her family produced. She could offer Sylvain Marquis an incredible opportunity.

And yet she felt so scared to try, she could barely swallow.

She kept seeing her family's most famous bar, milk chocolate wrapped in foil and paper and stamped with *her* last name—thirty-three cents on sale at Walmart. Those thirty-three-cent bars had put more money into her family's bank accounts than most people could imagine. Certainly more than *he* could imagine. And yet her soul shriveled at the thought of taking the one in her purse out and displaying it in these surroundings.

"*Bonjour,*" she said to the nearest clerk, and excitement rushed to her head again, driving out everything else it contained. She'd done it. She'd spoken her first word of French to an actual Parisian, in pursuit of her goal. She had studied Spanish and French off and on for most of her life, so that she could easily communicate when she visited cacao plantations. For the past year, she had also paid native French speakers to tutor her toward her purpose, an hour a day and homework every night, focusing on the words she had come here today to use—*samples, marketing, product lines.* And *chocolat.*

And now, finally, here she was. Speaking. About to put *la cerise sur le gâteau* of the whole new line she was planning for the company. *The cherry on the cake* . . . maybe they could do something with *La Cerise* as one of the new line's products. . . .

"*Je m'appelle* Cade Corey. I'll take five samples of everything here, one of each kind per box, please." Only one of those boxes was for her. The others were to send back to Corey Chocolate headquarters in Corey, Maryland. "And while you are boxing that up, I have a meeting with Sylvain Marquis."

Her French sounded so beautiful, she couldn't restrain a tiny smile of pride. It just came tripping off her tongue, with only the merest stutter getting started. All that homework had paid off.

"Yes, madame," the crisply attired young man answered in English as cool and precise as a pin.

She blinked, her balloon of happiness shriveling, humiliated by one word in her own language.

"M. Marquis is with the chocolates, madame," he said, still in English, making her back teeth clench. Her French was *much better* than his English, thank you. Or *merci*.

A young woman began to fill boxes with Cade's chocolates while the snobbish young man guided her through a door in the back of the shop.

She stepped into a magical world and almost managed to forget that slap of English in her face as her happiness balloon swelled right up again. In one corner, a lean man in glasses with the fine face of a poet or a nerd poured generous ladles of white chocolate over molds. In another, a woman with her hair covered by a brimmed paper cap used a paintbrush to touch up chocolate owls. Two more women were filling boxes with small chocolates. More women still were laying finely decorated sheets of plastic over chocolates grouped by the dozen and tamping down on each chocolate gently, transferring the decoration.

At the central table of rose-colored marble, a man took a large whisk to something in a bain-marie that looked as if it must by itself weigh forty pounds, a faint white powder rising in the air around him. Across from him, another lean man, this one with a tiny dark beard, squeezed chocolate from a pastry bag into a mold from which lollipop handles protruded. His wedding ring glinted in a ray of light from the windows.

They were all lean, in fact. Surprisingly so, for people who worked all day with chocolate only a bite away. Only one man, tall and burly, stood out for his paunch, and he seemed entirely cheerful with his weight. Everyone wore white, and everyone had a paper cap, styles differing according to role. It was a world with a hierarchy, clearly defined for all to see.

Over the sinks hung brushes, spatulas, whisks. On the marble counter stood a large electric scale and an enormous mixer. On a counter to one side were all sizes of containers and bowls. Filled with raisins, candied oranges, sugar, they surrounded those working at the great marble island.

Everyone glanced up at her entry, but most focused on their work again. Only one man, expertly stroking chocolate over marble, spared her a lingering gaze that held greater authority, and perhaps more dismissal.

Tall and lean, he had black hair that fell in slightly wavy locks to his chin. He had tucked it carelessly behind his ear on one side, clearly exposing his strong, even features. A white paper toque minimized the risk of any of the rest of it falling into some client's chocolate. Chocolate smeared the front of the white chef's jacket he wore.

He was beautiful.

She swallowed, her mouth feeling dry. All the scents, the activity, the realization that the best chocolatier in Paris was, in person, even more attractive than in his photos—it all swirled around in her, surging up in ever-heightened excitement. She was here. Living her dream. This was going to be so much fun.

And Sylvain Marquis was hot.

Maybe she was overexcited. He wasn't that great, was he? Okay, he had looked sexy in his photos, and that shot of his hand had filled her dreams for nights on end, but she had tried to take all that with a grain of salt.

But here, in person, she had a sense from him of energy and control, passion and discipline. It fed her excitement, provoking an exaggerated sensitivity on her part. She felt like a can of Coke being jostled, building up a fizz that was pressing against its limits.

"*Bonjour, monsieur,*" she said, as her French tutors had taught her to do, and she confidently walked forward to thrust out her hand.

He proffered an elbow in return, which threw her off. She stared at it, then stared up at him.

He raised his eyebrows just enough that she felt abruptly slow on the uptake. "*Hygiène,*" he said. "*Je travaille le chocolat. Comment puis-je vous aider, Mademoiselle Co-ree?*"

She translated all that in her head, growing more and more excited as she realized that she *could,* that this language thing was working. Hygiene. I am working the chocolate. How can I you help, Miss Corey? He sounded so elegant, she wanted to hug his voice up to her in delight. Instead, she found herself awkwardly brushing his elbow, flushing despite herself. How the heck do you shake an elbow?

It dropped away from her. He touched the back of his pinky finger to the chocolate he was tempering on the marble, concentrating. And none of his focus was on her.

That didn't make sense. He knew who she was. This wasn't a surprise visit. He had to realize she could up his income by millions. How could he not concentrate on her?

Yet he seemed to consider her less important than a batch of chocolate. She braced against the presentiment that someone might try to put her fizzed-up-Coke self in the freezer.

"Do you have somewhere we could talk in private?" she asked him.

He twitched his eyebrows. "This is important," he told her. Meaning the chocolate and not her.

Did he think she was just here as a professional tourist? "I'm interested in finding someone to design a new line of chocolate products for us," she said calmly. *Now who's important, Sylvain Marquis?* She had practiced that line at least fifty times with her French tutor, and actually saying it out loud in this place and for the reason she had practiced it made her feel giddy with success. "We're interested in going into premium chocolates and are thinking of something very elegant, very Parisian, maybe with your name on it."

There, *that* had gotten his attention, she thought smugly, as he stared at her, his long, thin spatula freezing on the chocolate. She could almost see the euro signs flashing in his head. Had he just added a few zeros onto the end of his account balance?

"*Pardon,*" he said very slowly and carefully. "You want to put *my* name on one of *your* products?"

She nodded, pleased at finally making an impact. Excitement resurged like Old Faithful inside her. This would be her gift to her family, this gourmet line. She would be in charge of it, and it would involve all the luxuriating in high-end chocolate making and Paris she could possibly want. "Maybe. That's what I want to discuss with you."

His mouth opened and closed. She grinned at him triumphantly. What would his hand feel like when they shook on the deal?

Warm maybe. Strong. Sure. Full of the energy and power to turn something raw into something sensual and extraordinary.

There she went with the fizzing again. She glanced around at the small *laboratoire,* a miracle of intimacy and creation, so different from the chocolate factories in which she had grown up.

"Vous—" Sylvain Marquis broke off whatever he had started to say, shutting his mouth firmly again. Something was percolating up into his eyes, breaking through that cool control.

Rage.

"You want to put my *name on* your *product?"* he repeated, trying hard to keep control of his voice, his expression, but his eyes were practically incandescent. *"My* name?" He flung out a hand to where box after enticing box stamped with that name was being filled, closed, and tied a couple of counters away. "Sylvain Marquis?"

"I—"

"On *Corey Bars?"*

Thirty-three cents at Walmart. She flushed down to her toes and thrust her hand into her purse to close it around a rectangle in gaudy gold and brown wrapping, using it as her talisman-strength and hiding its shame all at the same time. "It would be a different line. A gourmet line—"

"Mademoiselle . . ." His mouth hardened, freezing her fizzing Coke bottle so fast, she could feel an explosion building up. "You are wasting my time. And I am wasting yours. I will never agree to work with *Corey Bars."*

"But just list—"

"Au revoir." He didn't move. He didn't stalk off. He stood over his half-tempered chocolate and pinned her with eyes

the color of cocoa nibs and *made her,* just by the look, the words, his mastery of his own domain, made her turn around and walk out.

She was trembling with embarrassment and rage by the time she got five steps back toward the door into the shop and realized she had *let* him. She had let him keep control of his world and drive her out of it. She wasn't the kind of person who got dominated. She should have stayed put and stood up for what she wanted.

She tried to get herself to turn around and brave that humiliation again, but the door was only three steps away. She closed her hand hard around the Corey Bar in her purse and tried to make those three steps scornful. But you couldn't be scornful in retreat. Nobody was fooled by a scornful back.

To hell with you, Sylvain Marquis. There are other chocolatiers in Paris and probably better than you. You're just the fad of the moment. You'll regret it.

She let the door between the *laboratoire* and the shop slam behind her, garnering multiple disapproving looks from clients and employees alike, all of whom expressed their opinion of barbaric Americans by a subtle downturn of their lips.

America could buy and sell them any day of the week.

Damn it. If only they would put a price sticker on themselves and take the money.

She strode toward the glass door onto the street.

"Madame," said a young woman near it, a large sack the color of raw wood sitting beside her cash register, stamped with SYLVAIN MARQUIS. Her expression—neutrality buoyed up by an underlying conviction of superiority—made Cade want to smack her. "Your chocolates."

Cade hesitated. Her credit card might as well have been barbed wire, it galled her so much to pull it out and hand it to the clerk.

Glancing back, she saw Sylvain Marquis watching her

through the glass window, one corner of those supple, thin lips of his twisting in amusement, annoyance, dismissal.

She pressed her teeth together so hard, she was surprised they didn't break. He returned to his work, forgetting her.

Her own rage went white-hot.

She signed off on a credit card payment into his bank account of nearly a thousand dollars for five measly boxes of chocolate and strode out into the street.

She desperately wished to sweep dramatically into a limousine or at least stride off into a Parisian sunset. Instead, she walked ten paces across the street, through a dark green door, and into an elevator so tiny, she finally understood the *real* reason French women didn't get fat. Claustrophobia.

Her bag of chocolates squashed against her legs. The elevator creaked to a halt six floors up. She let herself into an apartment less than half the size of her bedroom back home, threw her bag of chocolates onto the bed, and glared down at Sylvain Marquis's shop below. She had been so excited to find this little apartment for rent right above his *chocolaterie*. It had seemed so much more real, so much more what she wanted to do, than a luxury hotel off the Champs-Élysées. It might come with some sacrifices, like the fact that she was going to have to figure out how to use a Laundromat, but that had seemed a reasonable price to pay.

Until now. Now here she was, stuck just above the *chocolaterie* of a real jerk.

She could still go to a hotel, she supposed. But then, what was the point of her being here, if she just went to a hotel like she did on all her business trips?

She snuck a glance at the bag of chocolates on the bed. *No,* she told herself firmly.

She went back to scowling down at the SYLVAIN MARQUIS sign below.

The scent of chocolate reached her from the boxes. Her hometown smelled of chocolate all the time. Not this kind

THE CHOCOLATE THIEF   11

of chocolate, though. Not this exquisite quality, the work of one person's imagination and hands.

Maybe she would try just one. To prove how overrated he was.

As flavor pure as sin burst in her mouth, and her whole body melted in response, she pressed her forehead helplessly against her window, trying to keep her mouth in a scowl. Which was hard to do around melting chocolate.

He was so delicious.

How unfortunate that he was such a jerk.

Chapter 2

She was *gonflée*, Sylvain thought, with a dismissive move of his lips, dumping all his chocolate back into the bain-marie and reheating it. *Complètement gonflée*. In fact, her opinion of herself was *so* swollen, he itched for a pin. He hoped the way he had looked at her had *been* a pin. He had grown up practicing the kind of look that could deflate somebody's ego. It had been honed in his country for centuries.

He poured a third of this batch of chocolate out onto the cold marble, running a long, supple spatula under it to scrape it up, fold it over, and smooth it out again, tempering it deftly. He was annoyed he was having to redo this stage. It wasn't like him to let a minor distraction like an arrogant billionaire make him mess up chocolate.

For no reason, as he stroked the chocolate, he imagined his visitor's shoulder stripped of the coat and cashmere and his hand running over it, tempering it deftly.

He flushed a little. He used to blush crimson, back in his early teens, when at the most inopportune times he first started to imagine women naked. A few memories of blushes while talking to female teachers or pretty friends were still residually mortifying. But by now he had embraced the way his mind worked. For one thing, it seemed as if most men's minds worked that way.

Strange and truly unfortunate that women's minds didn't

work that way—tangentially sexual and direct all at once, all the time.

His American visitor, for example, probably hadn't imagined him naked. She had just imagined buying all his life's work and achievements as if they were a nice pair of shoes in a shop window, and she could take them home as a souvenir of her Paris jaunt.

He gritted his teeth on a surge of fury.

What *did* they teach people in that country?

"I told you it was a barbaric country," Cade's grandfather, James Corey, better known as Grandpa Jack, said over the phone. "Did I ever tell you about the time I tried to get hired by Lindt so I could learn how they were making those little balls of theirs? Couldn't even get hired. There I was, running the biggest chocolate company in America—not that I told them that, of course; I paid some local boy to help me make up a good résumé—and I couldn't even get hired to roast cocoa nibs over there. Swiss snobs," he said with relish, anti-Swissness being a pleasurable hobby of his.

"I remember," Cade said. They had celebrated her grandfather's eightieth birthday two years ago, a huge celebration that had become a month-long cross between a chocolate festival and a country fair in their town of Corey. At eighty-two, he was still going strong, but he had taken to repeating stories. And her father had pretty much dedicated a corner of the factory to the weird flavor experiments Grandpa Jack had started lately. He had been trying to combine spinach with chocolate just before Cade left. Because their factory employees had a peculiar sense of humor, they had not warned her about this when she walked in hunting for him, and she had had to taste it.

Her mouth still flinched at the memory.

"I ended up having to bribe one of the employees already there for the secrets instead," her grandfather lamented.

"But . . ." he sighed. "I would have loved to have been in there myself. Just to *set foot* inside one of those Swiss factories. Not one of those stupid formal tours where they hide all their secrets, but really inside. Almost managed to buy out one of the little ones one time, but Lindt got wind of it and white-knighted me just to be ornery."

"Yes, but—"

"And my *daddy*—your great-granddaddy, Corey honey—the things he went through to try to get the secret of that milk chocolate. Disguises, bribes, blackmail—you didn't hear about that blackmail from me, Cadey—infiltration. It was a time, I'll tell you."

"But this is different, Grandpa. I'm working with small chocolatiers now. I'm offering one of them a deal worth millions."

She could practically hear her grandfather wince. "Now, don't go throwing millions around like it was spare change, Cadey. You kids. I always did have trouble teaching you to appreciate the value of a dollar."

"Grandpa! You harassed Daddy into only letting us earn ten cents a day for keeping our rooms clean. A long way that went at prep school, let me tell you."

"Spoiled," her grandfather said affectionately. "It did you and your sister both a world of good, let *me* tell *you*."

"We couldn't even afford to buy snacks, Grandpa!"

"You should have brought Corey Bars from home," he said implacably. "No granddaughter of mine needs to be buying Mars junk out of a snack machine."

She rolled her eyes. She had tried all the Mars products at some point during her life, but purely for research purposes. She still felt a certain wistfulness when she saw M&M's in snack machines and knew she could never allow herself to buy them. (The one time she had cracked during a solo business trip was her little secret.) She had had maybe a dozen M&M's in her whole childhood. Even her friends couldn't have them at birthday parties because their parents were afraid it would be rude to her.

"All I'm saying is, for millions, you'd think he could have been a little more polite to me."

"Oh, no." Her grandfather sounded alarmed. "You don't want a Frenchman to go and start being polite to you, honey. It will curdle your soul. You might never recover. The Swiss, they're clumsy with it—they can be all polite, and you never even notice. But the French—they're *good* at it. You finish with a Frenchman being 'polite' to you, and you're about ready to jump off that tower of theirs."

Cade knuckled her forehead in frustration. "I just—I just want to *be here,* Grandpa. You know? I want to learn how to do what they do. I want to *belong in Paris.* I want to have their chocolates."

"Oh, I know." Her grandfather sighed. "I guess it's our fatal flaw. I sure wish I could talk you out of wasting your energy on those snobs, though. They're just going to hurt your feelings and make you feel bad about yourself."

"I'm *not* going to let him hurt my feelings," Cade lied.

"Hmm. Just remember something, honey: they can act as snobby as they like, but back in '45, those were *our* chocolate bars our soldiers were handing out to *them,* and they were grateful to get them, too."

Cade had to grin. They had reproduced a big batch of those old chocolate ration bars as part of the D-day anniversary events, and they weren't exactly the best-tasting thing ever to come off the line—the military had insisted on too many nutritional components. "Maybe the source of their snobbery?"

Not to mention the source of her grandfather's obsession with getting spinach into chocolate bars.

Her grandfather huffed. "Well, they weren't too proud for it then."

Cade tried to embrace this old American World War II

pep talk: *they weren't so superior back* then, *were they*? But she kept seeing that incredulous dismissal on Sylvain Marquis's face, and her shoulders just shriveled into a slump again. Somehow she didn't think she was going to be able to take credit for something that had happened nearly seventy years before in order to change his dismissal into the enthusiastic acceptance she had dreamed of finding.

Bastard. Self-absorbed, arrogant jerk.

God, he made good chocolate, though. Once she had started tasting it, she hadn't been able to stop. She had even dreamed about it that night, the rich silk of perfect chocolate drugging her thoughts, the subtle flavors twining around her like an elusive striptease, luring her deeper and deeper into the trouble hiding behind the curtains in the back of a mysterious opium den. . . .

She yanked herself awake and jumped out of bed to shower briskly.

Unfortunately, the "brisk shower" turned into a battle with a handheld spray in a claw-foot bathtub. Who had designed this bathroom? With no shower bracket for the nozzle and no curtain, she ended up dousing the entire room and the fresh clothes she had brought in with her. She stared at the soaked, ancient, flowered wallpaper and wondered if this was some kind of setup to force her to pay for repainting the apartment in something a little more . . . plain. Classy. Maybe the tub had originally had a shower curtain, but somebody had Googled her name when she booked the apartment and seen it as an opportunity?

Splotches of water decorated her slim black sweater and elegant black pants when she pulled them on, too. She had barely started for the day, and already she looked ridiculous.

Your clothes will dry, she told herself. *Before any Parisians see you. Let's work on getting the makeup right.* Dramatic, lovely, subtle—that's what she needed. This was Paris, after all. And at the end of the day, she was just an average-looking young woman with a strong sense of herself. Strong enough, usually, to carry her straight, light brown hair, her even but unremarkable features, her clear blue-gray eyes, and make them something people remembered.

Usually. Usually, she felt quite confident in her ability to do that. She had done it for so long. But now she was in Paris.

She might own her little hometown of Corey. She might own a significant chunk of world business, in fact. But she didn't own Paris. Not yet.

Here, she had to compete with Parisians and the even more challenging *Parisiennes.* She had to stand out against the backdrop of a city so dramatic and romantic, it had kept eyes riveted on it for centuries.

She stepped out onto the sidewalk into the cold autumn air, nervous and afraid of another failure like that of the day before. A few doors down, the baker had his sign sitting out on the sidewalk, and the scent of pastries wafted to her on the cold wind. Otherwise, the street was quiet. It was early on a gray day. She had an hour to herself to walk around Paris before her meeting with the city's second-best chocolatier.

Maybe really the *best.* Sylvain Marquis had probably just had a lucky day when the Maire de Paris gave him that *meilleur chocolatier de Paris* award. What did the mayor of Paris know, anyway?

She reached the bakery just as a man was about to step out of it, paper-wrapped pastry in hand. Her eyes met Sylvain Marquis's, and she stiffened.

A poetically inclined wind stirred her red scarf at precisely that moment, blowing a lock of hair across her mouth. It stuck to the shimmery pale lip gloss she had just added in an effort to compete with the beautiful Parisian women.

Stuck like glue. She tried to shove it away with a gloved

hand. Lip gloss rubbed off on her glove, but her hair stayed stuck and even managed to get in her teeth. She stripped off the lambskin glove, pulling at the strands with her bare fingers, while Sylvain Marquis watched her in a coolly perplexed way. All elegant. All *together* and ready to dive, with all the passion contained inside that elegant coolness, into the rich world from which he was excluding her. He would be working in chocolate's heart all day, and she would be pounding the pavements trying to find someone who would let her do the same thing.

She could exclude him from *her* world, too, if she wanted to. The world of wealth and power.

Except it was hard to exclude someone who didn't want to come in. She *could,* but it kind of lost the point.

"The answer is still the same today," he told her as he stepped back inside to allow her to enter the shop.

If she strangled him, would he keep looking coolly disdainful while his face turned purple?

"I'm not asking you again today." She brushed past him into the bakery. Through their two wool coats, two sweaters, and two shirts, the brush still sent a rush of nerves and heat through her. She focused on the baker's selection, which should be enough to maintain anyone's focus. Good Lord, but Parisians were lucky. How did they manage to stay so rude and brooding, when on every block they could step into a refuge of warmth and gold like this?

Golden pastries filled the cases, in spirals, crescents, circles, and puffy rectangles from which winked almonds, powdered sugar, raisins, dots of chocolate. Red berries rested on beds of soft, pale custard and golden crust, in a perfect-sized circle for someone's hand. Slices of apple peeked delicately through something labeled *tarte normande.* Little chocolate-covered *choux* nestled on chocolate-covered cushions of larger *choux,* like fat little black-clad snowmen. Long, phallic éclairs in shades of coffee, chocolate, and pistachio stretched in rows like some nymphomaniac's dream.

She frowned sideways at Sylvain Marquis suspiciously. Since when had she started seeing phallic symbols in good éclairs?

If Marquis wasn't standing there with his infinite convictions of her inferiority, she could have chosen several pastries and gorged herself. Instead, she had to be embarrassed into self-restraint. What to pick? A croissant was boring and would make her look like a tourist. A *pain au chocolat*—she could get that back home. She sneaked a peek at the pastry he carried. A *croissant aux amandes*. So that was out.

She would be damned if she would copy him.

She didn't know the name for any of the others, meaning she would have to look ignorant again. "Um . . . that one." She pointed at random and found her finger indicating a delicate little tart entirely covered with fresh raspberries.

Good choice. She needed some more fruit in her diet with this cold weather.

"Pour le petit-déjeuner?" Sylvain Marquis asked, astonished.

"Did I ask you what I should have for breakfast?" she snapped. The baker gave her a minatory look. What, were they best friends? Great. Now for her whole stay here she would wonder if her baguettes and pastries had been spat on and dropped on the floor. Maybe she should look for another apartment.

One with a shower curtain.

One several *arrondissements* away from Sylvain Marquis.

"Américains," Sylvain Marquis said incredulously, shaking that beautiful mass of black hair of his. "You'll eat anything anytime, won't you?"

She curled her bared hand into a fist in the shadow of her coat sleeve, embarrassed once again. She purely hated him. Thank goodness she had learned how much so before she signed a contract with him that let him make millions off her blind idealization of Parisian chocolatiers.

"What are you doing here?" the chocolatier asked, apparently oblivious to the fact that his behavior hadn't left them on speaking terms. "My shop doesn't open until later. Did you come to steal my recipes?"

Had he been reading her family history? Those accusations of recipe stealing against her great-grandfather had never been proven. Primarily because those Swiss factories had been so hypervigilant about their security that he hadn't gotten the chance and had had to reinvent the chocolate wheel the hard way: lots of experiments, a couple of boiler explosions, and once a burned-down barn.

"I'm on my way to talk to Dominique Richard," she said coolly, accepting her beautiful tiny concoction of raspberries from the baker. "Why? Did you think you were the *only* 'best chocolatier in Paris'?"

His eyebrows flexed. That had gotten under his skin, hadn't it? *Good.* She strolled past him out of the shop and down the street, exiting fast so she could savor at least one point won in this encounter. She willed her back to try to do a better job at scorn this time.

She still waited until she had turned the corner at the end of the street and was out of sight before she bit into her raspberry *tartelette,* though.

It was so good. Not too sweet, fresh and full of flavor, with a thin layer of gently sweetened custard. What was wrong with eating something like that for breakfast? It was healthier than his *croissant aux amandes,* she would have him know.

Only she wouldn't have him know, because to do so she would have to turn around and walk back down the street and tell him.

And giving him that much attention would put the win definitively in his camp.

Chapter 3

Sylvain felt uneasy about that *gonflée* piece of capitalist arrogance hovering outside his *chocolaterie* at seven in the morning as if it was her next acquisition, but he tried to brush it away. At least she hadn't had the nerve to try to talk him into selling his name to her again.

Which was pretty annoying, actually. She could be a little greedier for him, couldn't she? Plus, there was nothing like an argument with a cute female who had a weakness for raspberries to brighten a gray day.

She *had* looked *mignonne* with her raspberries, too. It was a ridiculous breakfast, but he liked that she had chosen it, nevertheless. *Savor the flavors you want to in life*—that's what he thought. Plus, he could imagine her teeth sinking into the delicate, thin layer of custard, her lips closing over the perfect red raspberries, and the wind blowing her hair all over her face at the same time, driving her crazy.

He could imagine saving her from herself, laughing and pushing her hair back with his fingers, so that she could finish her bite.

Bordel. His imagination was going to get him into trouble again. He hoped the wind drove her *really* crazy. Dominique Richard? Dominique Richard might just murder her when she suggested buying him, for one. And . . . *bordel.* Dominique Richard? Was she trying to imply that Dominique

Richard was as good as he was? Or even nearly as good? *Imbécile de capitaliste américaine. Putain de* nerve. As if Dominique Richard wasn't cocky enough already without some idiot running to feed his ego. . . .

His anger eased a little as he let himself into his *laboratoire,* as his moods always did. Theobromine. Drug of the gods. *His* theobromine, his chocolate, his masterpieces that people lined the sidewalk to pay a fortune for.

It was a long way to come for a boy who had grown up *en banlieue,* whose rural parents had wanted him to apprentice to a farmer. Watching women who looked like a million dollars—women like the American capitalist, in fact—sink pretty little expensive teeth into a thumbnail-sized chocolate of his making was a long way to come, too. He had been a gangly, awkward adolescent with shaggy hair, so it was a good thing he had discovered very early in his teenage years What Women Wanted.

Chocolat. If you wanted to lure a woman who wouldn't otherwise have looked twice at you, good chocolate was better than a love potion. As an awkward teenager, he hadn't necessarily managed to turn those beautiful-friends-lured-by-chocolate into *girlfriends,* but he had at least earned the right to be in their orbit and torture himself with their nearness, and from there he had slowly learned a certain process. He seduced them with chocolate, and, in return, occasionally one of them seduced him. A fling, usually. A consolation prize for her when her real boyfriend was mean to her, before she went straight back to *le bâtard.* He was twenty before he broke out of that particular hopeless rut.

It hadn't hurt that the intensely physical apprenticeships in *chocolaterie* had taught him control and power and strength, or that he had filled in to his height, but the real key had been his mastery of chocolate, and he knew it. The way to a woman's body was through what she delighted in putting into her mouth. When a woman let his chocolate melt on her tongue, he thought of it as her letting a little bit of him melt there.

He smiled suddenly. So, how many of those five boxes of his chocolates had Cade Corey eaten? How much of him had she taken into her? And then he stood still, with his hand on the cold marble countertop, alone in his *laboratoire* in the early morning while heat blushed through him.

Chapter 4

Leaves blew across the gravel in the Luxembourg Gardens. Cade let the wind blow Sylvain Marquis out of her mind and tossed her chin up into it, thrilling to the fact that she was walking here. Ripples formed on the perfect circle of the pool in front of the seventeenth-century palace, but no little children's boats floated there today as they always did in pictures. Sun sifted softly through the clouds, light against gray behind the trees and the palace.

The park was nearly empty. The few people crossing it seemed to be using it as a shortcut, leading with their chin as they walked, hands in coat pockets, in a hurry to get somewhere early. A couple of joggers circled the periphery, looking starkly out of place in that classical landscape and rather awkward about their athletic endeavor.

Here she was, Cade thought, stopping in front of the pool to gaze around her. Her hands curled in her pockets in a little squeeze of the moment, milking it for its preciousness. *Paris.*

She dismissed Sylvain Marquis's refusal, a temporary setback. Her world would hold this city in it now, once she succeeded with this line. Her life would hold in it a *laboratoire,* a workshop full of handcrafted chocolate alchemy and fussy, passionate masters of their craft producing something superb. Both would become part of her.

Her soul seemed to grow up and out of her as she thought about it, bigger and bigger, richer and richer, to become as large as this largest of small cities and all it had ever held, as rich as a dark chocolate ganache gently infused with some new flavor she didn't know, being stirred over the lowest heat.

Her eyes stung, maybe from the cold wind or maybe from the sudden beauty of the moment. She might have lingered in it, except the odor of urine invaded her space. An unshaven man in stained clothes wavered toward her, mumbling something, his hand cradled near his body, palm up.

She gave him twenty euros and, on a whim, her talisman Corey Bar. She had a big box of them she could restock from back in her rented apartment, and she liked to give a Corey Bar with any money she gave out in the street. She always imagined it brought the recipient a little spark of pleasure.

She strolled on, feeling stronger, braver, freer, Sylvain Marquis's outrage and chocolaty superiority retreating to the back of her mind. Happiness surged through her, even when she had to dodge a man dropping a cigarette butt onto the sidewalk while his dog finished pooping in the middle of it.

Paris. She was in Paris. This city was hers.

Chapter 5

Dominique Richard didn't like the idea, either. He wasn't quite as unpleasant about it as Sylvain Marquis—or, rather, he wasn't as intensely attractive, he didn't make her fantasize she was the chocolate laid out on his counter being tempered by his hand, and he didn't have that same gift for minimalism in his initial dismissal of her, as if she wasn't worth a sneer. Dominique was rough, aggressive, his refusal brusque, although he looked her over while he gave it. As if she might not be worth the respect of considering her proposal, but he might be willing to have sex in his office with her if she was interested.

That type of insult was, somehow, easier to deal with than Sylvain's. It didn't settle under her skin and burn there like a fire she couldn't put out.

But on the other hand, it was the second rejection of her brilliant idea in less than twenty-four hours. She had started toying with this dream as early as her high school days, had kept playing with it through college, and had held it close to her heart for the four years since, while she built up respect for her ideas and her work in the company before she tried to take it "haring off into some new line," as her father liked to put it. Ten years at least she had been hoping for this.

She had always thought the only things that stood in the way of her dream were her family, their company, and herself. It had never occurred to her that the dream itself might reject her.

And Parisians had a way of saying no that was really discouraging. Couldn't they at least smile and pretend they were sorry to turn her down? They didn't have to act as if she had acquired some kind of odor just from asking the question.

She strode back through the Luxembourg Gardens, hands thrust deeply into her coat pockets, trying to keep her head and her courage up, trying to focus on the beauty of the gardens, on the pleasure of people-watching. A woman tried to keep her toddler from climbing into the great round pond, while the chilly breeze blew ripples across its surface. A couple stopped another passerby just in front of her to get him to take their picture.

She nodded at the homeless man from earlier, who was halfway through the Corey Bar.

"C'est de la merde," he informed her conversationally. "Do you think that just because I'm homeless, I'll eat anything?"

She hurried on, her hand clenching on nothing, since she had given away her talisman just so a Frenchman who didn't even have a roof over his head could look down his nose at it. Her eyes stung desperately. She focused on getting back to her apartment, on regrouping—on hiding—on getting back to her laptop, where she could lay out a list of the third- to tenth-best chocolatiers in Paris and make a plan.

Warmth closed around her as soon as she squeezed into the elevator. The place was barely heated, but it was out of the wind. Amid the ancient, flowered wallpaper in her tiny apartment, the giant box of Corey Bars that often followed her on her travels sat on the laminate counter of the tiny kitchenette.

She pulled an armful out of the box and sat down on her little bed near the window, letting the bars spill all around her as she started to cry.

Her phone interrupted her tears. "Cade," her father said abruptly, while she struggled mightily to make sure not a single sniffle escaped. "Could you look over the memos from Jennie and Russell that I sent you? Check your e-mail. I don't have all the background information on the discussions you've been having with the convenience stores, and I'm not sure they're making a good decision."

"They can't handle it? This should be good training for them."

"Yes, but . . . we'd all feel better if you would give us your assessment. You might have a couple of other forwards in your in-box, too. I'd appreciate it if you would look them over. How are you doing anyway, honey? Having fun?"

"Yes!" she lied enthusiastically. "It's fascinating to make contact with these little artisan chocolatiers. There's so much we could learn here."

"Mmm," said her father, considerably more tepid about opening a new gourmet line than she was. "The city is beautiful, isn't it? Your mother and I had our first honeymoon there."

Julie Corey, *née* Julie Cade, and Mack Corey had taken a "honeymoon" every year on their anniversary until Cade's mother died.

"Yes," Cade said.

"She always liked it. You remember when we took you with us sometimes as kids? She liked to just walk all over the city. She really never saw a cobblestone street or an old building she didn't like."

Cade smiled, thinking about her mom. That was so true of her.

"Well, we miss you over here, sweetie. I can't wait to have you back. Don't you go staying at the end of the world like your sister wants to. But you enjoy every minute while you're there, all right?"

"Yes," Cade said definitely. "I will." Especially since those moments were numbered. Her younger sister, Jaime, seemed determined to throw off all her family responsibilities in favor of saving the world, so Cade couldn't really do the same. She would be heading back to Corey, Maryland, soon.

Twenty minutes later she was back on her feet, restoring her hair and makeup to Paris-worthiness and plotting which chocolatiers to try next.

She eyed the heels of her boots doubtfully, because her feet already felt a little sore from the morning's walk. But her first full day in the city was not the moment to cave and put on flats. If Parisian women could do it, she could do it.

She walked and walked and walked.

The walking part was really nice.

Except for how badly her feet hurt.

And the time she stepped in dog poop.

And the time another pedestrian reached out suddenly and grabbed her breasts.

And the time she brushed too close to someone else on the sidewalk, and the cigarette he was carrying low by his side burned the back of her hand. At least *he* didn't smirk at her but reached out to steady her, apologizing in a quick, sincere rush. She glanced after him as he continued on, wondering if it was a sign of overabuse by Paris that she wanted to grab him and ask him out on a date just because he had been nice enough not to sneer at her when he burned her.

She sat down at the nearest café, defeated, flexing her aching toes, and ordered a cup of hot chocolate. The drink proved surprisingly dark and intense, not at all like the ritual Corey cocoa of her childhood, with its cute little snowman marshmallows. A thin cylinder of sugar lay on the saucer beside it, but was she supposed to dump that into her chocolate? Or would that make her look like a tourist? Maybe the waiter had given it to her because he'd already guessed she was a tourist. He would probably start speaking to her in English at any minute. Everybody started speaking to her in English. She had studied French all through middle school, high school, and college, and paid for years of private French lessons, and they all insisted on speaking to her in very bad English.

Scattered pairs of people talked here and there at tables, waving cigarettes over half-empty cups and glasses. Maybe they should sell fake cigarettes in a package with Parisian guidebooks so tourists could have a prayer of fitting in. Wasn't it supposed to be against the law to smoke in cafés now in Paris? She laid her coat and gloves on the seat beside her and cradled the chocolate cup in her hands, soaking up the warmth, her feet aching even more as she took the pressure off them.

Exhaustion pressed on her. Was this how defeat felt? She had never really tasted that feeling before and wasn't willing to admit she was tasting it now. She was just regrouping, that was all.

She had walked all day. Past gorgeous fountains, glimpses of hidden courtyards, store windows that were works of art. The buildings, the streets, the cobblestones that had ripped up her boot heels, they were all so, so . . . *Paris.* She had walked along the Seine, and it had been cold and brown and *gorgeous.* And there had been Notre-Dame rising up above it, and, and—

—she would arrive at the next chocolatier on her list. And she would brace herself—and brace harder each time—and she would go in. And the scent and sight of chocolate would wrap around her, so elegant and fabulous and extraordinary, and—

—the chocolatier would say no. Simon Casset flicked one quick, penetrating, steel-blue look over her and recommended she talk with Sylvain Marquis. However, the tiny twitch of those stern lips of his had made it clear he was saying that just to give Sylvain a hard time and *not* from any sincere effort to help her in her quest. Philippe Lyonnais had stared at her with eyes that quickly went as dark blue as a stormy sea, and he'd actually *growled* at her. Aslan-roared. Her ears had still been ringing when she left the shop.

Sometimes one said no kindly, as if she was a naïve young thing who couldn't possibly understand any better. Sometimes they turned her down with a baffled look, as if wondering where Americans got their wild ideas. Sometimes they were impatient, as if pretty fed up with Americans and their wild ideas. One rejected her offer flirtatiously, as if she might be able to talk him into it if she took the right route.

She had kept the flirting chocolatier on her list of possibles. He had been sixty, and she was pretty sure he was just leading her on, but she had to keep somebody on her roll.

She couldn't understand why they all said no. Sure, they had their principles about the art form of their chocolate making. That was what had drawn her here; that was the world she so passionately longed to own.

But how could they not be willing to sell it to her? They acted as if the sale would destroy it somehow. Like some little stubborn old lady in a historic cottage with her beloved garden, refusing to sell to the major construction conglomerate that wanted to bulldoze over it. That wasn't what Cade was trying to do *at all*.

Maybe she had gone about this all wrong. Maybe she should have come in with her cadre of lawyers and executives and assistants and overwhelmed them.

Would that have worked? A vision of Sylvain Marquis's stubborn, sexy, arrogant face rose up before her, and she had a suspicion its reaction to lawyers would still be indifferent dismissal.

And anyway, she hadn't wanted to bring any of those people. She had wanted this to be her adventure in Paris. She had wanted to be all alone, to go in and talk to people as one person to another, to . . . live a dream. This premium chocolate line was the only way she had found to fit the dream into her life and not betray a structure built by generations.

But it was Saturday afternoon, and she didn't have dinner planned in some superb Parisian restaurant with a passionate chocolatier so that they could talk about their plans excitedly while he told her what the best items on the menu were and they tried something chocolate for dessert. She was staring into another evening all alone. She couldn't remember the last time she had spent two whole days and nights alone. Solitary evenings were usually a choice, a relief from her busy, people-filled days. But she hadn't made this choice, and she didn't feel relieved. She felt like a failure, lonely and rejected by a dream.

Back in her apartment, she closed the refrigerator door on the boxes in brown, beige, and one turquoise that filled it, all stamped with the name and logo of the second- to tenth-best chocolatiers in the city. She wasn't going to stay in her apartment eating chocolates tonight.

She hesitated over her BlackBerry and then set it down firmly. She wasn't going to call any of the list of wealthy contacts her father had given her, people who would be glad to go out with her for the business opportunity. This was her adventure, her chance. She didn't want it to become just another day in her life, only in a foreign city.

No, she was going to go out to eat by herself. And then she was going to go to the Eiffel Tower and see the sparkling view everyone talked about. And then she would catch one of the famous *Bateaux-Mouches* that steamed along the Seine, providing tourists with yet more glimpses of the city. And then maybe she would walk along the river and watch the dancers and the drummers she had read about in her guidebook.

She deliberately limped several streets away, over the protests of her feet, to avoid running into Sylvain Marquis again. She left her BlackBerry and her laptop behind and went without the guidebook. She was in Paris. She could find her own good restaurant.

As if by magic she found herself on a street with no traffic, cobblestoned, full of unhurried people congregating before bars and restaurants and posted menus, people who all seemed happy to be there. Some people didn't even glance at the menus scrawled on chalkboards out on the sidewalk, instead entering their favorite restaurant as they might step into their own front door.

Cade stopped at a restaurant with a front of green and floors of old, smooth, burnt-red tile. Bottles of vinegars and oils climbed up its walls. Five tables crowded the small space downstairs, and black metal stairs led to a mezzanine above. The slim waiter in black pants and black T-shirt shook his head when she asked about the mezzanine; it was too early to start seating there.

He didn't look thrilled with the fact that she was dining alone, either, but maybe that was her own self-consciousness. He was kind enough to give her the window table for two, where she could sit watching the street.

She swallowed. She rarely ate alone in public. Meals on the road were usually packed with people and work. But surely she had the self-confidence for this. Even in Paris.

It just felt so horribly, awkwardly lonely. She smiled brightly at the waiter, who looked alarmed. She bent her head and focused on the menu he brought.

A couple in their early fifties came in and sat at a nearby table, speaking English all the while.

Great. In her attempts to embrace Paris on her own, had she come straight to a tourist spot?

She ordered the full *prix fixe,* three courses, determined not to shrink into a quick dinner and a flight back to the semi-safety of her little apartment. She was here to enjoy Paris. All three courses of it.

She played with the silverware as she waited for her wine, thought longingly of her BlackBerry, and resolutely pulled out the little leather-bound journal she had bought specifically for her trip to Paris.

A couple came in, the man tall and dark. Her heart froze even before she had lifted her head to get a better look. The waiter greeted Sylvain Marquis with friendly familiarity, he said something back, and the finger-sized, perfectly coiffed blonde with him laughed.

Cade closed her eyes against fate.

How could this be happening to her? How incredibly hideous that *he* should come in with his perfect little date to the very restaurant where she was sitting out her lonely meal.

He turned away from the waiter and stilled. She opened her eyes to stare at him defiantly.

"Do you have spies on me?" Sylvain Marquis asked incredulously.

"That would be a waste of company resources," she said icily. Really, who did he think he was? The, uh . . . *one* of the acknowledged best chocolatiers in the world? Talking to a part-owner of one of the biggest mass producers of chocolate on the planet?

It was, admittedly, eccentric of her *not* to have spies on him at this point, or bodyguards and lawyers and assistants on *her*.

"Spies?" the little blonde asked with a laugh.

Sylvain Marquis made a dismissive gesture. *"Ce n'est pas important."*

Cade burned.

"The mezzanine?" the waiter asked him. Apparently that rule about waiting until the downstairs filled up before seating the upstairs only applied to people with an American accent.

"Non," Sylvain said, ignoring the blonde's disappointed look. "Downstairs is fine."

There were only the five tables downstairs, and two of them were already taken. The waiter seated Sylvain and his friend two tiny tables away from her. Cade pressed the point of her silver pen into her journal until it broke through the paper, as she longed to shrivel into an old, dried mushroom that could be lost on the floor.

At least now she knew she had picked a good restaurant, she thought bitterly. She would bet Sylvain Marquis only put delicious things into his mouth.

Probably he thought that blonde was delicious. Her pen drove through another layer of paper.

The air around her seemed to hold scents just from the chocolatier's passing—cacao and cinnamon, citrus and vanilla. Of course. He would be imbued with those scents at the end of the day. It was possible he might never be able to completely wash them out of his clothes and off his skin.

She closed her eyes against a vision of water sluicing off his skin, failing to wash away the chocolate essence of him.

Cacao was so oddly reassuring to her, as if the very scent of it made all right with her world, returned her to her comfort zone. But she didn't need that vision of his naked skin to tell her that any sense of a comfort zone where he was concerned was completely false.

She bent her head, trying desperately to think of something to write in her journal, to make herself look busy and indifferent to his presence. And *not* lonely. She found herself writing *Paris* over and over just so her pen would be moving. Her name. The name of the restaurant. *Syl*— She slammed the leather cover closed.

She tapped it, not knowing what to do with herself. And finally opened it again. Being very careful to keep it half-closed so that he couldn't glimpse a thing.

"What are you writing?" Sylvain Marquis asked from his table only three feet away. "Memories of Paris? Chantal, have I introduced you? This is Cade Corey. She's in the chocolate field," he added, with a tone of great kindness, as if he was saying the custodian at a lab was in microbiology.

"Corey?" Chantal said. "Do you make those—?" Belatedly, she apparently realized her face was curling into a sneer, for she quickly smoothed it out. "How nice. Have you come to France to learn more about chocolate?"

Cade wondered what would happen if she hauled off and decked both of them. Surely it wouldn't be the first time an American in Paris had been provoked to violence by French "politeness," as her grandfather had called it. She *had* come to France to learn more about chocolate, but it didn't sound at all the same when *she* said it.

And who was Chantal, anyway? She noticed his Marquisness hadn't introduced her. Maybe she was so much a part of his life, he assumed everyone already knew.

Cade was never leaving her apartment without her Black-Berry again. At least she could have whipped it out and looked . . . probably even more pathetic. As if, even sitting in the middle of Paris, she had no other aspect to her life than Corey Chocolate.

Exactly what she was trying to make *not* true.

"Don't you know anyone in Paris?" Sylvain asked.

Cade turned her head and stared at him. Was it her imagination, or had he sounded a touch concerned? Was he about to include her in his party out of social pity?

Chantal looked worried about that, too.

"I know people," Cade said. At least, quite a few people here would like to know her. That list of her father's.

Sylvain looked doubtful. Cade had just made up her mind to stand up and walk out—pretend she had only stopped for a glass of wine—when the waiter appeared with a small white dish of ravioli swimming in a bath of basil cream and pine nuts. It smelled like heaven—and looked like the door locking her in to a long prison of an evening. She felt a little sick to her stomach.

She should have stayed in her room feeling sorry for herself. She should have dined on top of the Eiffel Tower.

(A sudden vision of herself dining on top of the Eiffel Tower with Sylvain Marquis flashed through her mind, just quickly enough for her to catch a glimpse of city lights, of dark sky and stars, of dark hair and a hand proffering her a taste of something delicious. She shoved the image out of her head.)

She should have taken advantage of Sylvain's night out to break into his workshop and learn all his secrets.

Now, *there* was an idea. Her grandfather would be proud. He would be so proud, the secret would probably burst out of his lips and right into her father's ears. Her father had a really funny attitude about corporate espionage. He thought it should be done discreetly, by people who couldn't be linked back to the Corey family.

"Then why are you eating by yourself?" Sylvain asked.

She glared at him. From buying his secrets with millions to becoming his act of social charity was a pretty brutal step down. Of course, maybe he wasn't concerned so much as trying to humiliate her.

"Because I don't really like people," she lied coldly.

There, that should shut anyone up and turn his attention back to his date. She wondered what it was like to date a man who could do what he did with chocolate and who had eyes as dark as . . .

"Vraiment?" Sylvain said, intrigued. "Do you just see them as dollars and euros, or how does that work?"

A second before she slapped her credit card onto the table and called for the waiter, Cade realized what a victory it would be for him to drive her out of the restaurant. The same way he had driven her out of his *laboratoire*. With just a few contemptuous words and a supremely disdainful look.

She took a slow breath, focused on her ravioli in its cream sauce so faintly tinted with green, and cut into it with her fork.

"Bon appétit," Chantal said kindly.

Seriously, Cade hated her. She would take spite a hundred times over kindness from that beautiful Parisian blonde sitting across from an equally gorgeous sorcerer of chocolate.

The *raviole* bloomed in her mouth: just the right amount of basil, salt, and melted butter, pine nuts, cream, perfect fresh pasta with something inside she wasn't quite sure of. All condensed into one thousand calories a bite.

She realized she had closed her eyes as she savored the pasta square, and she opened them to find Sylvain Marquis smiling a little as he watched her. As if he knew that moment, that first bite of this dish, and was enjoying it vicariously through her.

Enjoying the taste in her mouth.

She found herself blushing, a strange fever that spread through her mercilessly. She could feel it mounting to her cheeks, growing visible, and she could not for the pride of her get it to stop.

The smile slowly faded off Sylvain Marquis's mouth as he gazed at her. The waiter came up to their table, and Chantal answered whatever he asked, but Sylvain didn't even seem to hear him.

"Sylvain?" Chantal said. His name sounded so perfectly pronounced by her delicate French lips. The *ain* was so correct, like the breath of a whine.

He didn't respond.

Chantal glanced from him to Cade, and she didn't look very pleased at all. Cade turned her head to stare out the window.

"Sylvain," Chantal said again.

"Hmm?" Sylvain's voice sounded distracted.

"Tu as choisi, mon cher?"

"Pardon. Oui. Les ravioles," he told the waiter.

Heat roiled through her again.

This was pathetic and ridiculous, she told herself. Could she fake a seizure so she could get out of this restaurant?

No, a seizure would make her look bad. A heart attack? An allergic reaction to basil? That might explain the flushing. Maybe she could fake getting something in her eye and disappear to a bathroom, climb out its window, and never return to her table. She searched surreptitiously for signs of a bathroom but couldn't find one on the ground floor. Meaning it was either belowground or upstairs. She was pretty sure she couldn't carve a tunnel before someone came to look for her, but she wondered how much toilet paper it would take to make a rope.

For some reason, climbing out of a bathroom window on a rope of toilet paper seemed like a less humiliating plan than just paying her bill now and walking out.

"You aren't going to eat it?" Sylvain asked her incredulously.

Couldn't the man just talk to his date? Turn his back on her? Leave her alone?

"I'm not very hungry," she said. She had been when she'd ordered her three-course meal just before he walked in, but now she felt as if she were trying to get her food down past a horde of butterflies.

Sylvain's lips formed one of those tight, beautiful French Os but without a sound. He looked at her plate and then at her mouth. One eyebrow lifted a little in question, and he looked into her eyes again.

Just exactly what did he think he was figuring out about her? What questions were those eyes asking that were making warmth start to lurk in their depths?

"I ate too much chocolate today," she explained quickly, without thinking.

Sylvain looked smug.

"I was at Dominique Richard's," she added sweetly.

This was such a good hit that Chantal's lips parted, and she brought up a perfectly manicured hand to cover them. Cade's hands were perfectly manicured, too, but she didn't know how to make them cover her mouth so sexily. Did French women practice in front of a mirror, or what?

Sylvain's own lips thinned, and anyone would have thought she had reached out and smacked him. "And did he sell himself?" he asked disdainfully.

Caught between a lie and having to admit defeat to him, Cade remembered abruptly that she was part-owner of a multinational corporation. "I can't discuss contract negotiations," she said, with the same gentle coolness she had used in business meetings a thousand times before.

He didn't like that at all. He turned abruptly back to his date at last, but he was visibly simmering.

"Oh, have you been trying to buy Sylvain?" Chantal asked playfully, clearly trying to break the tension and recapture his attention and her enjoyable evening. "How much do you cost, *chéri?*"

Sylvain lanced Cade a glance like lightning. "*I'm* not for sale."

"Oh, I don't know," Cade said pleasantly, trying for a perfect little contemptuous put-down. *Which was a very hard thing to do in someone else's language,* she later tried to console herself. "I paid nearly a thousand dollars for a bite of you just yesterday."

Chantal's eyebrows went up. They even did that perfectly.

Sylvain's lips formed that beautiful French *O* again. Then they split into a grin.

Oh, God. What had she just said? Please let the earth open up and swallow her.

It took Sylvain a full minute before he managed to get that grin calmed down into something more urbane, a silky, gorgeously self-satisfied gloating. "Why, so you did."

She couldn't even stammer out something about "a bite of *your chocolates*" to correct the impression her words had left. She and he both knew that when she took a bite of his chocolates, she really *was* taking a bite of him.

She strove for a disdainful moue instead, wishing she had practiced that expression in the mirror when she was working on her French *u*. One needed a lot more than language skills to get by in France. "A bit overpriced, don't you think? But I suppose you can always fool some people into thinking anything is good if you charge enough."

A muscle ticked in his jaw. He fulminated.

"Sylvain is *the best* chocolatier in Paris," Chantal said coldly.

"Do you think so?" Cade raised her eyebrows. "Have you tried anything of Dominique Richard's?"

The glare Sylvain sent her could have made her burst into flame. She really couldn't shake that sorcerer impression of him, and right now the sorcerer looked like the kind that fed impertinent people to demons.

"Non," Chantal said loyally.

Cade shrugged and opened a palm, making her point without a word.

Sylvain looked as if feeding her to demons might not be enough of a punishment. He might want to kill her with his own two hands.

"I'm satisfied with Sylvain." Chantal smirked, catching his eye and winking at him.

Damn it. Depression out of all proportion to the comment settled on Cade. What a horrible, nauseating evening.

She refocused on her gloriously exquisite *raviole du Royan à la crème au basilic* and poked at it with her fork.

After a moment, she inevitably glanced sideways, to find Sylvain watching her again. His gaze was thoughtful, his anger visibly down at least three notches.

It occurred to her that she had been blushing so constantly since she met him that he might just assume she had naturally red skin. It was possible, right?

The waiter brought his basil cream ravioli, and he refocused on Chantal a bit, exchanging pleasantries for a few minutes before offering her a perfunctory *Bon appétit*. But when he took his first bite, his eyes closed a little in pleasure, too, if a bit more familiar and expected than Cade's.

When he opened them again, he looked straight at her.

Cade, who had finally gotten the butterflies suppressed enough to take another bite, got caught with her fork still at her lips, flushing again all through her. The taste on their tongues right at that moment was exactly the same.

Their eyes held. Was that a touch of color on Sylvain's cheeks?

Chantal sighed, looking subdued for a moment, then tossed her head in a sexy, *tant pis pour toi* way that made the perfectly feathered ends of her hair shiver and catch the light. She stretched out a little hand to close over Sylvain's, one of those beautiful, masculine hands that knew exactly how to manipulate . . . probably far too many things. And she tugged it, just a little.

He looked back at her, and she held his eyes, half smile, half query. He flushed suddenly and shifted his body to angle away from Cade.

Cade, too, shifted to angle her body back toward the window and tried to eat more of her ravioli. For something that had a thousand calories a bite, she would have preferred it to taste a little less like sawdust. Also, her throat felt horribly exposed every time she swallowed, as if everyone in the restaurant was focused on what an ungainly gesture swallowing was.

Well, not everyone, really. Just one person. And his elegant date who swallowed so beautifully, it was practically a sexual act.

It should have helped when another couple came in and took the table between hers and Marquis's. At least she could pretend that was what stopped him from pestering her, and not the tug of Chantal's hand.

Having the other couple between them now did mean that her every glance away from the window didn't land on him or Chantal. It meant that his every stray glance away from his date or dinner didn't land on her. The shield provided by the couple's bodies should have helped save some part of the evening.

Except that she was still the only person there who wasn't half of a couple. And one of those couples was *his*. The next hour might very well have been the longest in her life, stretched to infinity by her desire to be doing anything but eating alone in Paris two tables away from those two.

The waiter gave her second course, duck in a honey-apricot sauce, still three quarters-full, a look of deep concern when he unwillingly removed it from the table. "No dessert? *Mais, madame, vous avez le prix fix.*"

"It doesn't matter," she said. "I'll pay for it." The waiter looked offended that she should have mentioned money openly, even though she couldn't figure out why else he cared that she had changed her mind about dessert. "I'm just not hungry enough."

"Do you want a—what do you call it—a *doggy bag*?" Sylvain asked from his table, smirking at the possibility of seeing her do something he clearly considered revolting.

"Personally, I've always thought the 'doggy bag' would be a good thing to have here," Chantal said, being kind again, which really was just the very last straw of this miserable evening. "I can never finish the whole meal, either, and the dessert always looks so good."

The waiter gave Chantal an indignant look at the suggestion and made no attempt to pull out any foam boxes.

"I'm fine," Cade said, falling back on the cool, courteous tone she used whenever she had to meet with Mars company executives right after a particularly successful bit of marketing on their part. *"Mais merci."* Always pretend they really meant it nicely; that way they could doubt the success of their attacks.

She beckoned the waiter closer to her with a small smile.

His eyebrows rose, but he bent, and then bent still farther when she beckoned again.

When he straightened, he was quite openly, but playfully, disappointed. "*Vous êtes cruelle, madame.* When a beautiful woman dining alone wants to whisper in my ear, you can't blame me for getting my hopes up."

Beyond him, Sylvain was frowning.

Cade laughed, rather pleased at one of her first encounters with casual Parisian charm. "Well . . . maybe I'll come back for that dessert one day."

The waiter laughed, winked, and gave a tiny bow.

Sylvain turned back to Chantal. His frown lingered.

Cade signed the credit slip and left, adding a generous, American-sized tip. It was probably a stupid whim, but, having seen for herself how annoying the other couple's kindness was, she could only hope that when Marquis discovered she had paid for their meal, he would feel as galled and condescended to as she had.

She hoped he brooded over it, that muscle in his jaw ticking and his stress rising, the whole rest of the evening.

Although Chantal would probably prove a pretty good stress reliever. *Damn it.*

Chapter 6

"There you go again," Chantal said as soon as the door had closed behind Cade.

Sylvain watched Cade head down the street, her chin up, a slim, small figure with a long stride. Her heels took the cobblestones as if they were no obstacle, her tailored black coat hiding her body all the way down to the tops of her boots. The problem with fall and winter was that he always saw women's coats as Christmas wrapping paper. He wanted to take Cade Corey somewhere warm where he could push that coat off and see what Papa Noël had left him underneath.

Papa Noël had a nasty habit of leaving him coal, though.

"What do you mean?" he asked, irritated already by what he suspected Chantal meant.

He didn't want to admit how much of his irritation came from the fact that Cade Corey had left so early. What was wrong with her? Didn't she know how to eat? The waiter hadn't even brought his and Chantal's main course yet, and the whole evening suddenly looked flat.

Another idea snuck through him: had he made her that self-conscious?

He smiled a little, rubbing his fingers over the smooth wood of the table.

"Falling for some glamorous, rich woman who is just going to use you," Chantal said reproachfully.

"No, I am not," he said, deeply annoyed. Act like an idiot in high school—and, okay, through half his twenties—and your old friends never let you forget it.

Chantal gave her head her characteristic toss, a move she had started affecting way back in high school and had practiced until it became part of her.

He thought of Cade Corey again, with her unconscious arrogance and sudden blushes. He didn't think she had a head-toss in her. That chin led too straightly. Even when she was flushing, she tended to look at him straight on.

She did flush—a lot.

His mouth curved again, his thumb rubbing this time over the slender stem of his wineglass.

Guiltily, he realized he wanted to ditch one of his closest friends so he could linger in thoughts of exactly why Cade Corey flushed so much and ways he could make her flush even more.

"Then what, exactly, are you doing?" Chantal asked dryly, forcing her way into his attention.

"I'm *trying* to have dinner with a friend. Do we have to talk about Cade Corey? It's bad enough that she's following me everywhere I go."

It flattered the hell out of him that she was following him everywhere he went. That chin indicated a woman who knew what she wanted. A woman who *really knew* what she wanted. Talk about erotic.

Unfortunately, what she wanted was his name on her mass-market chocolate. But he couldn't help wondering if there was any way he could shift her focus a little and make *him* what she wanted. He had honed serious skills in luring women with chocolate.

"*Bon.*" Chantal tossed her head again. "We won't talk about her."

"No. Let's not ruin a good evening." He rapped his knuckles against the table a couple of times. "Do you know what she did?" he exploded. "She walked into my shop straight off a jet from America and tried to buy me. Buy *my name*, Sylvain Marquis, to put on *Corey Bars*. Can you believe that?"

Chantal's mouth dropped open. "*C'est vrai?* But, Sylvain, you would make a fortune."

He made a hard motion with one hand, as if he could chop Cade Corey's head off with it. "*Sylvain Marquis?* On *Corey* Bars?"

"True," Chantal admitted. "That would be . . . pretty humiliating." She was silent for a moment. "You could go retire in Tahiti if you wanted, though."

Sylvain stared at her. He and Chantal had been friends since high school. That is, he had had a crush on her, and she had used him occasionally in high school, and eventually that had developed into real friendship. It had never occurred to him that Chantal didn't even know who he was. "You can't make good chocolate in Tahiti. Too hot and too humid, and who is going to eat chocolate made in Tahiti, anyway?" He was the best chocolatier in *Paris*. Being the best chocolatier anywhere else seemed a sad and pitiful thing.

"*Bon, bon.*" Chantal held up a hand. "I get it. My apologies for mentioning the advantages. I know you can't let her buy you."

"Thank you," he said, partially reassured. Maybe a fifteen-year friendship had led to some mutual understanding, after all.

"Don't let her *use* you, either," Chantal said with emphasis.

Sylvain gritted his teeth. "I won't. Didn't we say we weren't going to talk about her?"

"You did say that," Chantal said very dryly.

He flushed. And managed not to talk about Cade Corey the whole rest of the evening, right up until he didn't get the bill.

"She did what?" he asked Grégory, the waiter, ominously.

"Paid for your dinners," Grégory said, amused.

"And you *let* her?"

Grégory looked taken aback. "What's wrong with her paying for your dinner?"

"Everything." Sylvain pushed back from the table.

The waiter shrugged. "I thought it was kind of cute. *She* was cute." He touched his ear as if he could still feel Cade's breath tickling it when she whispered to him. *"Son petit accent . . ."*

Sylvain caught himself just short of a snarl. He had the privilege of having this excellent restaurant five doors down from his apartment building. The last thing he needed to do was tackle the waiter and get banned from the place because of some spoiled billionaire.

Who wanted to buy him.

Who had just bought his meal with a little flick of her pen. Like she was tipping her shoe-shiner.

His jaw ground so hard, he could feel the muscles protesting.

"Remind *me* never to buy you dinner again," Chantal murmured, impressed by his reaction.

He forced the words between his teeth: "It's not the same thing at all."

Chantal looked away. "That's what I was afraid of," she said, oddly.

The gray, dim streets of Paris hesitated at dawn. Poetic and tentative, they clung to the night even as they were drawn inexorably out of it. Here someone left a doorway and forged, head bent, into the cold new day, aiming for the warm light of the bakery spilling out from under its burgundy awning. There a car engine started.

Still the streets hesitated, as people clung to warm covers

or warm showers or made a cup of coffee. It was all starting over, another intense Paris day. Were they ready for it?

Standing at her window, gazing at the dawn, Cade resisted the urge to check e-mail and hide in her responsibilities back home. She pulled her robe tightly around her, eyeing the windows across the street for signs of life. All up and down the street, lights were coming on, but sporadically, not as many or as simultaneously as they had the morning before.

It was Sunday, she realized. All the chocolatiers would be closed.

She would have no chance today of finding a way to fulfill her dream, but also no chance to fail at it over and over again.

She spun away from the window, delighted. She felt as if she had woken up and discovered that Santa had stopped by a month early and left her presents everywhere: she could go to the Louvre, skip stones on the Canal St-Martin, have bread at Poilâne, go see Mariage Frères. Just to browse and buy tea. No purchase of the entire business necessary. No pursuit of a dream and risk of its failure required.

She skipped the claustrophobic elevator and took the stairs, suddenly happy with her lot in life again.

In the street outside her building, a car the size of a shoebox nipped by, far too fast for a lane so short and so narrow. Sunday morning it might be, but the steering wheel of a car clearly acted like coffee on Parisian drivers. A gangly young man crouched, tightening in-line skates on his feet, unsmiling, focused on his own world. An older man, maybe someone with a family, came out of the bakery with a white paper bag in one hand and a white box dangling by its string from a finger of the other. He was smiling, slightly, at nothing, at Paris and a Sunday morning, as he headed around the corner. Cade imagined the family waiting for him, the man depositing the treasure of Sunday-morning pastries before the children in casual satisfaction.

A group of six women and one man milled awkwardly in front of Sylvain Marquis's store, some of them talking excitedly, others acting like people who didn't know one another very well. Three of the women were Japanese and formed their own tight, elegant group. Two others were clearly American.

"I don't think he opens today," Cade told them. The last person who needed to find groupies waiting all day for him was Sylvain Marquis.

"Oh, we're here for the workshop," a sixty-something American woman answered proudly. In a purple pantsuit and plastered with makeup, she looked as excited and pleased with herself as could be.

"The workshop?" Was Sylvain Marquis teaching the secrets of his artistry?

"We're going to learn how to make Sylvain Marquis chocolate," the woman explained excitedly.

"Really." Cade barely hesitated. "Um—could I ask you something in private?" She gestured to move them a little out of earshot of the others.

"Why?" the woman asked, immediately wary. "Are you going to attack me?"

Cade looked at her blankly and then down at her own elegant and expensive coat, boots, gloves. "Do I *look* as if I'm about to attack you?"

"Well—no," the other woman admitted. "But this is Paris. Muggers probably dress better here."

"No, I just—how much money would you want to give up your place in this workshop and let me pretend to be you?"

"None!" the other woman said, offended. "I've been looking forward to this for months! I planned my whole trip to Paris around it!"

"Two thousand dollars." Cade tried to blow aside all reservations with the first extravagant figure.

"Are you kidding?" The other woman looked outraged. "It costs more than that to take the class!"

His workshops cost more than $2000? Cade raised her eyebrows at the seventeenth-century stone walls that stood between her and that workshop, impressed and annoyed both at once. "Five thousand dollars."

"I said no!"

What was it with people refusing to let her buy them these days? "*And* I'll pay for you to stay in Paris another two weeks in a beautiful apartment and take cooking classes at the Cordon Bleu."

The woman hesitated. Finally Cade was striking a chord. Then the older woman frowned suspiciously. "Why? Why do you want my place so badly?"

Fine. Someone was going to arrive to open the doors to the workshop at any minute. Cade turned back to the others waiting there. The Japanese women were hopeless; from the way they were dressed, money wasn't going to buy a darn thing from them. Besides, Cade didn't speak Japanese. She focused on the Americans and French: "Does anyone want to earn five thousand dollars?"

Everyone stared at her blankly. She repeated it in French.

"What is that worth in euros?" the Frenchman asked. "Fifty *centimes*?"

Was it against the law to be helpful in France or something? Cade gave him an aggravated look.

"Now, wait a minute," the woman in purple interrupted. "I didn't say I was turning you down. But I'll take the two extra weeks in Paris and the course at the Cordon Bleu in cash, if you don't mind. What does that come to? Ten thousand dollars or so?"

Cade was never going to be able to put this on her expense account. "Fine," she said. At least this way she would know his secrets.

Know his secrets . . . The words whispered through her, tantalizing her on more levels than she had suspected. The secrets of that dark sorcerer, in his workshop full of magic.

Trade secrets, she clarified to herself. Secrets of the chocolate craft. That was what she was after. He could keep his other kind of secrets, the jerk.

"Um . . . I might have to write you a check," she told the woman.

The woman gave a snort and turned back to the others.

"I'm good for it," Cade said desperately. She didn't have time to renegotiate with anyone else. And with intense impatience, she didn't want to wait for the next workshop, whenever that was. It could be months from now.

The purple-pantsuit lady gave her a disgusted look.

"No, really," Cade said. She pulled out her ever-present talisman Corey Bar, a business card, and her US driver's license, holding them out in her open palms. "Look."

The woman glanced, annoyed and puzzled, at the Corey Bar, then at the business card. Her gaze slowed, and she gave the card a thorough read, then looked from the license to Cade's face and back. Cade wished she hadn't looked quite so much like a drug trafficker in that license photo, but money couldn't buy everything.

As this city seemed determined to teach her.

"I'm good for it," Cade repeated.

"I don't know. . . ." The woman's gaze flickered between Cade's face and the evidence of her identity again. "I—*really?* Are you really one of the real Coreys? Do you think you could . . ."

A man came around the corner down at the far end of the street and headed in their direction. Cade thought she recognized one of the men who had been in Sylvain's *laboratoire* that first day. She thrust her fingers back into her wallet. "I'll tell you what: you tell me your name and let me pretend to be you in this workshop today, and I'll let you use my credit card while I'm doing it."

"Done." The woman reached out to snatch the credit card before Cade could remember reason. "Christian Dior, here I come!"

"Meet me here at six, or I'm calling the police," Cade warned. Or, better yet, her credit card company to cancel the thing. "And what's that name again?"

By the time Maggie Saunders gave it to her, Sylvain Marquis's employee had reached the group. Everyone flooded around him when he said, *"Bonjour,"* looking slightly fatigued, as if he felt it should be someone else's lot in life to greet excited tourists at this hour of the morning.

Cade took advantage of the distraction to slip back into her building, mind racing as she tried to think of ways to disguise herself. Folded on her pillow were the loose black yoga pants and extra-large alma-mater sweatshirt she wore as pajamas in this cold apartment. She switched her elegant clothes for those quickly. She didn't have any white tennis shoes, but she could at least swap her classy little boots for her also-classy little black Pumas. Those were kind of like tennis shoes. She clipped her hair up into a sloppy twist, wishing desperately for a baseball cap. But the only one she had with her said COREY in bold letters on the front, which she didn't think would help the disguise.

She *did* have a beret. *Not* that she had thought Parisians still wore berets. She knew better. Of course she did. But *just in case* there would be an appropriate moment for her to put it on and stroll along the Seine with it, browsing through old books, she had packed it. Just in case.

She remembered the moment when she had tossed the beret into her suitcase, the quickening of hope and pleasure, her attempt to quell it with sophisticated cynicism.

She pulled it on now, covering most of her hair, not daring to look at the sweatshirt-beret combination in a mirror. If she had more time or more skill, she might try to make her features look different with different makeup. But that would take forever to figure out, so instead she just scrubbed her subtle makeup off entirely. At the last second, she tried to change the shape of her eyes with eyeliner but ended up looking vaguely Goth instead.

Well, hey. A Goth in a sweatshirt and beret. The only people likely to recognize her were those who had known her as a teenager.

The man who had opened the door was inside with the others, handing out pastry-chef hats and jackets to all the attendees, by the time she got back. With hair the color of straw, cut to a short spike, and a few days' growth on his jaw, he looked slightly younger than Sylvain Marquis and a little shorter but was good-looking in his own way. What was it about these French chocolatiers? His gaze swept her from head to toe and back up again, and his eyebrows rose just slightly in incredulity. What, he would have preferred the purple pantsuit?

"Hi," she said in English, in the longest drawl she had, as if she couldn't speak a word of French, which was what he would probably believe even if she was talking to him in his own language. "I'm—" What was that woman's name again? *Oh, right.* "Maggie Saunders. Sorry I'm late."

The man's look of stretched patience deepened, and he handed her a chef's jacket about four sizes too big for her. She grinned as she stuffed her hair more securely up under the paper cap he also gave her. Her own daddy would probably have a hard time picking her out of a lineup in this getup.

Cade Corey, chocolate spy. That had a nice ring to it, didn't it? *Chocolate spy.* She could imagine herself in World War II, some kind of Mata Hari takeoff, smuggling the secrets of chocolate out of France before the Germans got their hands on it.

Then she imagined Sylvain Marquis in a beret, snorting at the idea that the Germans would know what to do with the secrets of chocolate even if they did get their hands on it.

"Madame . . . Madame . . . Madame *Sewn-DAIRRRRsss,*" penetrated her consciousness.

She blinked at the man now standing directly in front of her, finally remembering her fake last name. "Sorry." She blushed. That was getting old, the blushing. She had too much self-confidence to blush back in the US.

"If you could take this station," he said, leading her to a great black marble counter squared around an empty space where someone could stand in its center. The other students had already placed themselves around it. The long, large room had a triple heart: this great marble island and another, and farther down at the other end, the Sollich enrobing machine and cooling tunnel. She recognized the German manufacturer, but this machine was nothing, a child's toy, compared to the great enrobing machines and cooling tunnels in the Corey factories.

Cade pressed her hands onto the counter's smooth chill, excited beyond measure. The sense of a dream on the brink of fulfillment took her insides and wrung them like a sopping rag, tighter and tighter until the water had to go somewhere and nearly sparkled in her eyes.

She had taken artisan-chocolate workshops before—at the Culinary Institute in New York, for example. With Alice Medrich on another occasion. But those had been *American.* Here she was in *France.* About to learn the secrets of the best chocolatier in Paris.

Well, he thinks *he is the best,* she corrected herself hastily, remembering the disdain on that handsome face. True, the mayor also thought he was the best. As did his lovely friend

Chantal. And most of the population of the city. But that did not mean he really *was* the best.

She had to keep that in mind, because he was clearly too stuck-up for his own good as it was. She stuffed her hands into the chef-jacket pockets, determined to get hold of herself, and her knuckles brushed against something startlingly hard and cold. She pulled them back, then brushed the item carefully with her fingertips. It was a key. She tried to keep her face expressionless as she wondered what that key unlocked.

"*Je suis Pascal Guyot, le sous-chef chocolatier* here, and I will be leading the class for you," the man who had let them in said, moving to stand in front of the class. Cade felt let down.

No, relieved. Relieved, of course, that Sylvain Marquis would not be sharing his secrets in person. This way she didn't run the risk of his recognizing her.

She bent over to tie one of her shoelaces, and while she was bent over, she slipped the key from her jacket pocket to her shoe, which was the only place she could manage to hide it subtly. They needed to start putting pockets in yoga pants.

"When we talk about the chocolate," Pascal Guyot said, "the first thing is to be clear what we discuss. For example, a *chocolat noir* at 70 percent does not react the same way a *chocolat au lait* does to anything—to heat, to tempering, to the palate. A *chocolat noir* at 72 percent that comes from the Caribbean will react differently than a *chocolat noir* at 72 percent that comes from the Andes."

Cade again pressed her hands onto the marble, focusing on the pleasure of that chill, the words blurring a little around her ears. She knew this stuff. The Corey chemists had the science of chocolate down to a hundredth of a degree. Chemistry had been one of her minors in college.

Her gaze swept the room, trying to take in everything. Liquors lined part of one wall, some of which she could pick out from where she stood—white rum and dark, and the bronze of Armagnac. Great burlap sacks slouched against the walls, black words stamped on their sides. What did those words say? What was in those bags, and from what lands had they come?

Bottles of opaque dark brown glass whose labels she could not read lined a shelf—what flavors did he have there? A chef pouch of vanilla lay open on a counter, beans glistening brown against its gold backing, with more vacuum-sealed pouches in a crate under the shelf of extracts. She could smell that vanilla even from where she stood. It provided the undertone to the chocolate, modulating it, giving it sweetness.

"With M. Marquis, we work with a supplier who roasts our cocoa nibs—to our own specifications, of course," Pascal Guyot said. "Most chefs buy their chocolate in bars, such as these here." He gestured to a pile of chocolate chunks in various gradations of color, clearly rough-hewn from larger blocks.

They roasted their own cocoa nibs to exacting specifications at Corey, too, Cade thought. They had been doing it for nearly a hundred years. Nobody gave *them* any credit for it.

"If everyone would come get their bars," Pascal Guyot said.

The weight of the chocolate chunks sparked excitement through her again.

She might have gotten in under a fake name and as a spy, but she was going to be working chocolate in a Parisian *laboratoire*.

Chapter 7

Sylvain shrugged off his coat in the entryway just off the workshop, smiling a little as he heard a heavy Japanese accent struggle with a question in French. Some chocolatiers left these things to their sous-chefs, but he always liked the workshops. Once in a while, they got a jerk, but usually the students were passionate amateurs of chocolate making, delighted to be there.

It was a pleasant feeling, to teach such eager and enthusiastic students and to know that they were eager and enthusiastic for *him*, for what *he* had to teach. They reminded him of himself when he was a teenager. And they made it very clear to him that he had come a long way from that teenager, *Dieu merci*.

He pulled on his white chef's jacket and the chef's cap that only he had the right to wear and came in, nodding at Pascal and scanning this new crop of students.

He spotted the Corey capitalist so immediately, it gave him a jolt of alarm. Surely he shouldn't have instantly penetrated her disguise of white cap and chef's jacket twice as big as she was.

She looked—*mignonne* again. She was busy trying to edge her cute little body so that the Japanese woman between him and her blocked his view. Unfortunately for her, the Japanese woman in question was even smaller than she was.

He gazed at her for a long moment as the realization of what she was trying to do sank in and started to simmer in him. First she had tried to buy him. Then she had said she preferred *Dominique Richard,* of all people. Then she had paid for his and Chantal's dinner the night before as casually as if she were tossing a coin to a beggar.

And now she was trying to *steal* his secrets.

He hesitated between smugness and outrage. It was nice to be pursued so desperately. She had to know it was a long shot. How many of his most prized recipes did she think he was going to reveal in a workshop for amateurs like this?

She gave up trying to fiddle with her cap and hide her face as he continued to look at her. Her hands dropped to the marble countertop and fisted there. A flush colored her cheekbones.

She had flushed last night. Repeatedly, as she sat there looking so lonely and recalcitrant, arrogant and vulnerable. She had closed her eyes in a moment of pure bliss the second those *ravioles du Royan* in their *crème au basilic* had touched her tongue, just as he had known she would.

And then she had met his eyes and flushed crimson and not eaten another bite.

She had been too busy being obnoxious.

He walked quietly past the other students, without interrupting Pascal, and stopped in front of her.

Her fists clenched so tightly on the marble, he wondered if she was going to bruise her knuckles against the stone. Her eyes were so intense, for a moment it looked as if she was biting back an urge to beg.

Beg?

Why do you want this so badly? he wanted to ask her. *What could you possibly be seeking here that would make someone like you bite back the word* please?

The Corey family owned something like 30 percent of the cacao plantations in the world. Owned them. They funded entire institutes that were the only thing standing between chocolatiers like himself and infestations of witches'-broom that might destroy all the crops. They were even famous for leading the movement to improve worker welfare on cacao plantations.

The knowledge of their power and generosity should have made him nicer to her, but . . . she had paid for his dinner as if he were a *beggar*.

No, worse, as if he was her chocolate gigolo or something.

"Mademoiselle Corey," he said urbanely, loud enough that her famous name could be heard by all the other students there. "Of Corey Chocolate," he added, just in case they hadn't made the connection. "What a pleasure to have you join us. Are you hoping to learn something new about chocolate?"

She bit her lip. She was a little bit stuck, wasn't she, since her eyes had just begged him to let her stay? She couldn't very well claim she *didn't* want to learn something from him about chocolate. Nor could she hit him, which it looked as if she might like to do.

For some reason, her clear desire to do him violence sent a lick of excitement through him.

He needed to get control of these licks of excitement. Last night had been bad, with that *crème au basilic*. He was such a sucker for a pretty, proud woman who savored the finer things in life.

He maintained a façade of cool superiority, but he could feel his heart thudding as he dueled for control with her.

"I would love to learn what you do with chocolate," she said in French, in a clear voice she probably used to carry across boardrooms when billions of dollars were in play, making sure everyone could hear her.

He pressed his lips together. She had taken the high road, honesty, which gave her moral superiority right off the bat.

"I told you so two days—" She broke off, fumbling for the right word in French.

Grégory was right, damn him; her accent was adorable.

"I told you so it was two days. Before. Two days before," she managed.

"Oh?" he challenged. "Not Dominique Richard?"

"If Dominique Richard is willing to teach me some of his secrets, I would be happy to learn from him, too." She made sure the name *Dominique Richard* carried just as clearly through the room as her last sentence had.

She was doing a hell of a job of keeping her dignity for a woman wearing some fairly ghastly eye makeup.

And Dominique Richard was a damn flirt. He would probably be willing to teach her quite a lot of things.

"I'm flattered you should choose me first," he said. Which was the truth. Flattered and insulted both. Mostly, it pissed him off that she had even *had* a second choice. Him or nothing—that's what it should be.

She bared her teeth at him. "Oh, you were just the only decent chocolatier offering a workshop at a time when it was convenient for me to be in Paris." Still that clear, carrying voice.

He narrowed his eyes. He was quite sure her name hadn't been on the list of students. He would have noticed. But he decided to take the high road, too, and not challenge her false pretenses. No, let that be the little sword he held over her head.

Decent. Decent chocolatier.

"Pascal, I think I'll join you today. Mademoiselle Corey, *vous permettez?*" He stepped closer to her, physically crowding her personal space.

Because she was stubborn, or arrogant, his body was actually brushing hers before she gave ground to share her counter with him.

Excitement leaped sky-high in him. Worse than last night in the restaurant. She was a good head shorter than he was. He could feel her smallness and arrogance all the way through to his bones, like a beat in him that was driving him crazy. And here, in his domain, he knew he had something she wanted.

Pascal began speaking again, telling the students to look at the blocks of different types of chocolate they had just taken back to their stations.

Sylvain picked up the darkest, the purest. Crumbs clung to it from when it had been hacked from a larger block.

He smiled, looking down at it in his hand. The finest crumbs were already starting to melt against his skin.

He had something she desperately wanted. His chocolate. Now he wanted to see if he could use that to make her desperately want him.

Chapter 8

Cade thought if her heart beat any faster or more blood rushed to her cheeks, she might pass out. To cool herself down, she drew up an image of Chantal, *la Parisienne parfaite,* and tried to mentally paste it to the inside of her forehead.

"This is one of my favorite moments," Sylvain murmured to her, his voice a brush of sound, too low to interfere with Pascal's lesson, too low for anyone but her. "The chocolate is untouched, virgin." *Chocolat,* he said. Not that clumsy, cute English word *chok-lat* but a caress, a mystery, *sho-co-la.* "I choose it. It is beautiful as it is, perfect; anyone could eat it forever. Yet I bring something else to it, blend it with another flavor that makes people encounter it in a new way, a richer way."

His voice burred over her skin. All the fine hairs on her arms rose to that voice and to the words that seemed to talk about more than chocolate. Made her want to *be* his chocolate.

"I pour it into another form worthy of it, something as beautiful as its essence, so that just looking at it fills people with desire."

She realized her lips had parted, her breath had grown shallow. She kept her lashes lowered, her gaze focused on that dark block in his hand. On his strong, square palms, on the long, adept fingers.

"*Tenez.*" He handed it to her.

She did everything she could to take it without touching him, but he shifted his hand at the last second, and his fingers brushed hers. She sank her teeth into the inside of her lower lip.

"We have here *criollo*—do you know it?"

"I probably produced it," Cade told him in a clipped voice. It was arrogant to say "I" and not "we," but he was provoking. Did she *know* one of the four major types of cacao? True, they didn't really use it in Corey Bars—too expensive for their market—but she knew what it was.

"No," he said definitely. "No, part of this came from a small grower in Venezuela. I liked their crop this year, *épicé et voluptueux.*"

Spicy, voluptuous. Oh, God. Why were even those words dissolving her?

"The rest came from Madagascar, and perhaps some of that may have been from one of your plantations." His brow knitted. "It's strange that a company capable of encouraging such a quality primary production could end up with . . . what you end up with."

Cade thought of the poor, maligned Corey Bar in her purse hanging in the entryway. Millions of people were biting into a Corey Bar right this minute, and it was making all of them very happy. Only one or two people were biting into one of his chocolates, she reminded herself. And they almost certainly had at least six-figure incomes. They could find other things to make them happy.

"In what percentages did you combine them?" she asked. "What kind of conch did you use, and how long and how hard?"

His lips curved in a very male smile that took her technical question in a completely different direction.

She tried to ignore that, but she could feel all her eroge-nous zones flushing with heat. "How much cocoa butter did you add?"

He laughed and shook his head. "You might be able to flirt that information out of Dominique Richard, but I think I can hold out a little longer."

Her skin burned. Had that been yet another contemptu-ous dismissal? This time implying that her flirting was not ef-fective?

Why was he accusing *her* of flirting? She was standing there in humiliating Goth eye makeup, a sweatshirt, and an enormous pastry-chef jacket. He was the one talking about *virgin* chocolate with which he could do anything he wanted.

"Now . . . what do you want to make of this *chocolat*?"

"Anything you tell me to," Cade said, trying to be flip, to remind him that she was taking lessons and had to do what the instructor said. But it didn't come out quite right. Her tone was too low, too absorbed.

"Anything?" Sylvain gave her a little smile that made her feel like the teacher's pet. *"Vraiment."*

Utensils had been laid out on each counter, waiting for the students. He picked up a great butcher knife, its blade as sharp as a stage whisper. His chef's jacket, of course, fit him perfectly, made for him, so that his straight shoulders and lean waist were clearly defined. Elbow-length sleeves revealed lean, corded forearms, the muscles of his profession. *"Veuillez m'aider à hacher ce chocolat, mademoiselle."*

There was only one knife. How was she supposed to help cut with it? She looked around for another one.

"Tenez." He physically took her hand and put it over the handle of the knife. His hand on hers.

Her skin felt sunburned, as if she needed to douse it in aloe and cold water.

"Do you know how to hold a knife, *mademoiselle*?"

Yes. She had taken artisan chocolate workshops before,

just not in Paris. And she liked to cook. At least once a month, she cooked. She always made it an elaborate, gourmet affair. But she kept silent, while his long, warm, agile fingers positioned hers, open, on handle and blade, so that she could shave off bits of chocolate without cutting off her fingers.

The blade looked wickedly sharp. In her currently rattled state, she probably *would* cut off her fingers if she tried to manipulate it solo. But his hands stayed strong on hers, linking with her fingers to keep them lifted away from the blade. Together, his deftness overpowering her clumsiness, they shaved chocolate off a corner of the dark block. It curled and crumpled and fell to pieces against the cold marble, piling on top of itself.

His arms brushed against hers, his biceps pressing against her shoulder. She could feel his lean, strong body. She could feel him taming himself for her, the speed and energy pent up and kept under control. He did not usually shave off his chocolate carefully, stroke by stroke, she knew. His knife would fly through it, thoughtlessly, as automatic as breathing; his muscles, used to this work, would barely be conscious of its resistance, its hardness under the knife.

He lifted a shaving on one finger and brought it to her lips. *"Goûtez,"* he said. "Tell me what you taste."

"Could you show *me* how to cut the chocolate?" one of the American women asked Pascal hopefully, eyeing them from across the table. "I think I might need some . . . help."

Pascal Guyot gave Sylvain Marquis a look of deeply tried patience. Sylvain didn't even notice it, focused on Cade.

The chocolate was melting already on her parted lips. She took it, perforce, her lips closing just barely, just briefly, on his finger.

His lashes lowered to hide some expression.

She tasted . . . She didn't think she should tell him what she tasted. It went beyond the chocolate, which was bitter, bitter on her tongue but extraordinarily smooth.

A little sigh ran through him. "Let us make something you would like," he told her, with heat in his eyes and a little, very male curve lingering around his mouth, as if he was playing a game he very much enjoyed.

She was his game, Cade told herself. Was that it?

Was he hers?

"What do you like in your *chocolat, mademoiselle?*"

He poured white cream into a small pot as he spoke to her and added inverted sugar. He had taken her lesson in a different direction from the rest of the workshop. Pascal was still showing the others how to cut their chocolate and trying to stay patient with the woman who was being particularly helpless and demanding of hands-on instruction.

"Cinnamon," she said.

"*Cannelle?*" He gave her a little smile, as if she had charmed him.

Charmed him how? Like a quaint child whose hair he wanted to ruffle?

"*Vous aimez la tradition,*" he said.

Yes, she supposed she did love tradition. Corey prided itself on being the chocolate of generations of Americans, and it had never once changed its original milk chocolate bar. So that was tradition. And the only way she wanted to break that Corey tradition was by sinking into a realm of chocolate that had been exquisite even before her country was born.

"Then we shall make you something with cinnamon." He moved away to the shelves where the brown bottles were, grabbing a handful of cinnamon sticks. On his way back to her, he picked up a brick of butter that had been set out to soften. "Say it again in English?"

"Cinnamon," she repeated helplessly.

Heat leaped in his eyes. "It has a *je ne sais quoi* to it in English, *cinnamon*. More mystery, more exotic, than in French."

"Because it starts with *sin,*" she tried to say. Only she couldn't think of *sin* in French. "*Pêche?*"

Supple black eyebrows crinkled. "Cinnamon and peaches? With your chocolate? I don't think . . ."

He paused, clearly unable to reject any combination of flavors out of hand without giving it serious analysis.

"No," she said. "No peaches. Just cinnamon."

"*Pêches confites,* perhaps," he murmured. *Candied peaches.* "But I don't have any on hand, and it's the wrong season to find them. I could perhaps order some from Nice. There's a market where you can find them in the autumn."

And did he do that? she wondered suddenly. Wander through markets, absorbing all the sights and flavors, his mind all the time spinning new spells of chocolate out of what he saw?

It made her want to take him to Morocco, to India, if he had not already been. It made her wish he would take her to Nice, to all the markets that he knew. They could walk through them, hand in hand, showing each other flavors.

What was happening to her head?

It could not possibly be healthy for all her dreams of Paris to be crystallizing around this one person.

He disdained her. And he had been out last night with a beautiful blonde.

"*Tenez.*" He handed her the cinnamon sticks and nodded to the pot of cream. She dropped them into it, watching white drops splash over the brown of the sticks. "À *feu doux.*" He caught her eyes just for a second. "One must start à *feu doux.*"

With a gentle flame.

If this was gentle, she didn't know whether to crave high heat or be terrified of it.

Terror and craving made a very powerful combination of flavors.

She set the pot on the burner nearest her, her gaze as she moved scanning the room, going over those great burlap sacks whose contents she did not know, those brown bottles, the doors to walk-in storage. Who knew what riches hid behind them? What word would unlock those doors? *"Open, cacao"*?

She tried to figure out what was a gentle flame according to French temperatures and how to work the controls of the stove. Let's see, she knew this. If the ideal storage temperature of chocolate was 17 degrees Celsius, then—

Sylvain's hand reached over hers, brushing it and half enclosing it, and pushed a couple of buttons.

Warmth ran through her. On its heels, wariness finally raised its head, and anger. What an absolute bastard he was. An arrogant absolute bastard. To be so sure of his attractiveness that he could use it to punish her.

That had to be his motivation. Why else would he be doing this?

For a wild instant, she thought about trying to turn the tables on him. Drive him crazy with *her* attractiveness. But she was wearing a sweatshirt and an enormous pastry chef's jacket, and she was currently made up like someone in an old silent film. And her magic talisman was a Corey Bar, which made his sorcerer's lip curl in disdain.

"Is this the same way Dominique Richard does it?" she asked instead in a breathless voice, trying to convey the impression that she was just using him to get nearer the true rock star around this town.

She didn't need quite that much breathiness to convey that impression, but that brush of his hand made it hard to keep steady.

The hand withdrew a fraction. When she snuck a glance, he looked very annoyed.

"I can't say I've studied the way he pours cream into a pan," he said dryly. "But it can't be that different."

She bet it could. Sylvain had a way of pouring cream into

a pan that made her feel like a cat. "No, I meant—all of this." She waved a hand to encompass the whole workshop and process.

"I don't know," Sylvain said, increasingly acerbic. "Maybe you should be stalking *him* if you would rather know his way of doing things."

Her lips snapped together, and she flushed at the hit. She was *not* . . . well, she was indeed stalking Sylvain, but it was obnoxious of him to say it out loud like that. "The restaurant was completely accidental." Did he think she would make herself that miserable on purpose?

"There are a surprising number of good restaurants in Paris that aren't in my neighborhood," he pointed out.

It was hard to carry on a conversation with someone who wouldn't politely refrain from calling her out on every possible thing that he could. Were all conversations more like fencing matches in Paris, or did she and he just have a special relationship?

"I didn't realize you lived near here, too."

He blinked, silenced for a moment. "You don't know where I live?"

She was sure she had it in her files. She just hadn't paid attention to his home address. "I'll look it up if that would make you happy."

Another pause. "You really are focused exclusively on my chocolate, aren't you?"

Cade gave him a blank look. What did he think?

What *did* he think? And did he like whatever it was he was thinking? And if so, like it how? With arrogant satisfaction or . . . ?

"I believe I mentioned my interest in your chocolate when we first met," she said pointedly. "In fact, I believe my assistant might have hinted at something to that effect when she set up our first meeting."

He made a vague gesture at the mention of their initial,

infuriating meeting. "I thought you were just asking to visit the *laboratoire* while you were in Paris. It seemed a simple courtesy to agree."

"You do things out of courtesy?" she asked blankly.

Indignation sparked immediately in those chocolate-dark eyes. "I'm being courteous to you right now!"

Was he brushing his finger against her lips as he brought exquisite, bitter chocolate to them out of courtesy? Because if he was, she was going to kill him.

Him and his kind girlfriend.

"I am making you a chocolate," he said. "I don't get any more courteous than that."

Was he really? she thought, utterly seduced and undone. Was he making up a chocolate on the spot, just for her?

"But if you sell it, or put my name on it, or in any way re-produce it in some mass, bastardized version of pseudo-chocolate, I will take my case straight to US courts, where I can sue millions out of you."

"Or we could skip the suing step and just sign a contract," Cade suggested. "You would still get millions, and I'm sure it would be less stressful."

His jaw clenched. He whipped up the butcher knife and shaved a second block of chocolate to bits in so little time, it was like watching *The Six Million Dollar Man*.

It gave a jolt to her stomach to think exactly how much he had been taming himself to go slowly with her a moment before. It gave a jolt to some other regions, too. This man made her melt all over.

"Exactly how much money would I have to sue out of you to make you regret something?"

Cade gave that some thought. "I think a few million would probably get the company's attention." Really, any lawsuit was a potential public relations issue; there was always the risk the media might pick it up and glorify the plaintiff.

"L'attention de la compagnie, je m'en fous," he said crudely.

He flipped the knife to scrape the shavings into another pot and set it over a bain-marie on a burner next to her cream, which was slowly infusing with cinnamon. Steam breathed gently up from the water. "If you do anything to me, I want you to personally regret it."

Cade could think of at least ten ways he could make her personally regret something right off the bat. But she managed to refrain from passing on a list of her weak spots to him. It was one thing to go kamikaze and quite another to commit suicide to no purpose.

Besides, she had a strong suspicion he was figuring out some of those weak spots on his own. In his pot, the chocolate shavings were melting helplessly over a flame so low, nothing else would even notice it.

The shavings were just like her, probably. He probably wasn't even trying.

"Am I not supposed to use cinnamon in any Corey products for the rest of my life, or what are you trying to get me to promise?"

He stirred his chocolate and looked aggravated.

Pascal Guyot, passing him to pick up vanilla beans for everyone else's workshop, gave him an ironic look. Sylvain looked a little embarrassed and focused more intensely on his chocolate. "She told me her name was Maggie Saunders," Pascal mentioned.

Cade remembered her credit card, and qualms seized her.

"You know what's strange?" Sylvain said, speaking more to her than to Pascal. "I would have thought a company the size of Corey would have other people to do your corporate espionage."

They did. And those people were very far removed from the top cadre of family members and executives. "You've seen too many movies," Cade dismissed him. "We're a very hands-on family, really."

The hands-on part was true, anyway. Who wanted to keep their hands off chocolate? Who the heck wanted to *pay* someone else to go learn all the secrets of a top Parisian chocolatier?

Pascal shook his head, with one last dry look at Sylvain, who ignored him, and continued back to the others, distributing vanilla beans as he went.

"I thought this workshop was full six months ago," Sylvain said. "They usually are. Did you sign up under a fake name before you even made me your offer?"

If he caught her in a lie, she knew darn well he wasn't going to ignore it to let her save face. But he probably didn't handle the day-to-day registration process for his workshops himself, right? That would be a waste of chocolate talent. "No, it was an impulse. There must have been a last-minute cancellation."

She wondered if it would be morally right to slip out and cancel her credit card now. Cade's assumption of Maggie Saunders's identity had ended up lasting only five minutes.

But if she slipped out, would she get back in?

Exactly how much was she willing to pay to learn how to infuse cream and melt chocolate, two things she already knew perfectly well how to do? This little tourist workshop was nice. It was sadistically kind of him not to kick her out of it, even. But it did not begin to be the immersion into the world of a Parisian master chocolatier that she wanted.

Sylvain Marquis leaned over her to examine her cream, and all thoughts of her credit card slipped from her mind. He picked up a clean spoon and dipped it into the cream to taste it. His eyes closed a little as he concentrated on the flavor, and she watched him helplessly, longing to know what he tasted.

He opened his eyes and smiled at her, then dipped a fresh spoon into the infusion and proffered a swallow of cream to her lips. "What do you think?"

It tasted sweet and strongly of cinnamon. His mouth would taste of cinnamon. She felt like that cream, slowly infusing with the warmth and taste he desired as he watched.

She tried to produce a coherent comment. "Too much?"

"The chocolate will overpower it quite a bit," he said. "I haven't worked much with cinnamon recently, so this is an experiment. Let's see how it goes."

"Why haven't you worked with cinnamon recently?" she asked as he fished the cinnamon sticks out of the cream. It seemed an obvious flavor combination to her.

"*C'est très datée.*" He dumped her chocolate shavings into the cream.

Cade hid a squirm. Really? Her tastes were dated for this top chocolatier? That explained the smile when he'd mentioned "*la tradition.*"

"*Et maintenant, fouettez.*" He put a sturdy whisk into her hand. "Hold it firmly, and whip it hard." He grinned a little at his own words but didn't share whatever they made him think of.

Cade, grasping the handle of the whisk and whipping the chocolate and cream into a glossy hue, suspected she could guess.

"Have you ever tempered chocolate by hand, *mademoiselle*?"

She had a couple of times, in US workshops, rather poorly. But if she said yes, he might not teach her, or, worse, he might let her manage on her own, so she shook her head.

"*Bon, d'abord, sur la table. Tenez.*" He put her hand on the pot handle. "Pour about a third of it out onto the marble."

The chocolate spilled over the marble, silky, warm, brown. Its gleam in the light made her think of that gleam in his eyes.

"*Et maintenant nous le travaillons.*" In one hand he picked up a long metal spatula three or so inches wide, in the other a much wider, shorter spatula, again flat metal. Expertly, he began to scrape, lift, and spill the chocolate between these two blades.

He had been doing that when she first met him. And she had been fantasizing she was the chocolate stretched out on his marble. She stared at it helplessly.

"You see? Now you try." He placed the spatulas into her hands, fingers brushing hers again.

She thought she made a reasonable imitation of his gestures, albeit much clumsier.

He laughed. *"Encore une fois."* He shifted behind her so that his sleek, muscled body enclosed hers, brushing against the whole length of her back. She felt his breath stirring the hair on the top of her head and lost all thought.

He closed his hands around hers on the spatulas. For a second, as he tried to guide her hands through the gestures, her own automatically sought control, their unblended gestures ungainly.

"Relax," he murmured into her ear. "Just let me take charge."

If she relaxed, she was going to so completely lose her muscle strength that he was going to have to pick her up and carry her straight to a bed. Or just stretch her out there on the counter and make everyone else leave.

His body was so warm behind hers. His forearms against hers were so lean and strong and perfect for his task. Across the great marble island from her, one of the Japanese women narrowed her eyes at her in open jealousy.

"Et puis touchez," he breathed into her ear. "Touch with the back of your hand. You should feel neither warmth nor cool. It should be exactly the same temperature as your skin. It should be . . . exactly matched to you." He dipped the knuckle of his pinky into the chocolate as she did hers. "Can you tell?"

She was not sure her current body temperature was a reliable indicator for chocolate tempering. She was too hot.

Not Sylvain? Was he still as cool as a cucumber?

"How long did it take you to learn to do that?" the
Frenchman who was taking the workshop asked from down
the marble counter.

Sylvain turned easily to answer him. It seemed to cost him
no effort to wrench himself away from her.

Cade wished they were alone. Not only because she didn't
want to be just another tourist among this group, but because
she didn't think she would let him get away with this if they
were alone. She would break, one way or the other, and
whether by grabbing him or by dumping a bowl of cream on
his head, challenge him to quit *toying* with her.

He *was* toying with her, wasn't he?

Like a shock of cold water, it occurred to her that maybe
he wasn't trying to drive her crazy. Maybe this was just the
way he was, and let the women fall where they may.

It was a good thing they weren't alone, Sylvain thought.
He wasn't sure, if they weren't watched, that he might not
crack, push too hard, reach for too much, too soon. He had
learned patience the hard way as a teenager, paying the price
whenever his control slipped and his greed showed before
the pretty girl in question was completely mesmerized by
chocolate.

He had grown into himself. Journalists liked to say he was
beau, and even Chantal insisted it was true these days, so he
supposed he was. But he actually had no idea how to attract
a woman without chocolate.

Ce n'était pas grave. Chocolate had proven extraordinarily
effective.

Its effectiveness right now was driving him crazy. Miss
Ruler of All Money Can Buy, so small and arrogant and in-

tense, swamped by her borrowed pastry-chef jacket, was letting him stand so close behind her as he showed her how to temper his chocolate. She was taking tastes off his finger, off a spoon held in his hand. Testing the warmth of the chocolate. Blushing. She kept blushing.

Money can't buy this, he thought at her, but it wasn't quite true. He had always been attracted to women who were rich and elegant, confident and together. Even in high school, when he didn't have a prayer of attracting them—before he learned chocolate—those had been the women who attracted him. So was he letting her money buy him?

She had walked into his own *laboratoire,* confident as could be that she could buy him and produce him in a factory, and he had put her quite properly and resoundingly in her place.

But here he was, two days later, letting her infiltrate his workshop. Giving her a hands-on lesson.

Very hands-on. He was reducing himself to a state of pure desire. Fortunately, a chef jacket could hide quite a bit.

Why was she letting him? he wondered suddenly. Why hadn't she drawn the line, reclaimed her personal space? She was letting him get away with everything.

She really hadn't struck him as the type to let anyone take her over very easily.

Was she, in fact, manipulating him? he wondered, as he showed her how to use a *guitare* to cut the chocolate into little bites. How big a fool was he making of himself?

He had had a tendency to do that over women like Cade Corey for a while. He had thought he had grown out of it, but last night, Chantal had made it clear he was making a fool of himself again. He remembered the friendly, pitying look in her eyes, the warning shake of her head.

He winced. Cade Corey didn't even know or care where he lived, only where his workshop was. She had said it herself.

He had had a lot of experience with being used. He knew that the women who were doing the using seldom even realized that was what they were doing.

So if Cade Corey was doing it on purpose, that was, in its way, refreshing.

That still didn't excuse him for being an idiot, though.

A hopeless, romantic, gangly teenager could be excused for being an idiot when he learned how to get the prettiest, classiest girls to look at him briefly by seducing them with chocolate.

Even someone in his early twenties could be excused for being an idiot, when things shifted somehow, and suddenly he seemed to be attracting women right and left. It had taken him a few years to adjust to that, and another few years to stop getting his heart broken repeatedly as he learned that just because a woman had glittered from a distance didn't mean she was gold now that he could touch her up close.

Many of those women who seemed so beautiful and classy were regretting husbands they still had and neglected to mention; some were unable really to think about anyone or anything but themselves; some were so needy, he felt as if he were being sucked into a black hole. In short, just because women fell for him easily now didn't mean they weren't using him.

Only in the past couple of years had he felt he had reached a degree of intelligence in his relationships, a certain centeredness that he hadn't had before. He had stopped falling for everything that glittered, had stopped handing his heart over on a silver platter. He had learned that if he wanted to find a treasure, he was going to have to hunt for it and be very, very careful as he did.

He hated it, though, being so careful. It was not his nature. He wanted to find that one person and just give her all of him, his heart, his head, his body. He wanted the sound and scent of her in their apartment, he wanted to be cooking with her in the kitchen, he wanted babies eventually, waking them up every two hours and leaving toys for him to trip over.

He wanted the true prize.

And he wasn't going to find it by falling for a billionaire who made no attempt to hide the fact that she just wanted to buy him and everything he had accomplished in life.

The class was breaking for lunch. He took a last breath of the scent of her hair and then did one of the hardest things he had done since he first opened the doors of his own *chocolaterie,* years ago. He stepped back from Cade Corey.

He didn't know whether it was to save himself—*idiot*—or to punish her for being so exclusively interested in his chocolate and not him, but he even managed to smile at her. "*Merci,* Mademoiselle Corey, for joining us this morning. I'm afraid I won't be able to let you stay for the afternoon session, as we will be covering things we don't want to share with a larger public."

She looked at him as if he had hit her. Or, worse, stripped her naked in a pretense of seduction and then smirked and turned her around to see a thousand ridiculing eyes.

She stared at him, something rising in her with a powerful force. His pulse quickened as he prepared for anything, anything—

She turned abruptly and strode toward the entryway. Without a word. Without letting him find out what that powerful force rising inside her *was.*

He found himself following, hoping she *would* say a word. He was kicking himself already. He hadn't really wanted her to *leave.*

He just . . . thought it would be in his own best interest to make sure she did.

"I believe you still have our coat, mademoiselle," he mentioned as she reached for the doorknob, trying to pry that word he wanted out of her.

Her flush deepened further, her jaw as tense as it was possible for her to hold it. Her hands trembled so much on the buttons, she couldn't get them undone.

"Tenez," he said, troubled, his own hands lifting. He *was* an idiot. There was more than one way to be an idiot, and he had just proven it. He had just cut off his own nose to spite his face. "May I help?"

"Don't. You. Touch. Me." So much anger vibrated through her voice that he dropped his hands, that fourteen-year-old teenager waking in him, the kind girls didn't want to be touched by.

So he stood there as she struggled with button after button, making her slow, miserable way down the coat, everyone watching them, her cheeks deeply red now. He wondered why she didn't just destroy it—rip it off, pop the buttons, drop it on the floor, and maybe drop a few bills on it to cover the damage as she stalked out. It seemed like something an American billionaire would do.

At last she got it off, to reveal the most ridiculous enormous sweatshirt. He started to smile despite himself. "What are you wearing? Did you come to my workshop in your *pajamas?*" *Americans.* All the money in the world and not a gram of taste.

She gave him a look like a slap, thrust the coat at him, and strode out.

He stood there holding it, staring after her. He had just let cowardice make him an *imbécile*. You couldn't fake blushes.

Plus, not having her there to drive crazy, when he knew he could have, ruined the whole rest of his day.

And he only had her secretary's phone number. What if she didn't come back?

Chapter 9

It was going to be his own fault, Cade decided, once embarrassment and something very close to heartbreak had subsided and she could nurture a proper sense of vengeance to take its place. He would have no one but himself to blame.

In the Halles, pigeons, tourists, lovers, and a diverse collection of ne'er-do-wells gathered around a great tower of a fountain that curlicued up and fell into a wide pool. Most of the shops were closed for Sunday, making the area even sketchier than it was on weekdays. Several men began making crude suggestions as she approached. Cade tried to ignore them as she sought the shop she had Googled earlier. She was relieved to find that its owner did, as advertised, take advantage of the loosening of restrictions on Sunday openings, and she stepped inside just before her hecklers could find the energy to stand up and pursue her.

Inside, an array of high-tech paraphernalia filled walls and display cases.

"I need to buy a pair of twins," Cade said as confidently as anyone could say something like that in a foreign language. That was what it said in the dictionary. "Female twins," she corrected herself. Apparently males didn't work as binoculars.

"Bien sûr," said the salesman, moving to a display case of binoculars. "What type do you want?"

"Just the smallest, most powerful thing you have," she said. Wait, how long did she want to stand there staring at Sylvain's door? Even his door was going to look smug and gloating through binoculars. "And a camera." That way, she could record the security panel without spending her entire day obsessed with Sylvain Marquis, and she would be able to rewind as often as necessary to get the exact code down. "With a good"—Now how in the world did she say *zoom*?

A half hour later, she stood at her apartment window, trying to find a way to angle the camera, *zoomer* it in to an exact reading of the security panel, and keep it from being too obvious from the outside.

Her phone rang. "So, how is it going?" her father asked.

"Ah . . . great." Cade hid her spy camera behind her back as if he could see it over the telephone.

"Really? Have you found a good partner for this line of yours?"

"I've—talked to several possibilities," Cade said. "I haven't come to a final decision yet. I want this to be perfect, you know."

"Ye-es. Now, don't promise anyone the moon, sweetheart. You know we'll have to give it a limited test-marketing first. We've been Everyman's chocolate for so long. I don't know how a foray into Parisian gourmet will be received."

"Doesn't Everyman deserve some gourmet options, too?" she said stubbornly.

"Maybe. I'm not saying it wouldn't work. But I'm starting to wonder if we might need our cash reserves for other things."

Cade's heart sank. She pressed her forehead against the cold window, gazing dismally at the street where people resolutely refused to go tap in the code to Sylvain's door so that she could film it.

She had spent years cultivating this chance, working up to

the opportunity to develop this line. Paris seemed to stretch before her just out of reach, as if this window were of unbreakable glass. "You're having second thoughts?"

Merde, what did it even matter when she couldn't talk a single chocolatier into even listening to her?

"The thing is, honey, I know we've talked about this before. If we really want to strengthen our foothold in Europe, the best way to do it is to buy someone out, like Valrhona or something. Not create a new line. And if we want to strengthen our sales in the premium chocolate lines in the US, we don't need some Parisian's name to do it. We just need some good marketing, maybe some fancy French words, but something people can recognize, like *Chocolat.* You know this."

But neither of those solutions got her outside the Corey factory doors. Neither let her live and breathe Paris, with all its rain and cold and cobblestone streets, its poop on the sidewalks and its impossible elegance in the store windows, its tense, rich culture and the warm luxury of fresh bread scenting every street.

Neither let her stand in the heart of a *laboratoire,* making chocolate out of sounds and scents from every corner of the globe. Making it with her own hands. Better, watching Sylvain Marquis make it and tasting what he made.

"Dad, didn't you agree to this?" She kept peering out the window, feeling like a hawk that was too hungry to blink—a bunny might get away.

"You've been wanting it for years, honey."

So, what did that mean? If he didn't think it was good business, what did it matter if she wanted it?

"Speaking of Everyman, tell me, is it normal you would be dropping $15,000 on clothes today? Your assistant said your credit card company called to check."

What was her assistant doing, talking about her private expenditures to her father?

Fifteen thousand dollars? Maggie Saunders hadn't been kidding about Christian Dior.

"Did she tell them to stop authorizing charges by any chance?"

"No, she said it was true you were in Paris."

Darn.

"But I thought I would check. Since I thought you were busy working, not shopping."

"I took a little break," she lied. Better shopping than getting caught lying and bribing her way into a workshop any day. If her father knew how slim this chance for a gourmet line was, he would definitely pull the plug. "This is Paris, Dad. I have to shop while I'm here."

"Huh. I guess you never know how that city is going to affect people," he said judiciously.

Someone approached the rear door to the *laboratoire*. "Excuse me, Dad, got to go." She clicked off her phone and grabbed her camera.

People didn't enter that *laboratoire* nearly often enough in the afternoon, she decided a boring hour later. And managing to catch a code entry in the one second it took them to enter it, while shoulders and arms blocked her vision, was a lot harder than she had expected. Maybe she needed to put into practice that plan about not standing there obsessing over Sylvain's smug door all day and leave the camera to do the work.

She stiffened. She recognized that person who had approached the glass panes of the shop and was now peering in. Gone was the purple pantsuit, but the feathered ensemble in burgundy stood out in its own way.

She kept the camera on its tripod fixed on the security panel, recording, in case someone with a code happened by, but she flew out of the apartment and down the stairs.

Five flights of stairs approximately two inches deep. In heels. She was pretty sure she was only alive at the bottom because God was on the side of Corey Chocolate in this battle.

"Just came to pick up my passport," Maggie Saunders chirped. The belt around her waist was broad, leather, and had a buckle in the classic Dior D. Did it just *look* as if it was made out of platinum, or was it the actual metal?

"Fifteen thousand dollars?" Cade said. "You didn't have a single qualm charging fifteen thousand dollars to my credit card to cover a day in a two-thousand-dollar workshop?"

Maggie shrugged and withdrew Cade's credit card from her purse. "You got to be me for a day. I don't see why I shouldn't get to be you. You wouldn't have had any qualms about buying whatever you wanted."

"I'm not Paris Hilton." Cade snatched her card back. She had met Paris, but the two of them had had nothing in common besides money. Which wasn't as much a common denominator as people might think. "And fifteen thousand dollars is a lot for one chocolate workshop."

"I think this watch might have cost more than that." Maggie eyed a diamond-studded piece on her arm, its band of white leather. "The exchange rate is just not that good, you know. But I bought it later in the day. It might not have shown up on your charges yet."

Cade stared at her. To think she hadn't stopped that card because of moral qualms about reneging on a bargain. "And you think that's a *fair* trade?"

Maggie shrugged again, looking supremely happy. "You have money. I had the forethought to enroll in the workshop when it first opened so I could get a space. You agreed to the trade, I'll have you know."

Cade ground her teeth. "I didn't even get to stay in that workshop the full day. And I can't even keep your place. You can go back tomorrow." Tomorrow, the *laboratoire* would be in full swing again, and all the workshop participants would be able to watch it. But not her. Sylvain Marquis had cast her into exile.

"Really?" Maggie beamed. "You know what? I've been so down in the dumps since my husband left me, but I *knew* I was right to come to Paris! I *thought* God was telling me to come here. My pastor wasn't sure, but I could just feel it. And He sent me you."

Funny, every time someone thanked God for her it was because they had gotten great sums of money out of her. Usually, of course, the great sum of money was for a worthy charity. A little of her annoyance started to ease out of her, though, because—what if God *had* sent her there to help this one woman in her purple pantsuit find a new direction in life? What if her own desire to learn Parisian chocolate making had all been to set her on the road to help this woman?

Wouldn't that be lousy?

"Plus, you're almost as good as alimony!" Maggie Saunders said happily.

"Oh, for . . ." Cade spun around and headed back toward her building. *At least you've done a good deed, even if it cost you close to $20,000,* she told herself. *You've helped someone recover from a divorce.*

"You're welcome!" Maggie shouted after her.

Cade refrained from banging her head against something and just let the door slam behind her as she limped back up the stairs. Her knees hurt after that downward slalom to catch her credit card.

Sylvain Marquis had a lot to answer for. This really was all his fault.

"*Thirty* thousand dollars?" Cade said over the phone, keeping one eye on the *laboratoire* door across the street below as she talked. "You got thirty thousand dollars in charges to my card in one morning, and it didn't occur to you to stop authorizing the charges?"

"But, Ms. Corey, we knew you were in Paris! Of course you would be spending money at Dior and Hermès."

Of course. Cade wondered if she was normal. Or if anybody in her family was. She did want to do the whole Faubourg Saint-Honoré thing eventually. She just hadn't gotten around to it yet. "Have I *ever* spent thirty thousand dollars in one morning?"

That blond woman coming down the street—was that Sylvain's date from the night before? Cade's stomach knotted, with hope and reluctance. Would she have the code?

"No, but you're in *Paris,*" the woman said, longing in her voice.

The same longing Cade had always felt. Paris, the universal symbol of a more romantic life.

"Do you want to refuse the charges?" the woman asked, as politely as if this wasn't a headache for them at all.

Cade sighed. "I'll accept them. Someone I know took my card."

A neutral silence suggested that the friends of the rich were something indeed.

"But can you stop this card now and FedEx me a new one?"

"Of course," the woman said, professionally neutral even in the face of ecstatic relief at not having $30,000 in charges refused by someone the company would hate to offend. "It will be there tomorrow morning."

"Great." Cade dropped the phone and whipped up her binoculars.

The blond Chantal had stopped in front of the *laboratoire* door. Cade steeled herself to not let her binoculars droop as the answer became obvious: Chantal did, indeed, have the code.

A perfect, beautiful, chic *Parisienne* had the open-sesame to the sorcerer's lair.

Sylvain Marquis *had* been toying with Cade.

Or worse, was not even conscious of his effect.

Chapter 10

Outside, Paris put on darkness the way her women dressed for excitement—a black dress sliding over skin, something glittering in its threads. Paris pulled black net stockings over her elegant lines, added high-heeled black boots to click against pavement. Buildings lit in strings of jewels—an earring here, a bracelet there, and a shimmer of something over the skin, a dusting of glitter.

Cade stood at the window, watching that glittering, promising night through that cursed pane of glass. She watched it until it got tired of itself, until the jewels started to come back off, tossed carelessly onto a bedside table—lights in apartments going out, heels stripped off, sore feet tucked under the covers.

She watched it until only the lamps still glowed on the street below and the last insomniac put out his light. The cars stopped passing. Long after the last person had gone by on foot, one more person stumbled by drunk, and then the street was quiet. Loneliness built in her; the later it got, the less likely she was to get up the courage to go out into the evening.

Here she was, spending another night in that romantic dream of Paris all by herself, this time in her room, too intimidated to go eat alone in a restaurant again or walk around under the Eiffel Tower at midnight.

Here she was, scared to step out into the Paris night and take what she wanted.

She hugged herself as she stared out the window at the street below, so frustrated at herself that she was sitting there lonely and doing nothing this night in Paris, that—

She stood up and headed toward the elevator.

The copy she had made of the key fit the door to Sylvain's *laboratoire.* It took her four tries to get the code right, from what she had pieced together from her camera and binoculars, but the fourth try was the charm.

She hesitated a long moment, the door pulled open just a crack, wondering if she was really insane enough to do this. She could feel the adrenaline racing through her. Her chest felt tight.

The darkness inside the *laboratoire* called her, with all its possibilities. When she breathed in, short, raw breaths, she could smell chocolate sifting out through the crack in the door.

She went in and pulled the door closed behind her.

Inside the *laboratoire,* silence. Her heart beat so fast, she had to press her hands against her stomach and force deep breaths. It would be a bad idea to faint right now, hit her head on a marble counter, and be discovered in the morning. For one thing, it would be a really lousy time to die from a fall, and for another, the scandal didn't even bear imagining.

Chocolate flooded her body with each breath, so strong she might as well have been sniffing a drug. A drug to which she had been addicted since she was in her mother's womb: theobromine. Natural antidepressant.

True, her father said her mother had had to spend much of her pregnancy with Cade at their beach house, because the sweet, acrid scent of cocoa in the air at Corey had made her so nauseated. Odd, given how much Cade had loved chocolate from her first breath. Her first three written words had been *Cade, Corey,* and *chocolate.* Her dad had framed the sheets of paper she had first written them on and hung them up in his office.

She wondered how long it would be before she saw her father if she got jailed for breaking and entering.

She pressed her palms hard into her belly and reminded Sylvain Marquis that this was all his fault.

Reminded him in her head, of course. Clearly his physical presence would have been unfortunate right at that moment. French prisons. She really didn't want to end up in a French prison.

Plus, Sylvain Marquis's actual physical presence tended to throw her off stride. The moment she got near him, she forgot pretty much everything, and that made her sound like an idiot. And *blush.* And just be humiliated. She was tired of being reduced to a forlorn American barbarian longing for a crumb of French civilization.

No, he was much more manageable in her head. Also, less likely to throw her into jail.

In her head, as if to disprove her attempt to make him manageable, he sneered at her with that sexy, subtle mouth of his. He didn't sneer at her in any dramatic way that she could caricature and render ridiculous.

No, with just a little quick once-over, head to foot, the tiniest tightening around the corners of his chocolate eyes and at one corner of his mouth, he dismissed her entire existence as worthless.

The way he had dismissed her from his workshop, for example. As if all that morning brushing up against her, holding chocolate to her lips, was *worthless.* That was what was the most infuriating about that sneer, how subtle it was. How calm. She didn't even inspire passion in his disdain.

Dismissal complete, he tucked one of those silky, chin-length locks of black hair behind his ear and concentrated on his luscious, submissive chocolate again, putting the fact that she marred his planet out of his mind.

She made sure he left an imaginary streak of chocolate across his face while tucking that hair away.

But it lacked something, as imagined vengeances went. She kept wanting to wipe it off. And then lick her finger.

She found herself, in fact, sucking on her actual physical finger. She blinked, jerked it out of her mouth, wiped it on her jeans, and glared around her.

She slipped the original key into the pastry-chef jacket she had borrowed, still hanging on its peg, and moved past the entryway, a copy of the key tucked in her back pocket.

In the heart of the *laboratoire,* she managed to forget Sylvain Marquis. No, that wasn't true. It was impossible to forget him, when she was melting in the heart of him. Say, rather, he retreated like a sorcerer into the shadows in the depths of her mind, his eyes glinting from time to time to show he was still there, the maker of all that lay before her.

All that surrounded her. By some magic like that in an old fairy tale, he had crafted here his heart, and she had stepped inside it.

She had been around chocolate all her life, and until she had stepped into Sylvain Marquis's workshop, she had never seen anything like this.

This place was so exactly as the world should have been, it overwhelmed her with its reality. Her heart started beating too hard, and it thumped up into her throat, and parts of it almost wanted to leak like tears through her eyes. She felt like a child who had dreamed of wonders but never seen them, suddenly in the middle of an Enchanted Forest.

In the depths of brown shelves and black shadows and glossy black marble, cauldrons had been stacked—tempering kettles cleaned for the next day. This day's finished magic was stacked in boxes and boxes of chocolates on one table. Tomorrow they would be moved to display cases or shipped out cold-packed and find their way into someone's luxurious life, changing it just for a bite or two.

She went to the shelf of extracts. Its contents were barely clearer tonight than they had been from the distance she had been forced to keep during the workshop. Darkness obscured their labels. She ran her thumb over one, squinting to make out the word *citron* in the faint light from the city outside. When she opened it, it was as if the genie of lemon escaped out of the bottle, its essence flooding the dark room, overwhelming for a second even the scent of chocolate. She capped it but in the process got a drop on her thumb that she carried with her as she moved down the shelves.

She went by aroma, as it proved easier than trying to read the words. Another jar rattled slightly and released a piquant scent. She touched her finger to the familiar small rounds of whole pepper. Another jar puzzled her for a moment with its licorice scent. She traced rough stars . . . star anise. Vanilla was easy. She picked up a bean because she could not resist it, running her finger down the glossy, wrinkled length of it, imprinting herself with the aroma. TAHITI claimed the crate of chef pouches, the brand so bold she could make it out even in the dark.

Trailing vanilla and lemon, she plunged her hand into a great burlap sack stamped with the word IRAN. Roundness slid over her hand, a curiously intense pleasure of texture. Pistachios. She closed a fist around some as she pulled her hand out and ate them, capturing the unroasted flavor inside her the way she had taken the lemon and the vanilla onto her skin.

PÉRIGORD claimed a crate full of almonds. She ate one of those, too, picking up a handful, letting them slide over her palm back into the crate.

All around her, the sorcerer lurked, in every darkest

shadow. He was not there, of course. Logic told her he was home asleep or maybe with Chantal and not asleep—she flinched. But logic had little to do with the feel of him. He was here. She felt him here. Watching her explore his lair. His eyes gleaming in the shadows.

She ducked away from his eyes, into the walk-in refrigerator, where she found great palettes of cream, *crème fraîche, crème fleurette,* some in cartons, others in glass bottles, as if they had come from someone's private farm. She wanted to pour these out into a cauldron, throw something out of a brown bottle into it, see what sparks she could make fly up, what magic she could create. She looked up, almost expecting to see Sylvain Marquis standing in the doorway of the walk-in, watching her.

No. No one. But the shiver of expectation and the shot of adrenaline it had aroused stayed with her.

Great loaves of butter sat by the cream, the paper marked in French with a name she did not recognize. Even his butter came from a small, carefully chosen dairy. He could probably taste the difference in the grass those cows had eaten and ordered accordingly.

She fled from this walk-in to the next, feeling as if a sorcerer's spell pursued her, its tendrils almost reaching her ankles. It would catch her and draw her down into his clutches, and who knew what he would do with her.

She ducked into the next walk-in, trying to shake him by the stupid act of plunging ever more deeply into him. She recognized the temperature against her skin like a wanderer recognizing home, the same temperature and scents of the vast factory storage rooms back home—55 degrees, the temperature of a wine cellar, a perfect temperature for storing chocolate.

Here, enormous loaves surrounded her. She used a tiny penlight, the beam tracing over white, dark, milk. Cases of *pistoles* were stacked by the loaves. She reached in at random and tasted one—black chocolate so bitter, it made her tongue water.

What would Sylvain Marquis do with that bitterness tomorrow? What would he turn that chocolate into, and how would the taste of it on her tongue make her whole body melt?

She moved deeper into the walk-in and stopped, hair shivering all over her body in delight. Here were the late-afternoon's products—rows on rows of chocolate molds, left in here to cool to 17 degrees Celsius. Tomorrow, they would be popped out in exquisite perfection, placed by gloved hands one by one into boxes, and sold for $120 a pound. She had just reached out to take one, when her cell phone rang.

She almost jumped out of her skin. She looked around frantically, half expecting someone to handcuff her on the spot. The sorcerer retreated, displeased.

"Dad!" she hissed. "What? It's after midnight!"

"I am always getting that time change switched around," her father said ruefully. "And here I was thinking it was just after noon over there. Did I wake you up, honey?"

"No, I—" She broke off, realizing it would have been much easier to say yes.

"Really? What have you been up to? Not working this late, I hope. Or have you been out to dinner? Did you get in touch with Claude de Saint-Léger yet?"

Cade stared around at the workshop. "I, uh—as a matter of fact—"

It was too bad it wasn't her grandfather on the phone. Grandpa Jack would have been delighted. He might actually have commandeered a plane and flown over to Paris to join her. Her father took the weight of being president of one of America's major companies seriously and tended to be more reluctant to indulge in corporate crime, at least the kind that could get you arrested and bring about bad publicity. A little marketing skullduggery against Mars was another story entirely.

"Really? You're still up working on a Sunday night in Paris?" Her father laughed affectionately. "That's my daughter. Cadey-C, do have some fun while you're there. It's okay." He said that as if he were also trying to convince himself that it was okay to not work sometimes.

Cade wriggled a fingernail under the edge of one of those molded chocolates and popped it out. Covering her phone with one hand so her father couldn't hear her chew, she slipped it into her mouth.

Oh, God. Maybe Heaven wasn't a place but just a bite. One bite.

Adrenaline heightened her sensations of gloss and smoothness, of melting and sweetness. Her body wanted to melt, too.

How could Sylvain Marquis do this to her?

"Listen, honey, I called because I'm interested in your analysis of Devon Candy. They look so tempting right now, but we would have to leverage ourselves quite a bit to buy it."

Devon. The international British-based confectionary company dominated markets like India and held a strong place among the cheaper, mass-market chocolates sold in Europe. Cade thought of all the bars she saw in London airports, the brightly packaged, chocolate-coated candy.

If they had Devon, there might be a need for her to stay here, based in Europe. Devon Candy. Billions of candy bars spouting into molds, wrapped by the millions a day. Just like Corey.

She massaged the bridge of her nose, depressed for no reason she could identify. "I need to look at it more," she said. "I thought we were more interested in opening up our own premium line as our next market move."

"Mmm." Her father's tone just reeked of enthusiasm for this Paris premium-chocolate venture, all right. "Go ahead and look more at Devon, and get back to me tomorrow. Do you think . . . ?"

Before she knew it, she was knee-deep in business discussions, right there in the middle of breaking and entering a chocolate shop. She felt disoriented, as if Aladdin in that cave had suddenly had to stop and go over the ins and outs of a corporate acquisition.

It took her half an hour to get off the phone, with some desperation.

By that time, she had tried a chocolate from each mold. Greedily, unable to stop, as if at any moment they might be reft from her forever. As if she might, at any moment, find herself back in factories and boardrooms.

She might, at the rate she was going, find herself in prison. They would almost certainly not provide her Sylvain Marquis chocolates in prison.

She tried the one printed with a tiny flower, the little glossy ribbed mound, the one shaped like a cone and decorated with bits of cacao bean, like some playful reference to a child's nut-studded ice cream cone. Its inside was the silkiest mint ganache, bursting into her mouth.

She turned off her phone completely and slipped it into her pocket.

Chocolate melted on her tongue, melted into her body. Its warm, rich sweetness combined with the pounding adrenaline until she felt . . . the closest she could think of was aroused. Desperately, intensely aroused, as if someone could come out of the shadows with his sorcerer eyes glinting and lay her down on the dark counters and . . .

She swallowed the chocolate with a shiver, the fine hairs on her spine prickling from her nape all the way down to her back's lowest, lowest point and maybe even a little farther, with the desire to be discovered by him.

She forced herself to continue through the workshop to what she guessed was the office door.

No recipes lay scattered on the desk for her to grab. She used the penlight to check the filing cabinets. No files were marked *Secrets*. There was one marked *Recettes,* which got her excited, since that could mean recipes, but it turned out to contain receipts. Other folders contained employee files and bills from different suppliers. She turned to study the laptop sitting closed on the desk.

She preferred the image of Sylvain Marquis writing recipes in sorcerous runes on parchment, but the laptop might be more likely. When she turned it on, though, a log-in screen showed. She tried the obvious: *admin, Sylvain, Sylvain Marquis,* password *chocolat*. But nothing worked. What was his birthdate again? She would have to look through her research on him and come back better prepared tomorrow.

She pretended to ignore the thrill that shot from eroge-nous zone to erogenous zone at the idea of coming back to-morrow.

She lingered a while, reluctant to abandon the sense of sin-fulness and power and the delicious hope of danger, that sor-cerer-coming-out-of-the-shadows fantasy she felt being in Sylvain Marquis's lair at night. Helping herself to some paper from his desk, she spent a long time writing down all the equipment she could find, in case the Corey Chocolate ex-perts could figure out more from it. But the sorcerer did not come out of the shadows, and she finally slipped out the way she had come, feeling oddly anticlimactic.

At the very last second, passing the stacks of chocolate boxes, she found herself reaching out and taking one, two, three, four of them, as many as she could carry. She didn't really mean to do it. But she couldn't stop herself. She wanted his chocolate, and she *didn't* want to have to come into his shop tomorrow and humiliate herself by letting him see her buy it.

She stopped herself from grabbing a fifth, but only because

she could envision them all toppling out of her hands as she tried to cross the street.

And she snuck back up to *her* lair, her tower, with her loot, to curl up with it, gloating.

Chapter 11

The first thing Sylvain noticed when he opened the work-shop the next morning was that there were four boxes of chocolate missing. He stopped, puzzled. He had been the last one there after the class ended yesterday, and he was the first one back, so—something immediately did not add up. Pascal and Bernard had their own keys and the security code, but why would they sneak back to steal chocolates?

"That's odd," he murmured.

"*Qu'est-ce qui est bizarre?*" asked Christophe. Sylvain had promised the food blogger he could come visit his *laboratoire* after the man had written up a visit to his shop with extravagant praise. *Justified* extravagant praise, *bien sûr*.

"Some of the boxes we prepped yesterday are missing." He looked around, expecting to find them set in another spot.

"A chocolate thief?" Christophe asked, intrigued. As the words sank into his imagination, his eyes grew dreamy. "I think I might just have discovered my third career. Imagine sneaking into *laboratoires* every night to steal the finest chocolates."

"To eat or for the *marché noir*?"

"Both, really," Christophe sighed blissfully. "You could probably make a killing on the black market if you didn't eat all your ill-gained goods."

"Well. The thief would have to steal more than four boxes

to manage that," Sylvain said arrogantly. No one had ever eaten just one of his chocolates. Not since he was sixteen years old.

Maybe the boxes had just been . . . just been what? He tried to think. He had been the last one out the door the night before and the first one back in. Who would have moved them, sold them, taken them home?

He went into his office to double-check his laptop, which lay untouched on his desk. Or . . . he stopped.

A chocolate thumbprint mark. There was nothing unusual in that; he often left chocolate thumbprints on documents on his desk. But this thumbprint was a lot smaller than his.

He laid his thumb beside it and studied the difference for a long, thoughtful moment.

When he came back out into the main room of the *laboratoire,* Christophe was running his hand over one of the marble counters, looking around, and smiling.

"What?" Sylvain asked him.

"I'm just imagining the kind of person who would steal chocolate," the curly-haired blogger said, quietly happy. "He certainly picked the right person to steal it from."

"She," Sylvain said, remembering the size of that chocolate thumbprint.

Christophe blinked in pure joy. "Oh, that's perfect."

Sylvain raised his eyebrows.

Christophe stared at him. "Doesn't that make you happy? A woman thief sneaking into your lair to steal your chocolate? Don't you want to hide out here overnight to try to catch her *en flagrant délit?*"

Sylvain opened and closed his mouth. Yes. He did. "I think we might be a little premature in deciding there's a thief. I'm sure there's a much more innocuous explanation."

None leaped to mind, but—a thief who stole chocolate but not his laptop? He might have to marry her. He could feel himself falling in love just at the idea.

He hoped she had worn black leather pants.

"Well, where would be the fun in that?" Christophe asked indignantly. "Can *I* hide out and catch her? If it's going to be wasted on you."

For a food blogger, however famous, who was here as a special privilege, Christophe wasn't showing nearly enough humble appreciation and respect, Sylvain decided firmly. Food bloggers were getting pretty *gonflés* these days. Full of themselves.

And if there really was a thief—which he very much doubted—then he was the one who should get to catch her.

Voleuse de Chocolat chez Sylvain Marquis? went up the title on Christophe's blog only a few hours after he left the *chocolaterie.*

Cade, who had a Google Alert set to go off whenever Sylvain Marquis's name showed up in a new posting on the Web, looked at it and jumped a foot. That was fast.

She read the post quickly, or as quickly as she could read things in French. Most of it seemed to trade in fantasy. *Is a thief stealing Sylvain Marquis's chocolates? When I was there this morning, Sylvain discovered four boxes missing and a small, feminine, chocolate thumbprint on his papers. Is someone breaking into his* laboratoire *to steal his chocolates? If so, this woman is my soul mate. I think I may be in love.*

She had left a thumbprint? Well, actually, she had probably left many, just not all visible in chocolate. But her fingerprints weren't on record anywhere, and it would spoil the fun if she had to wear gloves the whole time. She couldn't even imagine deadening her sense of touch to that smooth, perfect chocolate.

She noticed, with almost no guilt, that she had thought *would spoil* not *would have spoiled.* Yes, she was going back. If she didn't get caught.

The blog post passed on almost immediately to other details of the visit. Sylvain had taught this *Le Gourmand* blogger, Christophe, how to make chocolate-dipped candied oranges.

The details made Cade want to grab both the blogger and Sylvain Marquis by the hair and rip it out.

Those were all the things *she* wanted to do. Plunge her hand into sacks of sesame by the light of day, lay candied oranges from Spain out on a counter and learn how to dip their brilliant colors into dark chocolate. Be part of it, be welcomed into the secret.

Instead, she was fumbling around at night trying to figure it all out on her own.

It really was Sylvain Marquis's fault she had to steal what she wanted to own. She would have been happy to pay for it. Pay a really high price, too.

If money wouldn't buy something, you had to steal it.

Right?

So he had no one but himself to blame for not being willing to share.

Sylvain, who didn't have a Google Alert on his name but who had been e-mailed a link to the post by Christophe out of courtesy, read the first paragraph with deep annoyance. What did he mean, the thief was his soul mate? What did he mean, he might be in love?

Talk about presumption. *If* the thief existed, which was unlikely, then she was *his* fantasy. Not Christophe's. He was the one in love with her. Christophe could go try to talk himself into some other chocolatier's *laboratoire* for a one-on-one visit, that's what he could do. Not try to cut in on Sylvain's mystery.

The next time Cade checked her e-mail, after a long walk along the Seine and some meditation in Notre-Dame to try to get herself to focus on aspects of Paris other than Sylvain

Marquis's *chocolaterie,* there were twenty more e-mail alerts from Google. Mostly pingbacks to the first Chocolate Thief post.

She raised a horrified hand to her mouth. It turned out that this was a really popular idea among food bloggers. It had crossed the language barrier, too. *A Taste of Elle* had picked it up in English right away, adding lots of exclamation points, and the other English-language food bloggers in Paris and then their comrades in America and England hadn't been long to follow.

A Taste of Elle had even drawn a fairly sexy caricature of what the Chocolate Thief would look like, tiptoeing away with a bagful of chocolates in hand. It had some elements of Michelle Pfeiffer's *Catwoman* suit. Maybe Cade needed to get some black leather pants.

Another blogger, a Frenchwoman, had named a chocolate concoction she had just been working on the *Chocolate Thief.* An American, posting at nearly the same time, had a chocolate double-ganache cupcake called *La Voleuse.*

Her remaining fifty e-mails were work questions people were failing to handle in her absence. Cade turned straight back around and went shopping. If Maggie Saunders could go shopping, she could, too.

"What do you mean, you can't sell me . . . ?" Still not quite grasping the word for *extremely small spy video camera* in French, but having managed to convey the idea, Cade held up thumb and forefinger pinched to almost touching, the agreed-upon sign between the French salesman and her for these items.

What was it with the French and their refusal to sell things? It defeated one of the main points in having plenty of money.

"*C'est illégal,*" he said coolly. "We don't carry those anymore."

There was another thing about every time the French wouldn't sell her something. It was not only that they said no; it was that they seemed to take such a smug satisfaction in the ability to do so.

"What about things that listen?" She cupped her ears, familiar with the word *écouter* in French but carried away by the whole sign language thing.

Maybe Sylvain Marquis muttered his recipes aloud while he was working on them. Like a mad scientist.

"We have these." He showed her some listening devices about the size of an iPod Nano.

She pinched her forefinger and thumb again. *"Petit."*

"Non," he said smugly. *"C'est illégal."*

Cade wondered, if she called their corporate security for a little equipment, how long it would take for someone to let her father know. Five minutes?

"Fine," she said. If you wanted something done, you had to do it yourself. "Do you know where I can get some black leather pants?"

The salesman stared at her blankly.

She ended up getting her leather pants at Hermès, just to prove to herself that there was something money could still buy in France. Also, she felt a little odd that Maggie Saunders had spent more time enjoying the Paris fashion scene than she herself had. She wasn't sure she was an entirely balanced child of wealth and privilege. Was it normal that she bought chocolate instead of clothes?

She was keying in the code to her building, her shoulders tightening against the thought of all the responsibilities surely waiting for her in her in-box, when Sylvain Marquis stepped outside the back door of his *laboratoire* and, of course, raised his eyebrows at her.

He had a real gift with that eyebrow-raising thing. The urge to swing her Hermès bag and knock those eyebrows right back into place was intense. Lucky for him he was across the street.

Her phone rang, and she turned her back on Sylvain to answer it. "Please tell me this is you," her grandfather begged her on the phone. "The Chocolate Thief."

"Grandpa! Do you really think I would?"

"Well, I hope so," he said indignantly. "I think your father is the only white sheep in the family. No idea how it happened. You would think he would be at least brown."

"Has Dad seen any of the blogs?"

"I doubt it. He's too busy to read blogs, your father. Besides, if he had, you wouldn't have to ask me the question."

That was true. Her father would have been calling her at midnight again. About something other than Devon Candy, for once.

"Well, don't point them out to him."

"No," her grandfather promised. Then he added, unreassuringly, "It's hard not to gloat, though. Your dad was so determined to raise you right, but I knew one of you girls would turn out to be a chip off the old block of chocolate. Although—not to speak ill of the dead, but between Jaime getting arrested at G8 summits as an annual tradition and you acting like your goal in life was to wear a suit and sit in an office—I was starting to think some bad thoughts about your mother's gene pool. Tell you what, honey, what do you say to me flying over there and the two of us hitting up one of those Swiss factories, just for the fun of it?"

"Are you staying here?" Sylvain asked right by her shoulder, and she jumped so violently, he had to catch her to keep her from falling over.

"I'm on the phone," she told him severely and turned her shoulder on him. He let go of her so she could do that, much to her regret. She tried to pull the door open, but it stayed locked. She frowned and typed the code again. "Oh, no one,

Grandpa, it's just that Marquis chocolatier I mentioned to you."

"Really?" Grandpa Jack sounded delighted. "Is there any way you can make sure I hear what he's saying? Can you put your phone on speaker so he can hear me? I know some really good cuss words in French."

"No. And don't come flying over here. This is my thing." If Sylvain hadn't come nosing over, she might have tried to convince her grandfather she wasn't really stealing chocolate secrets, but she couldn't figure out how to do that in front of the person she was stealing them from. Probably just as well. Grandpa was so proud of her.

A moment of wounded silence came over the phone. "I would be a good partner."

"I didn't say you wouldn't, Grandpa, but I want to do this by myself. We can go to Switzerland next month."

"Switzerland," Sylvain said by her ear flatly, his mouth turning down. Did he have no sense of personal space, or what? Could he hear what her grandfather was saying?

She put a little more oomph into the cold-shouldering. Apparently it wasn't having much of an effect on him. Did he think he could just play with her emotions all morning, turn around and kick her out cold onto the street, force her into a life of crime, and then be on chatty terms with her the next day?

"What do you mean, next month? Don't you have to work?" her grandfather demanded. Then he audibly perked up. "Is your father letting you play a little? I always did think it was excessive that you worked so much. Go out shopping or something. It's not as if you were a boy."

Cade sighed and rolled her eyes. "I just bought something pretty at Hermès, Grandpa. Don't worry about me." What was wrong with the stupid code panel? Why couldn't she get the door to open?

"Who's Hermès?" her grandfather asked blankly. "I thought we were talking about shopping. You mean the chocolatier?"

"Are you going to see Pierre Hermé now?" Sylvain sounded very frustrated. The only effect her cold shoulder seemed to have had on him was that now she could feel his breath on the top of her head and not in her ear. "Did he let you tour his *laboratoire*? You smell a little of lemon and vanilla."

Were the scents from his *laboratoire* marking her like ink stains? "You're smelling yourself," she told him curtly and lifted the bag to wave the logo in front of him. "Hermès."

Sylvain stared at it blankly, despite the fact that it was one of the top names in couture in his city. He was as bad as her grandfather. And her. Why was her kindred soul such a jerk?

She tried to type the code one more time and froze. She had been entering the code to his *laboratoire*. Right in front of him.

She slid a glance sideways. He was staring at her hand on the code panel.

He didn't say anything.

Maybe he was just staring blankly, not paying any attention to what she was actually typing. She began typing in the correct code, angling her body ostensibly to block it from his view as if he were a suspicious person. *That's right, throw the suspicion back his way.* That had to be a good psychological trick.

"And you didn't answer my question," he said. "What are you doing here?"

"I live here." She pushed the door open at last. "When I rented an apartment in Paris, I had no idea you would be such a *con*."

She let the door slam behind her.

Chapter 12

That night, the scents of his *laboratoire* lured her everywhere, into everything.

As she tried the chocolates Sylvain Marquis and his people had made that day, she closed her eyes, trying to pretend she had been there for the making, that she had a right to test them to see if they were worthy of their name. Did the outside have the right bite to it? Yes, it always did. Was the inside an unctuous surprise that prickled the senses and made them long for more? Yes. It always was.

In the walk-in where the *pistoles* were stored, she tasted chocolates from black to white but kept going back to the bitter dark ones, closing her eyes and gleaning from her tongue exactly where this chocolate had traveled, from an island off the coast of Africa or somewhere in the Andes. Had she seen its pods being pounded on a visit to the cacao plantation where it grew? She tried to guess its journey, what had been done to it at Sylvain's orders to make it into the chocolate it was. The temperatures, the times, the rhythms.

What would this chocolate taste like coating candied orange slices from Spain?

She found the candied orange slices from Spain, still moist, and tasted one, her fingers growing sticky and specks of chocolate clinging and blurring against her skin under the residue of the orange. Sylvain had shown Christophe how to coat these in chocolate.

She imagined Sylvain's fingers growing all sticky. She sucked slowly on her finger, licking the stickiness off.

Abruptly, she opened cabinets until she found the components of a small bain-marie.

A giddy kind of pleasure rose through her as she began to heat the water and pour chocolate *pistoles* into the pot set above it, a pleasure something like that fizzing Coke bottle her first day here, only more alarming.

Sylvain Marquis might have refused to allow her a place in his workshop, but she would steal one, right here in the heart of Paris, and make her chocolate in the dark of night.

While she worked, she kept looking up into corners, expecting to find the sorcerer of chocolate waiting there, his eyes gleaming like fires in the dark as he closed the trap on her in his lair.

But he never did.

Sylvain felt his heart kicking into gear as he opened the door to his *laboratoire* the next morning, the rich scents flooding him. Had she been there, the thief?

He shouldn't get his hopes up.

His hopes? Was he *hoping* that outrageously arrogant woman had broken into his workshop and stolen his chocolate?

She had, he saw almost instantly. Thumbprints smudged the marble counter they always left so glossy and clean at the end of the day. He could track her across the room. Here, she had tasted candied orange slices from Spain. Here, she had dipped into all the chocolate *pistoles*. Here she had . . .

She had helped herself to at least one of every single chocolate they had produced the day before.

He grinned, his heart thumping. She couldn't get enough of him, could she?

He stopped when he found the components of a bain-marie dripping dry in a sink. Had she been making chocolate in his workshop? Exactly how nervy was this thief?

"So, did she come back?" Christophe asked eagerly just before lunch.

Sylvain, in the act of transferring a thirty-kilo *marmite* of chocolate to a heat source, considered dropping it onto the man's toes. He'd done the blogger a favor once, let him visit his *laboratoire* at his begging, and the man thought they were such buddies that he could come be nosy about Sylvain's thief?

"She did, didn't she?" Christophe said, delighted. His chest visibly expanded with joy.

So had Sylvain's, that morning. He put the giant pot of chocolate down before he could yield to temptation.

"What did she take? Do you know who it is? Do you know how she got in?"

"Somebody is stealing chocolate?" Pascal Guyot appeared at Sylvain's shoulder. Not a blog reader, Pascal. Sotto voce, he added, "Is it someone who works here, do you think? But we keep that platter in the employee lounge full of them."

"Oh." Christophe looked disappointed. "Really? Do you think it's an inside job?"

"*C'est possible,*" Sylvain allowed slowly. "One of the assistants, maybe. It was a small thumbprint. That makes more sense than imagining someone would risk breaking and entering for my chocolate." It did make more *sense*. If they were dealing with someone behaving sensibly.

His heart kicked into high gear again, and his body tightened as he imagined the thief losing her head for him.

For his chocolates.

Close enough.

"I'll tell you what," Christophe said. "You imagine the

suspect you want, and I'll imagine the suspect I want. Just tell me—did she come back last night? You can blink once for *oui* or twice for *non*."

Sylvain blinked once but at the pure effrontery of the man in trying to cajole him into an admission.

"Oh, she did!" Christophe clasped his hands, *ravi*. "You have made my life, Sylvain Marquis. *Merci, merci.*" He whirled out.

A few seconds later, he whirled back. "You don't have Wi-Fi here by any chance?"

Sylvain narrowed his eyes at him, starting to smolder. If the man was going to keep a public journal of his puerile fantasies, he could at least have the grace to make them different fantasies from Sylvain's.

"No, never mind. I'm sure the café down the street has it." Christophe whirled out again, exiting through the shop. Sylvain saw him buy a box of chocolates on his way out.

Voleuse de Chocolat, je t'aime, read Christophe's headline. *As I sit here biting slowly through the robe of Sylvain Marquis's* Caraque, *a delicate crunch and then silk ganache, I know I have found a kindred soul. You, too, think this is worth risking life and liberty for. . . .*

Well, maybe not *life,* Cade thought uneasily. French police didn't have a tendency to close in with guns blazing, did they? And as for liberty, maybe she should make another major contribution to the political party in power right now just in case she needed any intervention from the ambassador. This whole French prison thing didn't sound appealing at all.

The Chocolate Thief Strikes Again flew up in blog titles throughout the Anglophone world. French was no barrier to the food bloggers, who all knew in what language their bread was buttered with 85 percent butterfat. *Please, Can I Be a Chocolate Thief? A Taste of Elle* wrote, which was just greedy on her part, since she was engaged to chocolatier Simon Casset. Another posted *How to Steal Chocolate in Ten Easy Lessons. Number 1: If you're going to go to jail for it, make sure you don't settle for less than Sylvain Marquis.*

"That's funny," Maggie Saunders said, reading over another traveler's shoulder in a security line that had been stalled for two hours at Charles de Gaulle. "I was just at one of his workshops."

"Really?" The man turned.

"You know the strangest story?" Maggie said proudly. It was not every day, or even every decade, she got to share a story as juicy as this. Well, her friends' stories could be pretty juicy, but she felt guilty about sharing those. And they weren't famous, so no one cared. "You know the Corey family?"

The man's brow knitted. "The Corey family? The chocolate family?"

"That one." Maggie nodded enthusiastically. It was always better telling a story about famous people when the listener recognized their names. "One of them, Cade Corey, bribed me to let her take my place in Sylvain Marquis's workshop. She was spying on him! I probably shouldn't have let her," she added guiltily. She touched the platinum D on her wide leather belt to console herself.

The man's eyebrows shot up to the top of his head. "Really? How much did she bribe you?"

"I kept it under thirty thousand," Maggie said vaguely. "I think. I didn't buy any real jewelry," she added defensively. "And I could have!"

It was impossible for the man's eyebrows to climb any higher, but they tried. His eyes were gleaming. "Cade Corey paid you thirty thousand dollars so she could slip into a chocolate workshop run by the best chocolatier in Paris, in disguise?"

"She did better than that! She let me use her credit card

for a day. I could have spent a lot more, but I had moral qualms." And she was regretting those qualms already. One ten-carat diamond ring—that wouldn't have been so bad, right?

"My God, I wish the man had stock I could buy." The stranger propped his laptop on the top of his suitcase and began typing. "Now, when was this?"

By the time he had all the details, the line had still not advanced by even one person. He pulled out his phone to call someone and spoke into it. "Can I change my flight to take another couple of days in Paris? I mean, officially, as opposed to just standing in this security line that long? Because I think I might have a fun one here."

"You're leaving?" Maggie said, disappointed. In a security line like theirs, no one wanted to lose entertainment.

"Would you be willing to share your contact information by any chance?" he asked her.

She pulled back suspiciously. It had been all very well sharing the details of Cade Corey's story with a complete stranger, but she didn't want to have some weirdo stalking her.

"I'm sorry, I never introduced myself." He pulled out a card. "Jack Adams, *New York Times.* I usually write for the financial section, but I've been begging to get into Food."

"That's quite a jump," Maggie said sympathetically.

He grinned. "Yes, but sometimes God smiles on you."

"That's what *I* thought!" Maggie exclaimed in wonder. "Isn't that something? That means God's used Cade Corey twice now. I hope she appreciates it."

That *How to Steal Chocolate in Ten Easy Lessons* blog post had some good tips, Cade decided. Except for number one: *Make sure you steal from Sylvain Marquis.* That was just going to make his head even bigger than it already was. How well did he read English?

But number five, how to avoid a French prison—she might need to pay some attention to that.

Comments were more or less evenly divided between envy of the thief and outrage on Sylvain Marquis's behalf. "Shouldn't chocolate be accessible to all?" Cade wrote quickly and hit Submit before she could think better of it. She probably shouldn't be participating anonymously in debates about herself.

Besides, she didn't exactly want chocolate to be accessible to all. She wanted the end product to be accessible to most, but she wanted the hidden inner fastnesses to be accessible only to her.

And perhaps one sexy, dark-haired lord of the keep.

"You are my hero," her grandfather told her over the phone. "Are you sure it's a good idea to go back twice? You couldn't steal everything you needed the first time?"

Cade glanced around her. She was trying to combine taking advantage of Paris and combing through the reports on Devon Candy her father wanted her to look at by taking her laptop out to the Seine. The widespread availability of Wi-Fi meant she kept getting distracted by blog posts, though. And her fingers kept stiffening up. It was a little chilly.

From where she sat on cold concrete above the brown water, the flying buttresses of Notre-Dame soared up above her to her left, and bridges arched over the river to either side. "La Vie en Rose" crackled through poor speakers every time an excursion boat sparsely populated with tourists passed. Yellow-brown and burnt-sienna leaves swirled around her feet when a breeze blew, fallen from the plane trees that lined the upper and lower quays. Late autumn in Paris wasn't a brilliant last burst of color. Plane trees, so beautiful in the summer, didn't go out with a bang but, rather, leeched themselves into a gray-yellow-brown and dropped their leaves reluctantly. Paris retreated from the *joie de vivre* of summer into wistfulness, a cold chill, and longing.

"I can't find his recipes, Grandpa!"

"If he's smart, he locks them up at night. How are your safecracking skills?"

"A safe? That'd be kind of paranoid," she said severely.

"Maybe," he said. "I mean, ours are in a safe within a safe within a safe and written in code, but our chocolate is *important*. People use it to get by every day. His stuff is just luxurious fluff for people who already have everything else money can buy. Tell me something, though. Have you seen any signs he's experimented with spinach? Or kale. It's packed with nutrition, kale."

"Toute seule, chérie?" a male voice asked, and Cade turned from the Seine-backdropped laptop to stare at him blankly.

Having grown up in a town she owned, she hadn't been hit on by random strangers all that often. First, very few people were strangers. And second, if they were hitting on her, they had a multibillion-dollar agenda. She and her sister, Jaime, both knew there were very few people they could marry who couldn't later take them for alimony that would carve a slice out of Corey Chocolate and put it into the hands of a hostile man who had once screwed her into believing he liked her.

It was a nasty bit of knowledge, but that was just the way it was. There were only so many things money could protect you from, and, unfortunately, falling in love with a man who just wanted to use you was not one of them. Quite the reverse, in fact.

In fact, falling in love with a man who just wanted to *sexually* use her and not her bank account would be romantic as hell by comparison. Just not somebody who looked as slimy as this guy.

An image of Sylvain Marquis flashed through her mind. He didn't show any consistent interest in using her sexually, the jerk. But it was pretty safe to say he wasn't interested in using her for money. In fact, she imagined his face if there was ever even any suggestion that he might marry her for money, and she choked on laughter. *You—you want to put my name—on you? For money?*

The slimy man grinned at her laugh and stepped toward her.

"I'd better go, Grandpa," she said, because if he heard her trying to defend herself from some random loser on the Seine, he would be on the next flight out to protect her.

Any excuse to start breaking into chocolate factories with her—that was her Grandpa.

She slipped the phone back into her leather satchel, which the man apparently took as further encouragement.

Delighted, he sat down so close to her that his weight pinched her thigh. Cheap cologne and body odor assaulted her, mixed with the smell of lanolin from something glistening in his hair.

She jumped away, closing her laptop as she did so. Words failed her. It was hard to think how to say, "Get the fuck away from me!" in another language when she didn't have time to look it up in a dictionary. "Get the fuck," for example. How did you say that? She was fairly sure any attempt would have disastrous unintended meanings.

"Chérie, ne sois pas comme ça." He came up closer to her, reaching for her shoulders.

She twisted to the other side of him, rather than falling into the Seine. "When he takes me in his arms, he speaks to me so softly," serenaded speakers from a passing tourist boat. *"Quand il me prend dans ses bras, il me parle tout bas. . . ."*

"I'll take you in my arms," said the man and in fact tried to do that, grabbing for her waist. "That's what you're here for, isn't it?"

Cade slammed her laptop with both hands into his chest and shoved as hard as she could.

Apparently he didn't expect her to have any strength at all, because he fell back a step. Only there wasn't any step. His eyes opened wide, his foot sought frantically for purchase in midair, and he grabbed at the laptop for balance.

The laptop jerked from her hands. Water splashed back up from the surface of the river and splattered her in the face as man and computer went under.

Merde. Cade tried to remember exactly when she had last backed up her data.

Not since before she left for Paris. So the past week of cramming Corey work into days she wanted to fill only with Paris had just gone down into the Seine in the hands of a pig.

From behind her on the quays above came loud clapping and cheers. Three clearly Parisian women and a couple of guys stood in the gap between two green bookstalls, pumping fists into the air and giving her the thumbs-up.

She grinned.

The man resurfaced, the current pulling him downstream from her. No laptop was visible.

Not that it would have survived a dousing in the river anyway. The man cursed and coughed, and she gave him the finger and headed upstream to climb back to the upper quays. She arrived at the top of the stairs at the same time as the group that had cheered her. They were all grinning at her. A slim brunette with that sleek Parisian look, put together from black pants, high boots, a gray scarf, and the perfect touch of a silver bracelet, said, *"Sérieux, on peut t'offrir un verre?"* "Can we buy you a drink?"

Cade glanced back at her assailant, who had finally managed to grab one of those iron rings on the edge of the quay, about a quarter mile down, and was hauling himself out. "I—sure."

Within half an hour, they had adopted her. All five were students, even though they were close to her age. They seemed so much younger and freer than she felt that envy licked through her.

"You're here to see Paris?" the brunette, Nicole, said. "We'll show you the real Paris. Come out with us tonight."

"No, not tonight," Marc said. Funny, how he seemed so sophisticated and yet so young to her. "I've got a presentation for my Proust class tomorrow."

A presentation. On some guy who wrote about madeleines. She had to give her father feedback tomorrow on a decision about candy that could affect the entire global economy and directly impact the livelihood of tens of thousands of people. Maybe *that* was what had happened to her sense of youth.

"Bon, demain," said the others. "Tomorrow night? *D'accord?"*

"D'accord," Cade said, thrilled.

They were befriending her, and they didn't even know who she was. Maybe it had been a good idea to come to Paris after all.

It was too bad Marc had that presentation for the next day, though, because that left her with another night free to get into trouble.

Chapter 13

She could feel him lurking, even as she stepped into the workshop. Feel his eyes gleaming from the shadows.

The sense of him prickled over her skin, tightening it, making it long for a touch, as she moved through his domain. She searched the *laboratoire* for him, wishing he *could* see her, wishing he had a security camera set up that he was watching even now.

But wait, that shadow, there . . . no, those were pots and the gleam of copper.

That shadow . . . was an enormous mold in the shape of an egg, maybe five feet tall. Those shadows were a stack of crates from Sri Lanka.

She took a long, deep breath, stretching out her arms to let her chest expand, taking in the scents all around her. The whole world and all that was most magical about it seemed to be held in here, scents and flavors taken from everywhere and distilled into pleasure.

Tonight she wanted to make . . . hot chocolate. Spanish hot chocolate, like they drank in Madrid, or the hot chocolate French nobles had once used as a love potion. *Du chocolat chaud.* It was cold outside and cold in the *laboratoire,* where the temperature had been set lower for the nighttime hours.

Her skin kept prickling with excitement as she tasted *pis-*

toles to decide which chocolate she wished to use. Odd, that he would let her get away with this three times.

A colder fear seized her, and she scanned the *laboratoire* again, eyes higher up. Maybe he *had* installed a security camera. Maybe he was collecting evidence right now to hang her. Maybe the police would be waiting outside.

Was she nuts? She could go to *jail*. She could cause major damage to her family's company, in the form of a reactionary stock drop among their subsidiaries. She could lose all the privilege to which she had been so lucky to be born. She could find herself stripped down to nothing but her physical person in a prison cell with no way out.

Would he do that? A man who had flirted with her all one morning and then kicked her out into the cold again?

She didn't really know what he would do, did she? She just liked to imagine. . . .

Heat coursed through her, like and not like the heat she sought from her hot chocolate. She went to the shelves of spices, shadows upon shadows in the dark. She did her work in the thin light that came through the windows from a city night, the City of Lights that was never entirely dark. She did not want to turn on a light inside.

The spice jars felt cold and round under her hand. Hot chocolate should have a touch of vanilla, fresh from Tahiti. A stick of cinnamon from Sri Lanka. Nutmeg from . . . Zanzibar?

She hoped it was. In her opinion, every life should have something in it that came from Zanzibar.

Now what was the French word for *nutmeg*? She opened jars as she hunted, fingers sliding over peeling paper labels, releasing spice after spice into the air—whole cloves, anise, mace. And here at last the small football-shaped nutmeg. She pulled one out and began searching for a grater.

Her skin would not stop prickling. It was as if the spices

themselves were arousing her, or the danger and insanity of what she was doing. Or the pleasure. She felt aware of him in every fiber. She kept fumbling things, as one did when too conscious of eyes watching. She looked through the shadows and saw nothing and tucked her hair back behind one ear and flushed.

She poured milk into a pot, thinking of Sylvain Marquis simmering cream. She dropped in the cinnamon stick and a vanilla bean, then grated nutmeg over it. The scents were heavenly. Or diabolic. Anyone would sin for scents like that, for the promise of life and flavor.

She ran her hand over the cold silk of the marble counter, touched a spoon to the milk and to her tongue, a tiny bit too hot, almost a burn.

And looked toward the embrasure to her left, an alcove that held more sacks and crates and molds.

A shadow moved out of it.

The jolt ran through her. She froze, her heart beating so hard, it seemed to vibrate her whole body.

The sorcerer walked out of the shadows toward the invader of his lair.

He walked straight toward her, a long, menacing stride. Dark cutting through dark and seeming to leave a glitter in his wake of all that knowledge and magic and power he held in him and was denying her.

And danger. She had placed into his hands the ability to destroy her.

He froze her to her place. Just the sight of him. The way he moved through his workshop, such utter mastery. Arousal, burning low in her for hours, even for days, filled her until she could not think. Could only see his hands. The strong, perfect, masculine hands making magic out of raw cacao.

She ached as he walked toward her.

His size and the lean economy of his movement and the darkness of his body in the darkness seemed to close around her, leave her no escape.

He did not speak. Not one word. His hands closed around her hips, and she gasped and shivered, flooded mercilessly with desire. His fingers flexed into her leather-clad bottom, and he lifted her as he might lift a fifty-pound cauldron of chocolate and set her on the counter.

He set her well away from the burner. Even then. Some part of her noted that care. Some part of her might even remember it one day.

He stared down at her, the counter bringing her almost to his height. His eyes glittered. He had caught her, and the thrill of it had taken her over until she couldn't think, only breathe, long, clean last breaths that lifted her chest and filled her lungs with scents of cinnamon, nutmeg, vanilla, chocolate, and human.

"So, you thought you could steal me?" Layer upon layer of dark menace in his voice, a bite and a melt of it. And the sudden intimacy of *tu,* the abrupt abandoning of all the *vous* and *mademoiselle* with which he had so correctly kept her distant, even while he played with her in his workshop.

His face was so close to hers that she could feel every breath from his words against her lips. She was just going to lean forward. She was just going to . . .

His fingers flexed into her bottom, shattering her attention. *Oh, please, let him do that again.* "Are you stealing from anyone else?" he demanded.

No, she started to say, but thought better of it. "From Dominique Richard," she told him provocatively.

He kissed her for punishment. Ran one hand up her back hard, so that her body molded against his, tangled his fingers in her hair to hold her head, and kissed her.

His kiss. He was kissing her. He was *kissing* her. The glory of it poured through her. She rose to it, trying to capture every atom of his taste, his texture. Grabbing for his body, trying to pull herself in harder to him.

His wool sweater frustrated her instantly, too rough, too thick. She pushed under it, found cotton knit, and rushed past that, afraid she would lose this chance if she didn't take it as fast as she could. *Ah, there.* Skin. Sleek, hot skin.

He shivered as if her hands were icy. Or maybe something else made him shiver.

His skin felt so warm. It shifted under her touch, as if her fingers conveyed impulses that electrified his muscles. She climbed up those lean, hard muscles, her fingers working over ribs to his chest, feeling a soft fuzz of hair. Her arms pushed up his clothes as she went so that his torso was exposed to the air.

One hand rubbed hard over her thigh. He nudged her legs wider apart with his body. Her legs yielded to him; she yielded to him. He pulled her to the edge of the counter and stepped into her so that hips pressed against hips. So he *did* want her. He wasn't toying with her now. At least this once, right now, here, she could make him want her.

He pressed her own upper body against his, hard, rubbing her breasts against him with a force he had not shown in all his teasing games with her, that workshop morning full of bare brushes of his hands. His mouth closed over hers, all hot, all force, all silk, lips and tongue and a pull and nip of teeth with no mercy for her.

His hands flexed into her thighs, pushing them wider still apart, pressing his hips against her, so that she had to slide her hands under his arms to his shoulders to find purchase, to hold herself against the force of his kiss, to fight into it, back at it, and not be toppled over by it.

He made a sound that thrummed through his body. She knew she made one, too, a tiny shiver of a moan.

He could do anything to her, anything he wanted.

He wrenched his mouth free and pulled his head back, staring at her, as if he couldn't believe she was real.

She was and she wasn't, that was the thing. That was what she liked about this Paris night and the swirl of scents and possibilities.

Some part of her knew this could not be happening, not in any life she had ever known. But it was. And she had made it happen.

Hanging on to his shoulders, arched up to him, she stared back at him, not moving. He took a hard breath and brought his mouth back to hers.

Sylvain had walked toward her with a certainty he had never felt in his life before. This woman was his. This night was his. Any fantasy he caught in his *laboratoire* was his to keep.

À moi, he thought. *À moi.*

She had hunted him. She had tethered herself out there like some kid goat to his Tyrannosaurus rex. She had tapped the entry code to his own *laboratoire* over and over right in front of him, telling him with every press of that perfectly manicured little finger against a metal button where she would be that night and what she would be doing.

She had placed her chocolate thumbprint on his papers like some wordless signature on a contract with his body. She had lit a fire in his *laboratoire* to taunt him when he did not catch her fast enough, and made something with what was his, and did not even leave him a taste.

She had plunged her hands into his sacks of pistachios and coffee beans and let the textures roll over her skin; she had breathed in his scents and left the traces all over her body; she had tasted his chocolates and let them melt on her tongue. And with every trace he saw of her passing each morning, she had driven him one degree crazier, until he could not think beyond what pistachios felt like against the back of a hand plunged into a sack, what his vanilla and orange peel and almond oil would smell like against her skin, the scents she stole from his workshop every night and with which she was marking herself his territory.

He could not think beyond what it would feel like to melt on her tongue. Him. Not just the chocolate he made to seduce her, but him.

It seemed as if every classy, pretty girl he had ever lusted after in high school or since had been condensed into her, with her arrogance, and her raspberry tarts for breakfast, and her brown hair flying into her lip gloss, and her blue eyes looking up at him as if defying him to reach out and touch that hair and free her mouth for other things. Her sense of her own right to own the world was so bone-deep, she didn't even know she had it, but her attempts at masks of cold indifference toward others were so flawed, she couldn't sit at a restaurant table by herself without making him want to scoop her up and bring her to his table, looking so determined and alone.

She lusted after everything he produced and owned so intensely and sinfully. Surely she must lust after him.

Never in his life had he felt so positive of that. And yet, driven by some old, stupid weakness of his, he had still held back far too long, just in case she wanted to escape.

But she arched up to him. Her hands gripped his shoulders with that strange, feminine strength. Nothing like his strength. Nothing even approaching his strength. And yet he was the one who could not break away.

She could. She could yet. You could never trust a woman's desire. It was something you had to constantly seduce.

But she could have wrapped one strand of her hair around his littlest finger and held him with it.

Her *fesses* were supple and perfect under his fingers, and she was wearing black leather over them at midnight, sitting on the marble of his counter. He brought his mouth down to hers again and closed that window of opportunity for rejection and didn't open it even a fraction of a millimeter again.

She felt so gloriously perfect against him, the silk-cashmere of her sweater sliding under his hands as he found her skin, and the way her eyes closed at his touch in more bliss even than the way they closed when she bit into a raspberry *tartelette* or *ravioles du Royan* or even . . . maybe . . . one of his chocolates.

Leather . . . silk-cashmere . . . his hands pushed her sweater up . . . a texture that felt like nothing else—not rose petals, not silk; all of these were just pale similes for the fineness and the humanness of a woman's skin. Lace. Lace covered her breasts, a faint, raw rub between her soft fullness and his hands.

She opened her eyes again and stared up at him.

Thinking—what? Feeling—what?

But she was his fantasy. His to keep. Caught brown-handed. So he didn't try to guess what she wanted; he just did what he wanted: he dragged his thumbs over that faint prickle of lace, pressing into the softness underneath, rubbing her nipples hard, letting his fingers flex into her ribs.

Her body rippled in his hands, her lips parting as if begging.

But she didn't have to beg for him, his perfect fantasy. He would be glad to give her everything.

He kissed her again, delving into her, pouring himself into the moment. Not trying to calculate his next step in seduction. Just enjoying every atom of her being.

There in his arms. Yielding to him. Pulling at him. Yielding. Her mouth, her tongue, her body that flexed to him and grew softer and softer, as if all strength failed her, even as he grew stronger and stronger, too hard, hard to bursting with himself and his power over her.

He pulled the cashmere over her head and pushed it away,

revealing pale skin and black lace in the shadows lit just enough by the city night that came through the windows. She shivered at the touch of the cold air against her body, and he felt an instant's guilt that they were here and not in some bed with down comforters where he could keep her warm.

He wouldn't mind down comforters instead of marble and leather with his fantasy.

Dieu, but that could be beautiful, luxuriating in the softest white cotton on a cold November day, nothing but coziness and pleasure and smiles, and no fear of waking to second guesses driving one or the other of them out into the cold.

Beautiful, too. He would concentrate on the beautiful moment he had right here in his hands.

He ran his hands up her back, warming her, pressing her into his chest. She pushed his sweater and shirt up, insistent, until he had to pause long enough in touching her to take them off, and she buried herself against the warmth so exposed to her.

He grinned, hard and fierce, because he had that warmth to give her. He had that strength to hold her. He had that world of scents and tastes to lure her. He knew how to make her happy. Tomorrow, who knew, because women changed too much from night to day to say. But this woman—this thief here in his arms—he knew exactly how to make her happy.

That certainty filled his kiss, the way he molded her body to his. Her hands slid over and gripped his back, every tightening, releasing pressure built up over a hard day's work, every soft stroke making him feel stronger, surer, more wanted.

He kissed her and kissed her, unable to get enough of her mouth, the miracle of her skin under his hands, her breasts. He pulled off her bra and threw it toward the sweater.

Her breasts were so peaked and urgent for him. As urgent as her hips, twisting against his, lifting and subsiding. As urgent as her mouth, returning his kiss with so much passion, it soon became impossible to call it *his* kiss or to tell who had begun it, only that neither wanted to end it.

But she did, gasping for breath, melting instead onto his shoulders, his biceps, her lips pressing over and over against his skin.

With each touch of her lips, he felt bigger, harder, until he could do nothing but find the zipper hidden on the hip of her pants and push that exquisitely enjoyable leather down over her hips.

But skin . . . skin bared from leather . . . oh, that was exquisite, too.

And the way her hips jumped and jerked against him when her bottom touched the cold marble. And the way he slid his hands under her *fesses* and picked her up, protecting her from the cold and sinking his fingers into her roundness all at the same time.

She slid her arms around his waist and held on to him hard, her whole body trembling.

He pulled their sweaters back, spreading them where her body would lie on the marble, and eased her backward onto them.

She resisted. She did not want to let him go.

But *he* was the master here. He took her wrists and forced her down. As soon as his hands locked around her wrists, she stopped fighting him, her eyes huge, her breasts so peaked, her body so pliant.

He forced her down on the sweaters and brought her wrists together to hold them with one hand. She shivered and shivered, her body stretched out to him pale in the dark. Her sex, when he began to play with it, was already so moist.

It took her . . . almost too soon to come. He was enjoying his power to make her body buck and melt and moan. He could have kept doing that for hours.

But when she came so helplessly, her wrists twisting in the

hold of his hand, her hips jolting against the heel of his palm, her body shivering and shivering in some offering to him . . . then he couldn't keep doing this. Then he couldn't wait even another second.

He pulled his jeans open one-handed and pulled her onto him while he could still feel the aftershocks rippling through her body, squeezing him helplessly, in a rhythm beyond her control.

It was astonishing that even with that, he managed to rein himself in a little longer, not to come at once, but to press into her over and over, watch her eyes shut, feel her muscles again begin to clutch at him uncontrollably, as he made her helpless with his thumb, with his sex. She was so amazing, lying there across his marble, half in leather, all slim and white and his. He couldn't bear to end that quickly.

But she was so incredible. He couldn't make it last nearly as long as he would like, either. When she came again, he did, too, driving into her in an explosion of feeling.

It took a long time for Cade to figure out what to do next. You couldn't really cuddle on a marble counter. Especially not with a man who despised you and had used *tu* for the first time only a few minutes before, and that only because he was on the brink of having sex with her. For all she knew, he was going to kick her out at any second.

He was still standing, or rather sagging over her, letting his arms take his weight. His face, so hard and intent a few minutes before, looked utterly relaxed now, almost sleepy. But he didn't close his eyes. She would almost rather he had closed his eyes, but no, his gaze kept tracking up and down her body. Those French lips of his, usually so tight and precise from all those vowels he had to say, had softened into a curve.

He looked pretty happy with his life, in fact.

Of course, you would, if you were a man and had women throwing themselves at you or stripping naked and stretching themselves out the second you touched them. What was there not to be happy about?

She closed her eyes. His hands had felt exactly as she had imagined. So strong and sure and . . . delicate, when they needed to be.

They knew her melting temperature, that was for sure.

And now she was being tempered much too fast. The cold from the marble was seeping into her bones.

He shifted his weight to one arm and brought the other hand to rest on her tummy, fingers stroking idly.

That helped, a little.

She stopped feeling quite so isolated and awkward.

But it got cold. And she didn't know what to say. And he sure didn't bring up any ideas.

And then, from the slow trickling at her thighs, she realized with a shock that for the first time in her life she had had unprotected sex.

Oh, good Lord. She took the pill, but . . . he might even have a girlfriend, that Chantal. And who knew how many women he slept with, considering that supersexy mouth and hands and dark eyes and arrogance and all that chocolate.

Completely freaked out now and frozen so fast that she was a little sick to her stomach, she rolled away from him.

That slight curve to his mouth disappeared, and he stepped back from her. He rubbed his hand once hard over his face, pushing his hair back, and then just watched her.

It was unnerving to have him watch her so steadily without speaking. Couldn't he just look away?

She dressed, half turned away from him, her head bent. She didn't know what to say or do.

She kept trying to come up with something, but what

words fit? "Thanks"? *No way.* No way was she thanking him for having sex with her. "Well, that was nice"? *Oh, God.* "See you tomorrow?" *No, no, no!*

"I could still make you some *chocolat chaud,*" he said. The rough darkness was gone from his voice. It sounded—careful, not dangerous. Teasing sneaked into it, cautiously. "Probably better than yours."

She lifted her head and looked at him. "Really?" Make her hot chocolate? As in something he might do for someone he kind of liked?

"*Vraiment.* In fact, almost certainly better than yours." He grinned at her.

She narrowed her eyes. "You haven't tasted mine."

"You haven't tasted *mine,*" he retorted.

Were they only talking about hot chocolate?

"Here." He picked her up and set her on the marble again. "Watch how it's done. And put your sweater back on before you freeze."

But she noticed he didn't put his own sweater on, or even his shirt. Half-naked, seemingly indifferent to the cold, he tossed flavors into a cauldron, whisking milk and chocolate and cacao together, brewing her hot chocolate. His body was utterly beautiful in motion. Long and lean, it was the perfect masculine form of a flat stomach and broad shoulders, dark hair curling on his chest, his jaw-length hair tucked behind his ear on one side, falling to tease his cheek on the other. He mastered every motion so perfectly, so efficient and easy.

"Does your nutmeg come from Zanzibar?" she asked him, as she lifted the cup toward her mouth and felt its heat warm her hands and face.

His eyes met hers with complete understanding. "Sometimes it does."

She sipped it slowly. It really was delicious. Thick and

unctuous, an elusive hint of spices hiding in its depths, warming her right to the bottom of her chilled, newly awkward body. He had used the cinnamon and nutmeg and vanilla that she had gotten out, but she knew hers wouldn't have tasted this good.

When she finished, she stared into the smooth brown gloss that coated the bottom of her cup, but no one had ever read the future in the dregs of a cup of hot chocolate. "Are you going to call the police on me?"

"Have you stolen files that you're going to use at Corey Chocolate without my authorization?"

"Not yet. And particularly not if you give your authorization. That would make everything a lot simpler."

"You mean it would make it more efficient. Trust an American to get efficiency and simplicity confused."

"They're related."

"They're completely different terms." He leaned back against the marble countertop, holding his cup of chocolate, a white contrast to his matte skin and the dark curls of chest hair. If he had calculated every move to seduce her again, he could not have done a better job of it. "I don't know. Calling the police seems a waste of a good opportunity to me."

Opportunity?

"For blackmail." He gave her a slow smile.

The blood congealed in her veins. She had given him multiple chances for blackmail, hadn't she? The break-in itself. How much might Corey Chocolate have to pay to hush that up? And the sex on a countertop . . . *did* he have a video camera recording somewhere? Again she found herself scanning the room, trying to spot one of those little items she had looked for in that high-tech shop in the Halles. "What are your blackmail demands?"

His lashes lowered, and his fingers tightened on his cup. "I don't think I should give them to you right now, but . . ."

maybe tomorrow sometime. Somewhere . . . a little more comfortable. I could describe them to you in detail."

Her frozen blood got a little confused as heat began to pool simultaneously. What were they talking about, exactly? Hush money or hush sex?

For all she knew, both. He could be capable of asking for both at once. She knew nothing about him, really. Except that even right now, she wanted nothing so much as to take the place of his cup of hot chocolate, cradled against his bare chest, touched in a leisurely savoring from time to time by his lips.

What would he think if she just stepped up to him and nestled her head right at his heart?

That she was pathetic? Worth thirty-three cents at Walmart?

She set down her empty cup with a little click that made a strange, cold, final sound in the *laboratoire*. "Well. Thank you for the chocolate."

At least that *chocolat chaud* gave her some kind of exit line for the night.

He made a muted, incredulous sound, as if she had punched it out of his stomach. "*Il n'y a vraiment pas de quoi. No thanks are necessary, I promise you.*"

She didn't look at him, too much of a coward to see what expression might be on his face. She just walked toward the door, steadily. At least it didn't feel quite so much the retreat in inglorious defeat. It wasn't completely humiliating.

It was still embarrassing as hell, though.

He followed her and stood just hidden in the doorway as she crossed the street, making sure she went back where she belonged.

Or maybe just making sure she got back to her apartment safely.

A shadow shifted under the bakery shop awning, someone standing there watching her. She glanced that way, pulse jumping in a preliminary fight-or-flight instinct, but the shadow shifted farther back.

She relaxed. Whoever it was, he was no danger to her tonight.

Perhaps he had seen Sylvain keeping watch.

Chapter 14

"Sylvain. Sylvain."

Sylvain blinked, shaking his head and focusing on Pascal.

"We were trying to decide what chocolates to make today," Pascal prodded, indicating with a look the battered, worn, schoolboy binder in which were stored a decade of recipes. Well, the ingredients for the recipes. The technique, the timing, were all in Sylvain's head.

Sylvain rubbed his brow. "*Pardon.* I didn't get much sleep."

Pascal pursed his lips on a grin, as if a dozen possible jokes about lack of sleep had leaped to mind and he was restraining himself from uttering any of them. "Well, go over this with me, and then go home and get some rest, if you want. You almost never take a day off."

The door between the workshop and the shop opened, and Francine, his store manager, came back. "Sylvain, can you tell me what this thief story is about? People have been coming in for the last two days asking about it, and now there's one of the Americans who lives around here saying she saw an article on the *New York Times* site this morning. And someone from *Le Monde* is calling. Is some American chocolate baron stealing your chocolate? Co-ree?"

Sylvain blinked some more. "The *New York Times*? Today's *New York Times*? Is it out already?" Fuzzily, he tried to

THE CHOCOLATE THIEF 137

remember what time it was on the other side of the Atlantic. But since what was happening on the other side of the Atlantic had never been much of a concern of his, he had no idea. "And it mentions Cade Corey's name?"

Francine spread her hands. "I haven't seen it. But I assume it's online."

Sylvain abandoned the recipe binder without another word and went to the laptop in his office.

A Chocolate Thief by Any Other Name read the lead title of the Food section. He grinned. *Lovely.* Any time his name came up in the Food section of the *New York Times,* he made a fortune for the next couple of months in American-tourist sales. He already had a solid contingent of American celebrities and extravagantly wealthy patrons who had his chocolates airmailed over to them once a week, and he would certainly see a jump in that list, too. He felt intense satisfaction when he watched a movie by Steven Spielberg, or a role played by Cate Blanchett, or opened Microsoft Excel or Google on his computer and thought about those people biting into one of his chocolates as they worked on producing their masterpieces.

For the past two days, bloggers have been reporting a thief stealing world-famous Sylvain Marquis's chocolate.

World-famous. Sylvain grinned again. It was true but always nice to see it repeated by one of the accepted global authorities on news.

Can it have anything to do with Cade Corey, daughter of Mack Corey and part-owner of Corey Chocolate, currently in Paris? According to sources, she allowed one woman a day's use of her credit card—to the tune of $30,000—in exchange for her place in a workshop by Sylvain Marquis. And last night, she was seen slipping into and, a few hours later, out of, Sylvain Marquis's workshop in the middle of the night when no one else was there.

Sylvain had been there, he thought, losing track of what he was reading as he felt Cade Corey's body against his again, saw the way she had tilted her head back and looked at him as he caught her in his *laboratoire*.

Right about now, he thought, she must be fielding a lot of calls. His face couldn't quite decide whether to grin or raise eyebrows in alarm as he tried to imagine her reaction to this article.

His main worry, he had to admit, was that she might stop sneaking into his workshop to steal his chocolate in the middle of the night. He had already been worried about that, in fact. What if last night was a one-night affair, never to be repeated?

What two people might do in the dark without speaking, they might never do again or even want to admit to. He had learned that growing up.

He had given her more chances than he'd wanted to, more chances than he owed to a fantasy caught in his workshop. He had waited longer than he could bear too many times last night, to see if she would turn away or change her mind.

But she had never even seemed to hesitate. Not once.

And that meant . . . absolutely nothing today. You could keep a fantasy about as well as you could keep a butterfly. It was all too easy to want it too badly and crush the life out of it. His mouth shifted from a grin into grimness.

Ça, alors . . . ça serait vraiment con. That would be really, really lousy, in fact.

He had been stupid. He knew all about tempering chocolate; he knew all about the way he should have stroked her afterward, eased her back to normal temperature and normal life. And he had not paid attention. Too caught up in his own experience, thrown too completely, as if he had rubbed one of his bottles of vanilla extract and a succubus had popped out at him.

It was only after she had twisted away from him and started getting dressed, in that awkward silence, that he had

had the brains to save the moment by offering her hot chocolate.

He had done his best to recoup his carelessness. He had calculated every move and word, from then on, to try to lure her back into warmth and into his arms. He had almost frozen to death keeping his shirt off the whole time he made that hot chocolate. But if the sight had sent her mad with lust again, she had kept a pretty tight lid on it.

So he didn't know if that chocolate made up for . . . anything. With women, you never knew for sure what they were thinking. They seemed to have some instinct to go off in bizarre directions, get mad, get weird, just because they had sex. One would think sex would drive them in the other direction—into a blissful sense that all was right with the world—but no. You had to be careful all the time with women, and he hadn't been.

Some of his efforts to make a future out of that night *clearly* hadn't worked. He had thought a blackmail sex fantasy might appeal to a woman who dressed up in leather to break into his *laboratoire* and deliberately got caught at it, but she had seemed to get angry more than anything. He could still hear that empty cup clicking down on the marble like a dead bolt sliding shut.

If he lost her and it was his own stupid fault . . . *ça serait vraiment, vraiment con.*

His own phone started to ring.

Her phone buzzed and buzzed and buzzed, maddening her, as if she kept being stung by a bumblebee, until it finally forced her out of sleep. Such a happy, mindless sleep.

She looked at it, saw the quantity of missed calls from her father and grandfather and even Jaime, then rubbed her face hard and switched the messages over to her e-mail.

Her in-box flooded, downloading Google Alert after

Google Alert. *Good grief.* What had Sylvain Marquis done to draw so much attention this time?

She looked at the first one, a ten-word excerpt from the *New York Times* Web site, and saw not only Sylvain's name but hers and *thief.*

The bottom sank so far out of her stomach that she nearly threw up right there.

Her phone buzzed some more, like a beehive gone mad. She got up, walked into the bathroom, and braced herself over the toilet for a long time, until she could be quite sure she wasn't going to throw up the remains of last night's hot chocolate. Then she went back and read through the primary articles. Then she went back and hung over the toilet again for a while. And then she came back, opened the new laptop she had bought the afternoon before, and spent twenty minutes trying to get Skype working on it before she could finally face the music.

Her father, unshaven and his gray hair sleep-crushed, still rubbing drowsiness out of his blue eyes, was almost incapable of forming words: "I just . . . I can't . . . were you out of your mind? Cade. Why? We have *people* for this."

"You're not supposed to get caught," her grandfather pointed out over his shoulder. He was thinner than his stocky son, wrinkled and white-haired, and he looked as spry as if he had been up for hours, which might be true. He only slept a few hours a night. His blue eyes were paler than Cade's or her father, Mack's, having lightened with age, but they still held absolute confidence in every word he said and their typical glee at the world's twists and turns. "I told you not to get into a position where they could start sniffing at you."

"When are you flying back?" her father said.

She frowned, worrying a thumbnail. "I'm not. Not yet."

Flat silence. In the delay in the video, her father just sat still, staring at her. "Why *not*? What more damage do you hope to do there? Cade, I'm fielding calls from The *Wall Street Journal* here. I just made an extra political contribution in case we need to get you out of some French jail. You're not Jaime!"

Yes, and somehow Jaime always got to do what she wanted, wherever in the world she wanted to do it. G8 summit protests, tear-gassed on the front page as a poster girl for anti-capitalism, backpacking trips abroad while Cade had worked for Corey since she was a teenager. Jaime had even been able to *abandon* all the business and follow her *heart*, and her father and Cade herself had thrown everything Jaime wanted at her as a reward—Corey funding for her cacao plantation labor work, everything. Cade couldn't help thinking that if just once as a teenager she had had the chutzpah to get on the front page at a World Trade Organization protest, she too might be free, right at this moment. Free to pursue whatever dream she wanted. Ha, and maybe *Jaime* would be the one stuck with all Corey Chocolate on her shoulders, whining about how her older sister had ditched it on her.

"You know, France probably won't bother to extradite over a simple breaking and entering, so if you come home before they put an arrest warrant out, you might stay out of jail," her grandfather offered helpfully.

"I haven't gotten what I came for," she said stubbornly.

"I haven't figured out a way to incorporate spinach into chocolate yet, either," her grandfather said. "Some things you never do manage."

She gave the screen a narrow look. Her grandfather was being a turncoat, that's what he was. He had been totally behind her before the Corey name got out there. "Yes, but you're still trying. And Great-grandpa still tried for that milk chocolate, even after he burned down the farm with his experiments."

Suddenly, the memory of that was reassuring to her. However unhappy her family was with her, Great-grandpa's family had to have been even more unhappy with him when he burned down the place where they lived for some pipe dream. And look where they all were now, thanks to that experiment.

They all were . . . at the mercy of the sniff of a French chocolatier, thanks to her.

"Let me get this straight," Sylvain's mother, Marguerite, said over the phone from Provence, where Sylvain had helped his parents buy a house when they retired.

Just his luck. He had thought he was picking up a call from *Le Monde*.

"Some spoiled, rich owner of *Corey Chocolate* is breaking into your shop to steal from you?" Sylvain's mother kept her voice modulated and lovely as she always did, but her outrage vibrated through it until his ears prickled.

"*Maman.* How did you find out about this so fast?"

"I have a Google Alert on you, of course," she said promptly. "Also, I got ten calls from friends before I could get out of the shower this morning. Is it true?"

"She hasn't actually managed to steal anything but chocolates yet," he hedged. "She hasn't found my recipes." Not that they would do her much good. He just listed ingredients to jog his memory. The timing, the temperatures, everything else was in his head. *"Maman, une alerte Google?"*

"Why are you saying 'yet'?" his mother demanded. "Haven't you had her arrested?"

Sylvain tried to think of the best way to say *non*. "*Maman.* This is chocolate business." As in, *his* business. *Back off.* "It's okay."

Of course, his mother didn't get the hint about minding her own business at all. She never had. "You haven't had her arrested?" Again his ears prickled with the depth of outrage in that perfectly elegant voice. "You're going to just let her get away with it?"

Not only that, but he was hoping she would come back and steal from him some more. "It's complicated, *Maman.*"

"What is complicated about it?" she asked dangerously.

"Well. She's kind of cute," he said apologetically.

"Oh, Sylvain. *Please* don't tell me you're going to let some spoiled rich brat use you to steal what's most important to you. And break your heart."

"I won't," Sylvain said firmly. *Merde,* it already sounded like a lie. That wasn't a good sign for him.

"Sylvain," his mother said sorrowfully. *What the hell?* Did everyone have to start grieving for him *in advance?* "Aren't you *ever* going to learn?"

It was the kind of morning when Cade would have liked to take a very long shower before facing any more of it. But when she tried, she mostly just showered the wallpaper and froze herself. She finally ended up filling the bathtub and sinking into it until only her nose was exposed to breathe. She hadn't taken a bath in years, and it lacked something, as far as bracing effect went. Plus, she was pretty sure it was 60 degrees in this apartment.

She dressed with as much care as it was possible for a woman to put into her appearance—the perfect eye shadow, the perfect subtle mascara, a very, very long debate over the perfect lipstick. Quite a drawn out struggle over the perfect pair of pants that were both sexy and professional and would not even remotely make anyone think of black leather. She almost went with chocolate brown, and then the whole fact that they were called "chocolate" infuriated her, and she switched to a short gray pencil skirt with high black boots and gray pin-striped tights instead. A very deep burgundy sweater. A black pearl pendant.

And over that whole outfit, she had to pull on a long wool coat. It was too cold to go out without a coat.

But if that coat ever came off for any reason, she wanted the next layer down to look good. She chose the red wool coat defiantly.

There was a line out the door of the chocolate shop, and Cade thought briefly about using her stolen code in broad daylight and going in the back way. But she was pretty sure that was a journalist staked out over there with a camera. Either that or one of those damn food bloggers.

Instead, she adapted local custom and broke through the line with complete authority, striding into the shop. Okay, *trying* to stride into the shop. In practice, that turned out to be a lot of wiggling and squeezing through a packed crowd leaning avidly over glass display cases.

She grasped the door to the *laboratoire*.

"*Madame!*" exclaimed one of the women in brown aprons stamped SYLVAIN MARQUIS. "*Vous ne pouvez pas . . .*"

"*Vous êtes Cade Co-ree?*" she heard a man exclaim happily.

She ignored both of them, although her stomach flinched at her name being called aloud in that shop. Particularly her last name. Thank God their parent company was privately held stock.

Sylvain and Pascal leaned together over a battered brown binder, both in paper toques, Sylvain's slightly higher than Pascal's. Sylvain straightened immediately when he saw her and closed the book.

Energy seemed to surge through him, and he smiled at her, but warily.

She narrowed her eyes at him. "May I talk to—" She broke off, realizing that French left her with a really awkward choice right now. She could either talk to *vous,* perfectly formal and professional, or *tu,* a sudden switch to intimacy that would be like stripping naked in front of everyone who could hear her. To hell with pronouns. She pretended she was back in French 101 and couldn't remember to use them. "May I talk in private a moment?"

A beat too late, she realized she had asked almost exactly the same question the first time she had ended up scorned out of his *laboratoire*. If he raised his eyebrows in refusal and said, "This is important," she might very well burn the entire contents of that binder. And just where did he keep that thing when he wasn't looking at it? She had searched everywhere.

"*Bien sûr,*" he said. "May I come listen?"

She bristled, wishing she had some kind of riding crop to whip against her leg in a menacing way or something. He had caught her ducking that all-important *tu/vous* choice and pushed her on it. She noticed he had adroitly avoided any stand on the second person himself.

He had used *tu* last night. She couldn't remember what she had used.

"*Par ici, Mademoiselle Corey.*" Sylvain took her elbow. Despite her coat and sweater, a jolt of electricity ran through her. "I don't believe you've been in my office before," he said with a certain ironic showmanship, since they both knew she had broken into it several nights in a row. And he used *vous*.

She swallowed that cold pill.

Sylvain guided her into his office and shut the door. He let go of her to lean back against his desk and smile at her. "*Bonjour.*" He pulled off his paper toque and tossed it onto the desk, his black hair sliding free to caress his chin.

She hadn't even touched his hair last night. It had all happened so fast. Her fingers twitched now, regretting that lost opportunity to discover if it was as silky as it looked. She bet, if she just stripped off her gloves, she could sink her hands into that hair and . . .

"Let me explain something about blackmail to you," she said through her teeth. "If you want to blackmail someone with a secret, you can't tell the world about the secret first."

His gaze was drifting over her red coat. A tiny delay followed before he seemed to realize she had stopped talking. He looked back at her face. "What?"

"If you want to blackmail someone over something, you have to keep the something secret."

He was gazing at her chest as if trying to penetrate the heavy coat. "I'm sorry, what?"

"Are you listening to me at all?"

"I'm trying," he admitted. One corner of his mouth kicked up. "But I didn't get much sleep last night. And I'm thinking about the reasons."

Thank God for the coat. At least he couldn't see her nipples tighten or her thighs clench.

"I *thought* you said you were going to blackmail me. I was counting on that!"

The curve of his mouth deepened. His eyes darkened. "So you liked that idea? Are you wearing pajamas again under that coat, or what—"

He caught himself and tried to focus.

He had dropped into *tu* again, she noticed. Was he trying to drive her mad? She had no idea where she stood with him.

Well, two could play that game. No one here even seemed to entirely accept that she spoke French. She could mash *tu* and *vous* together within one sentence and act as if it was all in complete innocence. "I liked it a lot better than being called a thief in the *New York Times*. Maybe you should have given that some thought before you told them."

His eyebrows rose. "You think *I* told them? Do you think I am an *imbécile*?"

"You turned down a contract worth millions and then decided to blackmail me instead. I'm still trying to decide how smart you are."

His eyes narrowed. "I wasn't born the best chocolatier in

Paris, so I must have had some brains to get here. I believe you were born to own Corey Chocolate?"

That was both infuriating and cruel. People thought that all the time about her, that she had inherited billions, and those hereditary billions made *her* worthless. But she worked her butt off for Corey, and the fact that she had been born to own it was true in more ways than one. Running the family firm had been her life's purpose from the moment she was enough of a presence in her mother's womb to make her start throwing up from the smell of cacao.

This stupid effort to own a little dark chocolate chunk of Paris was one of the first choices concerning her destiny she had ever managed to make.

Before she could speak, he stopped her. "Wait. What does blackmail have to do with that ridiculous contract idea of yours? Did you think I was going to blackmail you for *money*?"

She hesitated.

Outrage smoldered in his eyes. "Last night—when I said—you thought it was all about *money*?" He shoved away from the desk abruptly, which brought him only a foot from her in the small office. "And you think I'm the one who isn't very smart? Is that because you define intelligence as the ability to keep track of six zeros after a number?"

Nine zeros, she thought. She did manage to bite her tongue before correcting him, though. "And how do you define *intelligence*?"

"The ability to recognize something of value when you see it," he said promptly. "Or taste it. Or touch it."

She began to blush. Was he talking about a general life philosophy or her? Was she something of value? In a non-financial sense?

Then again . . . she had certainly tasted and touched him. Her blush deepened almost to the shade of her sweater as she remembered his taste, his feel. Maybe he meant *he* was the something of value *she* should be recognizing by taste and touch.

That would be just like his arrogance, wouldn't it? "I do recognize value," she said, her words clipped. "That's why I've been breaking in here trying to steal your recipes for chocolate."

For chocolate. Not for you.

Whatever she'd meant to accomplish with that sentence, she was going to count it a failure, because he almost visibly pulled all his emotions back from her. They just seemed to retreat back into him.

"Or get Dominique Richard to sell me his," she added perversely, driving the wedge in deeper.

His mouth set. "So, tell me something. Would you have sex with Dominique Richard for his chocolate, too?"

No. Because Dominique Richard was only good-looking, in a rough, wham-bam way. She didn't lose all capacity for thought when she looked at his hands. Or his mouth. He wasn't *beautiful*, his every movement perfect.

But she wasn't going to tell Sylvain Marquis that. Especially not as his insult sank in and her blush fled, leaving her white and cold and sick. "I don't want your chocolate. I don't want you." *Yes, I do, yes, I do*, she shouted to herself inside. *Shut up, shut up.* "I withdraw the contract offer." She could barely remember how to say that in French. It had shown up in one of the business-language textbooks her tutor liked, but she hadn't paid much attention to it. She hadn't entertained the possibility that she might need to use it.

And there was another thing she had never learned how to say in French, so she switched to English and bared her teeth at him: "Fuck you, Sylvain Marquis."

She turned around and strode out.

Chapter 15

"**M**erde," Sylvain said aloud in his office. *"Putain de bordel de merde."*

She was right, he was an *imbécile.* Why was he so stupid specifically around her? Every time he told himself to be careful, reminded himself of the rules of seduction, he turned around and did something worse.

She had come to see him, *non?* She hadn't hidden. She had come in fighting, but she had come; she had sought him out again.

Why had he let that comment about valuing his chocolate get to him? He *knew* that was the way it worked.

But something had rebelled inside him. Something had said, *Wait, if the chocolate is the only thing that matters, why did you have sex with me?* Dominique Richard had been *meilleur chocolatier de Paris* last year. True, that had been an error in judgment on the part of the mayor, who happened to be from Dominique's neighborhood. But . . . surely there was something else she saw to distinguish him from some of the other top Parisian chocolatiers besides how well they made chocolate.

He had yielded to a sudden, furious desire to make her admit it—to herself, at least, even if she wouldn't admit it out loud.

And what he had accomplished was just like a child in a

temper tantrum destroying the beautiful model airplane he had had the good luck to receive for Noël and had just spent days building, all because he couldn't get some decal to fit on it right.

He went back into the *laboratoire* but found himself completely unable to concentrate on his recipes.

"I'll decide," Pascal said finally, frustrated. "You're useless today."

Useless, indeed. He thought of the way that deep, inexplicable blush on Cade Corey's face had paled and paled, until there was nothing left of it, and only her eyes glittered with color.

"I'm going to take a walk."

He stripped off his *tablier* and chef's jacket in the room off the entrance and pulled on the leather coat he had worn that day in honor of his Chocolate Thief. He went to the Jardins du Luxembourg. The November wind stirred branches stripped of leaves and chilled his cheeks. His feet crunched on gravel.

The gardens were mostly empty, compared to the spring and summer flocks that filled them, but even in the cold there were always people who sought refuge here. They took pictures of the large perfect octagonal pond before the Palais, tourists in Paris even in November, or they huddled and brooded on chairs or stairs, or they just walked.

A homeless man had pulled eight chairs together to make a kind of bed and installed himself there with worn blankets and a brand-new jacket picked up somewhere. Blissfully happy, he was scarfing down something from a very familiar-looking box.

Sylvain's jaw dropped as he realized the man was eating from a box marked with his own name. And not only that, he had a large bag marked with Sylvain's name, and it was filled with at least eight more boxes of chocolates.

"Where did you get that?" he asked tightly, although already, even as he was asking the question, he was starting to guess. Fury simmered up, despite all his reminders of self-control.

"Une femme." The man waved vaguely down one of the paths. "She gave me some *chocolat de merde* the other day, and I told her what I thought about that. She must have felt guilty, because she gave me a box of the good stuff the other day. Sylvain Marquis," the man said appreciatively. "Never thought I would be eating Sylvain Marquis."

"That's more than a box," Sylvain said. A part of him felt guilty, too, at seeing a homeless man so grateful to eat his chocolates. He needed to do something about that. But another part was rising to a boil. She wasn't eating his chocolates herself? She wasn't up there in her apartment savoring bite after bite of him insatiably?

The man closed his hand protectively over the sack, imagining a threat. *"Ouais,* she just handed me this a few minutes ago. She must have a real complex over that Corey Bar she gave me the first time. Gave me this jacket, too." He hugged it around him possessively, clearly reveling in its warmth. And then he sniffed. "It's too bad she's so interfering and bossy. She tried to convince me to go to a shelter, when I have this whole beautiful garden to myself."

She had broken into his *laboratoire,* stolen his chocolates, then given them away casually to a homeless man in the gardens? What was she, Robin Hood *du Chocolat?*

Sylvain gave the man ten euros and strode in the direction the man had vaguely indicated, soon spotting a red coat. Cade Corey walked between chestnut trees and empty green benches, past white statues of French queens. She had a long stride for someone her size. The wind tugged at her hair, and she walked with her hands in her coat pockets, her head down. Once or twice, he saw her pull her chin up, but inexorably it would sink again.

She stopped at the edge of the Fontaine Médicis, standing

at one end of the long *bassin d'eau,* staring at the dark waters and the statue of lovers surprised by a Cyclops in a grotto at the end of it. Garlands of ivy roped in trained green beauty between bare plane trees. Some late-fallen leaves trailed on the dark water.

Approaching her from behind, he saw her hand lift and wipe across her face at eye level.

Was she crying?

Putain. His stomach clenched as if she had just hauled off and punched him.

Non, he thought, remembering the delicate game of her strength against his the night before. It felt like a punch from someone stronger than she was.

Maybe she held a lot more power than he realized.

Maybe he needed to learn fast to tighten his stomach muscles against the next blow.

When an arm brushed Cade's shoulder, she moved away automatically. Stupid, slimy lowlifes who kept hitting on her everywhere she went. She glanced at the lowlife and nearly jumped out of her skin when she saw it was Sylvain.

He turned toward her, keeping his hands in his coat pockets—was the fact that it was a leather coat some kind of mockery of her thief pants? He had been wearing wool the other day. *"Ne pleure pas."*

Don't cry.

She gave him a furious look. "I'm not crying. It's cold, and it's windy."

"Ah. Let me block the wind for you, then." He shifted so that his torso shielded her from the worst of it, standing very close.

She pinched her lips together, determined to get her eyes and nose to stop stinging. It must take a minute to get eyes to stop watering from the wind. That was it. That was why the tearing seemed worse now that she was sheltered by his body.

There was something extraordinarily touching about having him physically place himself between her and the wind.

Bastard.

He was probably calculating that, too.

He started to speak, stopped, started again, and finally took a long breath. She could see the rise and fall of it just in front of her eyes, lifting the leather of his jacket. "Was it a bad batch of chocolates or something?" he asked, with disappointing mildness.

If she had imagined his reaction—*which she had not*—to her giving away all his chocolates to the homeless man, she would have hoped the gesture would turn him incandescent with rage. "No." She curled her lip at him. "They were just making me sick."

"*Vraiment.*" He rocked back on his heels to study her face. She had hoped to insult him, and instead he looked as if he had gotten a very intriguing glimpse of some gaping holes in her armor.

She turned her shoulder on him. "Go away."

"*Je m'excuse. Pour tout à l'heure.*"

He was apologizing? *Complete and utter bastard.* She clenched her fists in her pockets, head bent, fighting against that cold wind stinging her eyes.

"But you wouldn't, would you?" he asked.

"Give away your chocolate? I would give a piece to everybody in the world, if I could."

One hand left his coat pocket to make a quick, brushing gesture. "Sleep with Dominique Richard."

She remembered, vividly, the successful dunking of the man the day before in the Seine and wondered how deep this *bassin* was. "You're the one who is so obsessed with him. You sleep with him."

He gave her an indignant look. She pivoted and continued on her way, not exactly sure where she was going. But he was a good head taller than she was. He had no trouble stretching his legs to fall into step beside her. "Does that mean you're obsessed with me?"

She didn't stop walking, but she gave him a puzzled look. He said that as if it was a joke, but . . . it seemed as if her obsession must be humiliatingly obvious at this point. She flushed, drove her hands deeper into her pockets, and focused on the gravel.

He said nothing more, but when she snuck a glance at him a moment later, he looked quite happy with his lot in life again.

Well, wasn't that wonderful. Someone was.

He walked her back to her apartment and stood watching the numeric panel unabashedly as she entered the code for her building.

Something stirred, hot and dark, in her. What did his focus mean? That one good break-in deserved another? She was never going to be able to go to bed in comfortable cotton panties and an old sweatshirt again.

He leaned in close to her, almost the prelude to a kiss. "Do you still have the key to my shop?"

Her hand clenched around the copy she had had made of it, in her pocket. She stared up at him, silent.

He held her eyes for a moment, until the key began to burn against the palm of her hand. Her breath tightened until she started to feel that the only way she could get oxygen was through mouth-to-mouth.

He did not ask for the copied key. He turned away and hesitated.

He turned back and brushed away the lock of hair that had blown across her lips. One gloved thumb rested just a moment on the bow of her mouth.

Then he walked across the street to his *laboratoire*.

Chapter 16

That key drove her completely crazy during her evening out with the students.

The evening was great. Going out with real Parisians who had no idea who Cade Corey was, people her own age who seemed to have few responsibilities beyond enjoying their student life while they could. They went from a bar to dancing at some party full of people in their twenties who acted like teenagers. Or rather, they gave a whole new perspective on what other people in their twenties got to act like. It was a lot of fun.

And it was *Paris*. And she was part of it.

But she kept thinking about that key question. She kept wondering if he was waiting for her in a dark shadow in his *laboratoire*. Or breaking into *her* apartment, with plans to ravish her in her bed.

The possibility lurked in her all night, calling her away from the partying, pulling at her darkly.

She tried to ignore it. She tried to focus on the fun evening that was much healthier and better for her than any stupid obsession.

But the possibility drove her mad. She spent the whole evening aroused, on edge, trying not to show it. Her nipples kept peaking against her silk top, as thoughts of darkness and skin would sweep through her, their continual arousal confusing one of the students who started trolling to see if she was interested in him.

She wasn't. She couldn't even spare a thought to him.

When a taxi dropped her off at four in the morning, she was all one maddened, thwarted longing as she climbed the stairs to her apartment. She kicked her boots off her throbbing feet and fell into bed in her smoke-filled clothes and told herself firmly that she had made the right choice for her evening.

But she felt like a drug addict making the choice to spend one evening straight.

Which was ridiculous, because surely you couldn't get addicted to anything on just one dose.

Sylvain had it all planned. He would make her one of those chocolates that fascinated her so much. He would guide her step by step through simmering, melting, stroking, spreading, touching, tasting, shivering with the pleasure of a flavor. He would seduce her so slowly, tormenting them both deliciously with the slowness, his fingers on hers as they stirred melting chocolate, his body brushing hers from behind, his hands stroking up her ribs, down to her belly, up to her breasts as he gave her own hands something to stir, teased her by blending her chocolate obsession with the feel of his hands.

And he wouldn't forget the tempering this time.

He had thought of the scents he wanted her to smell, the flavors he wanted her to taste, as he seduced her. He had the jars and *pistoles* and bags of them strewn across the marble counter.

But she never came.

He was there all night. He kept trying to give up, to admit she wasn't coming and go back home. But then a doubt would seize him. What if he missed her? What if five minutes after he left, she finally came?

And he would take his jacket back off and wait.

But she never came.

Chapter 17

"**Y**ou were here all night?" Pascal asked incredulously. He looked around at the dirty pots, the strewn materials, the new chocolates gleaming in the form of great near-black drops, not yet cooled. The autumn-morning light came through the high windows and sparkled above them on the walls. "What were you, inspired?"

"I don't really want to talk to anyone about anything today," Sylvain said. "I'm sorry."

Pascal gave him a searching look and opened his mouth, probably to ask if he was all right, but Sylvain held up a hand. "About anything. *Pardon*."

Another searching look, but Pascal gave him the respect a *maître* chocolatier deserved in his own lair and didn't push it. He left him alone and nodded the others away when they came in. He even intercepted Francine when she tried to tell him there were more calls for interviews.

Sylvain finished cooling the chocolates he had made at the end of the night, when he had to have something to do besides failed waiting. He went back among *les petites dames blanches,* taking one of the small bags they used to package individual chocolates for dinner parties or weddings. He tied the bag with his trademark twine and went out to the front of the shop to intercept one of the clerks who was handling the lines.

Yes, lines already, first thing in the morning. They did love that Chocolate Thief story.

He pulled the clerk out of hearing. "Could you take this across the street and leave it at a door? It's on the sixth floor. I'm not sure of the apartment number, but it will be the apartment facing this way. Here's the entry code."

Cade slept very late. She woke still reeking of the smoke from the party and feeling stale and deeply let down.

Showered and dressed, she spent some time trying to get her new laptop's e-mail to work. In French, because she couldn't figure out how to switch the default language on the computer. She normally had tech staff to do this kind of thing.

She finally handled the bulk of the messages via her phone, including one message telling her tech staff to overnight her a new, English-speaking computer.

Hunger drove her out of her apartment in the end. Even she couldn't live on chocolate forever. She had started to make herself sick.

Inspired by the student party and the fact that a Chocolate Thief should have a certain dress code, she pulled on patterned lace leggings and a clinging gray knit tunic dress shorter than the leather jacket she shrugged on over it. High leather boots and large, dramatic earrings in lapis lazuli completed the ensemble, her hair up on top of her head to show those earrings off.

As she shut the apartment door behind her, her fingers closed around something. A little bag hung from the doorknob, tied with twine and stamped with a miniature version of the SYLVAIN MARQUIS brand.

Her heart jumped. Her breath grew short, her thighs clenched, and sensation rushed to all her erogenous zones, as if she had just discovered him standing there in person.

She took the bag and held it a long time in her hand before she opened it, very carefully. The chocolate was, of course, beautiful. The form was new, nothing she had seen among his chocolates before. It was round but not perfectly so, a ripple and a flip at the top giving it that sense of an artist's work and not a machine's. The outside was perfectly black, or so close to black as made no difference in the poor lighting on the landing.

She stared at it a long moment. Maybe it was poisoned. Death by Sylvain Marquis's chocolate.

She brought it to her mouth, lips brushing smoothness, teeth meeting the faintest resistance of the exterior.

It was bitter. Good Lord, it was bitter. Dark, dark, dark, with almost no hint of sugar. But it was quality bitter. Her teeth bit through the delicate crunch of the *robe* to the softest, silkiest, smoothest bitter that could ever melt across a tongue. It left just a trace, just a hint of cinnamon, an elusive promise of sweetness, as it melted. Quickly overwhelmed by the bitterness, that melting, smooth bitterness. She had never in her life thought anything that bitter could be that luscious on her tongue.

She pulled the other half away and stared at the mark of her teeth against the ganache, which was as dark inside as out.

She reached the street to find him in jeans and jacket before the door of his *laboratoire,* giving what seemed to be an impromptu interview to several people with high-end cameras, microphones, and recorders. ". . . desperate." He shrugged. "I can understand her desperation for good chocolate."

As usual, whatever her thoughts and emotions on seeking him out, finding him managed to put her in an instant rage.

He looked a pretty pathetic victim for that rage right now, hair mussed, unshaven, his eyes red in that distinctive lack-of-sleep way she recognized from many an all-nighter over an urgent Corey Chocolate problem. Sexy still, though. She bet he showed up well in the newspaper photos, haggard from the attacks on him by the nasty multinational corporation but still upholding the ideal of French sex appeal.

She tried to think quickly of anything she could do to improve her own image in those photographs but knew she was pretty much screwed. Whether she looked good, bad, strong, or weak, she was going to be the villain in the piece. She tried to slip back into her building before the journalists spotted her, but the door had locked behind her.

It would take her a few seconds to enter the code. If they caught her slipping back into her apartment and cornered her there, she didn't know how long she would have to hole up. It seemed the ultimate in failure, to be cornered in her apartment in Paris, afraid to go out, slowly maintaining life by eating her way through Corey Bars.

She headed briskly toward the nearest corner, hoping no one would spot her. How well would they have studied photographs of her, anyway? She wasn't someone people recognized on sight, typically, and her looks were pretty neutral—straight, light brown hair, blue eyes, even features.

Of course, Sylvain Marquis recognized her instantly. His face closed, his gaze pinning her.

She could still taste the bitter chocolate on her tongue. She might have a dark print of it on her fingers.

"She's like the poor little rich girl of chocolate, when you think about it," Sylvain said, pitching his voice clearly.

Making her what, his charity case? Was he trying to imply to her that he had had sex with her out of pity for her clear desperation?

She stopped walking and pivoted, burning.

Before she could do something really suicidal, like challenge him before all these journalists still oblivious to her presence, someone grabbed her elbow. A man of medium height, with dark, curly hair, smiled down at her with delight.

"*Mademoiselle Co-ree,*" the man said, very low, pitched not to carry across the street at all. "*Je peux vous offrir un café?*"

She supposed she would have to talk to the media sometime. And there was something wonderfully Parisian about doing it over a cup of coffee. Plus, it might marginally improve her odds of being portrayed in a positive light.

"If you can keep blocking the view of me from your colleagues, yes, you can," she said.

"If that would make me an aider and an abettor, I would be such a happy man." He sighed longingly and kept his body between hers and the journalists as he escorted her around the corner. She kept wanting to turn back to see Sylvain's expression, but with the help of that hand on her elbow, she managed to restrain herself. Mostly because her journalist-captor kept too firm a grip to let her twist so far, as if he was afraid she would try to get away.

In the café that formed the corner, they moved past the *tabac* with its wall of cigarette packs and a man scratching lottery tickets, to a table by the great glass windows that looked out on the other street.

Her semi-captor ordered coffee, and she asked for a glass of milk, because her stomach was growling at that point. She had been living on chocolate lately. A glass of cold, pure milk sounded wonderful.

The waiter stared at her as if she was just off a spaceship from Mars. "This is a café. We don't have milk."

The unknown man looked discreetly the other way, as one might when forced to witness a friend losing face.

"You have milk somewhere for the coffee, right?" she said. "I'll pay whatever you want for it."

"We don't sell milk," the waiter said.

"Would you sell it for twenty euros? Thirty euros?"

"There's an *épicerie* down the street," he said politely. "If you want to get milk."

"Maybe a *chocolat*?" the curly-haired man suggested diplomatically. "Or some juice?"

Cade thought of the *chocolat chaud* Sylvain had made for her. "Juice. This is a really strange country to be wealthy in."

"How so?" the curly-haired man asked, confused.

She gestured. "I can't buy anything."

"Well . . . not milk in a café," he said as if she had tried to buy fruit in a jewelry store or something.

"He has milk. He could make an exorbitant profit off it. It just—what?—goes against his principles to sell it to me?"

"I think he probably just doesn't want to give Americans ideas. You people are always asking for milk in cafés, and once you let someone get away with something like that, who knows where it might lead?"

"Into another profitable product on the menu?" Cade asked dryly. Hunger was putting her in a bad mood. Plus, she kept seeing Sylvain Marquis's closed face, tasting his bitter chocolate on her tongue, hearing him say, "desperate."

The curly-haired man brushed all this away before it could spoil their conversation. "Speaking of getting away with something, you're my hero." He grinned at her. "I'm Christophe. Christophe, le gourmand."

For a moment, she thought only in France could someone's last name be Gourmand. Then she realized: "Of the food blog, *Le Gourmand*? You're the one who started this whole Chocolate Thief story!"

"I have to admit, I liked the idea better when I thought it was some poor, impoverished, would-be food blogger breaking in to steal secrets, *mais ça va*. That story Sylvain was spinning about the poor little rich girl of chocolate has a nice ring to it."

Cade pressed her teeth together and tried to remind herself that snapping at this man would not improve her image

as the villain of the piece. She was pretty sure Corey Chocolate would rather she came across as the villain than the poor
little rich girl of chocolate, though. The entire executive
bodies at Mars and Cadbury must be smirking their heads
off.

"So, tell me, how did you do it?" he asked eagerly. "Did
it involve any rappeling in leather from one of those high
windows of his? Please tell me it did."

"How did I do what?"

"That's right, of course you can't admit it. We wouldn't
want you to end up in jail." He lowered his voice to a hush.
"Do you . . . do you happen to have one of the stolen
chocolates on you?" He glanced around to make sure no one
was in earshot. "I won't tell anybody, I promise. But just to
see it . . ."

The door to the café opened, and a very familiar male
form entered.

"I give all of Sylvain Marquis's chocolates away to the
homeless people in the gardens," she stated clearly. Well, as
of yesterday afternoon, that was her official policy. She was
not going to mention the number of boxes she had eaten before she had decided to disavow the man. "Not that any of
those were stolen, of course."

"*Oh-laaaa.*" Christophe clutched his chest. "I think you
just put a knife into me. You *steal chocolates to give them to the
poor*? Seriously, I think I might hyperventilate. Can I rename
my blog after you?"

Cade blinked. "I—"

"Promise me you eat at least a couple on the way out, in
the dark, hanging from your rappeling cord, when no one
can see. Before you steel your heart to give all the others
away, for the sake of those who suffer."

"No, I eat Dominique Richard's," Cade said as Sylvain
reached them. "I can't steel myself to give those away."

Sylvain pressed his lips together, looking down at them. "No rappeling cords, Christophe."

"How do you know? Have you seen her?" Christophe exclaimed enviously. His eyes gleamed. "Caught her in the act?"

"It's *my laboratoire*," Sylvain reminded him, but with a peculiar emphasis, as if he wanted to drive the fact that it was his *and not anybody else's* into a really thick head.

Her head, presumably. "Why don't you go get some sleep and leave us alone? You look as if you need it," Cade said.

He gave her a look as bitter as the chocolate he had left at her door.

She swallowed. Even the darkness of that look made her breath shorten, made her insides stir and melt.

"I would be tired, too, if I had such a beautiful thief breaking into my *laboratoire*," Christophe said blissfully. "I wouldn't be able to sleep a wink."

Sylvain looked as if he was seriously considering doing the other man violence. Cade had no idea what the food blogger had done to alienate him so much. It seemed to her his story about the Chocolate Thief had done damage to her— and her family, and 30,000 employees, and their suppliers and merchandisers—and no end of good to Sylvain.

The waiter reappeared with Christophe's coffee and her apricot juice. Sylvain shook his head at the juice. "How do you get away with consuming so much sugar?"

"I tried to order milk," Cade said defensively. "They wouldn't sell it to me."

Sylvain raised his eyebrows and went over to the bar. Cade saw him exchange a few casual words with the man behind it, then push two minuscule coins across the counter in exchange for a small carton of milk. He came back and set it down in front of her without a word.

When she closed her hand around it, she had a sensation

strangely similar to when she closed her hand around her talisman Corey Bar—as if she held something that made her feel special, cherished.

She really had to get a grip.

He had used *tu* when he spoke to her, she realized. *Tu,* like a stamp of ownership, while Christophe had to use *vous.*

Tu and milk and the bitter, bitter chocolate. She smiled a little, fingering the corner of the milk carton.

Sylvain sat down with them without being asked, took the tall, slim cylinder of a glass that had been provided with the bottle of apricot juice, and poured the milk into it, then slid the glass into her hand. Cade stared at it, feeling once again like a cat. Which would make him—what?—her owner, if he was pouring out milk for her?

Under the small table, his leg crowded hers.

Funny how she knew so absolutely it was his and not Christophe's. She wished she could think he was doing it on purpose. But the fact was, it was a tiny table. Where else was his leg supposed to go?

How was she supposed to feed Christophe some kind of better image of her to propagate to the media when Sylvain was there distracting her, shattering her focus? She wondered if she could hire someone to become a famous food blogger who only disseminated positive images of Corey Chocolate.

Of course she could. It was called advertising. No one bit the hand that fed them. "I've been thinking that Corey Chocolate should take more advantage of the advertising potential of food bloggers," she said, with a sneaky smile. "You take advertisements on your site, don't you?"

"That's interesting," Christophe said. "Mars contacted me just yesterday about that."

Those snakes. She could just see their smirky faces as they thought that up.

"But I think it would be a conflict of interest," he said.

"Honestly, I would rather just keep the advertising from small, *artisanat* places. It's more in keeping with who I am."

Cade slumped, defeated. Was there a single problem money could solve for her in this country?

A silence fell. Both men gave each other frustrated looks. But neither one seemed willing to get the other's message and leave.

The waiter appeared with a double espresso for Sylvain. He gave it a jaundiced look, as if he would much rather have a bed than coffee right now, but he took it and drank a large swallow.

"Tu as aimé ton chocolat?" Sylvain asked her.

She shivered all over, with pleasure and darkness. "It was very good," she said slowly. "But it was very bitter."

"Would you want another one after eating the first?"

I think I would take anything you gave me. Her eyes held his a moment. Then she forced herself to look away. "As a customer? Perhaps one, at the right moment. But then I would want something a little sweeter."

"Have you created a new chocolate?" Christophe inserted with interest. "A bitter one? How fascinating. Could I try it?"

Sylvain drummed the fingers of one hand hard on the table, likely in lieu of Christophe's head. "I'm not planning to sell it in the shop."

Bullets bounced off Christophe's exuberance. He lit from within. "A one-off chocolate that I would be one of the few people to try? And you said it was bitter? A bitter chocolate? Could I?"

Had he made it just for her? Cade thought. Just once, just for her?

She studied that tired face. He had just told a group of journalists she was desperate for him, a poor little rich girl of chocolate. Then gotten her milk.

What, exactly, was she supposed to think about him?

★   ★   ★

Sylvain hadn't planned to follow her or even to say a damn word to her ever again. He had waited all night for her, and she hadn't bothered to show. He wasn't going to crawl after her now.

And he was tired. He had not slept all night, and only four hours the night before.

But then Christophe had scooped up her elbow as if finally catching his very own fantasy, and he had watched the man escort those slim legs in black lace and leather down the sidewalk. Fixated on those legs and the apparent lack of skirt to cover them, he had had to watch until Christophe disappeared with her into the café on the corner. He had to walk past that café to get home to his apartment and get some sleep.

And now the man was being so irrepressible that Sylvain wanted nothing so much as to sit on him. Hard. Of course, he would probably feel as if he had kicked a puppy if he yielded to the urge. "Don't you have a blog to write or something?"

"Oh, I've got my laptop," Christophe said cheerfully. "In fact, we could do a little live interview right now if you want. Built-in Webcam."

"Are you recording me right now?" Cade asked sharply, scanning the blogger for signs of any other small camera or recorder.

Sylvain didn't think it was the man's style to record her without permission. But since he didn't have the responsibility for a multibillion-dollar revenue on his shoulders, he didn't have to be as paranoid as she did. He felt no urge to say anything in Christophe's defense. Let her be suspicious of him. Invasive, bubbly, pseudo-journalist fantasy thief.

"No, of course not," Christophe said, taken aback. "But if you ever want to agree to an exclusive interview on my blog, you would make me a very, very happy man."

Why the hell should Cade Corey want to make *him* a very, very happy man?

"How do you manage to make tens of billions of dollars off Corey Bars?" Sylvain asked, to change the subject from Christophe. He had looked up the Corey Chocolate revenue the night before, among the many other things he had done to try to pass the time while he waited for her. It was hard to imagine, tens of billions of dollars in responsibility. When he Googled her name, it showed up everywhere, and other than some references to donations or an appearance at a charity function, the mentions were usually in articles about company negotiations and initiatives. Working, in fact. She seemed to take her role in the Corey family very seriously. Seriously enough to get about 50,000 results from a Google search.

He had to check his own name after that, the first time in his life it had ever occurred to him to do so, and discovered that he got over 250,000. He tried hard not to be smug about that.

One wasn't supposed to be smug about the natural order of things.

"I don't understand," he continued. "That would mean people would have to *buy* tens of billions a year. There are only five billion people in the world. Surely most of them realize there's better chocolate out there."

Cade gave him a simmering look. *Good.* At least her focus was on him and not Christophe. "Well. We have a lot of subsidiaries that sell other products besides chocolate—"

"Oh," Sylvain said, relieved. "That explains it."

He could see her perfect little teeth grind together. Was she getting as frustrated as he had been the night before? *Hardly, damn it.*

"But, yes, we sell billions of them. It's the most popular chocolate bar in the US, for one. There are millions and millions of people who eat hundreds of them a year."

"America is a very strange country," Christophe said, in the tones of someone repeating a commonly accepted proverb. "It couldn't even be called chocolate here until a few years ago, when the idiotic European Union passed that law."

"Corey Bars do *not* have any other vegetable fats in them," Cade corrected tightly. "Only cocoa butter. They have *always* been legal chocolate in this country. And to set matters straight, we lobbied very intensively *against* the passage of that law allowing vegetable fats. If your people had let money buy something for once, other vegetable fats might still not be allowed under the label of chocolate to this day."

"Do you have one with you?" Christophe asked. "I don't think I've eaten one since I was a kid."

Cade hesitated a long moment before she reached into her purse and pulled one out.

Sylvain almost sympathized. *He* wouldn't have liked to show off a Corey Bar. If she had shown up the night before to rob his workshop, Sylvain might have tried to distract Christophe to save her. If she had shown up the night before, he wouldn't even be here; maybe they would both still be in a nice, cozy bed. The sheets on his were crisp and clean and smelling of laundry soap, just in case.

He remembered changing the sheets the day before, in happy hope, and decided she deserved what she got. She was making billions off the product; surely she could defend it in public.

She took a long, long swallow of her milk, the muscles in her throat working, her eyes closing as she drained her glass. Then she opened her eyes, braced her shoulders, and waited.

"I like the wrapper," Christophe said. "I always have. Gold, brown, plain font, clear stamp of a name. It's pretentious in its very lack of pretention. It makes no show; it is what it is, naturally. You do the same thing, Sylvain, only in a more sophisticated way."

The man was so aggravating. Sylvain was never going to be nice to another food blogger ever again.

Cade said nothing. Her hand lay so that her fingertips still brushed the edge of the paper wrapper, like a sleeping child might keep some contact with a teddy bear, just enough to know it was there.

Experimentally, Sylvain pulled it a little out of her reach. Her fingers stretched automatically before she caught them back.

Interesting. Of all the attitudes his chocolate evoked, he was willing to bet that a child's affection for her teddy bear was not one of them.

His mind started turning automatically, wondering what chocolate he could invent that would incite such affection, or be a nostalgic wink and a nod at chocolate loved as a child.

Christophe unwrapped the bar neatly, careful not to tear the paper or gold foil. He broke a square marked with C off the bar and bit into it.

Cade looked at Sylvain.

If he ever thought he would come to this—eating Corey Bars to compete with an annoying food blogger for a woman's attention? He broke off the O and bit into it.

Christophe's face screwed up. "I just don't get it. Why do they like it so much? It's got that sweet-sour taste to it."

"If any of those Swiss chocolatiers had let my great-grand-father steal their secret to milk chocolate instead of having to reinvent it himself, we wouldn't have it. And now the way we create it is our most closely guarded secret."

"Why?" Sylvain asked, dumbfounded. "Who would want to steal it? You've got to have figured out how to make proper milk chocolate by now."

It excited the hell out of him when she looked at him like that, all silk and luxury and control but her blue eyes bubbling with the desire to strangle him. *Go ahead,* he thought. *Launch yourself across that table and go for my throat. We can grap-*

ple together anytime you like. He wondered what he could say to make her actually snap and do it.

The fantasy distracted him, her body struggling against his, his hands sliding over her as he tried to control her, maybe her weight in the lunge toppling him backward so she was on top of him. . . .

"People *like* it," she said. "They grew up with it; they prefer it. It makes them feel—warm. Happy."

"It's got a decent mouth-feel," Christophe allowed. "You're right: no other vegetable fats," he told Cade.

The look on her face at being told she was right about the ingredients in Corey Bars was priceless. It almost made up for the fact that Christophe had drawn her attention from Sylvain to him.

Couldn't the man just go home? Instead of trying to grab Sylvain's fantasies for his own?

Then Sylvain could go home. And sleep. Instead of sitting here chasing after a woman who had not bothered to break into his *laboratoire* and steal from him the night before. He slouched back in his chair uncharacteristically, letting his legs jostle hers more aggressively. And incidentally bump Christophe's legs well away from hers. Her boots rubbed against his calf through his jeans, shifting his mind into fantasies again.

"Your professional opinion?" Christophe nudged Sylvain.

He wanted to take a bite of his new bitter chocolate to clean his mouth of the milky, pale, faintly sour flavor—that was Sylvain's professional opinion. But he also wanted to wrestle and tussle with Cade Corey among his freshly washed sheets, or in his *laboratoire* on cold marble, or in her apartment, or anywhere she wanted. So he tried to be diplomatic. "It's a mass-produced chocolate for children with a minimal cacao content." He shrugged. "What do you expect?"

He didn't know why that earned him such a burning look. How much nicer did she expect him to get about Corey Bars?

"Children and Americans," Christophe corrected.

Sylvain spread his hands, feeling that any attempt to distinguish the two groups for their gourmet awareness was splitting hairs. He did do a strong business with tourists, expatriates, and a contingent of wealthy Americans who had his chocolates cold-packed and shipped to them once a week, but he had always assumed their appreciation of quality was an exception to the norm.

Cade Corey was definitely an exception, on so many levels that he wanted to grab her and hold her as his prize more than anything he had wanted in a long time. He felt as if he was reliving his days of burning, desperate, high school passions.

Which had never ended well for him. They loved the sex, they loved the chocolate, but women always, always had other things on their mind.

Where had she been last night? How could she have not come?

"People love them," Cade said. "They write letters to us telling us how much they love them. We've got a wall at our headquarters with a collage made of our favorites."

"*Vraiment?*" Sylvain said, disturbed. "They write letters to me telling me the same thing." Often signed at the bottom by someone very famous, including a French president, an American one, and multiple movie stars on multiple continents. He read them and smiled, shared them with the others in the *laboratoire,* and filed them discreetly away. It had never occurred to him to splash their contents across a wall. Sounded like someone's desperate desire to reassure themselves.

How was it that Corey Bars were receiving the same kind of letters his chocolate was?

There really were a lot of gustatory idiots in the world.

"It's fascinating how much you two have in common, in fact." Christophe smirked.

Sylvain turned his head and glared at him.

At his open resentment of that comment, Cade tilted her head and gazed at her hands on the tabletop. Sylvain caught himself. She looked . . . tired, maybe. Sad? *Merde,* had he hurt her feelings again?

Mostly he seemed to infuriate her, in a way that perversely aroused the hell out of him. But that was twice now he had hit a sensitive spot. She had this fragile side to her indomitability, as if part of her strength was that she cried when she needed to and then picked herself back up and went straight back at it.

"I think I'm going to have to go get something to eat." She reached for her purse. "Christophe, it was nice to meet you." She slid a card across the table to him. Sylvain stiffened. Had she just given out her direct numbers and e-mail? To *Christophe*?

He didn't even have those things. He had chased her out of his *laboratoire* that first day before she got a chance. Note to self: never get so annoyed that you drive a pretty woman away without getting her cell phone number. You might live to regret it. For example, it would have felt awkward the night before to call her secretary and find out why the hell she wasn't breaking into his *laboratoire* again like she was supposed to.

Almost as bad as the gift of her private contact information, she waited a moment with hand extended until Christophe realized what the gesture indicated and found one of his own cards. Under the table against his thigh, Sylvain's fist clenched.

Both men stood automatically when she did. Just for a second, as she reached for her jacket, he could glimpse the full effect of her outfit—the gray knit that clung to her slim body, the slender neck so vulnerably exposed and highlighted by those blue earrings, the challenge of the black lace leggings and the high boots, the stretch and flex of her muscles as she pulled on her leather jacket and left only those legs for a man's focus.

She shook hands with Christophe, in that firm, confident American handshake she had, but only nodded at Sylvain.

Of course, what was she supposed to do? A handshake or *bises* seemed completely false, and a kiss on the mouth gross presumption. It was like the *tu/vous* dilemma. Exactly what were they to each other?

He kind of liked that dilemma. It was exciting. It was a fun edge to play with. But he wasn't sure how long he wanted to stay there.

"Wow," Christophe whispered as Cade and her legs reached the door of the café. Sylvain shot him a glare, but the man wasn't watching her legs. He was staring at Cade's card, cradled in both hands, held up to his face so that Sylvain couldn't even get a glimpse of the number on it. "When I wrote my first blog post, I never, ever thought that I would end up here."

Suddenly, Sylvain had to laugh. If it hadn't been for Cade Corey, he would have liked the man. "When I made my first chocolate, I didn't think so, either."

Mostly because his first try had been a disaster. By the time he had made his third batch, he had known exactly where he planned to end up in life.

He had always had a very good eye for what he wanted. And the persistence and focus to go after it.

Cade Corey had exited the café in the direction of his apartment. He got to his feet, then turned back. "Don't follow me," he told Christophe firmly.

The food blogger laughed. "Sylvain, I love your chocolate as much as the next man. But I would be following *her*."

"You know damn well that's what I meant." Sylvain headed out the door.

Chapter 18

She had disappeared. Where the hell had she gotten to? He walked up and down the street, checking restaurants and stores and the *épicerie*.

"*Coucou*," a cheerful voice called. He looked up, startled, from his attempts to peer through a plate glass window into the dark depths of the bar a couple of doors down from his building.

Chantal waved from the sidewalk in front of his apartment building and came toward him to give him warm *bises*. "Do you want to grab a drink?"

"I—not this evening, sorry." He scanned the street. Maybe he should check the neighboring blocks.

Chantal curled a hand around his arm, her delicately plucked eyebrows knitted. "What's wrong?"

"Nothing." He wanted to wrench his arm away from her and keep hunting. Who else was hunting those legs right now? He would bet she had every loose male in the quarter on the prowl. How likely was she to fall for one of those lame tourist lines about her charming smile and let someone buy her a drink?

She seemed too arrogant and too cool for that type of vulnerability, but then, she sure had been a pushover for him.

Chantal continued to study him. The easy cheerfulness faded from her face. For a moment, she looked somber.

Then she arched her eyebrows and gave him a searching, teasing look. "I read about the Chocolate Thief. Isn't that outrageous? Is it really Cade Corey? That rich American woman from the restaurant the other night? She's trying to *steal* your recipes?"

"Chantal, *pardon,*" Sylvain said abruptly, bending down to press a quick, apologetic kiss against each cheek. "Let's have lunch together in a few days. I've got to go."

The teasing expression died. She looked at him very seriously, the way she might look at someone going to a funeral. At the last second, as he moved away, she let her hand slide down his arm and caught his hand. "Sylvain." She tugged him.

He glanced back, trying hard to be polite to this old friend, to be patient.

Her eyes pleaded with him. "Don't get hurt. You know you always do."

He never did find Cade. He checked surrounding blocks, peering through windows until finally he felt so ridiculous and so desperate for sleep that he went back to his apartment. There he fell onto his bed in his clothes, not waking up until the next morning.

Whenever he went to bed without a shower first, his comforter always smelled of cocoa for days.

He came in late to his *laboratoire* the next morning and discovered that his employees had left a wide space of marble undisturbed, like a crime scene. On it sat a very strange concoction: two flat brown *biscuits,* a marshmallow, and a square from a Corey Bar, all sandwiched together. At some point, the marshmallow had been half burned.

His heart began to beat faster. "What is this?"

Bernard, nearest it, shook his head. "We don't know. We found it when we got here this morning."

She had been back. Maybe in those leather pants again, or

those high boots with those lace leggings. His body temperature rose at least three degrees, and his heart slammed into overdrive.

And he had missed her. *Putain de bordel de merde.*

He picked up the weird sandwich and eyed it doubtfully. Had she poisoned it? Why else would she deliberately leave such a ruined effort for him? "I wonder how she managed to burn a *chamallow?*" he wondered, half-aloud.

No one attempted to answer. He wondered where she had even found a marshmallow, or the *biscuits,* in his *laboratoire.* She was bringing in her own ingredients now?

What did that mean? He thought she was supposed to be desperate for his world. A thief who left very strange presents instead of taking anything . . . what was that?

He bit into it carefully and grimaced as crumbs fell clumsily and the marshmallow clung stickily to his lips. "It's very sweet," he said. He looked up to find the whole *laboratoire* gathered around staring at it, rather as one might a snake. "I guess, points for creativity?"

He had no desire to take another bite of it, but he couldn't quite bring himself to throw it away, either. He took it into his office to set it on his desk, then headed straight across the street and up her stairs.

She wasn't there.

Cade was in Christophe's apartment, learning how to make the chocolate *tarte* that he claimed he was going to name after her. *La Cade.* It made her smile. He made her laugh. His enthusiasm for everything was so unabashed and infectious.

She spent the morning there, feeling like a child at play, and even let him take a little ten-second video clip of her grinning and tasting his *tarte* for his blog. Then she caught the TGV up to Brussels. Her father wanted her to feel out the Firenze brothers, off the record, about their attitude toward a shared bid for Devon Candy.

Devon Candy. One of their candy bars had a bright pink wrapper. The very thought of it depressed her.

Sylvain, reading the blog post that evening, felt as if the top was going to blow off his head. Christophe had *spent the morning cooking with her*? He had named something chocolate after her? That was Sylvain's role. And he could do it a lot better.

And in that video clip, which he only played ten or twenty times, she looked so sparkling and happy.

He really might murder the man.

Cade caught the nine p.m. train back, and it got delayed by a problem on the line that had them stopped over half an hour, so it was close to midnight by the time the taxi dropped her off at her apartment.

The taxi pulled away before she even got her code entered. When a shadow detached itself from the greater shadows of the doorway across the street, she nearly screamed.

Relief rushed through her when she realized who it was, but not just relief from that first primal fear. It was relief that he was there, that she was there, that they had not missed each other again. That she didn't have to try to figure out what she should do—break into his *laboratoire,* stay in her apartment, or do something normal and call him.

Her body could just . . . melt into another dark, intense night, no questions asked. It was melting already as he crossed the street.

Without a word, he put his hand over hers and entered her code for her. Cade just wanted to turn to him and bury her head in his shoulder in overwhelming gratitude that he was there. She didn't want to have to resist him another night by staying out late. She didn't want to have to break into his *laboratoire* and have him never show. She didn't want to wonder or doubt or hope. She just wanted to do.

And be done to.

Over her shoulder, he pushed the door open, his arm and body holding her captive. "You shouldn't be out so late alone," he murmured, voice dark and rough. "This is a big city. There have been several break-ins across the street."

"Why don't you set a trap to catch the thief?"

"I did once. But I think I made a mistake by not putting her in handcuffs at the time."

His voice blended frustration, humor, and sincerity so darkly and perfectly that she couldn't be sure he didn't have velvet handcuffs in his back pocket, ready for use.

She felt disoriented. She had been working twelve hours straight now: facts, figures, decisions, e-mailing on the train. She was so used to working like that, it had seemed to set her back into her own world, an ocean's width from a sorcerer's lair in Paris.

Finding it still there, a world not completely shut to her, she wanted to sink into it completely. She backed up, tentatively, trying to make sure she didn't open any sudden gap between them to discourage his pursuit.

He came with her, into the dark foyer of the apartment building, his body staying so close, she could not have broken free. He let the door close behind him, its blackness shutting out the pale city light. Only a tiny orange spot of light indicated the button they could push to light the stairs.

She reached for it automatically. He caught her hand. "Just a minute." He pulled her into his arms, turned and pressed her back against the door, and kissed her.

Her whole body responded to him instantly, tightening, lifting. Her arms wrapped around his shoulders, gripping the leather coat. He took a breath and kissed her harder. His pleasure responded to her pleasure, and hers fed his, while the kiss deepened, lightened, changed. Kisses learned each other.

"I can't believe you're real," he breathed, his fingers rubbing over her back and ribs, where her skin yielded to his hands and where it didn't. It surprised her that there was any point it didn't; she felt as if her very bones were melting. "And yet you are."

That was good to know. She hadn't been sure the last time. But she wanted to be real here. She felt very, very real.

She felt so soaringly, intensely real, it was as if the person she had been until she got on that plane for Paris was some poor ghost finally invested with a life.

And able to taste and feel and touch and breathe and hurt and hate and *live*.

The feel and touch and taste of him, and sometimes even the spitting, furious hate of him, was so heady that once again she forgot everything but him immediately. His lean waist, the muscles of his back and torso under her fingers. His thigh pressing between hers. His hair brushing her cheeks. His mouth. His hands.

God, his hands were extraordinary. She had been right to have a crush on them before she even met him.

Today he smelled of chocolate, of course, and rum, and fleetingly, on the fingertips that stroked past her cheeks and pushed her hair back, vanilla.

She rose to his mouth, seeking him passionately, seeking all of him, seeking to absorb him into her in every way she could. He made a rough sound and obliged that need, everything escalating out of control.

She loved the feel of his breaths going deeper and faster, as he pressed her against his chest. She loved the way his fingers flexed and tensed and rubbed as if they could make their winter layers of clothes disappear. She loved—but maybe hated—the fact that he could keep just enough respect for her, or control, to pull his head away at last and look around. Now that her eyes had adjusted, the small windows at the stair landings allowed in just enough dim light from the city to make out, barely, the line of his chin, the shadow of his shoulders against deeper shadow.

He didn't say anything. He just lifted her up in one easy motion as if she weighed, well . . . no more than a giant pot of chocolate . . . and set her down on the first stair.

Cade leaned into him, liking this new height that made his mouth, his face, more accessible to hers, that brought her hips right on level with his, that . . .

He grasped her hips and rotated her, until she faced up the stairs, his hips now rubbing against her bottom. When she didn't immediately grasp the message, he nudged her with his hips and his aroused sex. *"Monte,"* he whispered. "Go up."

She grasped the banister for support, feeling her way up the dark stairs slowly.

As she climbed, his hands began to slide. Over her hips, her legs, as he let her get steps above him. He allowed the distance between them to grow, letting himself get several steps below her, as his hands drifted downward to the very edge of her boots, one finger slipping in, tracing her calf, and then back up. Then he came closer again. She could hear his tread on the stairs, in the dark an even darker presence behind her. He slid under the neat, knee-length pencil skirt and pushed it up, his hands tantalizing the sensitive insides of her thighs.

Cade tightened her hand on the rail and stopped, incapable of forming enough coherent force in her body to go forward. One finger teased just one split second against the crotch of her tights and then withdrew to push her bottom. Push her up, toward her apartment.

She started forward again, and his hands rose for a few

steps to unbutton her jacket, to find their way under her sweater, to stroke and stroke her breasts until she was almost in tears of desire for him to do more. To take her on the stairs—she didn't care.

He did care, though, apparently, because a lightly stinging slap against her bottom made her realize she had stopped moving again, lost in desire. The slap on top of it drove her almost frantic. She wanted nothing so much as to double over the banister, let him spank her mad, do anything to her, as long as his hands returned between her legs, as long as he took her.

And then his hands were gone. Nothing of him touched her at all. She breathed in a gasp of frantic air, as if she had been knifed.

"Continue," he whispered. "Or I'll stop."

Oh, cruel. She was nothing but desire. Nothing. *Touch me, take me, feel me, make me, do anything to me, please.*

But he kept to his word, not touching her. She stumbled forward.

They were halfway up the second flight now, and three more flights to go.

He rewarded her. His hands stroked and teased up her inner thighs again, promising to touch her sex but then retreating, stroking up again closer, retreating again.

She made a little sound that was no words, just begging, and stopped.

He took a step downward again, breaking all contact.

Again, a little sound from her, wordless pleading. She forced herself forward, craving the reward and loathing the punishment.

His hand came all the way up to the crotch of her tights this time and played with her for a full five steps, pressing and rubbing the lips of her sex through tights and panties, telling her what a good girl she had been.

"Sssy . . ." She thought she started to say his name. She just couldn't get her mouth to function for anything as coherent as a word.

As if to reward her for the effort, he began to ease her tights and panties down, an inch per step. She learned the rhythm quickly, that for each step she took, a little more of her skin was bared under her skirt. And his fingers, his beautiful, deft, masterful fingers that could take the raw elements of the earth and turn them into something wonderful, brushed against that skin.

They were halfway up the fourth flight of stairs, one more flight to go, when his fingers finally slipped around to her naked, madly damp sex. He made a low, approving sound when she clenched around his hand so frantically, and the sound itself made her clench again.

She was almost insane, on the edge of coming at that point. When his thumb pressed hard against her clitoris, she bit into the arm of her jacket and began to shake. As a last cruel torture, he tried to pull his thumb back as he realized, to make her wait still longer, but she grabbed his hand and forced it back against her, wave after wave engulfing her.

She came uncontrollably, body shattering in a dark, narrow staircase, his palm against her clitoris, his other arm holding her up as she fell against it, her own arm stuffed against her mouth to keep in her cries.

He held her until she finished coming, pulling her in tightly against him.

Then he picked her up, holding her in his arms as he took the last stairs swiftly. She fumbled, limp, mindless, for her key. He took it from her and opened the door, not fumbling at all. The apartment was small. It took him no time to find the bed. He dropped her onto it and fell onto her, one thumb driving her helplessly into waves of pleasure again as he took her, hard and fast.

He came almost immediately, hard, wrapping his arm under her shoulders and pulling her into him as he did so. His arm flexed around her until, just for a second, she could not breathe as his climax shook him.

He held her, held her tight, his faced buried in her hair, as his body slowly relaxed.

They both fell asleep together, Sylvain with one hand curled gently on her waist.

It was still dark when they woke. Sylvain made a low, pleased sound, as if drifting up from a dream to realize it was true. He stroked her clothes off, all of them, left her naked among her sheets, completely naked to him for the first time. So she did the same to him. She couldn't help it. His long, naked body was so beautiful. Stroking her hands over his bare skin and finding nothing, anywhere, to impede her, was such sensual pleasure.

He stroked one hand leisurely up her body, starting at the foot from which he had just removed the tights, all the way up the naked length of her, over her hip, her ribs, her arm, which he stretched above her head, linking his fingers with hers to imprison her hand. Light from the city came clearly through her windows. His eyes seemed to glitter in it.

"You can do anything to me you want to," she whispered.

"I will," he promised.

Chapter 19

When she woke in the morning, her bed smelled of chocolate. It smelled, in fact, of home, of Corey, where the very air smelled of chocolate, always. She came out of sleep smiling a little, nuzzling at the smell, whose source eluded her.

Bright daylight burned through the room. That disoriented her and combined with the achiness of her body to make her wonder if she had been ill. She never slept late. Not even when she was traveling.

By degrees, she became aware that she was very, very far from home, naked and completely exposed on her bed, under a thin sheet. And sticky. And the night . . .

She blushed all over, from head to feet, and fought against opening her eyes but finally had to.

Despite all the training of her hook-up period in college, she expected to see Sylvain standing there. She expected to have to face him, naked and crimson.

But the small apartment was mercilessly, brightly empty in the late-morning sun.

And outside her apartment door, the stairs were creaking as someone descended away from her. The sound that had awoken her had been her closing door.

* * *

"Cade," Mack Corey said reproachfully. Over his shoulder, her grandfather studied her. With gleaming eyes, knowing her grandfather, but it was hard to tell via Webcam.

Cade felt miserable. Guilty, rebellious, unsure of how to become herself. Like an adolescent, perhaps, except she hadn't felt that way as an adolescent. She had fit in perfectly in their world as an adolescent, known exactly what to do to be the best next Corey, and done it. Despite her own desires to sink into a simpler, sweeter world of artisan chocolate, she had assumed her responsibilities with no instant of rebellion, unlike her sister, Jaime, who had pretty much refused them from the get-go and set off to save the world from big, bad capitalists like her sister.

"Are you okay? I worried about you when you didn't respond to any messages yesterday."

"I was working," she said quickly. "I went up to Belgium."

"Still," her father said firmly, "you should have answered your messages."

She was trying to wean her father from needing to hear from her quite that frequently. She felt like Marie Antoinette playing at being a farmer in the Petit Trianon. *Please, I don't want to run the world anymore. Just—can I be something else, for a little while?*

"I had to make some calls to make sure you hadn't gotten arrested for chocolate theft."

"I—don't think Sylvain Marquis plans to press charges." It wasn't the sex that made her trust him. Far from it. It was the way he had shifted his body to block her from the wind in the gardens.

"Is it working, then?" her grandfather asked. "Are you luring him into the fold? Is he going to sell himself to us?"

Oh, yeah, sure, any millennium now. "No."

"Just as well, really," her father said. "I'm not convinced anymore that it's a good time to start a new line. But if *you're* that sure, why are you still there? I could use you back here right now, sweetie."

"Can't you ever let her have a vacation?" her grandfather asked him. "What is it with you and making her work all the time? I don't see why I made us billions just so my grand-daughters have to work instead of gallivanting around Paris."

Mack Corey turned away from the Webcam and stared at his father. "First of all, you made us millions. I made us billions. And second of all, what are you talking about? You made *me* work 24/7!"

"I was younger and stupid when you were a kid," the older Corey said impatiently. "And we still only had millions. And the Mars family was getting uppity, and we needed to make sure they didn't beat us. Plus, you were a boy."

Cade sighed. It was fairly annoying that her grandfather's sexism was her best defense.

"*And* I made sure you had a year to tour Europe, the way my dad did me, I'll have you know," her grandfather said. "It's not my fault it was wasted and you never tried to break into a single *chocolaterie* the whole time you were there."

"She had a semester abroad when she was in college! It's not *my* fault she wanted to double major and couldn't find time in her curriculum to stay a year. She travels all the time for Corey. And she's been in practically every country in the world! Except a few of the ones where we have to hire an army to make sure she doesn't get kidnapped. It's so hard to get a reliable army these days."

Her grandfather folded his arms. "Either that only whet-ted her appetite, or it isn't what she is looking for at all, *or* you need to cut her enough slack now that she can spend one whole day not working while in Paris without your hav-ing conniptions. She graduated four years ago. That's a long time to go without a few hours' vacation."

"I didn't mind that she wasn't working," her father said sulkily. It was one of the side benefits of being a member of a closely-knit billionaire family that she got to see the head of one of the Fortune 500 act sulky. He didn't do that in public. "Although it's not a good time for that, to be honest. I just wanted to make sure she was all right. It's not like her not to answer her phone or take care of problems as soon as they come up. She knows I want her opinion on the Firenze brothers."

"What could have happened to her?" her grandfather scoffed.

"A car accident, kidnapping, food poisoning, getting mugged, tripping and falling on stairs, hitting her head, and not having anyone find her until it was too late, an enraged French chocolatier, or, most likely, the way she's been behaving, jail."

Her grandfather studied his son. "Being a father is rough, isn't it?" he asked sympathetically.

"Yes," Mack Corey said definitely, completely missing his father's real meaning. His father punched him in the shoulder to try to make sure he caught it, but his son only glanced at his punched shoulder blankly.

Cade hid a grin, feeling homesickness well up in a strange, split-personality way. Because she really didn't want to go home.

Cade went to the Louvre. She spent the whole afternoon at the Louvre. She stood staring at giant Assyrian griffins. She wandered among the Italians, trying to remember if any of those artists had gotten syphilis, and if they had, whether staring at their extraordinary art should make her feel better about herself. Maybe she needed to be over in the Musée d'Orsay with van Gogh.

She got a little bit lost among Egyptian sarcophagi, found herself wandering among thousand-year-old foundations underground, and finally came out into the light pouring softly through the inverted pyramid in a great courtyard one level down from the surface. She folded her legs under her on one of the stone benches there and sat, almost Zen style, for at least an hour. The murmur of people moving through the courtyard surrounded her like running water as she soaked in the soft, luminous paleness of the courtyards, the great marble statues that had once stood in gardens.

The guards kept a casually suspicious eye on her, which was kind of funny. No one kept a suspicious eye on her in Corey. Maybe her descent into crime and kamikaze behavior had created an aura for her. If there was one place where you would spot auras, it was in this calm, calm space. Except that anyone who sat here too long would have his aura purified by beauty.

She imagined everyone coming up the escalators out of the museum, into the crisp, cold November courtyard of the palace, surrounded by white auras. Taking on life again, slowly turning back into their old colors.

She was crossing the wood-planked pedestrian bridge, the Pont des Arts, across from the Louvre, when her phone rang.

"Do you ever eat anything besides chocolate?" Sylvain asked. "Where are you? Do you know how inconsistent you are? You break into my *chocolaterie,* you try to buy it, you bribe people—is it true you paid that woman thirty thousand American dollars for that morning in the workshop?—but when I invite you, you don't even call back."

"The thirty thousand dollars wasn't intentional." There hadn't really been any intelligent analysis of possible results when she'd handed a stranger her credit card. "What invitation?"

"I left you a message this morning."

Really? No messages were required in a hook-up. That was one of the basic rules. Her thumb stroked over the back of her phone. She began to smile. "How did you get this number?"

Evening was falling earlier and earlier as November advanced, and the lights came on all around her as she stood there, looking at the tip of the Île de la Cité, with its bare trees and couples still sitting there, despite the cold and the failing light. The street lamps sprang warmly to life against the winter dusk, and luminescence softly woke around the Louvre and Notre-Dame and the Musée d'Orsay, its great railroad clock glowing faintly green. The wind blew a drizzle across her, nudging her home.

Unfortunately, she didn't have a home here. She only had a short-term apartment rental from which she could look out at things she wanted.

And Thanksgiving was coming, and Christmas after. Maybe she should be heading toward her real home.

Her eyes creased, her heart troubled, as she got an inkling of another side to her current conflict. Where should she be, as the holidays came round? She had agreed with her father to take no more than a month here. A month, which had seemed an enormous amount of playtime to her when she had first bargained for it, now seemed very, very short.

"I took a card out of your wallet while you were still asleep," he said matter-of-factly.

"You stole from me?" She was outraged.

There was a long, incredulous pause. "Are you *kidding* me?"

"Did you steal anything else?" Her stomach clenched in old, learned sickness. A credit card, for example. If all this nose-dived straight down to her money . . .

"Like what? *Ton passeport*? So you can't disappear—with all my secrets?" Had she imagined it, or had that "with all my secrets" been tacked on quickly? The rhythm of the question had barely broken. She had probably imagined it. He didn't care if she disappeared, just if she stole his secrets when she did it. "Do people who fly in private jets even have to show their passports?"

"Yes, but the immigration stamps are in gold leaf."

He laughed. "I've got something for you. Do you eat anything that doesn't have sugar in it? I can make dinner."

Standing there in the drizzle, gazing over brown waters at the winter-bare tip of an island and Notre-Dame, she felt her whole face split into a smile. She tried to keep her voice more neutral, though. "At your apartment?"

"You don't have anything in your refrigerator worth eating," he said firmly. In fact, she had a sample box from every important chocolatier in the city—besides him, of course. His had all gone to the homeless man in the gardens. From his tone of voice, she suspected he had opened her refrigerator while he was there and seen all those other chocolatiers' boxes. "So it will have to be mine."

Chapter 20

He met her at the *chocolaterie,* where the *laboratoire* had closed but the shop was still open until nine, with a long line out its door.

"Do you think I should pay you a commission?" Sylvain asked wonderingly. "Having you get caught stealing my chocolates is the best thing for business—other than myself, of course—that has ever happened to me."

She gave him an aggrieved look.

He pressed his lips together in amusement and led her to his apartment, stopping to pick up a baguette at the *boulangerie.* She watched him enviously. He did that so easily, as if it was as natural to him as breathing to stop in a bakery and pick up a baguette on the way home. Which, of course, it was.

"They just came out of the oven." He held it out to her to share the pleasure. She pulled off a glove and closed her hand over it, feeling the warmth of the long, thin loaf through the small square of paper the baker had twisted around it.

He broke an end off and handed it to her, crackling and warm. She smiled as he broke off another bite for himself. He smiled back. "Nothing like catching the loaves when they just came out of the oven."

He lived in the *rue piétonne* where she had run into him in the restaurant, a couple of blocks over from his *chocolaterie* and on the far end from the restaurant itself.

The apartment seemed nice. It was as clean and uncluttered as his *laboratoire,* everything put away in its place. But he obviously wiped down the counters in the *laboratoire* much more often than it occurred to him to dust the shelves here.

The living room was spacious and during the day must be luminous, with large windows that could be opened inward like great doors and that gave on to wrought-iron railings. A warm-colored rug graced the polished hardwood floor. The couch looked well-loved, as if someone liked to stretch out on it to read a good book or watch the moderately large flat-screen TV. She could see the indentation on the arm on which his head always lay, so that he was facing the windows. Tucked under the table at that end of the couch was a photo album in brown leather, embossed with his initials. It must have been someone's idea of a gift.

All the doors down the hallway were closed. She picked up the photo album and came back into the kitchen. The kitchen, too, was spacious, or at least spacious for a single person's apartment in a crowded city. And, of course, it was very well equipped.

Sylvain began pulling things out of the refrigerator— mushrooms, shallots, meat wrapped in paper. From a wine rack tucked under the edge of the counter, he brought out a bottle of wine. He paused when she came to lean against the dark granite counter and watch him. *"Tiens."* He handed her a tiny paper bag that looked recently crushed by someone's back pocket.

"What's this?"

He looked—awkward. Sylvain, awkward? Half smiling, half-embarrassed, as if not sure how his gift would be received. "Just something I saw while I was out for lunch. It made me think of you."

She blushed immediately. And opened it cautiously, half expecting velvet handcuffs.

A tiny, hand-knitted beige teddy bear peeked up at her, its

eyes stitched by hand with two strands of black thread. It wore a minuscule backpack, into which an even tinier beige teddy bear was tucked. It was a finger puppet. She slipped it onto her finger, smiling as she eased the baby teddy out of the backpack to examine it and slipped it back onto the mommy bear's back. It was completely and utterly charming, and it made no sense. She wasn't a child, and their relationship wasn't childish.

She looked up at him. He was smiling more, less awkward, as if the sight of it on her finger reminded him why he had bought it.

"Why?" she finally asked.

He pulled out a wooden cutting board and a chef's knife that gleamed sharp enough to shave. "Because I didn't think you would already have it. And I thought you might need it."

"Need it?" Was she missing something about this teddy-bear finger puppet?

He nodded. "It accomplishes nothing. It is completely and utterly frivolous and childish. It's just for the pure fun of it. For pleasure."

He thought she needed more frivolity after the irresponsible way she had been behaving? She turned and bent her finger, liking the feel of the teddy bear on it. Who wouldn't like a teddy-bear finger puppet?

Especially one that had no point. There were so few things in her life that had no point.

Or, wait . . . that *was* its point.

"This may be the most romantic present anyone has ever given me," she said out loud before she thought.

Black eyebrows shot up. *"Vraiment?"*

"Vraiment."

"Dis, donc." He shook his head, turning back to the counter. "Those other guys will be easy to top, then, won't they?"

She studied the back of his dark head, the easy set of his broad shoulders, the ease of all of him, all that lean, long body, as he cooked so casually. Did he want to top other men's romantic gestures? He was doing a great job of it, but . . . was he doing it on purpose? Sex didn't have to mean romance.

He dampened a cloth and began to rub each mushroom clean. "You mean, no one has ever brought you flowers?"

"Oh . . . flowers. Yes, of course." She got flowers a lot, actually. They were an unnervingly fake gift. Easy to order over a phone at the most casual opportunity a man could find to increase his acquaintance with her money.

"No one's ever given you chocolates?"

She laughed. "No. No one has ever given me chocolates."

He looked sympathetic. "That must have been tough on you. Always wishing someone would give you real chocolates, but no one ever daring because of your family."

There was maybe a teensy grain of truth in that, but she narrowed her eyes at him nevertheless.

He whipped his knife through the mushrooms in about five seconds and set the knife down long enough to fish in the pocket of the jacket he had draped over a chair. He produced the smallest-sized box from his shop, the kind that held only four thumbnail-sized chocolates, took the lid off, and held it out to her.

In it nestled four plain, square chocolates, completely unadorned. She looked from it to the broad hand holding it, the strong wrist, the straight, dark hairs on that strong forearm. Her gaze skipped up to his eyes, almost exactly the color of the chocolate and smiling just a little at her.

She got distracted by his eyes for a moment, wanting just to look at them in this moment of calm. He didn't seem to mind the delay, studying her, his hand still patiently stretched toward her.

She pushed her hand through her hair and looked away,

focusing on the chocolates. When she bit into one, it was dark, of course, lustrous in flavor, elusively cinnamon-y. Ever since she had told him she liked cinnamon, he kept playing with it.

"What do you think?"

She thought that, yes, as naturally as breathing he topped the romance of every other man she had ever dated or slept with.

How easy was this for him? Was it a formula, his seduction routine? Was she supposed to even care if it was a routine or just enjoy the moment?

His smile faded at her silence. *"Non?"* He closed the box. "It was just something I was playing around with today. I'm sure it needs more work."

"No." She shook her head helplessly. "It doesn't need more work." He was perfect exactly as he was. Perfect.

She turned away to the photo album, opening it in self-defense and also in deep curiosity. What would Sylvain's more personal photos, not the ones that were in magazines, look like?

She felt more than saw the gesture he made toward the album, as if to grab it. He broke that gesture off and turned to the shallots instead. He minced the small shallots so finely and so quickly, she was sure he would lose a finger.

Of course, he didn't. He tossed them into a pan and made an automatic gesture toward his front, as if to brush his fingers on a chef's apron, then remembered and switched to his jeans.

It was a little scary how much she loved his fingers. She wanted them to do other things besides drive her crazy. Stroke her hair, play with *her* fingers, brush a fleck of something off her cheek.

She looked back at the photo album. "Who made this for you?"

"Ma maman," he said, resigned.

The whole notion of a mother in connection with the man who had walked her up those stairs the night before made her jump, as if the woman might pop out from behind one of those closed doors. "Where does your mother live?"

"She and my father moved to Provence a few years ago when they retired."

Cade's shoulders relaxed. She flipped through the pages, smiling a little at baby photos and missing teeth, and one of a boy about five, with his face covered in chocolate, which his mother had marked *Ça s'annonce bien* in shiny silver pen. The album seemed to have been designed as a trajectory of his life. He had been a well-loved child, she thought.

She studied a photo of him as a teenager. He wasn't one of those teenagers who blossomed early. As a seventeen-year-old, he looked lanky and awkward, his hair falling into his eyes—she slid a glance at the chin-length smooth locks he still preferred and had to smile. He had a better stylist these days, that was all. He was still that same boy who had preferred the romance or sensuality of slightly overlong hair. In the photo, he had spotty skin and eyes that seemed too big for his face, and, over all, the form was there, if you knew to look, but he clearly hadn't hit his peak during his high school years. He looked shy and self-conscious in front of the camera.

He looked shy and self-conscious right now, to see her looking at what that camera had caught. His hand flexed, and his fingers stretched out toward the corner of the album and then quickly folded back into his palm, as if he had to restrain himself from snatching it away from her. She grinned up at him, and he hunched up one shoulder and turned away, focusing on his cooking.

"You ate too much chocolate when you were a teenager, too, did you?" she laughed.

"Chocolate is not bad for your skin," he retorted, more annoyed than the lightness of her joke deserved. "That's a myth."

"I know. We funded the study." She flipped to the next page. His mother had taken one of him in what must have been their kitchen—a cramped space with stained linoleum counters—making a total mess with chocolate. In the photo, his face was bent over his work with the same intensity he still showed in his *chocolaterie*. The angle of his head was even the same, and that clean line of his jaw.

"You were cute as a teenager." Like a nerd, but obsessed with cooking instead of math or computers. She would bet some other shy girl in his class had had a killer crush on him, and he had never realized it. "I would have flirted with you."

His mouth set. "No, you would not have."

"I might." She grinned again, wondering why this moment kept failing to be as light and cozy as she thought it should be. "I've always had a weakness for men who can work wonders with chocolate."

That was true. Just the memory of him, all lovely and distant and intense, focused on some magical cauldron of chocolate, was enough to make her hormones jump alive, make her want to taste it, taste him. He was pretty darn cute even right now without chocolate involved, just focused on his red-wine reduction. Or he would be cute if he would stop frowning. She had never been particularly turned on by frowns.

"Yes, I can tell," he said dryly.

Now, what did that mean? It didn't have a good feeling to it, whatever it meant. "Actually, I don't think I've ever dated a man who knew more about chocolate than I do," she said, to turn this conversation down a safer path—one where they could fight.

He raised an eyebrow and glanced sideways at her, finally allowing her enough attention that she could catch his eyes with a little grin.

"And I'm not sure I am now, either." She wasn't sure she was dating him, for one thing.

He turned. *"Pardon?"*

She set her elbows back on the countertop and just grinned at him.

"You think you know more about chocolate than *I* do?"

She probably knew more about some aspects of it. But she craved *his* knowledge—the mastery of the magic and mystery and intensity of chocolate. And . . . she craved him. "Well. I know how to sell it," she said impudently instead of admitting that.

"You know how to sell it for—how much are people willing to pay for that—?" He made a gesture toward her purse on the table that was similar to the way someone might gesture toward a mousetrap that held a dead mouse to be disposed of.

Thirty-three cents at Walmart. "A dollar," she said. In movie theaters it sold for a dollar. Or in machines in airports.

He shook his head, as if people would never cease to amaze him. *"Américains.* So. You know how to sell it to Americans for a dollar. Do you know how to sell it to Parisians for a hundred euros a kilo?"

Or nearly $4.00 an ounce. At that rate, her Corey Bars would sell for over $12.00 each. "Three dollars a bar is what I'm thinking," she said. "Enough to let people know it's special, but not enough that they can't afford it."

He looked ill. It wasn't all that pleasant to make a man want to throw up while he was cooking you dinner. "With my name on it," he muttered. *"Dans les supermarchés."* He gave his wine reduction an incredulous look, as if suddenly wondering how he could possibly have ended up making dinner for someone like her.

"Why not? Would it kill you to be accessible to the masses?"

By the revolted expression on his face, it just might. "You're a chocolate anarchist!"

She grinned, delighted at the term. She would have to tell her grandfather, just to see his matching grin. Jack Corey would love to be called a chocolate anarchist.

Sylvain raised a reproachful eyebrow at her delight, but as he plated the steaks, he had a smile on his face.

Who wouldn't be smiling? The scents of seared steaks, red wine, and shallots filled the apartment. Inside was light and warmth; outside in the dark, fine rain fell, glistening on the windows. Now that he had gotten her out of that photo album—a sweet gift on his mother's part, but he needed to remember to keep it and its adolescent photos of him well out of sight of beautiful female guests—Sylvain felt supremely happy.

He couldn't really ask for much better than this out of life. To be cooking good food for a beautiful woman who turned incandescent with passion in his hands, to be inside and warm with her on the kind of cold, wet night that would really discourage her from getting all funny about something and leaving. To know that she so intensely loved his chocolate that he held an irresistible lure for her in the palm of his hand if she did decide to get upset. To be arguing with her and making her laugh.

They could eat, drink, laugh, fight, curl up on the couch, read a book, fall asleep. They could wake up in the morning or in the middle of the night with a smile. He would like that. He was so worn out after the intensity of the past twenty-four hours that he might really just fall asleep.

Then again, if she did curl up on the couch with him, all trusting and cozy and her body nestled against his, he might not.

It didn't matter, either way. There could only be one bad way for the evening to end, and that was for it to end. Anything else was just fine by him.

He poured her a glass of wine as they sat down at the table, to encourage everything to be fine by her, too.

"Did you like the s'more?" she asked suddenly.

"The what?" *Suh-more?*

"The *s'more*." She tried to demonstrate it with her hands. "The thing with the—the—thing and chocolate and wafers I left you the other night."

The—the—thing must be the half-burned *chamallow* concoction. *The Thing* was probably a good name for it.

"Why?" he asked warily. Had it really been poisoned? Was she wondering why he hadn't died? Or was she testing him to see if aliens had snatched the real Sylvain Marquis and put an impostor in his place? She couldn't possibly think that *he* would have liked that thing.

"It's one of these fun things everyone does when they're kids in the US. Did you like it?"

Good God. There was a spark of hopefulness in her eyes. Sylvain wondered how to say it had tasted like *merde* diplomatically and got bogged down in the search for words.

Her spark faded. *Merde,* he had to spit something out. "It was . . . ah . . . I can see why children might like it." Not *his* someday children, of course. He hoped to teach them better taste.

Her face fell. He kicked himself. "The wafers weren't right. I couldn't find *gram crackers,*" she said, or something like that. "And it's really not good cold. You have to eat it when the marshmallow is all hot and sticky and the chocolate is all melting."

Sylvain struggled to keep the pain out of his expression.

"I'll show you how to make it sometime," she decided positively. There were times when it could be a real problem that no defeat ever kept her down for long. "You'll see. It's fun."

He liked her having future plans for them. And if he was careful, he might be able to distract her from the sticky-marshmallow aspect of that plan indefinitely. She seemed to be vulnerable to sexual distraction. He grinned a little.

She brightened up again at the grin, misunderstanding. "Is that a working fireplace? I could show you after supper."

"Fake flames." He tried to make relief sound like regret. "You're not allowed to have real fires in Paris. People cheat sometimes, but this chimney is blocked up."

She looked disappointed again. And then, true to form, she bounced right back up. "You have"—she broke off and made some gestures again as she tried to replace a missing word with a visual—"things to heat fondue pots, right?"

Maybe. Sylvain tried to duck the question. "I don't have *chamallows* or cookies." Or Corey Bars, for God's sake, but she was bound to have at least one in her purse. She always did, didn't she?

She looked toward the wet, dark window and hesitated. Sylvain started to relax. Then she squared her shoulders. "We could run out and get some. The *épicerie* is just down the street."

She was like a combination of a pit bull and a *Culbuto,* a Weebles toy. She went down and came right back up. She set her teeth into something she wanted and never let go.

Not that he was complaining. She had set her teeth into the idea of getting his chocolate, and here he was, taking every advantage he could of it. That resilient determination of hers was erotic. It was exciting. It made him want to kiss her and see if that might distract her enough to save him from eating sticky marshmallows, cookies, and Corey Bars mashed together.

"Next time," he said, and her blue eyes flickered. He felt a chill of fear. Despite her earlier use of "sometime," "next time" apparently wasn't a foregone conclusion.

He would have to work on that. He still had plenty of chocolate lures to use on someone as obsessed as she was.

She took a bite of her steak and closed her eyes for a moment in almost exactly the same expression he had seen on her face for those *ravioles du Royan.*

He smiled in fierce, sexual satisfaction.

"This is delicious."

He tried to look modest, but he'd been told it wasn't one of his strengths. "It's nothing. *Un petit truc.*"

"And the wine is perfect." She twisted the bottle to look at the label, a very rudimentary one, probably designed by the teenage nephew of some friend of the *vigneron.* "Where did you get it?"

"When I visit my parents, we go around to different tiny vineyards in the area. I'll"—He caught himself, cold with alarm. He had nearly said, "I'll show you sometime," but if they couldn't even confidently refer to "next time," he could make a disastrous error in assuming out loud that months from now they might be making trips south to see his parents. She helped run a company that earned over thirty billion dollars a year. Right now, this was just a vacation for her. "*Non, attends,* I think that one came from Jacques."

She queried with a blue look. He loved those blue eyes of hers. Every straight look from them made his skin tighten, his muscles try to override his mind and just reach out and grab her.

"This little man who knocks on my door every fall and talks me into ordering cases from small vineyards he represents."

Her lips split into a smile again, and he felt quite pleased with himself, although he had no idea what he had just said to make her look so happy. "A man comes around and sells you wine from little, unknown vineyards? Really?"

It seemed pretty normal to him. Especially since Jacques knew what a sucker he was. Sylvain, *la bonne poire.*

It was too bad this apartment didn't come with a bigger *cave.* Last year, Jacques had talked him into ordering so much, he had had to stock cases in his bedroom. He had ended up giving a couple dozen bottles out to everyone at the *chocolaterie* for Christmas so he could get his space back.

Something rode up through the happiness in her expression, changing it to something so wistful and full of longing, he wished it were for him. For one thing, if it were for him, he would have left his seat and his meal and satisfied her right then and there. God, to be longed for so intensely . . .

"What do you think would market Corey Bars to Europeans effectively?" she asked suddenly.

What? Was *that* what she was longing for? Did her mind just have a business track that was running all the time? *Probably,* now that he thought about it. His mind had a chocolate track that was running all the time. "Nothing, I hope," he said baldly.

She narrowed her eyes and went visibly chilly. "I'll bet Europeans would go for a premium-chocolate line with your name on it."

"If they want something with my name on it, they know just where to get it."

She flexed a frustrated fist. "I hate for Mars to win the market in Europe. Or Total Foods." She grimaced. "And I know Dad does, too."

He took a big bite of his steak as the best way of preventing himself from giving his opinion on Corey and Total Foods battling it out for the tastes of his fellow countrymen. "We might as well sell the country to McDonald's and be done with it," he muttered. *Damn, not big enough.* "Do you want to bring in processed cheese while you're at it?"

She pressed her perfect teeth together and glared at him. "I'll ask Christophe. I'll bet he would have some ideas."

Sylvain stiffened. "You know, if you want to blame someone besides yourself for becoming known as the infamous Chocolate Thief, it's Christophe who gossiped about other people's private lives"—*and fantasies*—"on a blog."

"I know, but he's a nice guy. He's fun."

Sylvain simmered.

"And he's smart, and he understands Europeans, and he might help me if I ask him."

"While I won't," Sylvain said crisply. He fantasized about picking up Christophe and shaking him like a wet dog. No, better—giving him a box of poisoned chocolates, then watching the betrayed look on his face as he keeled over. Preferably writhing in a slow, painful death. That, at least, would be a proper vengeance. "Christophe is a pushover. I've got standards."

"Maybe I *should* just buy somebody out," Cade said, as if thinking out loud. "That's what Dad thinks. Valrhona, maybe. That might be more efficient."

"More efficient at what?" Sylvain demanded. He knew he should keep his mouth shut, but even to have her slim, passionate intensity in his hands, he couldn't sell his soul and his country's with it. "Reducing everything that's good about this country to that?" He gestured at her purse and the Corey Bar it surely held.

She frowned. For a second, he didn't know whether she was going to get mad or get even. Then she bent her head and rubbed her crinkled forehead. She looked tired and exceptionally grave. Fragility again.

But he couldn't help her. He could not, would not, help her figure out how to take over the French market for chocolate, nor to mass-produce some bastardized version of his art and soul back home.

"Why do you need it, anyway? Don't you have enough money?"

She made a gesture with one hand and didn't answer. The grave look hadn't diminished. She just didn't want to talk to him about her reasons.

Women *always* had something else going on in their heads. Couldn't she simply enjoy the evening? He sighed. "Do you want me to run out and get some marshmallows and *biscuits*?"

Her face brightened. The distraction had worked. He felt as if he'd used his own palate as the sacrificial bait, though. "Do you want me to show you how to make s'mores?"

"Sure," he lied. He was *such* a pear. He liked that happy look so much better than that grave, tired look, though.

And that was how Sylvain Marquis, widely held to be the best chocolatier in Paris and therefore in the world, found himself making s'mores with marshmallows, Lu butter cookies, and cheap supermarket chocolate he wouldn't feed to a three-year-old child.

God, it sure did make her happy, though. They sat on the floor in front of the fireplace into which she had placed a Sterno can—because she insisted s'mores had to be made on the floor. She was like some excited kid, proudly showing off a crayon drawing of a crooked smiley face to da Vinci.

He being da Vinci, of course. He had no qualms equating his mastery of chocolate to da Vinci's mastery of art.

Sylvain didn't eat his. She was so gleeful as she smushed the *biscuits* together over the gloppy marshmallow and held the first one to his mouth that he reached up, took it out of her hand, and began to kiss her. They were on the floor already, so it wasn't long before sitting changed to lying, and he was braced above her on his elbows, and . . . he turned out to have more energy than he had earlier believed.

The Sterno can had burned out by the time she thought of it again. Mentally, he gave himself a congratulatory pat on the back.

But the sense of self-satisfaction soon faded.

Lying there on that hard floor, with cookie crumbs itching his bare back and her head on his chest, Sylvain stroked that straight, silky hair of hers and gazed broodingly at the white embossed ceiling. He could feel her long, even breathing against his skin and perhaps just the faintest suggestion of a ladylike snore. He should be beaming, all right with his world, but the post-sex letdown had left him somber.

She loved sex with him. She loved his chocolate. He wasn't sure she cared one iota about any other aspect of him, although, admittedly, those two were pretty dominant traits.

But he would take that. He didn't care. He had spent his whole life trying to make his chocolate irresistible; he wasn't going to complain when it was working on a prize like her.

The problem was, she didn't even have to buy a ticket to leave. She could climb straight back onto her private plane the second she decided to move on. And that had to be pretty soon, right? Because she was just here for a visit.

Chapter 21

Cade woke to daylight and the sounds of Sylvain moving cheerfully around the apartment, singing something under his breath, some French tune she didn't know. He had a good voice, a nice, rich tenor.

"I'll go get some *pains au chocolat,*" he told her, voice slightly muffled by the comforter in which her ears were buried. She liked it under there. It was cozy and warm and dark and smelled of chocolate and two human bodies, and she halfway wished he would just say "Ciao" and walk out so that she could stay there and not deal with anything.

Like him and herself, for example. And like her responsibilities in life. If she couldn't get this gourmet line idea to work, she knew she needed to go home and go back to her real job.

"Or do you want a *tarte aux framboises* again?"

She made a wordless sound that he must have taken however he wanted, because a moment later she heard the apartment door close. She got up and found his shower, determined not to be caught at quite the same disadvantage as the day before. He had a *real* shower. Enclosed in glass and attached to the wall so she didn't have to hold it herself. He even had a nice series of jets up and down the side of the stall. She soaked in the warmth and steam blissfully, taking her time.

She had her face raised to the spray and started when she heard a rap on the glass. Sylvain was holding a thick brown towel and gazing at her wet, naked body with an unexpectedly possessive smile on his face. "You should go ahead and get out," he told her with a grin. "I'm exhausted. I need a few hours."

She flushed, wondering if he thought she was a nymphomaniac.

Since during his entire acquaintance with her she had felt and acted like a nymphomaniac, odds were high that he did. Being a man, he probably wasn't complaining, just enjoying the ride.

Literally, she thought, with a wry twist of embarrassment.

It was those hands of his. They were so exactly the fantasy she had carried with her ever since seeing that photo on his fabulously artistic Web site of his right hand setting a bit of cocoa nib on a tiny chocolate. They matched so perfectly the tall, sexy, dark-haired, passionate man who lived with all his senses, who was so arrogant and so sure, who mastered her with tastes and textures. She wanted to meet his passion with her passion. She wanted those hands to manipulate her. She couldn't get enough of them. She couldn't get enough of him.

And then, just when she thought pure and passionate sex was an end in itself, and that was fine, and they didn't need anything else but chocolate . . . then all of a sudden he did something, and it *wasn't*. It wasn't an end in itself, and she did need something else.

Like now. She dressed in yesterday's clothes and came out to the kitchen with her hair damp and caught in a ponytail, and no makeup. And he looked at her a long moment, his face going closed and contained in that way he had, as if the sight of her caused him some kind of pain.

Why? Did it cause him that many qualms to be sleeping with someone from the Corey Chocolate family?

The scent of fresh baking, butter and yeast, came from the

white paper sack and rectangular box that sat on the table. The paper sack held three *pains au chocolat,* double bars of chocolate peeking generously from each end of their golden flakiness. The rectangular box opened to reveal a selection of three *tartes,* including a *tarte aux framboises.* "Just in case," he told her.

"What's this one?" She pointed to an apple-studded yellow tart in the middle, the texture of which seemed almost omelet-like. "Does it have eggs and fruit in it? That's almost breakfast where I come from."

He looked at it and then at her. "Americans are very strange. It's a *tarte normande.* Maybe someone in Normandy invented it to make some American soldier happy." He shrugged.

"It's not that similar," she told him dryly as she took a bite. The base, almost like a mildly sweet quiche, blended perfectly with the apples. It reminded her a little bit of a German apple pancake, but in the context of World War II, maybe it was better not to raise that origin as a possibility. "And it's probably healthier for me than that *pain au chocolat.* More protein, some fruit, less fat and sugar."

He shrugged again. "I have yogurt in the refrigerator, if you want it. And the rest of those chocolates, if you're having withdrawal symptoms from going almost eight hours without chocolate. Without *my* chocolate," he clarified, with a deliberately smug smirk. "Are you regretting giving it all away yet?"

Yes. Especially since it would be a real loss of face to go back to his shop and buy more from one of his snooty clerks. And if she couldn't live without it, and she couldn't bring herself to lose that face and buy it again, she was going to have to go to him for every piece she wanted.

And he was going to so completely master her.

Her eyes dilated, and her mouth watered, and she looked down at her *tarte normande* quickly.

"I should go," he said. She blinked and flinched inside. She tried to detect a tone of regret in his voice but didn't. "I have a *stagiaire* coming in today, and I'd like to be there when he is, in case I need to interpret."

"What language?" she asked, surprised. Did Sylvain speak another language? A *stagiaire* was an intern, a trainee—she remembered that word.

He shook his head. "Dialect. Between worlds. The *banlieue* he comes from is very different from the sixth arrondissement in Paris."

"Then how can you serve as the interpreter?" she asked, confused. She knew vaguely, from his biography, that he had been born in the outskirts of Paris, *en banlieue,* but the outskirts hadn't seemed an important distinction from Paris itself at the time.

"I grew up in the same *banlieue,*" he said briefly, rising. He clearly didn't want to expand much on his childhood with her, did he?

She supposed that was good. He wasn't trying to use sex as a springboard to intimacy. No effort to insert himself into her life and marry billions, at least.

It was romantic, but it was also confusing. Her billions had always been there to guarantee that men were interested in her. Without them, she felt as if she had been dropped into a foreign city with no business cards, no phone, no name, just the clothes on her back and her wits to survive on.

He rinsed the *pain au chocolat* crumbs off his hands and stopped in front of her where she sat holding her *tarte normande.* He hesitated, then leaned down and kissed her very quickly, a brush of his lips across hers.

And left.

Cade was still sitting there frozen a few minutes later when her phone rang. This time, she recognized the source. "You can come, if you want," Sylvain said. "I'll show you how to make something."

A smile bloomed across her face. She went to the window to look down and saw him standing in the middle of the pedestrian lane, looking up at the window. She wasn't sure he could actually see her there, or if the reflection of the light acted as a shield.

"But I'm showing you, not Corey Chocolate," he said. "So don't sell it. And please God, don't put my name on it if you do."

Chapter 22

In the *laboratoire,* a dust rose as Pascal coated a batch of truffles in finely ground crumbs of caramelized almond, shaking them on a wide, sievelike rack in a gesture exactly as if he was winnowing the harvest. Far enough away that he avoided any risk of contamination from stray crumbs worked a teenager who stood out not only for his youth but because he was the only black person in the room and seemed caught halfway between pride and awkwardness in his work. He was stirring a giant pot of chocolate.

A woman was applying a three-pronged fork expertly to little rectangular chocolates as they came out of the Sollich *enrobeuse,* glistening in their newborn chocolate skins. As the fork lifted, it left behind a pretty pattern that Cade recognized instantly as that of the *ganache vanille.* Another woman was spraying molds from a *pistolet,* coating each shell with the faintest sheen of *chocolat.*

Not far from the teenager, Sylvain himself was using his thumb to flick something that looked like pale green paint off a toothbrush onto a supple sheet of plastic. He picked up another toothbrush and dipped it into a darker green batch of what must actually be colored white chocolate, not paint.

He glanced up when she came in and gave her a long, searching look, then suddenly smiled. Pascal Guyot also looked up, rolled his eyes, sent Sylvain an ironic, sidelong glance, and focused back on his work, ignoring her. The teenager, who must be the *stagiaire,* raised his eyebrows right up to his hairline, glanced over at Sylvain, and grinned.

Then he started to lift his huge pot of melted chocolate confidently but faltered as the weight of it caught him by surprise. Sylvain dropped the toothbrush and caught the cauldron from him easily and carried it over to the *enrobeuse,* laughing as he poured it into the machine, manipulating the weight without even seeming to notice it.

"Et les muscles dans tout ça, Malik?" one of the other men called, laughing.

Malik, as the teenager must be called, looked a little embarrassed and flexed his shoulders self-consciously, as if to try to make sure his biceps were visible through the pastry jacket he wore. "I don't have time for the gym anymore; I'm always over here!" he protested.

"Maybe we need to give you more pots to carry to keep you in shape," the thin man with glasses joked. "Here, try this one." He handed him a metal bowl the size of an ordinary kitchen-mixer bowl.

"Or this one, if that's too heavy," said the burly man, pulling down a tiny pot that seemed to be too small for any practical purpose in this *laboratoire.*

"Okay, okay," Malik groaned. "I *can* carry it. I was just surprised."

No wonder almost everyone here seemed so lean and in good shape, Cade thought, trying to judge the weight of the original chocolate pot. Over fifty pounds, certainly. Eighty? How many times a day did they move something like that? Probably too many to keep count.

Sylvain stopped by Cade, his face still alight with humor. Looking up into that laughing face, she felt something run through her like a long, long sigh of brightness. "You can borrow one of my jackets today," he told her. "You looked as if you were drowning in Bernard's. And tuck your hair up into this." He handed her the plain paper cap that everyone but he and Pascal wore. "No one is ever going to find a hair in one of *my* chocolates."

Cade supposed that Bernard was the burly man. But it wasn't as if Sylvain's coat was a good fit. She rolled the sleeves up and up, wondering why he hadn't let her borrow one of the women's jackets. Maybe he just felt more comfortable lending his own things.

The fact that she was wearing his jacket made her smile to a puzzling degree. She felt fragile, still, to be standing near him in public after all their wild private sex, but in not quite the same way.

"What is this for?" she asked him, standing in front of the plastic spattered delicately with two shades of green.

"I'm experimenting with a new décor for my *chocolat, Curiosité,*" he said. "*La ganache au basilic,*" he added, in case she had eaten her way through multiple boxes of his chocolates without realizing that *Curiosité* was delicately flavored with basil. Truthfully, she wouldn't have been able to figure out the flavor if hadn't been for the glossy little insert explaining each chocolate. Basil, of all things. No wonder he thought her preference for cinnamon was so *datée*. "Once it hardens, we'll apply it to the top of the ovals that come out of the *enrobeuse*. And see whether we like the look."

"How many different kinds of ganache do you have?" she asked, because she liked hearing him say the word *ganache*. Like *chocolat*, it sounded like the caress of temptation.

"Twenty-four *ganaches au chocolat* currently," he said.

Ganaches au chocolat. The two words together licked heat up her body, flickering little tongues of flame against her sex, her breasts, the insides of her wrists, the nape of her neck.

"Nineteen *noirs,* of different degrees and flavors, and five *au lait*."

"Which one is your favorite?" *Say it again,* she wanted to beg. *Say* ganache au chocolat *again*.

He shook his head. "I don't have a favorite. If I didn't believe they were all the very best, I wouldn't be selling them."

Cade gave a tiny sigh and reminded herself that Corey Bars were the best of *their* type. The type that got sold by the billions by being within hand's reach in the checkout line at the grocery store.

No, it wasn't just that. The type that built up an affection in people, a coziness, that gave them a sense of security as part of their childhood. The type that got them sitting happily in front of a fireplace, laughing and making s'mores.

"Which one do you eat the most of?"

"I don't actually eat much chocolate for leisure. There is always something I am tasting here. Or occasionally a new chocolatier earns critical attention, and I want to taste what he is doing. There's so much to test all the time that I don't think it's the same pleasure to me as to you to sit down and open a new box of chocolates and think which one I will try first."

No, probably not. She always felt she was opening a treasure box after searching the world for it.

"For me, the delight of discovery is in the beginning, when I first create it and am tasting it as it is finished, deciding if it is perfect as is or needs something different." He took a fresh sheet of plastic as he spoke, setting it in front of her, and put the toothbrush in her hand, closing his hand over hers to show her how to flick her thumb. Green splattered too thickly on hers. There was a trick to it, getting that flick just right. He rubbed her knuckle with a thumb roughened by years of handling all kinds of equipment, and showed her again.

"I love that phase. But if anything compares for me to the way you feel when you open a box of chocolates, I suppose it's to sit down in an excellent restaurant for the first time and look at the menu of all the possibilities of what I can eat that someone else will have imagined and prepared for me."

Cade wondered what elegant restaurants in Paris he hadn't tried yet. Her heart gave a little sparkle of happiness at a fantasy that flitted through her brain of them both sitting down in an elegant restaurant, him scanning the menu intently, savoring each item in his imagination as he tried to decide which to order. She'd bet he did wonders for any elegant clothes he wore. She would take him to any restaurant he cared to name. She would order up a helicopter and fly him down to a three-star restaurant in the south of France, if that was what he wanted. She would . . .

"I think the chocolate I most want to taste again right now is the bitter one I made for you," he said reflectively.

"Did you really make it for me?" He could be like a rock star, making every woman believe he had written his love song for her.

"Oui, bien sûr," he said, clearly puzzled she could ask.

Whether in the raw or refined, Sylvain didn't seem to have much time for faking things, she thought. He did it real and the best, one hundred percent, or he didn't do it.

What did that mean, in regard to her?

"Have you thought about selling it?" she asked.

"I hadn't at the time. But I keep wanting to taste it again. Which means, yes, it could please a certain segment of our public. I could call it *L'Amertume.*"

Bitterness.

"Or *Déception.*"

Disappointment?

He pulled her blotched sheet of plastic away from her and gave her a new one. "Try again. So, what do you think? Should I offer it to the public?"

"It is oddly compulsive eating," she allowed. "Even now, I keep thinking I would like another bite of one."

A flicker across his face—humor, surprise, wariness. Also, was that a slight flush on his cheekbones? He looked at her. "Are we still talking about the chocolate? Or life? Or . . . ?"

She met his eyes straight on. "Chocolate." She did not seek any dark, bitter moments in her life. But that last, open-ended "or . . ." made a blush climb to her cheeks. "But once you have it, it stops you. You don't want more of anything at all. Which in my world is bad marketing, but in your world, who knows? You could probably sell each one for five hundred euros, and people would buy it. And then it wouldn't matter if you sold more."

"Not five hundred euros, but you have a good idea. We'll sell it in individual wrappers for twice as much as our other chocolates." In a tiny bag, exactly the same way he had offered it to her, in fact. She wondered how she felt about being an inspiration for this darkest, bitterest, smoothest, richest chocolate.

Good.

"I bet it becomes a fashion for a little while," Sylvain said with satisfaction, once again musing aloud without being conscious of his audience. "Especially as a gift between troubled lovers."

Cade looked immediately at her sheet of plastic, as if the word "*amant*" had brought them onto fragile ground. A bridge of eggshells over a long, plunging gap, maybe, and who knew what was on the other side, because no one ever made it to the other side without breaking through.

She was Cade Corey of Corey, Maryland. A lot of people depended on her. Even to think about the possibility of another "side" was to create an impossibility. And if something was impossible, you might as well give up on it and go home.

She flicked her thumb over her toothbrush, and a speck of green chocolate hit her right in the eye.

Sylvain laughed, low, took her chin, and turned her to him.

She went still under this casual, public possession of her. She thought it was safe to say that every other man outside her family who had ever tried to establish public possession of her had really been trying to establish possession of her fortune.

Her feet felt very bare on those eggshells.

"You've got green dots all over you." He rubbed his thumbs over her cheekbones, then her eyebrows, cleaning her. He was laughing but with something very like affection. She stood motionless almost to the point of not breathing, her eyes open on his face, closing only when his thumb brushed a dot off her eyelashes.

Can I step into your arms and press my body against your body and just stand there, however long I need to? she thought. Because if he would let his arms close around her, she might be able to stand there forever. *Would that be okay?*

But, of course, okay with whom? With what? He would probably take it in stride. He seemed to take women throwing themselves at him pretty well in stride. But would *she* take it in stride?

She turned back to her green spatterings, feeling the brush of his thumbs against her cheeks, eyebrows, eyelashes, for a long time afterward.

Chapter 23

"Are you ready to finish your vacation?" Mack Corey asked hopefully.

"Dad! I've been working most of the time!" At least half the time. "You call that a *vacation*?"

She had just spent the afternoon visiting Chacun son goût, a medium-sized, family-run, French producer of chocolate bars with a reputation for quality. The kind of place her father had recommended they buy out, rather than pursue the Sylvain Marquis premium-chocolate line. It wasn't what she wanted, but it might provide an excuse to spend more time in France.

She wondered what Sylvain would say to her thinking about buying out an entire company just for a personal excuse to stay with a lover in Paris.

He was the lover in question, and it would still probably put his back up right to the skies. Her father wouldn't be too happy about it, either, come to that.

It was, admittedly, deeply irresponsible and self-absorbed behavior. Exactly the kind of thing you might expect of a spoiled billionaire brat.

"Well, you know." Over the Webcam transmission, a hand waved choppily. "Finish visiting Paris and Parisian chocolatiers, and come home. It will be Thanksgiving soon. We miss you."

Thanksgiving was a nice time in the Corey family. Cozy. Full of laughter. It had been a big deal for them, ever since her mother's and grandmother's deaths, to keep those holiday traditions warm and alive. She drew through her fingers the twine that had once tied a bitter chocolate gift. Slowly she wrapped it around her pinky, then unwrapped it. "Dad, don't you think we really have to do something in Europe? Mars is winning the entire market share here."

Mack Corey frowned. "Europeans are so stuck-up, that's why. I can't believe they would go for some chocolate-brushed candy bar instead of real, solid chocolate."

"They don't like our real, solid chocolate. I think we need to either hit them on the fun front, the way Mars does, or go for a solid chocolate that's more sophisticated and closer to their idea of what chocolate should be." She took a quick, deep breath and clutched the twine in her fist. "Maybe that's something I should take on."

A long silence ensued. Long enough for her to hope the Webcam transmission had frozen but also to know it hadn't. "What do you mean, 'take on'? What do you want to 'take on,' exactly?"

Another breath. "Europe."

He stared at her. "I thought you were over there trying to find a new chocolate line to bring back *here*!"

"Yes, but . . . maybe this is more important. We do need to introduce a strong premium chocolate in the US. But it will cost us a fortune to grab any shelf space in Europe against Mars and Total Foods if we don't act soon. If it does work in Europe, we could try introducing it in the US, too, to recapture that growing sophisticated-chocolate-consumer demographic."

"I need you *here*! Your sister is wandering around in the Côte d'Ivoire on a moped again, for God's sake. Who is going to take over this company when I retire?"

Her. Of course, her. That was always understood. She would do a great job of it.

The twine felt damp in her fist. She did not want to go back to her wide, straight road at Corey. She wanted to run off down some twisty path in the woods and see what she found.

"You're fifty, Dad. I'll have plenty of time to catch up. Running Europe would be excellent training."

Running Europe. She saw Sylvain's face at that phrase, his eyes glittering in passionate dispute.

She didn't *want* to run Europe, to fight for shelf space, to visit factories. She wanted to sink her hands into sacks of pistachios and wander markets looking for exotic products. She wanted to visit *laboratoires* and learn their magic. She wanted to build more of what Sylvain had created—beautiful, rich, magical chocolatiers. She did not want to drive them out of business with her superior financial firepower.

There was another long, grim silence. "Look, when you get back here, we'll talk about it. We'll get our market research teams on the idea. Don't forget, we're still keeping an eye on Devon Candy. That would change things considerably in Europe."

It would make their role in Europe exactly what it was in the US—mass producers of baseline chocolate. Of course, she could probably make an argument for staying here if they had Devon Candy.

"I'm not coming back just yet," Cade hedged.

"Sure, take another week. Dad's right: you need to play a little. Plus, I'm sure you're learning a lot about our options. All that groundwork will help if we decide to do anything a few years from now."

"A few years from now?"

Her life suddenly loomed before her like some dark abyss, no Sylvain in it for an indefinite future. Her stomach leaped up into her throat as if she'd been thrown off a cliff into that abyss and was flailing against the fall.

"Depends what we do with Devon Candy, don't you think? Take another week, as I said. Let's talk about it when you get back home for Thanksgiving."

Two more weeks.

Cade felt so sick when she finished the call that she had to leave her apartment to flee the feeling. She walked through the Sixth, trying to feel her way without thinking.

Thinking wasn't working for her. When she thought about things, her father was right.

People brushed past her indifferently as she stopped to gaze at a shop window full of old toys, or to breathe in the scents pouring out of a bakery. Nobody talked much about the scents of Paradise, but if she were designing Heaven, bakeries and *chocolateries* would both contribute. The sewer odor of a *fromagerie* swept over her in contrast, and, trying not to breathe too much, she went in among all the great wheels of cheese and slabs of butter from which the man there carved slices off for her. She watched the *fromager's* face as he told her stories about each cheese and talked her into trying different ones, watched his humor, belief, and passion in his work.

When she got back to her apartment building, Sylvain was just leaving his *laboratoire,* his head tilted back as he looked up at the window of her apartment.

She liked the way his body, when he saw her, seemed to change.

She stopped a foot or two in front of him, still not sure what their greeting was supposed to be. *Bises* on both cheeks? A kiss on the mouth? She opted for thrusting her hands into her pockets and keeping an awkward distance.

His mouth took on that pressed, thin look only the French could do so well.

"You know what I would like to do? I would like to go for a walk," Cade said assertively, so that it didn't come out as if she was *asking* him. She was just stating her preference, that was all. He could join her or not; it was a free country. Well, it was France, but they seemed to think they were a free country, too. She wasn't *asking* him to go for a walk with her—that was the important part.

She wasn't exposing herself that way, putting down shields so that a cool, distant look could batter her fragile insides. He gave one sharp, astonished movement that braked right at the end, as if he wished he hadn't made it quite so sharp and astonished. His dark eyes studied her intently, as if he were chocolate and she was, say, maggoty cheese, and he was wondering what the two could possibly mean when put together.

She felt the flush rising, sneaking up from under her scarf and over her face. Her insides shriveled in the hope that, if they shrank enough, they could disown her entirely, squeeze into that small elevator, and go hide upstairs in her apartment while her outside went around doing things like this that made them regret they had ever been born.

"Tu veux faire une promenade?" he repeated, as if checking her use of his language for possible errors. Those dark eyes continued to study her as if they wanted to melt her down into something he could figure out, but otherwise that inherently controlled, contained face of his gave nothing away. Certainly gave away no sense of sudden overwhelming pleasure at her proposal. "With me?" he checked.

She would just go by herself. Or maybe she would just go up to her apartment and hide. Except it was right over his workshop. Maybe she would curl into a huddled ball in her private jet back to America. Maybe that would be the next best step.

"You want to do something with me besides—?" He broke off. With his hand at belly level, he made a tiny finger-gesture between her and him, between his *chocolaterie* and then upward toward her apartment. Then that same hand turned palm up, open, in blank confusion.

And here she had thought their dinner the night before had shifted their relationship from pure sex to something, maybe, a little more emotional.

Apparently cooking for her was just another way to get sex.

Now that flush of hers felt as red as her scarf, and something even worse created pressure against her eyes: tears. She was always crying in this stupid country. She never cried back home.

"Forget it," she said in English because she couldn't remember how to in French, and she turned on her heel to her door, fisting her hands in her coat pockets.

He caught the sleeve of her coat, yanking her to a stop. "I would like that," he said carefully in English.

She blinked rapidly, setting her jaw against those stupid, wounded tears. His accent and his use of her language totally undid her.

He wormed his hand into her coat pocket until he managed to close it around her gloved one and pull it out, holding her hand in his, two pairs of gloves between their skin. The last time their hands had linked, it had been when he stretched her arm above her head and pinned it to the mattress. With a strangely scared shock, she realized this was the first time they had ever really held hands. "It's a good afternoon for a walk," he said.

That depended. It was cold and gray, with a wind chilling the skin, and with a hint of snow in the air that would probably turn out to be just cold rain. It was a good afternoon for walking hand in hand, nestling something warm and special between two people, knowing that you could go home and curl up with that someone, that you were not alone as winter set in.

Did they know that? Did they know they were not alone as winter set in?

They walked down streets that seemed barely dried from the past night's rain. They passed shops filled with things it might be hard to even imagine anywhere else. One store window showed old wooden stamps for embossing one's own butter, churned from one's own cow. Another held the finest linens, embroidered by hand in purple and filled with lavender. Another store displayed vanilla. Nothing but vanilla beans, from Tahiti, Madagascar, Martinique.

Dusk was falling by the time they reached the river. It was cold, but they were dressed warmly. Sylvain turned their steps left along the upper quays, crossing over the Pont Neuf. The green statue of the equestrian Henry IV rose above them. From below came the sound of a boat chugging, ready to depart with its half load of Paris visitors for a nighttime trip on the Seine.

Cade just looked at things. She had been here only ten days. Every second of evening falling on Paris was a wonder to her.

The lowering light touched the two cones of the medieval Conciergerie, turning them rose and then dark, as if they slipped into a fairy tale. Boats passed, sending shimmers over the night-black water. The occasional skater flew past them, his or her skates making a slick, slicing sound on the pavement. Cafés started to fill as people got off work and stopped to warm up and meet friends. Soft illumination showed off the Louvre, one of the glories of Paris, to all who passed.

The Eiffel Tower gleamed down on the city, sending its searchlight out like a beacon. All at once, it started to fizz. Cade's hand tightened on Sylvain's. "It's sparkling!"

She stopped and leaned against the concrete wall of the quay, watching it. She had only managed to catch that famous hourly ten minutes of sparkling twice before.

He leaned beside her without speaking. When she glanced up at him, her face lit with happiness, he was looking down at her, not the tower. He was smiling a little, but his eyes looked wary, very dark and guarded.

Why?

Maybe he would have just preferred they go straight to the sex and skip the walk.

The Eiffel Tower finished sparkling, and people who had stopped to watch it started moving again. Most hadn't stopped, going about their affairs with that fast, tight Parisian stride. Down the sidewalk from them, a man stood up from a bench, trying to hassle a woman passing in black coat and boots.

Sylvain straightened, but the woman never broke her brisk stride or even looked at the man, and the man shrugged and turned, searching for another possibility.

"I pushed someone into the Seine the other day," Cade confessed with embarrassed satisfaction.

Sylvain gave a startled crack of laughter. *"Vraiment?"*

"He tried to sit on my lap! And grab my—" She gestured at her chest.

He began laughing so hard, he had to clutch his ribs. "So you pushed him into the water? Seriously? *C'est bien fait pour sa gueule, alors.* I wish I could have seen it."

"It probably wouldn't have happened if you could have seen it," she pointed out dryly. "I notice they only go for women by themselves."

"Connards," Sylvain muttered, giving the man in the distance, who had returned to his bench, a dark look. "But it still would have been something to see."

"He grabbed my laptop for balance and took it in with him," she said, still annoyed about that. "Do you know how hard it is to set up a new laptop in French?"

"Ah . . . non," he said, amused. "Do you need help?"

"I got Corey's technical services to overnight me a new one," she admitted.

He raised an eyebrow at her.

"I can't just let the guy in the store set up my computer, you know," she said defensively. "Company security."

"I could have helped you. You couldn't possibly think I would try to steal any of your secrets."

He didn't say that as if it was a question of his honesty, but a question of some more important honor—Corey Chocolate didn't have any secrets Sylvain Marquis thought worth stealing.

Not even, apparently, the secret to how to make serious money.

She shook her head ruefully. She didn't doubt him. But helping set up her computer sounded like something someone in another life, a life without a horde of assistants, might have a boyfriend do.

She slid him a glance. Chantal seemed very far away right now; it was inconceivable that she could be his girlfriend. But inconceivable also that Cade would ask him about Chantal and risk spoiling this moment.

"So why are you by yourself?" he asked suddenly. "Speaking of security. Shouldn't you have a bodyguard?" He gave the man on the bench another dark glance as they passed him. The man never noticed, eyeing a woman on the opposite side of the street with casual avarice.

"Not in Paris. There are a lot of wealthy people in Paris. And I'm not recognizable. I always thought Paris Hilton was nuts to go that route. Do you know that she actually could have had a private life?" Cade shook her hand in wonder at other people's choices.

"I don't think there are *that* many people here as wealthy as you," Sylvain said dryly.

"I bet if you calculated it, Paris has a higher percentage of the rich or famous than anywhere else in the world. Some of those Dubai princes who have apartments here probably think I'm middle-class. And you're pretty well-off yourself, from one perspective, and more famous than I am, I think."

"Well . . . I don't know about *famous*." Sylvain completely failed in his attempt at pretend modesty. He shook his head incredulously. "And to think I grew up *en banlieue*."

What was that non sequitur about? He had mentioned it before. "So did I, I guess. Corey is not a very big town, really. It's all suburbs, in a way."

Sylvain gave her a very dry look. "If you grew up in a *banlieue*, it was one like St-Germain-des-prés, which doesn't even properly deserve the name. I grew up in Créteil."

"And what was Créteil like?" Cade asked carefully, because obviously she was missing something.

He shrugged. "*L'exemple classique*. Bad schools, drugs, violence, no jobs, no prospects, no money, no way out; people burned cars pretty regularly. But the thing was, it wasn't everyone. You just had to work your way through that image people had of your life and become something else. That's what I try to remind Malik."

Cade stared at him. She would never have imagined this lean, elegant man, with his hands that could turn raw ingredients into something beautiful, with his unshakable arrogance when it came to his art, with his beautiful, perfect French that made her accent seem so embarrassingly awkward and American, with his passion, with his discreet but clear sense of style, with the way he kept such civilized control of his expression most of the time . . . she would never have imagined him as coming from anywhere but a cultivated, elegant milieu.

"You don't know how strange it sounds," he said, "to hear you say that someone would consider you middle-class."

Okay, maybe she had exaggerated. Cade felt herself flushing as she realized how that must have come across.

"But you have money now," she pointed out. "Surely." She saw the people lining up at his store, and she could do the math on one hundred euros a kilo. She was good at profit-margin math.

"Of course I do. I have all I need. But it's not the same class of income at all. You don't become a multimillionaire with chocolate, you know."

Cade stared at him until it became obvious that she was going to have to spell it out. Preferably by pounding the letters into his head with a large hammer. "No, I don't know that," she said instead with what she thought was commendable mildness.

"With real chocolate," he corrected himself.

She gritted her teeth. "Have you ever given serious thought to how much money multiple millions *are*?" Because maybe if he gave it some proper thought, she could talk him into accepting them for the right to create a chocolate line in his name. She would bet *that* would gain her a foothold in Europe. And she could run the European division, from Paris. . . .

"Not really," he said. "I can't really imagine anything I could buy that would make my life better."

Wow, was all she could think. He said that so calmly, so easily, as if he really had made his life that good, good enough that he spent no time envying someone else's greater wealth or possessions. That was so rare in life.

He hesitated, opened his mouth, then closed it again.

"Imagine something?" she said dryly.

"I—don't think I could buy it," he said slowly. Then he grinned suddenly, a small, quick grin that flashed through her like lightning, leaving silver traces of pleasure on her emotions. "Or if I could, it's with something I have plenty of."

Meaning—what? He wanted something that could be bought with chocolate?

A weird hope stirred deep within her, and she immediately started smacking it out as hard as she could. Because *she* could be bought with chocolate, or at least strongly tempted. But she hardly thought she was what he had in mind.

They kept walking, strolling through centuries of history,

between the Palais du Louvre and the old railway station of the Musée d'Orsay, past the gilt and glamour of the Pont Alexandre III, with its golden statues and ornate lamps that made Cade feel as if she should be wearing bustle and button boots and stepping out of a carriage at the opera. Twingos and Smarts and Porsches passed them, lights slicing through the dimness. A biker went by, serious, equipped, his head bent low, expensive orange gear protecting him from the cold.

They walked through quiet, as the activity in the streets pulled back from the Seine and shifted a few streets over to the Champs-Élysées. Although it was still early, it felt like true night by the time they reached the Trocadéro opposite the Seine from the Eiffel Tower. Cade's booted feet were killing her, but she never mentioned it.

Sylvain tugged her hand, leading her up to the esplanade above the extraordinary Varsovie fountain. From that vantage point, the fountain cascaded over steps and played in great jets below the gleaming iron symbol of romance and civilization that dominated their view.

"So why chocolate?" she asked.

It seemed like a silly question. Why did everybody else in the world not choose chocolate as a life path: that was the more logical question. How could they resist it?

"I've always loved it. I love working with it." He gave her a teasing look. "Women can't resist it."

He said that as if to make her laugh, but it didn't make her feel like laughing. "The way to a woman's heart?" she said dryly, trying not to show how much it bothered her to be just one of many women whose hearts were reached so easily.

His hand flexed on hers through their gloves. He studied his city's glowing tower. "Women's hearts are a little more complicated than their senses. So, no. I can't say I've figured out the way to a woman's heart."

"Have you tried?"

He didn't answer. He gazed across the water at the Tour Eiffel and glanced down once at her and didn't say anything.

A clean, elegant jaw in profile softly lit by a street lamp, dark eyes darker in the night, and black hair being stirred in the breeze—maybe that was a poetic enough response all by itself.

It didn't give her a clue, though.

Chapter 24

They stopped to eat in a bistro neither of them knew. Warm light and noise spilled out of it into the street, its small space stuffed full of people who looked happy.

It bore no resemblance to the formal dining experience she had imagined taking him out for. It was better. There was no quiet, no elegance in this bistro. The food ran to *pavés de boeuf, frites,* and *sauces au Roquefort.* It was a little over-warm, and people's butts kept bumping them every time someone had to squeeze in or out of a table nearby. The wall past Sylvain's head looked as if someone had started to paint a scene on it once, ten years ago, gotten distracted halfway through the first leg of the Eiffel Tower, and never gotten back to it. The wine the waiter brought to their table had no visible dust on it and was only a few years old, not the usual type of bottle brought to Cade's table.

It was perfect. She couldn't remember ever feeling so perfect.

They lingered for hours. Sylvain took the check absently, not making sure she would notice, not even really caring, and then they finally could linger no longer in the warmth, amid the tables of laughing, happy, well-fed people, and stepped out again into the cold. Cade shivered violently at the first impact of it, and Sylvain smiled and tucked her scarf up to her chin.

"Shall we catch a taxi?" she asked reluctantly. It was a long walk back and must be after eleven, and her feet were throbbing angrily, bitter about her attempts to imitate Parisian women with her high-heeled boots. But she did hate for this evening to end.

Near the bistro was a row of heavy, awkward-looking, plated bikes, all lodged safely in their rental stations, all with handlebar baskets and marked with *VÉLIB* and the logo of Paris. Cade had seen these before, in her discovery of Paris, the bicycles the city made available free to anyone who wanted. These particular ones were sporting pink latex seat-covers and the sign, *ET VOUS, VOUS FAITES QUOI POUR VOUS PROTÉGER? And you, what do you do to protect yourself?*

"A group of AIDS activists has been here, I think," Sylvain said at her confused look. He nodded at the handlebars, which sported a different sign. "An anti-hunger association has passed, too, I see." He paused before the pseudo-condom seats and suddenly smiled and caught her eye. "Do you know how to ride a bike?"

She wasn't really dressed for it, with her long coat and her boots, but by dint of much bundling of the coat under her butt and around her legs, she managed an uncomfortable seat on what must be the world's heaviest bike. She left the pink latex on it. If she had started running into bicycle seats wearing condoms, odds were good God was trying to tell her something about sex and stupidity. "These things must weigh over ten kilos!"

He nodded. "To make sure no one wants to steal them."

It was freezing cold with the wind chill on the bike, even with her nose buried as far as possible in her scarf. But it was crazy fun. She kept laughing, and he kept glancing over at her and breaking into a grin of pure delight.

They dropped the bikes off at a station near his apartment and fled the November night into warmth.

"Oh, my God, that's cold," she kept saying in his apartment, unable to stop shivering as the warmth hit her frozen skin. "That's cold, that's cold, that's cold."

He stripped off her clothes over her protests and bundled her into the bed, still laughing. He buried her under the heavy down comforter, dropped his own clothes onto the floor, and joined her under there, wrapping her up in his body until she went from shivering to melting.

He sure did know how to control the temperature of things, she thought later as she fell asleep, nestled in the curve of his arm, perfectly warm, perfectly content.

Chapter 25

"I have good news and bad news," Sylvain said the next morning.

Her heart lurched. She had known he would let her know he was just playing with her eventually. He was simply too sexy for any one woman. "What's the bad news?"

He hesitated. "Maybe I should just tell you the news, and you figure out which part you think is horrible and which part sounds like fun."

She braced warily over her yogurt. Her barely sweetened yogurt. The first time in ten days that she tried to be healthy for breakfast, and he chose that moment to break mixed-up news to her. That was just wrong.

"We're invited to a birthday party."

She looked even more suspicious. "By whom? What do you mean 'we'?"

His lips pressed together. "Okay, so I'm invited to a birthday party. Typically, I can bring someone with me. Is that a problem? You would rather not come?"

She didn't really date much. She hadn't in a long time. This sounded like a date. No, this sounded like introducing a girlfriend to a group of friends.

Maybe they did that kind of thing casually in France?

"Whose party?"

"My cousin Thierry, who's turning fifty."

Introducing a girlfriend to *family*. She felt as if she had been driving along on a rather twisty road and suddenly found the bottom dropping out of the world and realized she was on a roller coaster.

She didn't really do family meetings. She had avoided them assiduously since her high school years, because the pure, avaricious pressure of a date's family could be so ghastly. She didn't really do any kind of thing, actually—neither dating, nor meeting friends and family, nor even sex—since swearing off hook-ups when she got out of college.

Until . . . whatever she was doing now, of course. Maybe if she were more normal, she would *know* what she was doing.

"Who will be there?"

He waved a hand vaguely. "Oh, *tout le monde.*"

"What do you mean, *everybody*?"

"The whole family. Friends. It's his fiftieth birthday."

"Is your mother coming up from Provence?"

"It's his fiftieth birthday!"

"She is." Cade wrapped her arms around herself protectively. "Does she know who I am?"

"Cade, everybody knows who you are. My mother has a Google Alert on my name. If you don't want to become notorious, you need to think twice before you start breaking into someone's business and trying to steal his chocolate."

Cade blinked a few times. "I actually was wondering if she knew my alternate identity. Not the Chocolate Thief one."

"Tu as une identité alternative?" Sylvain looked confused.

Cade drummed her fingers and tried for patience, without much success. "You know, I wasn't best known as a Chocolate Thief until a couple of days ago."

He studied her the way a psychologist might study a very perplexing patient. "You consider Cade Corey and the Chocolate Thief as two separate identities?"

"Can you just answer the question? Does your mother know how much money I have?"

"C'est possible," Sylvain admitted. "Is it public record? Could she find it on the Internet?"

In other words, yes. Cade slumped. "I didn't mean an exact figure."

There was a moment of silence. "Are you surviving?" Sylvain asked acerbically. "Because I haven't even gotten to the part *I* thought you might think was bad news yet."

She put her hands on the edge of the table and pushed herself back against the chair, bracingly.

"The party is at their *château* in Champagne, which is about an hour's drive—"

"A castle?" she interrupted. "Weren't you telling me about your *banlieue* childhood?"

"Are *châteaux* expensive in the US or something? You could buy about six of them for what this Paris apartment cost. Good luck with the upkeep, though. Anyway, Thierry PACSed with a CEO."

"He did what with a CEO?" *Pax Romana?*

"PACS. It's a legal ceremony," Sylvain added at her blank look. "Between two people who don't quite want to go as far as marriage or, in their case, aren't allowed to by law. They're gay."

Cade rubbed the ridge between her eyebrows, trying to find her footing. "I'm still waiting for what you think is the bad news."

"Ah." He took a breath. "Brace yourself. We have to go disguised as farmers."

Cade couldn't stop laughing. They had stopped at a big store off the Paris *périmètre* and found the most hideous green waterproof ensembles that enclosed them ankle to wrist, *en vrai paysan,* as Sylvain had said. On top of that, they had added old-fashioned little brimmed caps. Over their feet, they had pulled on rain boots in vivid yellow. Under it all, they wore normal, attractive, comfortable clothes, which Sylvain said they should be able to unveil eventually. He didn't say when.

"Why do we have to wear these things again?"

"I believe I may be the only person in my family to not be a complete show-off at every opportunity," Sylvain said darkly, making Cade burble with laughter again.

"What?" he asked blankly.

"You think you don't show off?" She tried to make her snorts of amusement come out halfway delicate and refined. The yellow rain boots were affecting her risibility, she decided. It would be damaging to the morale to keep a straight face while wearing those.

"I was very shy as a teenager," he said loftily.

Cade thought of the showmanship with which he worked chocolate. She thought of the completely unabashed way in which he had seduced her that morning she had gate-crashed his workshop. "It must have been a very brief phase."

He gave her a puzzled look, making her wonder if she was missing something important about him. "I'm still shy."

She burst out laughing, unable to help herself. "*You* are shy?"

He shrugged and focused on the road again, not trying to argue her into believing him.

What *was* she missing? Why did he think he was shy? Was he being shy with her in some way? "So what does showing off have to do with wearing these ghastly outfits?"

"They like to dress up. Last New Year, my mother and sister made the three of us all wear cow costumes. Complete with udders." He sounded completely put-upon, but she felt quite certain no one could make him do anything he didn't want to do.

Cade tried to imagine the elegant, passionate Sylvain Mar-

quis in a cow costume with udders. It was surprisingly easy
to do. In her image, he was having the time of his life, grinning at the dark-haired sister she had seen in his photo album.

Something about the image made her body clench on a
sense of free fall, as if suddenly discovering her heart had
been yanked right out of it.

"And for Papa's retirement, we had to do a skit that required me to act out the roles of a gangster, a cowboy, and a
brown spotted mongrel—Papa's first dog—in the space of
five minutes. All my sister's fault, I promise you."

Yeah, right. She would bet he had come up with half those
roles himself. So *why* did he think he was shy? "You should
see the skit my sister and I did for my grandfather's eightieth
birthday. If you get me drunk enough, I might show you the
video."

He raised those demonically expressive eyebrows at her.
"You think I have to resort to liquor to get what I want out
of you?"

She pretended to hit him. But they were both smiling.

"The farmer aspect of the showing off is because my
cousin has always dreamed of having goats."

Cade blinked a few minutes, trying to imagine dreaming
of having goats. Then she tried to layer that onto previous
imaginings of the French castle they were driving to. Either
way, her imagination quite failed at the goats.

"So we have all joined together—to give him goats. Also
a flock of ducks. He wanted a donkey, too, but his partner
begged us to show reason. And in keeping with the theme,
we are all dressing up as farmers."

A crazy and enthusiastic family that lived life to the fullest.

If they never learned who she was, she could have fun.
"Can you introduce me under an assumed name?"

Sylvain didn't dignify that with an answer.

The van cut through the smooth, gently rolling countryside. Stone houses clustered in tiny villages, laundry hanging out to dry even in November. Poplars lined the road, something about their straight, endless elegance evoking a deep, soft pleasure in Cade. Sylvain had given his little Audi a wistful look but taken the shop van because it could carry the elaborate and enormous sculpture in chocolate he was bringing, a fantastical structure almost impossible to believe in. Had he been making that all afternoon while she was visiting Chacun son goût? She wished she had been in his *laboratoire* to see him as chocolate sculptor.

She would guarantee he would have done it intensely, with care and passion, and imagining his hands at the work sent warm sensuality curling through her.

Her phone buzzed, surprising her that there was reception.

Her grandfather burst out with no preamble: "What have you been telling your father? You're supposed to be taking a break! Exploring! You're not supposed to try to stay over there!"

"Grandpa, I thought you always complained that Dad didn't let me see the world enough." She glanced sideways at Sylvain, wondering how much English he understood.

"I'm eighty-two years old," Grandpa Jack said petulantly. "How many times do you think I'm going to see you again if you *live* in Europe?"

All her life, she and her grandfather had seen each other every day. They all lived in different wings of the great white house on the hilltop above Corey. He stopped by her office at work. He barged into her room at home and woke her up to sample his latest experiment, his blue eyes gleaming with delight.

And if she moved to Paris, the times she would see him again would be countable. Plane trees flew by, blurring in front of her vision as she stared at them without tracking.

"I'm sure I would be flying back and forth all the time," she said weakly, around what felt like a knife in her heart.

Sylvain's hands tightened suddenly on the wheel. He glanced sideways.

"Plus, you have to come over here, right? I have to show you the trick of breaking into some of these French *chocolateries*. If I did stay in Europe, which . . . I'm just talking about options, right now. "

Sylvain slid another sharp glance at her.

"Europe is full of snobs," her grandfather said definitely.

Yes, but she liked those snobs. She studied the strong, clean line of Sylvain's jaw, the thin, sensual mouth, the eyebrows that could be so expressive. In a collage around him, she seemed to see the faces of all the other chocolatiers she had met, and the bakers, and the *fromagers*. She liked their attitude and belief in individuality and being the best.

"Who would you rather see every day?" Jack Corey asked with a wheedling tone. "A bunch of snobs or your grandfather?"

Cade felt as if her stomach had been stuck between two stones that were now slowly grinding together. "Grandpa, I just . . ." She just what? What part of this did she want to even try to articulate to herself, much less to her grandfather? "I'm just looking at options."

Sylvain's mouth flexed hard and grimly.

"Well, look at them in a few years! When I'm gone," he said bluntly. "What's your hurry?"

Oh. Those stones grinding her stomach hurt. "Mars," she mumbled. "Market share." And if Sylvain . . . if Sylvain what? She glanced at him again. Damn it, she was so *goal*-oriented sometimes, she didn't even know how to have a casual affair with a man.

"You know, Cadey, I used to care about Mars. Turned your father into a damned workaholic over Mars. I don't mean to bore you with the fact that I'm old enough now to be smarter than all of you, because, well—you know that already. I still want to beat Mars. But I'll put family before market share any day."

There was a careful silence after he disconnected, and Cade slipped her phone back into her purse.

"You're thinking of staying in Europe?" Sylvain asked at last. His voice was very neutral.

Would it have killed him to express bright hope and delight? "I'm looking at options."

His hands flexed around the wheel. His mouth tightened.

She pressed her forehead to the cold window and stared out at the plane trees.

To reach the *château*, they ducked off the highway down a tiny street between stone houses, Sylvain driving with complete confidence, despite the fact that from her vantage point it looked as if they had an inch to spare between the side mirrors and the stone walls. The street twisted for about two hundred yards, right up to a tall green gate only just wide enough to fit through.

"Apparently the previous owners were afraid to have a wider gate because it made it easy for thieves to bring in a truck and clean them out," Sylvain said. He parked the van on white gravel by the edge of the courtyard, and they climbed out.

Cade gazed at a beautiful white façade, peeling here and there but over all well maintained, white lace veiling dozens of great windows behind iron railings. "Napoléon III," Sylvain mentioned. It loomed stately and graceful above the mob of peasants that milled below it.

Gleeful peasants.

Who were suddenly swarming them. Cade ducked at the onslaught of bobbing pitchforks.

"Oup, pardon," said one pitchfork wielder and planted the prongs in the gravel. She suddenly found herself in an extensive round of *bises* with more would-be farmers than she had ever met in her life. Some wore overalls and carried straw in their teeth. Some wore great floppy hats and huge sunflowers. Some had colorful suspenders and rain boots. Some, a little abashed, wore jeans and an apologetic baseball cap as the best they could come up with. From the far end of the courtyard, a tall, thin man appeared loaded with hoes and shovels to pass around.

"Seriously, don't tell them my name," Cade begged one last time in Sylvain's ear.

"Maman!" Sylvain exclaimed, ignoring Cade's comment for the pitiful attempt it was. "Where's Papa? How was the trip?"

A woman who looked as if the quintessence of elegance had been trapped in overalls three sizes too big for her embraced Sylvain hard, pressing her cheek for a long time against each of his, four times over. *"Ça va, mon petit choux?"*

"Maman, this is Cade Corey."

Bastard, Cade thought. She had always known he deserved to be robbed blind.

The woman looked like an older version of Chantal—hair a little shorter, as suited her age, and the blond was probably dyed but perfectly coiffed and elegantly feathered. She was dressed in the thrifty chic Parisian women seemed to do so well, as if elegance had everything to do with taste, and nothing to do with money, although at a guess, Sylvain had given her that Dior scarf which added the perfect touch of color to her outfit. Her makeup was subtle and effective, and glasses helped disguise the laughter and smoke lines around the corners of her eyes. She gave Cade two air kisses, not letting their cheeks touch. "So you're the thief," she said flatly.

Sylvain, *the complete and utter bastard,* was already turning away to clasp some man's hand, to be kissed by someone else, laughing.

"It's complicated," Cade said.

Perfectly plucked eyebrows rose. And waited.

"I had to do something dramatic to catch his attention," Cade said hurriedly. "He said the chocolate was more important than I was."

"And was he right?" Marguerite Marquis asked unanswerably.

Cade was still stuck trying to figure out the answer when a bright voice exclaimed by her shoulder: "*Bonjour!* Are you the Chocolate Thief? I haven't heard nearly enough about you. *Je m'appelle Natalie.*"

"My sister," Sylvain reappeared to explain, as a slim, dark-haired young woman around twenty kissed Cade's cheeks.

The man who had been distributing hoes and shovels stopped before them. He wore a big floppy hat, from under which peeked perfectly cut, perfectly silvered hair. His huge black rain boots were splattered with mud and straw, old and new, as if they clearly got a lot of use. "You must be Cade Corey. I'm Fréd—Fréderic Delaube. Welcome to our *château.*" He bent to kiss her cheeks with such perfect, urbane hospitality that Cade relaxed all over. "Would you like a hoe?"

"*Tiens.*" Sylvain handed Cade a pair of old work gloves. "To complete the look. Have you met Papa yet? Cade, *je te présente Hervé, mon père.*"

A tall, graying man with plenty of laugh lines around his eyes gave her *bises*—four *bises*—that more than made up for his wife's in enthusiasm. "Trust Sylvain to always find the prettiest women around!" he exclaimed, so warmly that Cade couldn't help liking him for his attempt to compliment her.

Then she thought that compliment through. How many

pretty women did Sylvain routinely show up with at his family parties?

"*Merci,* Papa," Sylvain said, looking rather pleased at the praise, oblivious to the fact that she might not care to be one of a plethora of pretty women. "Can you help me carry the sculpture in? Fréd says Thierry will be here in fifteen minutes."

Oohs and *aahs* greeted the appearance of Sylvain's fantastical sculpture, great wings and whimsies of white, dark, and colored chocolate curling and soaring around a small female goat curled up in the center, her legs folded under her, all carved out of chocolate. The crowd of pseudo-peasants gathered around it in a corridor of acclaim, cameras flashing, as Sylvain and Hervé started toward the *château.*

"So, how much longer are you staying in Paris?" Marguerite asked Cade in the sweetest and friendliest of tones, as the two men disappeared into the house. "You can't stay away from your business very long, can you? You must be going back any day now."

It was going to be a long weekend.

While Sylvain and his father were settling the sculpture onto a red-draped table in the center of a nineteenth-century salon, Marguerite kindly took her on a little tour of some of the other pieces in the room. Period glass-faced cabinets displayed precious crystal and family photos.

"This is one of my favorites," Marguerite said, opening the glass to pull it out so Cade could get a better look. "Last New Year's. We all dressed up as cows—it was *à mourir de rire.*"

It apparently was, in fact, *à mourir de rire,* because everyone in the photo was dying laughing. All three cows—Marguerite, Natalie, and Sylvain—plus a fourth person. In this photo, Sylvain was not, as she had imagined, grinning at his sister. He was laughing down at Chantal, who wore not a cow costume but something black and sexy, and who clung to his cow hoof as she laughed up at him.

Cade looked up from the photo to study Sylvain's mother a moment. Marguerite looked innocently back at her.

"Amazing," Cade said mildly.

"What is?" Marguerite asked happily.

"How anyone could look so good in a cow costume." Cade handed the photo back to her and left Marguerite trying to figure out whether she should take the compliment for herself or on behalf of her children.

The goats and farmers were a huge success. Thierry, as short and stout as his partner, Fréd, was tall and lean, was so delighted to find a horde of peasants awaiting him when he drove up that he nearly cried. Cameras flashed from all directions.

"Cade Corey!" Thierry exclaimed when Sylvain introduced them. "*Vraiment? Ta voleuse de chocolat, Sylvain?* I'm impressed. You've finally brought someone interesting."

It was all Cade could do not to let her shoulders slump. She was starting to feel like a fighter who had taken one too many to the gut. So. It clearly wasn't uncommon for Sylvain to bring women he was dating to family parties. She was as pretty as the others and maybe a tad more interesting, according to his family, but she wasn't any kind of special case.

Her feet felt heavy, pulled down by ubiquitous mud, as they tramped through the gracious, soggy gardens to a fenced area that held four little goats and a brand-new goat house with a heart carved in its door.

"So, tell me a little bit more about breaking and entering." Natalie leaned beside Cade on the fence. "Do you use a rappeling cord?"

"Actually, officially, I haven't been breaking and entering."

"What?" She looked disappointed.

"Her lawyers don't want her to admit to it," Sylvain explained, reappearing by Cade's side. "Cade, please don't tell my sister how to break and enter."

"I would only do it for a joke, Sylvain," Natalie said indignantly. "I don't have time for that kind of thing. I'm always studying. Has he mentioned I'm getting my degree in business?" she asked Cade ever so casually. Sylvain, who seemed to be widely loved amid his family, had already had his attention claimed by another cousin.

"Really?" Cade felt as if she had been parachuted straight back to her comfort zone. Talking to a woman whose son she was dating—that was horribly uncomfortable. People trying to establish their careers via party talk with her—that she understood. "What area interests you particularly?"

"I'm still exploring," Natalie said cheerfully. "Doing different *stages*."

Ah. Cade fed a handful of hay to a little goat with big, mischievous eyes. "Internships, huh?" She—well, Corey Chocolate—had been considered a source of them since she was in middle school.

"And I've got some chocolate experience. Sylvain let me do an internship with him when I was in high school. So I combine qualifications in both business and gourmet chocolate."

"And she's irrepressible," Sylvain mentioned dryly, reappearing. "That's a warning, not a selling point."

"Excellent." Cade laughed. "I like that in an intern."

If there was one thing worse than being a woman's "option," it was being grateful for it, Sylvain thought, his hand flexing too hard around the butcher knife, giving an unfamiliar awkwardness to his cutting.

But at least surrounded by family and laughter, he could ignore that for a while. He set Cade to slicing mushrooms beside him, partly because whenever he left her to her own devices, he didn't know what would happen next. His mother might slip poison into her wine. His sister Natalie might hand her a CV. And there seemed infinite potential for fatal combinations of too much alcohol and too many pitchforks. It was pretty much impossible to get his entire family to behave for a whole weekend.

But mostly, he just liked having her cut mushrooms beside him. He liked being able to let his body graze hers from time to time. He liked the careful concentration with which she cut, as if she was afraid she could get a slice wrong if she didn't pay attention.

He just liked having her be a part of this warm, happy, boisterous kitchen, as they all helped get the buffet tables filled and the guests fed.

This was the kind of thing he loved. He wouldn't miss a party with his family for the world. Everyone was in a good mood, everyone was laughing, everyone was pouring out energy in order to give Thierry the best fiftieth birthday they could.

"Yes, you keep an eye on that thief of yours! Don't let her steal anything!" one of his cousins shouted.

Sylvain laughed, and Cade looked rueful. Unable to help himself, he slipped a hand around the nape of her neck and kissed her, hard. He surfaced from that to find about five people openly analyzing them—including his mother, his father, and his sister. None of them looked in the least abashed. His mother didn't even have the grace to look away, just continued to study them critically.

He left the kitchen to add a tray of hors d'oeuvres to the great spread set out on the tables in the nineteenth-century salon. When he got back, one of his uncles had taken over his cutting board next to Cade.

"I understand you're interested in artisan food production. My son wants to become a baker," his uncle was saying.

"A baker *and* a chocolatier in the family?" Cade smiled. "How much better does it get?"

"But it's hard to get the financing to open his shop," his

uncle said delicately. A slight flush rose to his cheeks. Sylvain realized what Tonton Fabien was trying to do for the sake of his son—ask a barely-met billionaire to invest in the twenty-year-old's future bakery.

He flinched for his uncle.

Cade, however, seemed to take this conversation as a matter of course. "Yes, financing for small businesses is tricky. In France, it's not that easy to open a business, is it?"

"Something like that would be a great investment for . . . somebody," Tonton Fabien said gamely. "He's a good baker. He's just about finished his apprenticeship."

"Can I nudge you aside, *Tonton*?" Sylvain asked easily, reaching an arm between the two for his chef's knife. "I need to slice these lemons for the salmon. Oh—would you mind checking in the *cave* to see if they have more *crème fraîche*? I don't see any in the refrigerator."

His uncle left with an expression of relief, and Cade raised an eyebrow at Sylvain.

"Does that kind of thing happen to you a lot at parties?" Sylvain asked, keeping his voice low enough to not embarrass his uncle in front of the rest of the family.

"What kind of thing?"

"Strangers trying to get you to finance their projects?"

"Sure." She thought about it for a moment. "Just out of curiosity, what do other people get to talk about with strangers at parties?"

"In France, usually food."

She laughed. "Well, see, I got both at once, then." She finished cutting her mushrooms and moved around Sylvain to rinse her fingers. Sylvain shifted imperceptibly so that her arms ended up grazing his body. "But he raises a good point," she mentioned seriously. "*Boulangers, fromagers,* chocolatiers—maybe artisan food making needs what other artists need—people willing to invest in it to make sure it can continue to flourish. A patron, in a sense."

"A *patron*? As in *noblesse oblige*?"

"A patron of the arts." Cade looked a little annoyed.

"No one patronized me," Sylvain said coolly, deliberately changing the word. "And I didn't need anyone to, either."

"Well, of course, *you* didn't," she said impatiently, oblivious to the compliment inherent in that impatience.

He tried to keep his mouth straight and stern, just so no one could see the foolish pride that licked from his toes to the roots of his hair.

But his father, reaching past them for the *fleur de sel* just as she said it, smiled a little.

"I can't believe you brought her here," Marguerite Marquis told Sylvain indignantly later in the evening, having dragged him out on her smoke break. Sylvain didn't smoke. Around the time most teens started, he was getting into chocolate. His senses of taste and smell were too precious to him. "The woman who stole from you! And I'm supposed to be nice to her?"

Inside, people were still lingering at the buffet, but Natalie was trying to get some speakers hooked up and music going.

"You could try, *Maman*." Actually, Cade seemed to be handling his mother's barely veiled hostility quite comfortably. Did that mean she didn't care what his mother thought of her, or that she had expected worse?

"I like her," his father said unexpectedly.

Marguerite gave him an indignant look. "*Juste parce qu'elle est jolie.* He's had much prettier girlfriends, don't you think?"

Maybe technically. But they didn't blush the same way when he looked at them, and to get what they wanted, they only flirted and looked pretty. They didn't break into his heart.

"First of all, I like the fact that she seems to think extremely highly of him," Hervé said calmly.

"*Tu penses?*" Sylvain sent his father a sharp look, wondering what his father had observed that he hadn't. He could feel himself starting to blush. *Putain*. In front of his own parents.

"And I like that she took such a risk for him. Prison, public scandal. What did she tell you, Margo? That she couldn't get his attention any other way?"

Vraiment? Sylvain felt a jolt of electricity run through his entire body.

"True," Marguerite admitted, tilting her head consideringly. "Open crime is certainly a dramatic gesture." She said that like a Roman empress still hesitating on which way to turn her thumb over a dramatic gesture. "Blunt, though. They don't teach women how to flirt in her country?"

"Her way works for me," Sylvain said cheerfully. "Did she really say she did it to get my *attention*? Not my chocolate?"

His mother gave him a disgusted look. "Do you *like* getting your heart broken?"

"No," Sylvain said flatly. "I really, really don't."

"I blame you for this, you know," Marguerite told Hervé.

"*Moi?* I told him at least twenty times to improve the security on his *chocolaterie*."

"Not that. The fact that he's so *naïf* about women. You were exactly the same way."

"It's true," Hervé confided to his son. "I haven't wanted to tell you this about your mother until you got older, but she was and is . . . *difficile*."

"And I don't even try," his mother said proudly. "It comes naturally."

"*Naïf* I may be, but I like your Cade," Hervé said again.

His Cade. Sylvain wondered what she would think of the possessive.

"She knows how to be diplomatic to your mother, she can negotiate international business deals, she went down into a spider-filled *cave* to help us haul up Champagne a few minutes ago, and she can break in to places. Those are good skill sets. I think the only one of those we already had covered in the family was the ability to haul up Champagne."

"*I* am the one being diplomatic *to her,*" Marguerite argued, annoyed. "Just in case."

Sylvain caught his mother's eyes, smiling a little. "Just in case what, *Maman?*"

Marguerite sniffed, indignant at being pushed. "Just in case she does turn out to be . . . worthwhile." Offended at having had to admit that she considered that a possibility, she stubbed out her cigarette and strolled away loftily to speak to people less likely to force anything annoying out of her.

Father and son looked after her. "Do I seem *naïf* to you?" Hervé finally asked Sylvain indignantly.

"According to *Maman,* how would I know?" Sylvain asked dryly.

"*Enfin, bon.* I guess I can't guarantee you won't get your heart broken, but maybe at least it will be mutual this time. I have to say, a Chocolate Thief seems worth breaking your heart over."

Inside, Natalie had gotten the speakers working, and his twenty-year-old sister's selection of music suddenly blazed out. Sylvain laughed and grabbed Cade's hand, pulling her onto the dance floor of white marble tile surrounded by delicate, spindle-legged sofas and age-softened brocade chairs pushed back against the walls.

Natalie had gone all out in her playlist of music from the past fifty years. It boomed through one speaker and crackled erratically through another as they did line dances and tugged up the collars of pretend leather jackets to ham it up to songs from *Grease.* Sylvain and Cade danced without stop. Cade's *joie de vivre* seemed indefatigable. She did a really excellent chicken dance, too.

At around one, they slipped outside into instant peace and

tranquility, feet crunching on white gravel beneath the starry skies.

Sylvain led Cade down through the gardens that sloped below the *château* to the Marne below. They slipped out a gate beside a little fairy-tale conical house that might once have been a chapel and found themselves on a muddy path running along the great, wide river.

"It's freezing." He adjusted her scarf to make sure no bare throat appeared. "But I wanted you to see this."

Under the light of the full moon, the Marne flowed dark and deceptively slowly, the light shining off its water. A weeping willow trailed bare, fine, winter tresses over the bank beside them. Cade leaned against him as they watched the water.

Maybe she was seeking contact with him, or maybe she was only seeking warmth in the cold. Maybe her feet hurt. He didn't ask and didn't care, because he liked being her warmth, the strength against which she rested.

His life had felt so different only two weeks before. It had felt like a great life. And now, if or when he had to go back to that life without her in it, it was going to feel like the most miserable, wretched life in the world.

"I like your family," she mentioned.

His eyebrows rose. "Really? Even my mother?"

"Yes. She doesn't seem to like me at all," Cade said wonderingly.

"And that's an endearing trait?"

Cade nodded. "Most mothers like me right away, whether or not their sons would be happy with me."

Sylvain gave that considerable thought. "You're used to being able to buy even *mothers*?"

She shrugged.

"No wonder you keep thinking you can buy Paris."

She sighed. "Just a spot in it, really."

He didn't know what to say to that. He wasn't for sale, but he would be her spot in Paris anytime she asked. Surely that was obvious at this point?

God, he couldn't take much more of this, the fear that she would leave him. But how could he ask someone he had known less than two weeks to promise to give up her life for him?

He tightened his arm around her and stared at the water, willing himself to patience. *It's just like tempering chocolate,* he told himself. *Just like that. You have to take your time.* Maybe he could ask her after *three* weeks. Was that long enough to foster a commitment?

A thin stream of cloud drifted across the moon, creating a play of light and shadow over the water. He felt a long, long sigh run through Cade's body, pressed against his.

She closed her hand around his on her waist. "Seriously, I can't persuade you to give me your name?"

For two whole, thick, thudding heartbeats, he thought she meant something else. He almost said yes.

His lips had parted on it when he remembered what she wanted from him. "You mean, sell you my name for a chocolate line." He moved away from her abruptly, to the edge of the dark, gilded water. The side against which her warmth had been pressed felt very cold.

Her eyebrows flexed at the clarification, and at the way his tone of voice had darkened. Maybe she had figured out the other meaning of her question, because her eyes widened. She flushed, sending him a quick, searching glance and clutching strands of willow in her fingers. "Yes."

He shoved the hand that had been holding her, the hand she had just touched, into his pocket. "Can't we just enjoy the moment here? Why does this matter to you so much? You don't need the money. And you don't need Europe."

Her face emptied. She retreated back behind the bare strands of the weeping willow. In the spring or summer, she would have been veiled by their tiny leaves, but there was no hiding in the winter. "You don't want me to have Europe."

"You know I don't."

"Or you."

"Cade—" He broke off. "Are you *able* to keep the business and the personal in this separate?" It occurred to him that he had been born a person and chosen to become a chocolatier when he was in his teens. She had been born a business, and this might very well be her first try at becoming her own person.

"Do you want me to go home?" she asked, very low, very cool.

Sometimes open honesty was the only way to go, no matter how risky it was. *"Non."*

She stood there watching him warily, one hand holding those bare strands to the side, like some confused nymph who had been startled awake before spring.

"You can be part of something without owning it, you know." He held her eyes. "You can be part of my life without owning it anytime you want."

Her eyes widened. She searched his face. Her eyes widened still farther, and her lips parted, as if she were almost afraid.

Well, *merde,* what wasn't there to be afraid of?

"I don't understand you," he said. "Can't you do anything you want?"

Her eyebrows drew together. "Just randomly *whatever I want*? No. Do you realize how many people would suffer the consequences if I just acted according to whim?"

"I don't mean any whim at all. I meant, can't you decide what you want out of life and go after that?" He took a risk: "You seem to have been doing that so far here. Can't you stay the course?"

She frowned.

"In school, we learned that was an American ideal—the *pursuit of happiness.*" He turned his tongue around the English phrase, with its awkward *r* and breathy *h*. "It doesn't even translate well into French."

"It doesn't sound like an ideal in French; it sounds selfish," she retorted. "That's why. People depend on me."

"I didn't say to keep behaving completely irresponsibly." But she had been doing so. Interesting, given that she was so clearly opposed to letting herself be irresponsible. He reached for her, with an intimate, teasing smile. "Although I don't mind personally if you break into *my* business and get your family name splashed all over the place and run the risk of getting arrested."

"I've probably used up my allotment of irresponsible behavior for the next twenty years with that," she muttered, visibly depressed.

Sylvain's stomach knotted. "Don't say that. I'm the one who grew up *en banlieue,* and you're the one who acts as if you are caught by your circumstances and can't realize your own dreams. Cade, you don't seem to *want* to buy Europe or run Europe. Maybe you're just playing, but I could swear you love being in my *laboratoire,* you love sinking your senses into everything. You must be turning half of yourself off when you focus on factories and finances."

And it was a half filled with so much joy and passion. If she couldn't stay in Paris for him, surely she could stay for his chocolate.

She stared at him for a long moment. Then she looked out across the wide Marne. "My grandfather is eighty-two years old."

"Ah." That, he couldn't say anything about. He could tell her to pick Paris—*pick him*—over her life as a damned mass-market producer of *merde,* but he couldn't tell her to pick him over someone she loved.

Even if she let herself one day love *him,* he couldn't do that to her. Couldn't tell her to choose between him and someone she had loved since birth.

"And—I can do so many things. *So many.*" She said it as if it was a curse, not a gift. "I can save people. I can change lives. I can affect working conditions in entire countries. Working with chocolate in Paris—I'm not good at it. I'm never going to improve anyone's life doing it. I just—love it. But it doesn't do anything for anyone but me." She sounded, very briefly, exhausted.

"Have you ever done anything just for you?"

Her eyebrows flexed together, as if the question puzzled her. He could see her racking her brain to come up with an answer, which was answer enough. "I broke into your *chocolaterie,*" she finally said.

"*I* thought that worked out rather well," he said with a little grin. "Maybe you should try it for a while. Stop thinking of all you could or should be doing. Just savor what you want to be doing. Surely you're allowed a couple of years of just living what makes you happy."

She rested her head against his shoulder, gazing out at the water, and said nothing.

After a long time, she tilted her head to look up at him, her hair spilling across her face. "Are you living what makes you happy?"

He gazed down at her face, pale in the dark, felt the weight of her against him, seeking his warmth. The only thing missing from this moment was the surety that he could keep it.

"*Ah, oui.*" He stroked her hair back from her mouth, the way he had wanted to do that very first morning in the bakery. "*Je suis très content.*"

Chapter 26

Cade was cursing the handheld spray in her apartment's bathtub Monday morning, still a little hungover from all the family partying, when her phone started buzzing like mad. At the same time, her laptop turned itself into a carillon service, rippling out chime after chime as multiple messages came in one after the other. The phone had gone to voice mail and immediately started buzzing again by the time she got a towel and reached it, shivering as she got farther from the radiators and the cold air hit her half-dried skin.

"Total Foods has made a hostile takeover bid for Devon Candy," her dad said, and all her nerves fired to two hundred percent, adrenaline jerking through her as if she'd just gotten out of her shower to find a raging tiger leaping at her.

"Merde," she said. "I'm on my way."

She threw items into a carry-on with her phone clipped to her ear, delegating to her assistant in Maryland the job of booking her the first flight out or a private jet, whichever was most efficient. She slipped her teddy-bear finger puppet into her purse. She left most of her things in the apartment and flagged a taxi as she crossed the street to the *chocolaterie,* her pace long, fast, just short of running.

"Attendez," she ordered the taxi driver. "I'll pay you, don't worry."

Adrenaline had taken over, her mind turning almost its entire focus to this tiger. But she needed to see Sylvain. She needed . . . to take him with her.

But she couldn't do that. She couldn't buy him off an elegant display table, pack him up, and take him home with her. For one thing, if she removed him from his *chocolaterie* and his city, it would be as if she took an axe and cut off his limbs.

"You can be part of something without owning it, you know. You can be part of my life without owning it anytime you want."

"Get me . . . ten boxes," she told the nearest clerk as she passed. She knew her world, and she knew what it was going to be like for the next few weeks. They wouldn't sleep, and they wouldn't really eat; assistants would bring them food and coffee while they kept going. She had twenty boxes of chocolates from other chocolatiers upstairs in her refrigerator. But she hadn't thrown any of those into her carry-on. She wanted a little something of Sylvain Marquis with her every day. Or a lot of something, depending on how bad it got, back home without him.

Under and through all the adrenaline, her stomach was starting to squeeze with anguish.

They didn't even . . . where were they, in their relationship? Would he care? Could they call each other and make kissing noises into the phone? They probably couldn't. *Oh, God.* Would he even . . . well, where *were* they, exactly? He had introduced her to his family, but apparently he introduced many women to his family.

Would he just shrug and move on? There were other women who loved chocolate and sexy men, who could throw themselves at him with the same desperate longing she had. There were two beautiful, supremely classy *Parisiennes* in his shop right now.

Cade looked at them with a thin, hard line to her mouth. They looked back at her coolly and sniffed.

You can be part of my life without owning it anytime you want. Was that a statement of liberty—she could see him but better not think he was hers and that he wasn't seeing anyone else?

She stopped in the *laboratoire,* scanning it, unable to find the dark head she was looking for. Her stomach was now in a knot so tight, the struggle in her body between that and adrenaline was starting to make her feel sick and choppy, as if she'd just downed four too many energy drinks.

"Sylvain n'est pas là," Pascal said, pausing in the act of setting the pots of a bain-marie together. "He had a meeting with the mayor and some of the other chocolatiers in the city about this idea of his to set up a *Journée du Chocolat* with schoolkids, an exposure to the different food professions."

She looked at her watch. "When—?"

"Probably not until this afternoon."

If there was anything worse than wondering how he would react to her being gone for a few weeks, it was not being able to even see him one last time and at least have an idea. Would he kiss her hard, ask her not to go, or just say, "Ciao"?

She went into his office, pulling out one of her personal-info business cards in lieu of notepaper, trying to think what to say. Good God, what in the world was she supposed to put down on paper?

But she couldn't call him and interrupt him with the mayor. That wasn't cool. She wouldn't want him to do that while she was in a meeting with Devon Candy shareholders.

"Are you going somewhere?" Pascal asked from the doorway, his eyes very narrow and cool.

"There's been a—" How in the world did you say *hostile takeover* in French? "Ho-steel take-o-veer?" she tried. You never knew with French. Sometimes these English business words worked if you gave them the right pronunciation.

Pascal looked at her as if she had sprouted two horns and

started speaking in Demon. He did not look as if he understood anything whatsoever. On more levels than one.

She turned her shoulder to him and wrote, *Je t'appellerai* on the card. *I'll call you.* She signed it with her initials, *CC*. If he didn't recognize those, she was going to come back for the pure purpose of smacking him.

She wished she could leave him something, something just as powerful and rich and symbolic as the dark bitter chocolate he had left on her doorknob the other day. But she didn't have anything.

She hesitated, her hand clenching around the Corey Bar in her purse. Corey Bars held no value for him. But abruptly she pulled it out and put it under the card. For whatever he would make of that. Probably nothing.

She turned, her carry-on pivoting with smooth luxury behind her as she went back through the shop.

"Mademoiselle Co-ree." The young, elegant clerk who had once snubbed her look distressed. "I don't know if M. Marquis would want me to let you pay for this."

"It's okay." Cade handed over a card. "Charge me for ten more and promise to give one of them to the homeless man with the new jacket in the gardens every day until I get back, okay?"

Winter was setting in, and clearly only the best would help get the man through it. That and the wool socks and silk thermal underwear she had picked up for him the other day. She wondered what would convince that man to go to a shelter.

"M. Marquis already asked me to do that, *mademoiselle*. I can't charge you for it."

Had he? A smile brightened her face. When she got back, she would have to talk to him. She had an idea about an awareness-raising Chocolate for the Homeless Day, and if he had time left over from his schoolkids' day, she'd bet he would be the perfect partner.

When she got back. She was going to just keep telling herself those four words.

She stuffed her boxes into her nearly empty carry-on and climbed into the taxi.

Two hours later, she was back. *Shit, shit, shit.* How could she have managed to misplace her passport at a time like this? She always carried it with her. Had she forgotten and left it in a different purse? No. Had she slipped it into the pocket of her larger suitcase? No. Where the hell was it?

She looked and looked, everywhere in her apartment she could think of, on the phone with her assistant, telling her, no, she had missed the first flight, to get her another one in two hours. On the phone with her dad and her excited, half-gleeful grandpa, getting all the details of the Total Foods bid and what was going on, as she had been doing in the taxi, she went on looking and looking.

Finally the glimmer of a suspicion touched her. Not really a full suspicion. Just . . . she had looked in every possible and impossible place. Either it had been stolen and she had never noticed and she needed an emergency passport from the embassy, or . . . well, she would just check out one last idea.

She went back to the *chocolaterie,* barely conscious of the very cold looks everyone in it gave her.

Sylvain was at the marble counter. Pascal might have lied to her about how long he would be gone, or he might have finished with the mayor sooner than expected. Either was possible. But he was here now.

He was just standing there, his palms spread flat on the marble, his head bent, staring down at it. He didn't seem to be moving or doing anything. He hadn't even put on his white chef's jacket and toque and apron, and she had never seen him indifferent to professionalism in his own *laboratoire.*

A huge surge of relief swept through her, a desire to throw

herself into his arms and just hug him as hard as she possibly could.

Then his head lifted, and his eyes met hers.

He was furious.

He was furious in a way that made his outrage over his name on Corey Bars seem like a casual expression of annoyance over a minor matter. Maybe, in perspective, that's what that outrage had been.

"Did you miss something?" he asked, every word pure and precise, as if fury could be crystallized into some kind of intellectual diamond. Which in French it probably could.

"My . . . passport," she said. Looking for it here suddenly stopped seeming such a ridiculous idea.

He reached into the back pocket of his jeans, pulled it out, and threw it onto the marble. In the motionless *laboratoire,* the slap of the passport resounded loudly.

"I knew you would do that," he said, very low, so that it would not carry even in the muffled, unaccustomed quiet of the eavesdropping *laboratoire.* "I knew you would just hop back onto a plane the instant the mood struck you. At least this way you had to tell me to my face."

"I was going to call you," she began but stopped before the surge of fury her words provoked. His other hand lifted from the marble and from it fell, crumpled into nothing, her business card with the same promise.

"Merci," he said, that final *ci* in the word slicing like a sword. The curse came after it like a battering ram: *"Va te faire foutre."*

"No, you don't understand." She came toward him, reaching for his arm.

He pulled it away from her as if she were a plague victim.

Okay, answer to one question: he did care. On the other hand, everything had just gone to hell in a handbasket.

"It's an emergency. Total Foods has just made a hostile

takeover bid for Devon Candy. Do you know what that means?"

He just looked at her, his jaw set. "No."

Which wasn't surprising, since she still didn't know how to say it in French. "We can't let Total Foods get Devon Candy. We can't. We've got to figure out something." Even while she was saying it, a part of her brain was turning: They had three billion in cash reserves. The Total Foods bid was 17.6 billion and was probably not their final offer. Financing might come from . . .

"That's more important to you than—?" Sylvain caught himself, shutting himself up with a slicing gesture of his hand.

She hesitated, trying to think this through, to figure out the implications of what she was saying before she said it. He had stopped himself. But he had gotten halfway into his question before he rethought it, so she knew it was there. "Are you saying that I have to choose? That I can be Cade Corey of Corey Chocolate, or I can be your"—his what?—"here, with you, but I can't be both?"

His jaw was so hard, the purity of his profile was heartbreaking, like a work of art she had just shattered. "I'm here. You're going to the US. It's a big ocean."

She rubbed her fingers between her eyebrows, running on too much adrenaline for tears, full of only urgency and anguish. "I've got to go *now*. Will you—?"

Will you not go out and pick up one of those pretty Parisiennes *in your shop; will you wait for me?*

How did you earn the right to ask for that from someone you had known only a few days? Was she insane? What were they? She still wasn't even entirely sure he didn't have anything going on with Chantal. So if she couldn't even know for sure whether they had a monogamous relationship—of less than two weeks' duration, in which the focus of their relationship had been sexual—then how could she ask him to wait for her?

Her own jaw firmed. "I'm coming back," she promised, holding his eyes. She might not have the right to ask for anything, but she knew how to make promises for herself. And she knew how to keep them. She had partial control of the destinies of so many more people than Corey's thirty thousand direct employees, she had stopped counting when she was a child because of the vertigo it could inspire. She knew how to back up her own words.

She stretched both hands toward him. "You do . . . what you decide to do. I don't have any say over that. But I'm coming back."

He straightened from the marble and gave an abrupt, scorching look at the motionless laboratoire. "*Ça vous dérange?*" he asked his employees icily. *Do you mind?!* A couple of them stirred or otherwise moved halfheartedly, all still focused on them.

He came around the counter, took her arm, and half pulled, half escorted her out to her waiting taxi. Wind rippled his thin cotton shirt. He must have felt the cold, but he didn't react to it. He looked down at her, with no perceptible softening in the line of that hard jaw.

"*Je suis tombé amoureux de toi,*" he said, his voice angry, as if he was fighting a wound he had always known was coming. "You do . . . what you decide to do. I don't have any say over that. But I think I love you."

Cade stared at him, feeling as if a bomb had gone off in the distance and the wave of it had just hit her, as if she couldn't hear, couldn't see, could only feel, stunned. "Is there something going on between you and Chantal?" she asked abruptly.

He stared at her. "No." As the question sank in, his mouth grew, if possible, even grimmer. "You mean you thought there might be, and you only just now asked?"

She hunched her shoulders in a yes, flushing.

His hand clenched on the roof of the taxi. "Are other people just toys for you to pick up and shake a little bit and then drop on the ground?"

Her mouth dropped open in shock. That wasn't what she was doing *at all*. She had just—she had just wanted this so badly, she hadn't wanted to ask any questions. Hadn't wanted to let anything—like his responsibilities or hers or whether or not she was setting either of them up for hurt—get in her way. "I just—tried to take what I wanted," she said in a low voice. Why did it sound really bad when she said it out loud?

That clenched fist slid off the roof of the taxi. "Seriously," he said, almost conversationally, as if the rage showing in his eyes was too intense to risk letting into his voice, *"va te faire foutre."*

He turned and headed back to the shop.

Cade, sinking amid this utter disaster into the taxi, paused halfway, clutching the edge of the door. "Didn't you?" she cried after him. "Try to take what you wanted?"

Sylvain's long stride faltered. He turned back and watched as the taxi pulled away.

Cade Corey rode all the way to the airport without thinking about Total Foods or Devon Candy once.

Chapter 27

She had just handed over her boarding pass when her dad called again. "There's a new development," he said. "We've been talking with Firenze about a co-buyout of Devon. It's a good thing you're in Europe. Your French is going to come in handy, sweetie. Get up to Belgium right now. I want you to talk to the brothers."

The third day out, Cade and everyone around her were surviving on coffee and, in Cade's case, Sylvain's chocolate. She didn't share. The Firenze brothers offered her pots of their famous chocolate spread and local artisan Belgian chocolate, and her entourage of accountants, lawyers, and assistants, all flown in from Maryland or pulled from Corey Chocolate's small business center in Brussels, shared Belgian fries indiscriminately. When she flew over to London, everyone at Devon Candy tried to feed her Devon Bars and fish and chips.

She made secretaries bring her fruit and salads and whole grains and for the most part ignored the junk food. Instead, she kept a box of Sylvain's chocolate with her and just once in a while, whenever she needed to feel a part of him—every fifteen minutes or so—she ate a piece.

Every bite gave her a little burst of sweetness and hope, as if she could figure a way through this. Through this cooperative buyout, through Total Foods, through all her responsibilities and the fact that a part of her thrilled to them, through to what she wanted out of life, through back to him.

But she didn't know what to *say* to him. When she pulled her head out of discussions with the Firenze brothers and Devon Candy and looked at her phone, she didn't know what to call and say or text or e-mail or anything. "Really?" That seemed kind of a chancy start. "Are you sure?" Well, how could he be *sure* if they had only known each other a few days? Was there such a thing as *sure* with the words "I think I love you"? Maybe, instead, "What do you mean by that?"

That seemed hard to ask on the phone. And, of course, there was always the possibility that he was still mad at her. He had sent her one word via text message since she'd left, a word she had received on the TGV ride up to Brussels: *Oui*.

She assumed it was an answer to her last question: *Yes, I tried to take what I wanted, too.*

It could be a mad *oui* or a let's-not-cut-off-all-communication-over-a-fight, olive-branch *oui*. It was hard to tell over text messaging.

Finally, though, she couldn't *not* call him; she was quite sure that would be a very bad mistake. So she tried an intro line a little more awkward but time-honored. "Hi."

She heard him draw in a breath. "Cade."

She melted at the way he said her name, the precise French *a* that seemed to make her name half as long as it was in English. Instantly, she stopped being afraid he was still mad.

She put her feet up on one pillow and sank her head back into another. Her feet ached; her brain felt exhausted. She wanted desperately three separate and mutually exclusive things: to sleep, to go out for a long, long walk to clear her mind, and to just curl up here talking to Sylvain.

"I'm eating one of your chocolates." The conical one with

its sprinkling of cocoa nibs at the flat end, the one he called his nod to the pleasures of a child's ice cream cone. Except there was nothing childish about it, the nibs instead of peanuts, the thick, dark exterior, yielding to one of his softest, silkiest, most liquid ganaches. She had to eat it carefully, biting into the cone and sucking the insides into her mouth as she did, so that it didn't melt all over her hands. Exactly like a child with an ice cream cone.

"Ah." His voice was just a breath, a whisper in her ear. She might have woken him up. It was late. He might be lying in his bed now, naked except for briefs, his shoulders matte and muscled against the white sheets. Had he had his phone lying within reach, hoping she would call? Had he, too, stopped being angry the instant he heard her voice? "Is it good?" he murmured, warmth and sensuality stirring between them, across the distance.

"It's always good," she whispered.

A little sound on his end like a smile. "Which one are you eating?"

"The *cornette de ganache*."

"Ah." Just the breath of a murmur. Even over the phone, the sound stroked her skin. She had a feeling he was imagining with complete and utter accuracy every taste and sensation on her tongue. He knew the softness, the sweetness. He knew the gentle sucking of her lips so that the ganache didn't spill onto her fingers. He knew the imprint of chocolate left on her thumb and the way she had to lick it off.

And he knew that he had put it there.

Good God, he was so sexy. How could he be that sexy over a phone?

"What are you doing?" he asked.

She groaned. "I'm about to fall asleep. Someone is supposed to drag me out of bed in exactly six hours. We have this theory that by the third day everyone needs at least one full REM sleep."

"So, do you own the world yet? I checked the news, but I didn't see anything."

"We can't let Total Foods get Devon Candy. It's not exactly a question of owning the world." More a question of being disowned, really. Maybe they shouldn't get into this topic right now, over the phone. "And no, we don't. What are you doing?"

"I was asleep, but just barely. I doubt I'm as tired as you are. But it's five weeks before Christmas, so we can start producing our Christmas chocolates next week." Sylvain Marquis did not sell *old* chocolate in his shop. Certainly not four weeks or even two weeks old. But people would start buying and offering gifts early in December. "And I've been working on the Christmas decorations for the shop."

Five weeks before Christmas. She would probably spend all Thanksgiving Day locked in meetings with Devon and Firenze. How was that for irony?

Her eyes brightened as she tried to imagine what he might concoct out of chocolate for his windows and counters. "Will they be up by the time I get back?"

A little silence. "It depends on how soon you return."

She rolled over, burying her face in her pillow in lieu of him. She had no idea when she would get back. And she was so wiped out. But his voice in her ear was perfect.

"How do you like the Firenze brothers?" he asked.

"I'm not tempted to break into their *laboratoire,* if that's what you're asking."

His low laugh made her feel like a cat that had just had a hand run down its back. "That's what I'm asking. Eat another one of my chocolates, Cade."

She closed her eyes for a moment and just breathed in the thought, the feel, of him, hundreds of miles away.

A box of his chocolates lay a foot or so from her face on the table by her bed. Through her mind flitted questions like: How often did he fall in love? How often did he fall out of it? When he'd said "think," his hypothesis was based on what experience of how it felt to love someone? Instead of asking any of them, she opened her eyes and studied the array of glossy brown bites, each one signaling its contents in some subtle difference in marking, and asked, "Which one?"

His voice stroked over her like his callused hand. "Whichever one you want."

She was tired, so tired, and yet arousal seemed to caress all through her, as if she could fall asleep on a bed of it. "Whichever one you want me to," she whispered.

A sound from him as if she had stretched out her hand and grabbed the most sensitive part of him. And as if she hadn't. As if the phantom nature of that hand was pure torment. "Cade, where are you? Are you in Bruxelles? I could take the train up."

"London," she said reluctantly. "I'll be back in Brussels to-morrow."

"Night? Tomorrow night?"

Oh, God. She curled around the arousal he was creating in her, the frustrated longing. "I won't have a second for you. And I'll probably be exhausted."

"I can keep myself entertained, Cade. I know people in Bruxelles." He laughed. "Quite a lot of people, *en fait,* or have you forgotten that that misguided country thinks *it* has the best chocolate? It's only an hour and a half away. I'll have to see if I can get away from this winter forest I'm creating." A beat of silence. "Or would you prefer I not?"

"No," she said. "Oh, no." But it depended on how the fantasy played out. All their encounters had been pretty heated up until now, and pretty much . . . encounters. She didn't want him to be disappointed if she did nothing but fall asleep on him, crumpled and stale, at the end of another long day.

He changed the subject. "So, what are you wearing?"

"My clothes," she admitted regretfully. She had fallen into

bed in them. It would have been much better to either *be* in a sexy something or have the presence of mind to pretend she was.

Sylvain laughed. "Now, that's an interesting challenge. How to get your clothes off from five hundred kilometers away."

Heat flushed to her cheeks. And some other places. She wiggled for a second, letting her boots thump to the floor. "I took off my shoes," she offered.

"Ma chérie." He sighed. "I like your willingness to cooperate. But I think if you were so tired you hadn't gotten your shoes off yet, I should probably let you go to sleep."

"I know but . . . I was looking forward to finding out how you would get everything else off."

"Ah . . ." There was a long silence.

When he spoke again, his voice had lowered, deepened, roughened, a breath tempting her into a dark, warm room with a lock on the door. "Will you promise to do everything I tell you to?"

She turned off the light and sank under the covers. All pitch-black now. Nothing but his voice, the hard feel of the phone against her ear, the softness and weight of the comforter. "Yes," she whispered.

"Everything?" that dark voice insisted, mastering her as he always did.

Her voice was barely a sound: *"Oui."*

Chapter 28

"Please don't tell me you are going to take the train up there to be her gigolo for the night," Chantal said flatly.

Sylvain stared at her. As usual, Chantal looked lovely and classy. Too classy to accuse him of being a gigolo, but they had been friends for long enough that she spoke her mind when she thought she should speak it.

"I don't think I had thought of it in quite those terms, no."

They were in one of their favorite lunch spots, a tiny Vietnamese restaurant that one had to find by word of mouth or, rather, intense curiosity, as it didn't look like anything much from the outside or in: dark red velvet, barely lit. His had been the intense curiosity, back when it first opened, and his and Chantal's had been the start of the word of mouth that now made it so popular.

One of the quiet owners set *saki* in front of them, on the house, as she had for years now. The little china cups showed tiny and excruciatingly bad pornographic pictures if looked at through an alcoholic haze. Gender-specific, too; Chantal's would be of a man.

"Sylvain. Can't you see you're doing it again? I thought you had gotten over letting women use you and break your heart."

He was getting heartily sick of this subject. "You're sure Cade is using me?" He thought of her breathing the night before on the phone, what it had done to him to have her respond that way to his voice. He thought of her holding his gaze, saying, *"I'm coming back."*

"Absolument," Chantal said firmly.

"You don't think there's any possibility she could be a little bit in love with me? *Merci,* Chantal." People who knew you in high school never did learn to respect you, did they?

"Of course I think there's a possibility she's in love with you," Chantal said, flushing for no reason Sylvain could figure out. "Who wouldn't be?"

What? Deep inside, Sylvain started.

"But you can be in love with someone and still use him."

"You would know," Sylvain said dryly. She was beautiful, and she had an extensive history of letting assholes use her and then turning around and using nice guys to make her feel better about herself. She had been, in fact, one of those friends he had fantasized about in high school and whom he had successfully seduced once with chocolate when he was sixteen and she was eighteen.

The next morning, she had treated it as a blip in their friendship, kind and rather condescending about it. He had forgiven her because he was crazy about her—wounded, but crazy about her—and she had gone straight on to one of the jerks she'd liked to date so much at that time.

Chantal stiffened. "You know, Sylvain, I am—nearly a decade older now."

He was fourteen years older, but time flowed a little differently for Chantal, who was resisting hitting thirty.

She touched her fingertips delicately to the back of his hand. "Don't you think I might have learned to appreciate you?"

Chantal had always had a dog-in-the-manger streak with him, when it came to the women he dated. She was comfortable as a friend whenever he wasn't dating someone, but she always wanted to grab him back when he was. She needed a nice guy in her life; she just didn't know how to make a commitment to one. Chantal had had a pretty screwed-up home life back as a teenager. He liked her, and he understood that about her, and so he was able to tolerate some things. But there were limits.

"She knows her mind, though," he said suddenly.

"What?" Chantal looked wary.

"You've got to hand it to her. She may want to use me, but she wants to use *me*." And he wanted to use her. Use her and use her, in all kinds of ways. But he also wanted to make her smile. He wanted to let her curl up in the shelter of his body when the wind was cold. He wanted to set her up on his counter and feed her hot chocolate to warm her. "She wanted me or my chocolate from the start, and she went after it, and she never once thought she might want someone else instead."

"What about Dominique Richard?" Chantal asked defensively. "She told me she liked Dominique Richard better."

"She was lying. She's a very cute liar." She was a very erotic liar, was what she was. It made him want to capture her and . . . mmm, push her up against the wet wall of that shower of his—they hadn't tried that yet—and make her admit the lie.

"How can you be so sure?"

"Chantal." Sylvain looked at her and just shook his head. "I'm sure she was lying about Dominique Richard, yes. Very sure. But sure that I won't get my heart broken, sure this will end well? I think the chances are about one in a hundred."

"You think that, and yet you'll go chasing after her?" Chantal demanded furiously.

"Of course."

The security guard at the Firenze headquarters in Brussels couldn't get Cade on the phone for permission to bring him up but was too much of a romantic to turn Sylvain away.

The romantics in life had to stick up for each other. He finally decided to escort Sylvain to her, keeping a sharp eye on him to make sure he was who he said he was and not some fanatic out to strike a blow against globalization by throwing a bomb.

So Cade had no advance warning of Sylvain's arrival into her world. He felt his stomach muscles tighten as he approached the doorway, preparing to protect his soft, mushy *chamallow* insides from a blow.

Cade stood to the side of an oval table, by a window looking down on the old town. Dusk was falling, making the window a dark backdrop to a large, well-lit room. In the center of the table were the remnants of some kind of orange pie, that seemed to have been shared at some point. Cade looked very professional—black pants, boots, a fitted pale blue shirt, hair at the end of a long day having lost wisps from its chignon to frame her face but still remarkably smooth. None of that lip gloss she favored was left on her lips. A black blazer he suspected to be hers hung over a nearby chair. She was talking to one of the Firenzes, gesturing sharply with one hand and looking frustrated and intense, when the movement in the doorway caught her attention, and she glanced his way.

She froze, her lips still parted in whatever she had been saying, her hand stilling mid-gesture.

Then her face lit. The professional, intense energy fragmented under an explosion of happiness. "Sylvain."

The joy in it took his breath away. She left the group as if they had ceased to exist, her arms lifting up to him as she came toward him in such obvious delight that the security guard stopped trying to block him and let him meet her halfway. The woman who had previously infuriated him and made him deeply wary by her refusal to greet him with even the *bises* of a casual acquaintance threw her arms around him and kissed him with so much joy, he would think . . . well, he would think all kinds of things.

When he could think again. Right now, he just wanted to kiss her back.

"You came," she said, when she finally surfaced. And in complete contradiction to every other message she was sending: "You shouldn't have come. You'll be bored."

He gave a low half laugh, incredulous. He would have flown around the world to learn what he had just learned. He would even have done it two weeks before Christmas or Easter, when he could spare not a second from his own work.

"Why did you come?" She reproached his choice even while pressing her body into his as if she could never get close enough.

Because he had a one in a hundred chance, and he wasn't stupid enough not to take it.

He bent down with a smile to whisper into her ear: "To get your shoes off." Last night had driven him pretty insane with desire. And he wanted to make sure she was still real. To see a little of what her world was like. And to see her reaction to his walking into her world.

Sa réaction était magnifique.

She was still staring up at him with her eyes sparkling like the damn, giddy Eiffel Tower.

She blushed suddenly. Because she had, in fact, done everything he'd told her to the night before. Sylvain gave her a slow, slow smile, and her blush deepened. He pulled her hard against him, feeling himself grow instantly aroused.

Not a great thing in a room full of her business associates. He pushed her far enough away from him that she was no longer touching him but kept hold of her hips so he wouldn't lose his human shield before his arousal subsided.

When he was safe for public view, he shook hands with

the Firenze brothers, whom he had met before, and with a few other people who suddenly wanted to be introduced. At first that amused him, because he could see why a good corporate ladder-climber would want to meet the person one of the Coreys was publicly kissing. Then, belatedly, alarm penetrated the amusement. It had never occurred to him that a consequence of dating Cade was that he might gain power in her world and have to learn how to use it wisely.

It was a sobering thought. It gave him the tiniest glimpse of how she felt, with all that power, how worried she was about ignoring it and focusing, at least for a while, on what *she* wanted and not the infinite number of things she could or should be doing with her power. It was a wonder her sense of self wasn't fragmented to pieces. He remembered again Googling her name, and all the references that came up—business articles or charities, every single one.

She didn't know how to get out from under all that she could or should do. When he walked out of the meeting to let her finish it, he felt almost as if he was abandoning her to quicksand without even tossing her a rope.

He met a friend of his for a local Belgian beer in a pub on the Place St. Catherine but sat there uneasy the whole time, nagged by that illogical feeling he should go back and rescue her. And knowing she would be outraged if he even tried.

Cade came to join them an hour or so later, much to his relief. At least he could shake off that stupid quicksand image.

At night, cafés and restaurants filled the Place St. Catherine with lights and action, and the Église St. Catherine glowed against the dark sky, beautiful. The chalets for the Christmas market were just starting to be set up but had not yet filled the space. Sylvain and Cade took a slow walk through the square after his friend headed home.

"So is she?" she asked abruptly.

Since in French, "she" could be anything from a place to a person, he scrambled. "Is she what? Who?"

"A girlfriend? Do you sleep with her?" One of her heels wobbled on the uneven cobblestones. He took her arm more firmly to steady her.

"Chantal?" he finally guessed. That was the only other woman Cade had ever seen him with. *Enfin.* To his knowledge. She might have had some private investigator taking photos of him for the past year, for all he knew.

Her mouth set. He wanted to bend down and sip that stubbornness right off it. She nodded.

"No. A couple of times in high school."

That mouth set harder. "Why only a couple?"

Because he had been ditched, of course. Now, how to admit that to a woman he wanted to impress? "Well . . ." He tried a cocky grin. "It might surprise you to know that I haven't always been as cute as I am now."

It shouldn't surprise her, thanks to his mom's photo album, but she had seemed to see his old gawky teenage self through a flattering haze.

They had reached the Grand Place, and Cade stood there in the light of the Brussels Town Hall, her mouth slowly forming a perfect *O* of disbelief as she deciphered what he meant. "You mean she ditched *you*?"

Cade was really, really good for his ego.

"I think she was young and stupid." Sylvain pretended arrogance and mock sorrow for his friend's error in her ways.

"I think she was young and stupid, too," Cade said flatly, with no pretense at all. "And I think she realizes *how* stupid now."

That . . . might be true. But if their friendship had survived Sylvain's long-ago crush on Chantal, it could survive Chantal's current crush on him. Chantal was just lost again and turning to him the way she always did when she was worried about being lost. She would figure out her love life eventually and find the right person. He had an idea, in fact—maybe he could get her together with Christophe le Gourmand and kill two birds with one stone. He frequently fantasized about hitting Christophe over the head with a stone, these days.

"So, no lovers?" Cade checked. A bulldog, Sylvain remembered.

"I wouldn't say *no* lovers."

She looked as if she'd just been slapped. By him.

It made him want to strangle her. He reached out a finger and tapped her a little too hard on the chest. "What do you think you are?"

"No *other* lovers," she said impatiently.

"*Right now?* Is this some kind of French stereotype? That whole idea about our casual infidelity is *not* true, by the way."

She heaved an annoyed sigh. "It's nothing to do with your being French. You must have women throwing themselves at you all the time."

He grinned. Very good for his ego. "I thought you had figured this out about me, Cade—I only ever put the absolute best into my mouth."

That both shut her up and made her blush crimson.

He squeezed her hand, satisfied with the effect. *"Alors, comment ça va?"*

She was silent for a long time. "You know how sometimes you have to work so hard for something, and you don't even want it, but you have to do it anyway?"

"No," he said flatly. He worked for what he wanted. He didn't waste time on what he didn't.

"Oh." She was silent again for a while. "Well, that's how it's going. I don't know if we'll win this one or not. I'm working on an agreement with Firenze, but the problem is, we both want the same parts of Devon Candy and don't want the same parts. So we might not be able to share this merger. And no matter what we put together, Total Foods will probably up their first bid and beat it. It will be a bidding war, and I don't know how high we will be able to go. My dad is working on the financing angle."

"Let's go back to what you started to say, about working for something you don't want. That's more interesting. I want to know how *you* are doing."

Cade gave him a puzzled look, as if either French had suddenly failed her or he had started speaking Flemish. Did that happen to her a lot? That when people asked her how she was doing, they meant how the company was doing?

"Because I thought you said . . . you were looking for something different. You didn't want your life to be this way anymore." She had wanted her life to be his way. What he had to offer.

She stopped in front of the *Maison du roi,* or Bread House, as the Flemish preferred to call it, and stood with her head tilted back, gazing at its ornate, symmetric Renaissance front. Laughter and casual conversation drifted around them as groups passed. More Belgians than tourists were crossing the Place at this time of year, most of them friendly and relaxed, post-pub.

She was silent for a long time, before she finally spoke, low and fierce: "If I win this, I can stay here. We'll need someone to run the merging of the companies, the selling of parts, the new Corey Chocolate in Europe."

"Cade. Why would you do that? When you don't want to run Corey Europe. You want desperately to do something else."

She bit her lip but held his eyes. "Because I could stay here," she whispered.

"What does it mean to stay here, if you bring with you the world you wanted to escape?"

She clenched and unclenched her fists, kneading her palms with her nails. "Sylvain," she whispered, as if it hurt her. "Why do you think?"

It hit him like a body blow. "For . . . me? You would do what you don't want for me?"

"It's a compromise. I stay here. I stay Corey."

"What about you?"

"What?"

"Don't misunderstand. I want you here. But where are you in all that? You stay here for me, you stay Corey for your father and Corey Chocolate. What do you do for you?"

"Stay here," she said low. "With you."

He drew her into his arms and held her hard, his heart soaring. "Besides that. If you want to be in *chocolateries,* then you should be doing that."

She pulled away from him and shoved her hands into her jacket pockets, hunching her shoulders. "I'm good at this kind of thing. And it's a family company, and I have a lot of responsibility to a lot of people. Maybe I should have chosen my sister's route and refused any of that responsibility from the start. But now I have it, and . . . I can't see any other way."

"Why not? If you can chart five-year plans and how to negotiate a joint counterbid for another multibillion-euro company, it seems as if you should be able to plot out any personal exit strategy you want to. You can't tell me you don't have the brains to figure out a solution."

Cade scrunched her eyebrows together and gave him a long, thoughtful look, as if trying to see herself reflected in his eyes.

Good. As far as he could tell, he had a pretty damned accurate idea of her character and intelligence and passion, and it might do her good to take a second look at herself through him.

He gazed down at her for a long moment as she stood in this beautiful Grand Place, surrounded by guildhalls. Her heeled boots brought her up to his chin instead of his shoulder, but he doubted she wore them because she felt any need for more height. Like the people who had built the halls framing this place, she seemed pretty confident of her right to dominate any situation.

She could probably dominate in jeans, but she made sure to dress well for business. Perhaps it was an expression of her own pride. Perhaps it was a little bit like his insistence on wearing professional attire even in his own *laboratoire,* even when he would rather come slouching in after a late night.

Besides, she did like to look good, he thought with a smile, remembering some of her sexier outfits. She liked clothes.

One of these days she would probably get around to hitting the designers on Faubourg St-Honoré, like most wealthy women did. It charmed him how incidental clothes shopping was in her priorities, well below the important things like chocolate. But one day she would do it, and he was looking forward to seeing what she came home with.

He fisted a hand in his coat pocket, schooling himself to caution with that vision, because it involved her coming in through his apartment door with her arms laden with frivolity, dumping it onto his living room floor, showing the purchases off to him. The home she came to, in other words, was his.

The problem was that whenever he imagined her doing something in the future, he wanted to be somehow part of it—whether he heard about it at the end of the day or was with her when she did it. In his favorite view of the future, she was there with him.

In his view of what he wanted from the world, there were an infinity of moments that were beautiful, as this one was beautiful, with the light from the town hall gilding her jawline and shining off her hair in the cold northern night that made him want to pull her in and warm them both.

"And you know what else?" she said, her voice wobbling

just a second, as if it was the last straw. "It's Thanksgiving. And the Firenze brothers don't even know what a damn pumpkin pie is."

"Thanks-gi-ving. That's a big day for you, right? The only day of the year Americans eat a real meal, or something like that?"

"Sylvain. You're not helping." But she sounded as if he was helping, a certain frustrated humor steadying the wobble.

He wrapped an arm around her shoulders. "Where's your hotel?"

"I'm going to fall asleep as soon as I hit the bed," she warned him ruefully.

"A vulnerable victim. That's what I like."

She was indeed luxuriously sleepy, smiling and pliant, as if every touch of his hand stroked the last bit of tension out of her and with it all her energy. She was almost his own doll, but more human, warmer, yielding with soft sounds to every touch.

That, too, was erotic. When she came, it was as if the waves of her orgasm rocked her to sleep. By the time he came, only a few seconds later, he thought she might already be asleep, receiving him in her dreams.

He eased onto his side, still inside her, propped on one elbow watching her, one hand lightly caressing her back and bottom.

Her body felt small against his, fragile, although he knew she wasn't, very soft, very, very fine. Her straight brown hair, free now of its chignon, slid and caressed her skin and his with his every breath. In that moment, she was all his, but she was already slipping away from him, her dreams taking her to places of which he had no idea.

She had once asked him if he had ever tried to reach a woman's heart. He supposed that, like his final smooth chocolates, it was good she couldn't see the effort behind it.

Chapter 29

Three weeks later . . .

In the windows of SYLVAIN MARQUIS, *Chocolatier,* grew great
rustic fir trees of chocolate, branches rough-hewn as if chis-
eled from a solid block, dusted with white. The suggested
primitiveness of the way in which they had been carved, the
depth of field, the quantity, and the lighting made them dramatic, mysterious, as if the viewer hovered on the edge of
some vast, ancient, snow-hushed forest. It was beautiful, al-
luring, and just slightly dangerous, like a snow-filled night; it
made one long to step forward and get lost among those
trees. Tucked in the forest was a cabin, the chocolate shaped
into something old, worn, a little lopsided, a shape at its peak
that might have been a star. It could have been a place for *le
Père Noël* to stop, or a subtle nod to a starlit stable, or it could
have been just a cabin in the woods on a snowy evening. Despite its primitive appearance, the detail, when one looked
closely, was exquisitely fine—a candle, a bird's footprint on
the windowsill.

And everywhere, everywhere, were signs of passage, signs
that could mean gift or theft. Someone had left a footprint in
the powdered sugar "snow." A chocolate nut had rolled from
a hollow in a tree, as if someone had snuck into a squirrel's
nest for his stash. Sleigh marks traced the rooftop of the cabin

hidden in the trees. In extraordinary miniature, on the table in that cabin, lay a box of Sylvain Marquis's chocolates—the tiny box itself made from tinted white chocolate. Its lid was open and one chocolate missing.

The eye looked and looked through the scene for the person or the creature who had passed, whose trace had been left. But she or he was nowhere in it, only a mystery.

Cade stood a long time in front of that window, one hand loosely clasping the handle of her carry-on. It had been a tough week. A tough month. They had failed. Total Foods had beaten their bid, and they had lost Devon Candy.

Lost Europe. Lost her right to it.

Out of excuses, she had had a very long talk with her father, who was still grappling with the additional loss she had dumped on him.

She had not seen Sylvain for any of that week. The demands of the Christmas chocolate season on him, and the Devon Candy bid on her, had made trips from Paris to Brussels scattered and difficult to manage. She always knew when Sylvain woke up, because he texted her first thing every morning, something funny or sexy or just *tu me manques* (*miss you*), and he called last thing at night or she called him. She hadn't, though, told him she was coming back to Paris tonight. She hadn't really done anything or talked to anyone but her father and family since the Devon Candy failure crystallized.

She needed the scents and tastes of Sylvain's *chocolaterie* around her.

She broke into the *laboratoire* with the copied key that Sylvain had never asked back from her and the code he had never changed. Inside the *laboratoire,* the scents made all the hair on the nape of her neck prickle and a shiver of release run through her, like the first touch of heat when coming in from the cold. She stood still for a moment, her eyes closed, just breathing.

Then she walked through the empty *laboratoire* and into

the shop, studying the display windows from behind. The signs of passing could be seen from this side, too. Inside the shop, she was immersed in the winter forest; customers would be touched by something magic that was gone now, that they could not find. In the display cases, "her" chocolate was on sale, the dark bitter one he had offered at her doorstep.

He had called it *Amour.*

Oh. She felt the name like a blow against her solar plexus, driving out breath. Dark, rich, bitter, melting-smooth love.

In his office, his laptop was closed and the desk cleared, everything neatly filed. But a Corey Bar lay in front of the laptop, where it might be if it was the last thing fingered before the person sitting at the desk got up.

She reached out to run her fingers over the wrapping, tracing the letters of her name.

"So, you're back," a voice from behind her said.

Cade felt the hair shiver on her arms and the nape of her neck. The way it always did when the sorcerer surprised her in the dark. "You know I couldn't stay away."

He came up behind her, until her body was trapped between his and the desk. The nape of her neck felt very exposed. "I don't know if I've told you, but I'm looking for a new apprentice."

Sorcerer's apprentice. His voice, rich and dark as the night and his art, made it sound as if she was bartering for body and soul. The scent of his chocolate was everywhere, flooding into his office from the *laboratoire.*

"Are you in need of a . . . *maître?*" Very deliberately, he drew pauses and shadows around that last word. Very deliberately, he did not say *maître chocolatier.* Only *maître.*

Her body arched involuntarily. Her head fell back to touch his chest. He took her hips, refusing to allow her whole weight back against him.

"*Tu es cruel,* Sylvain," she whispered. "I haven't seen you in weeks."

"I know," he said. "I can't help myself." He wrapped her hair around his hand and pulled her head back farther, arching her body from him like a bow. A bow to his arrow. His other hand ran up the body he had thus stretched to it, from between her thighs to cup her breast. "Come let me be cruel to you."

Fire bloomed everywhere under the stroke of his hand. "Oh, God," she whispered, barely audible. "I love it when you're merciless to me."

"And I love having you *à mon merci,*" he whispered into her ear. Still holding her head bent with his hand in her hair, he pulled her hips back, arching the bow of her still further. He used the pressure of his hand between her legs to force her *fesses* against his sex. His breath was barely a sound against her earlobe. "Because I am at yours."

She was trembling with desire. The disaster of their loss to Total Foods, her last conversation with her father before she came back to Paris—all that was pushed far away, fleeing from the deep shadows and the brightness of this moment. "Shouldn't an apprentice have to please the master?" she whispered.

His hips jerked and pushed hard against her bottom, his palm holding her prisoner by his pressure against her sex. She shivered all over. "You do," he said, low, guttural. "Already."

She twisted away from him and pushed him back against his desk.

He gripped the edge of it, watching her, his eyes a black burning.

She reached for his jeans.

His hands tightened on the edge of the desk. "Cade. Don't do this to me. Do you know how long a real apprenticeship *lasts*? Don't play with the idea unless you're planning on staying at least that long."

"I'll do what I want to you." She freed him from his jeans.

His head tilted back until she could see all the strong muscles of his throat. "You do to me."

. He closed his eyes. "Cade. *Ne me touche pas. Bordel.* Cade. *Arrête.*" But he did not grab her and stop her. "If you can't promise you're going to stay, let go *now. Putain.*" His hips thrust helplessly. It was so strange to see every muscle in his body taut, to know exactly how much stronger he was than she, and yet to feel so much power.

"You're not used to it," she said wonderingly. Were other women insane?

He made a sound. It couldn't really be understood as a whole word.

"You're not used to having someone seduce *you.*"

"More subtly," he managed hoarsely. "A lot more subtly. More like—pouty lips subtly. *Are you really going to stay?*"

"I can do pouty lips," Cade said, sinking to her knees.

"Ah, putain." Sylvain's breathing was so labored. He was so helpless to her. She was giddy with her sense of power.

"I *know* I love you," she said and tasted him.

"Ca—ade."

"Do you want me to stay?" It was a trick question, to ask it right at that moment, she knew.

He gripped her shoulders so hard, those strong fingers hurt her, finally holding her back. His eyes were open again, blazing far hotter than chocolate ever could. "Cade. Every dream I have has you in my apartment, has you in my *laboratoire,* has you with my babies, has me making supper for us on a cold night, has us laughing, and dancing, and . . . together. Every chocolate I've made since I met you, I've made for you. I've seen your gaze on my hands while I did it; I've thought of the way it would melt on your tongue. *Don't— you—toy—with—me.* I can't take it."

She stared up at him, no longer giddy with her own power but helpless in wonder at it. "Really? You want that, too?"

He gave a sudden, exultant laugh and pulled her up his body with one easy surge of strength. "You can even have my name," he said into her mouth, between kisses, wrapping her legs around him, wrenching at her clothes. "But please don't put it on Corey Bars."

"Oh!" Even at that second, as he pushed her jeans off her, Cade was distracted by a sudden, beautiful idea. "*Cade Marquis* bars!"

He drove into her hard, vengeance for the idea mixed with desire. "*Non,*" he said hoarsely and firmly. "*Mon Dieu, qu'est-ce que je t'aime.*"

"*Moi, aussi.*" She wrapped her arms around the lean, taut muscles of his back. "*Moi, aussi.*"

Chapter 30

If Cade kept finding his *chocolaterie* such a turn-on, he might have to start looking for an apartment closer to it, Sylvain thought a little later. Or maybe install a bed in his office. Two blocks from his apartment to his *laboratoire* was all very well when he was just walking to work and back, but on a freezing December midnight, it seemed a long way to go post-sex for a cuddle.

And the apartment Cade had rented to spy on him left a lot to be desired in the comfortable, cozy bed department, he thought, squeezing in on its stiff mattress beside her. But for now it would do. It had a memorable staircase, and a delicious tight squeeze of an elevator, he had just discovered.

Maybe Cade could buy the entire top floor and turn it into a penthouse, or something. He would design the kitchen.

The light they had turned on when they came in the door shone now too brightly into the bedroom area. He pulled her comforter over them completely like a tent, like children at play. He did feel as excited as a child, but he had never felt so intensely, joyously adult.

His finger traced over her shoulder and down her arm. "My name on *you*," he said wonderingly. "Really? Did you mean that?"

She, too, looked wondering and puzzled. "Do you know,

we've known each other less than two months? And I haven't even dated anyone that long since high school."

His heart sank like stone. "You mean you want to wait longer, test this out." *Putain de bordel de merde.* Why couldn't she feel as absolutely certain as he did?

"No." Blue eyes met his, that straight look that charged him with electricity. "I've tested everything that needs to be tested. I know what I want."

Sylvain stared back into those blue eyes, so wide and dilated in the shadows under the covers. "And that's me."

She reached out a hand to touch just her fingertips to his bare chest, in possession. He could feel his heart thudding against them. It might be possible to die of pride at this woman's claiming of him. "And that's you."

"Dieu." He pulled her hard into his arms. "How could any man be so lucky?"

"Luck had nothing to do with it."

"Of all the *chocolateries* in Paris, you walked into mine."

"The last thing I would have thought you of all people would credit to luck is me walking into *your chocolaterie.* Who else's would I walk into?"

He pressed his forehead against hers. "You misunderstood. I know what's to my credit, Cade. I know why you walked into *my chocolaterie.* And I know exactly how much effort I put into getting you to want something besides my chocolate, too."

"Good. It would confuse me if you suddenly started being humble."

He did feel humbled, though. Not humble about his accomplishments—quite the contrary—but humbled before God, or fate, or destiny, whatever force it was that had brought her into it. "My luck is that of all the people who could have walked into my *chocolaterie, you* walked into it. You."

Her smile bloomed. "I'm special, then?"

"Cade." He squeezed her helplessly. Women's hearts were inexplicable things. "How could you not know that?"

She did not answer, moving her fingertips in tiny, stroking motions through the hair on his chest.

"Did you mean it about becoming my apprentice?"

She smiled a tiny, impudent smile, seemingly focused on his chest.

"My chocolate apprentice," Sylvain clarified. "In the *laboratoire*."

She looked up brightly. "Will you have me?"

This was trickier ground by far than marriage. He felt entirely, one hundred percent sure about the marriage. "Will you sign a contract not to use what you learn in Corey Chocolate?"

"Yes. I quit, anyway."

He just stared at her. No, gaped at her, caught completely off guard.

"I'm still available for consultation, something my father is sure to take far too much advantage of, and I've still got the same amount of shares, which leaves me a very interested party, but we're going to have to hire someone to take over my day-to-day roles. It's a blow to my father." Grief shadowed her face. That blow to her father was a blow to her, too. That, too, humbled him, the choice she had made. "And to my grandfather. But the competition for top executive positions is pretty cutthroat. I'm sure we'll find someone who will excel at the job."

He continued to stare at her. "You've had a hard week."

"A little bit, yes." He felt the rise and fall of her long breath against his body. "But"—she opened her hand with simple finality—"I knew what I wanted."

He framed her face in both his hands and just stared at her in amazement. She had known, without a shadow of a doubt, what she wanted—him.

"The most," she corrected herself after a moment. "I knew what I wanted the most."

"So you *will* be my chocolate apprentice," he said when he could speak again, thoroughly charmed by the idea.

"Part-time," she agreed. "Part-time, I might do some small-time venture-capital work. Working with individuals who want to succeed with their own *chocolateries,* their own *pâtisseries.*"

He tugged one lock of hair reproachfully. "You just couldn't manage to give up all sense of responsibility to the rest of the world, could you?"

"Existential guilt." She shrugged self-deprecatingly.

He rolled onto his back, pulling her to pillow on his chest, stroking her hair, dreaming dreams of a life like this. "You know, I may make a Cade Marquis bar, after all. We'll call it an engagement present. A special, *artisanal* Cade Marquis bar we sell only in my shop."

Her arms squeezed him suddenly so hard, he could barely breathe, making him rather smug about the success of that gift. But all she said, into his chest, was a provocative murmur: "When the demand gets too high for it, and you want to sell it for a fortune to a corporation that can handle its mass production, let me know."

He laughed and used his finger to script an invisible word over her back, lightly, delicately, as if he was inscribing a chocolate: *Je t'aime.*

Epilogue

Two days later, Sylvain was chiseling a Christmas tree—soon to be decorated with ornaments full of ganache for the Élysée Palace Noël festivities—when two men barged into his workshop. At first, he didn't even look up. He was considered the best chocolatier in Paris, and it was *the Christmas season*. People needed to stay out of his workspace. But Cade, who had been circling his sculpture, watching him chisel with an utter absorption that was making him fumble and grow clumsy, stiffened.

Sylvain glanced sideways at her, picking up on the nerves instantly. Not even his mother had managed to make Cade *visibly* nervous. He straightened and paid attention.

Neither man was tall, although the fifty-something man had some heft on him, but both carried themselves exactly like Cade—as if they owned the entire world.

"Sylvain Marquis," said the fifty-something one with the well-cut gray hair, his voice firm. "I'm Mack Corey. So you're the man who's trying to steal my daughter."

Sylvain shrugged. "She wanted to steal the best. So did I."

Cade's stiffness melted.

"And I'm not trying to steal your daughter. I've already done it. So if you've come here to try to undo it, you're going to have to get out of my *laboratoire*."

Cade stopped melting, staring at Sylvain in horrified

shock. Maybe she was used to people being a lot more careful around her father.

Mack Corey studied him for a long moment and finally grunted. "Well. At least I like you. That's something."

The man who must be her grandfather, James Corey, was looking around the *laboratoire* greedily. He seemed awfully spry for eighty-two years old, wrinkled and white hair thinning but upright and proud. Sylvain hadn't realized milk chocolate was that healthy. Must be those stearic acids.

"A real, honest-to-goodness, French, holier-than-thou, chocolatier snob," the elder Corey said delightedly, looking Sylvain up and down as if Sylvain was a painting to be bought and added to his collection. The family had a really annoying knack for that look. "I've got to hand it to you, Cadey. I never thought anyone would manage to bring one of those into the family. How did you get him to stop being polite to you?"

"Family?" Mack Corey went alert. "Are you two talking about family already?" He gave Sylvain a speculative look, as if analyzing his genes for the capacity to produce future CEOs.

"I'm sure they are," the elder Corey said. "She doesn't lose her head easily, but once she's lost it, it's kind of like one of your guillotines." He made a slicing gesture across his neck, accompanied by what was probably supposed to represent the noise of a blade. "It's gone for good."

"What are you talking about?" Cade demanded indignantly. "When have I lost my head before?"

Sylvain grinned. He couldn't help himself.

"Never," James Corey admitted. "You're usually so cool and controlled."

"She's *what*?" Sylvain interjected. Cade had acted so helplessly hot and out of control since the moment he had met her. Had she been that way *just because of him*?

"I was starting to worry that she was going to turn out just like her father," James Corey confided.

Mack Corey gave his father a frustrated look. Cade must have decided her father had had about as many kicks this week as any man could stand, because she left Sylvain's side to go give him a hug.

When her father's arms wrapped around her, Sylvain stiffened against the unreasoning fear that the other man was going to haul her off into his limousine and disappear with her.

"Did you come to Paris to try to talk me out of it again?" she asked her father.

"No, to hunt for an apartment. Your grandfather and I were thinking it's about time we had a *pied à terre* here."

Until he saw the incredulous happiness blossom on Cade's face, Sylvain didn't think he had really understood how much leaving her family had cost her.

"Plus, we had a lousy Thanksgiving, so I thought it would do us good to get the whole family together in Paris for Christmas. Get to know the new family. It's closer to the Côte d'Ivoire, so we may even get Jaime up here for the holiday."

"I'm eighty-two years old, and I've never spent Christmas in Paris," James Corey said. "Can you believe it?"

Sylvain's mother was fifty-three and had never hosted four billionaires for Christmas, either, but she was going to have to get used to the idea really fast.

"You're not going to try to talk me out of it?" Cade asked wonderingly.

"I already tried that," Mack Corey said, rather bitterly. "It didn't work."

"Don't beat yourself up about it, son," his father told him sympathetically. "It didn't even work for me, so you can hardly blame yourself."

Mack Corey gave his father a look of much-tried patience

and declined to take the bait. "Plus, you spent the whole time lying to me about it, Cade, which wasn't helpful. You could have talked about it in other terms than as a business decision once in a while."

Cade looked completely dumbfounded.

"So, we'll come visit. Have you found a good real estate agent here yet?"

Cade hugged herself, blinking slow, delighted blinks. Father and daughter might have worked all her life together, but her father, with thirty years experience on her, had clearly still managed to catch her by surprise.

Sylvain began to smile. "So, just out of curiosity, what do you want out of life?" he asked his new *beau-père*.

"For my daughters to be happy, for Corey to dominate the chocolate market, and to let my family inherit the earth," Mack Corey said promptly. "I don't think that's too much to ask, do you? Not much point having money if you make your own kids miserable with it. *Right, Dad?*" he added rather acerbically. "Meanwhile, if you two could get to work on the family bit, so I don't have to wait until I'm ninety-five to retire, that would be great."

Sylvain stiffened. "Wait. Why? You don't think one of *my* children is going to run Corey Chocolate, do you?"

"Children?" said a voice from the shop door. He looked past the Corey men to see his mother and Natalie advancing, Christmas shopping bags draping from each arm. Behind them, Chantal, similarly accoutered with shopping bags, had stopped still in the doorway. The three women were long-standing co-shoppers. "Are you two talking about *children?*" Marguerite studied Cade as if analyzing *her* genes. All hostility had dropped from her gaze, to be replaced by absolute delight.

"Your—son, I presume—wants to marry my daughter," Mack Corey told her, holding out a hand.

Marguerite gave the hand an utterly confounded look, bypassed it, and pressed enthusiastic *bises* on Mack Corey's cheeks. Four enthusiastic *bises,* in her excitement. *"Mariage? Sylvain, tu veux te marier? Enfin? Enfin!"*

Beyond delight, she turned and planted multiple *bises* on Cade's cheeks. "Nobody in your generation gets married! Sylvain, I never thought you would! Are you going to wear white?" she asked Cade eagerly. Clasping her hands again, she looked toward Heaven, making Sylvain suspect his mother had been praying for him: *"Un mariage."*

"Vraiment?" Natalie looked excited. "This will be fun. Can I be a *demoiselle d'honneur*?"

"Un mariage?" one of Sylvain's least favorite voices said. Christophe. Seriously, he was never going to allow another food blogger into his shop as long as he lived. The guy was worse than fleas. He just kept bouncing right back into Sylvain's *laboratoire.* Christophe stopped beside Chantal in the doorway and studied Cade a little wistfully. "I suppose I should have expected it," he said to Chantal, as the closest available ear. "They both have to be so melodramatic about everything."

"Yes," Chantal said, resigned. "I suppose I should have expected it, too. But I didn't."

"Well, who gets married? That's so old-fashioned."

"He's a romantic," Chantal said. "And nobody can talk him out of being one."

Christophe turned his head to really look at her for the first time. He blinked. Then he suddenly bent down for introductory *bises.* "I'm Christophe. A friend of Sylvain's. Do you like romantics?"

A friend? Sylvain thought, outraged until he got distracted. Cade had curled a hand around his wrist and was gazing up at him, looking so completely and utterly happy, he wished he could bottle this moment and bring it out for her every time she was down for the rest of her life. "Really, no one gets married here?" she murmured.

"It's not that common," he admitted. "Most people just live together all their lives. But you already promised, so don't start backing out now."

"You had better not!" Marguerite interjected, outraged. Her hands clenched into fists of excitement. She was practically bouncing on her toes. "*Un mariage*. Wait until I tell my friends. None of *their* children have gotten married. Can I help you shop for the wedding dress?" she asked Cade.

Cade cast a quick, analytical glance over the plethora of shopping bags. "Yes," she said very firmly. She apparently knew now exactly how to make friends with her *belle-mère*. "On the Faubourg St-Honoré, in fact." She mentioned the street in Paris most packed with outrageously expensive designers.

Sylvain's mother had to go sit down. Any minute now, she was going to have to put her head between her knees so she didn't pass out, in fact. Chantal took Christophe's arm, and they both fled this talk of weddings to go stand with heads bent toward each other in the front of the shop.

"Good Lord," Cade muttered in English, gazing after Marguerite. "I think money might have finally bought me something in this town."

"Can I come shopping, too?" Natalie asked, thrilled. But she didn't allow herself to be distracted long. She thrust out her hand to the most powerful business contact in the room for a very American business-style handshake. "So, are you Cade's father? I'm Natalie Marquis. I'm thinking about interning for you this summer."

Cade grinned and glanced at Sylvain, who had to admit being rather proud of his sister. Irrepressibility was an excellent trait.

"You know what I would like out of life?" the spry voice of another irrepressible person announced in Sylvain's ear. "To break into a Swiss chocolatier, which Cadey's going to help me with, now that you've got her trained. And to blend spinach with chocolate. Which sounds to me like *your* area of expertise, so . . ." Behind him, Cade's eyes widened in alarm. She put a hand up to her mouth as if protecting it from gustatory assault and started shaking her head at Sylvain in warning. *Too late.* The old man grinned fiendishly. "I'm sure you won't mind helping your new *grandpapa* with a little project, now, will you?"

"I think the spinach project sounds like a good idea," Mack Corey said, proving conclusively that CEOs of multinational corporations had no morals or conscience. "Especially the part about doing it here in Paris in Marquis's *laboratoire*. But no breaking and entering. No getting caught spying in a Swiss factory. My God, if both of you get all over the media as chocolate thieves . . ." He flexed his large, square hands in impotent strangling motions. "And Jaime will probably get arrested in some World Bank protest right around the same time." He brought both fists to his forehead and groaned.

James Corey slung his arm over his granddaughter's shoulders. She grinned up at him quickly, her eyes lighting in a way that showed instantly exactly how much she loved her grandfather. "It's really tough being the white sheep of the family," he told his son sympathetically. "I don't know how you do it. But don't you worry about Cade and me. First of all, now it will be the Marquis name that gets splashed all over the media as a chocolate thief."

Sylvain had a sudden, horrible vision of his name being associated with an attempt to steal another chocolatier's secrets.

Cade's grandfather grinned diabolically at him. "But I probably won't find those Swiss factory owners sexy, so we won't get caught."

Laura Florand's Favorite Chocolate

Worth a Trip to Paris

Okay, *Paris* is worth a trip to Paris. But if these chocolate shops were in the world's ugliest city and it was being bombed by aliens, they would be worth a trip *there*.

Jacques Genin
133, rue de Turenne
75003 Paris, France
011 33 1 45 77 29 01

The first thing you notice as you step into this *chocolaterie* is the sublime space. Rough arches of exposed stone blend with red velvet curtains, white rosebud-embossed walls, and a spiraling metal staircase to create a setting of exceptional beauty. (It's the inspiration for the setting in my third book, in fact.)

While Jacques Genin has supplied chocolates to the top hotels in Paris for years, he is a relative newcomer with the general public, as his *salon du chocolat* only opened in 2008. Considered by many to be among the best in the world, his chocolates are presented in flat metal boxes that frame the beautifully printed squares of luscious ganache infused with herbs and spices—ganaches that melt in your mouth in sensuous ecstasy. Take your time the first time you bite into one of his chocolates, because the memory will stay with you for the rest of your life. But don't stop with the chocolates. If you have the joy of being in Paris, sit down at his tables to sample his famous *millefeuilles* (made to order and worth the wait), his *éclairs au chocolat,* and all his other delicious pastries. And if you have never considered yourself a lover of caramel or *pâtes de fruit,* try his and you will be converted.

For some behind-the-scenes looks at Jacques Genin's *laboratoire,* check out my website, www.lauraflorand.com, where I share some of my research for the Chocolate series books. With generous enthusiasm and a true passion for his work, Jacques Genin welcomed me into his chocolate workshop and answered every question I could ask. And he has, without a doubt, the most beautiful *laboratoire* in all of Paris, in itself worth a look.

Michel Chaudun

149, rue de l'Université
75007 Paris, France
011 33 1 47 53 74 40

Michel Chaudun's tiny shop in the 7th arrondissement of Paris provokes the giddy delight of stepping into some old museum crammed with artifacts from around the world—only in this case, they are all in chocolate: from the massive sculpture of a Mayan warrior to the bust of an Egyptian pharaoh, from a Hermès purse to strings of sausage so utterly realistic you could offer them at the dinner table and no one would realize the trick until they tried to cut into them and the chocolate fragmented around the knife.

Another of the world's very best chocolatiers, he is famous for his chocolate sculptures as well as his whimsy. And as for flavor . . . take one bite of his very famous *pavés* and you will melt right at the feet of that Mayan warrior. Sensuous bites of ganache delicately dusted with cocoa, these are as simple and as sinful as chocolates get. Don't try to hoard them for months or even weeks. (You know you want to eat the whole box anyway!) They are at their best when you buy them and need to be enjoyed at their peak.

The utterly charming Michel Chaudun also welcomed me into his world for my research for the Chocolate books. Take a look at www.lauraflorand.com for glimpses of his tiny *laboratoire* and this passionate, generous man in action.

As you'll notice, the preceding chocolatiers are so good, so famous just on word-of-mouth, and so very focused on local artisan production that they don't need to have websites. And as of this writing, they don't. For chocolates you can order, read on.

Can't Make It to Paris?
When I can't, I order my chocolate from these . . .

La Maison du Chocolat
www.lamaisonduchocolat.com

La Maison du Chocolat is a legend. It was founded in 1977 by Robert Linxe, who came up to Paris from the Basque region in 1955 and changed the taste of Paris chocolate by replacing the popular nut- and fruit-laced fillings with pure heavenly ganache and, in so doing, became my personal hero. By bringing ganaches into the forefront of French chocolate-making, he has made the world an infinitely better place.

These days, La Maison du Chocolat has boutiques all over the world, and that's our good fortune, because the quality has never faltered and it is possible to order these legendary chocolates shipped straight to one's door. (The price, you say? Hmm . . . perhaps you thought I was exaggerating Sylvain's assessment of his own worth when he sells his chocolates for over a hundred dollars a pound? No, no, I'm *toning him down*.) Michel Chaudun was chef chocolatier here before he set off on his own over twenty years ago. Jacques Genin was head pâtissier here when he was 33.

These days, the creative director is Gilles Marchal. Try his tender, intense ganaches, and the way you think about chocolate will never be the same. And if you're in New York? La Maison du Chocolat has not one but four beautiful chocolate shops that you can step into to experience your own magic moment in Paris.

L.A. Burdick
www.burdickchocolate.com

Whenever anyone in the United States makes me very, very happy, I order them chocolate from L.A. Burdick. Born and raised in Boston, Larry Burdick spent time both in Switzerland and France before establishing L.A. Burdick Chocolate in 1987. His cafés in Cambridge and New Hampshire have been around for a while, but they have two recently opened spaces in Boston's Back Bay and New York's Flatiron district as well.

For the rest of us, best of all is that they operate a thriving mail-order business and you can have chocolates only my heroes could snub (because, you know, nothing another chocolatier can make is as good as what *they* can do, ever) shipped to you. Tiny bites of dark chocolate, laced delicately with fig and port wine; exquisitely delicate chocolate-enrobed salted caramels; truffles infused with lemon, pepper, and rum . . . and if that isn't enough, each box comes with at least one of their impossibly cute, tiny chocolate mice. If you have a child in the house, you may as well give up on tasting the mouse yourself right now.

The classic mice can be varied through the holiday seasons with the cutest chocolate ghosts known to the living, turkeys, snowmen, adorable tiny bunnies, or, my personal favorite, honeybees.

Or let me let you in on a little secret . . .

Miel Bonbons
www.mielbonbons.com

Ferrandi- and Le Nôtre-trained chef Bonnie Lau opened her shop, Miel Bonbons, three years ago in the very out-of-the-way corner (for chocolate) of Carrboro, North Carolina. Since then, she has drawn followers from all over the United States. There is something delightfully charming and comforting about these chocolates—despite exotic flavors like mango mint and coconut curry—as if exoticism and quality have been synthesized in a chocolate you can cozy up at home with. They are larger than the thumbnail chocolates so popular among Parisian chocolatiers, and you can savor over two or three bites unafraid that they will disappear in your mouth before you have quite finished enjoying the flavor.

Rich, dark ganaches pair with whimsical and sophisticated flavors, giving the whole jewel box of a shop the appeal of finding the treasure in Jeunet's *Amélie*. And amid all the ganaches, don't miss Bonnie Lau's dense, intense salted butter caramel chocolates. Every chocolatier gives her chocolate the stamp of her personality, and Bonnie Lau's are fanciful, warm, adventurous, and reassuring.

Check out my site, www.lauraflorand.com, for more tours of chocolate shops, behind-the-scenes looks at chocolate making, and even occasional giveaways of the best chocolates out there.